PENGUIN BOOKS

BRIDGEPORT BUS

Born in Bridgeport, Connecticut, Maureen Howard is a
novelist and teacher who lives in New York City. Her
short stories have appeared in *Hudson Review*, *Yale Review*,
and *Kenyon Review*. Critically acclaimed for her literary
virtuosity and emotional precision, Ms. Howard has distinguished herself as a writer through her novels, including
Not a Word about Nightingales and *Before My Time*,
which is published in The Penguin Contemporary American
Fiction Series, and through her autobiography, *Facts of
Life*, also published by Penguin Books.

Maureen Howard

Bridgeport Bus

PENGUIN BOOKS

Penguin Books Ltd, Harmondsworth,
Middlesex, England
Penguin Books, 625 Madison Avenue,
New York, New York 10022, U.S.A.
Penguin Books Australia Ltd, Ringwood,
Victoria, Australia
Penguin Books Canada Limited, 2801 John Street,
Markham, Ontario, Canada L3R 1B4
Penguin Books (N.Z.) Ltd, 182–190 Wairau Road,
Auckland 10, New Zealand

First published in the United States of America by
Harcourt, Brace & World, Inc., 1965
Published in Penguin Books 1980

LIBRARY OF CONGRESS CATALOGING IN PUBLICATION DATA
Howard, Maureen, 1930–
    Bridgeport bus.
    Reprint of the 1965 ed. published by Harcourt,
Brace & World, New York.
    I. Title.
[PZ4.H8524Br 1980] [PS3558.O882] 813'.54 80-13560
ISBN 0 14 00.5566 5

Printed in the United States of America by
Offset Paperback Mfrs., Inc., Dallas, Pennsylvania
Set in Janson

Parts of chapters 1 and 6 appeared originally,
in different form, in *The Hudson Review*.

For George and Bobby

Bridgeport Bus

1

Ornamental divider

First I will write:

When I go home I walk through all the dim two-family-
house streets where the colors are brown and gray with
what they call cream trim. On the route I take—eight-thirty
in the morning, five at night—there are four houses which
are repainted in pastels, pink and pale green, with aluminum
around the doors and windows: their front stoops are faced
with quarter-inch fake stone. When my nerves are raw from
the meaningless day at work I see nothing more than four
ugly houses, their vulgar shapes, their sameness defined by
the light colors and bright metal. On better days I think

these houses have beauty, reflect some hope shared by the Italians who own them: I suppose their blank painted faces would look fine in the Mediterranean sun or in a summer town on the Long Island shore.

I turn and walk up the hill where I live. Here the dark houses are equally bad, though presumed to be better, with an extra bedroom in each flat and the upstairs flat bulged out over the downstairs porch. When I look up the hill there are dirty window-eyes and huge indolent growths on each idiot brow—a row of monster heads to greet me. I turn back and see the city stretched out dead at my feet; I think about New York or San Francisco or Paris—the scene in which young Gide (it's the first entry in his journal) looks down on beautiful mist-gray Paris across the imaginary writing desk of an artist. I started reading that book, but something happened—my brother's children, my mother's gall bladder; something happened so I never finished.

The actor says: "You see all that down there . . ." (panorama of city at night) "all that," he says to Rita Hayworth, "will be yours." When I look down I see my city on the banks of the exhausted Naugatuck. There is a line of rust along the shore that smells of rubber—the gardens, if I may be allowed, of factories; and then the hills with all the streets of brown houses coming up toward me and toward my street of superior brown houses.

When I go home my mother and I play a cannibal game; we eat each other over the years, tender morsel by morsel until there is nothing left but dry bone and wig. She is winning—needless to say she has had so much more experience. She meets me in the front room, hiding behind the evening paper, a fat self-indulgent body, her starved mind hungry for me. I am on guard when I first come from work —what means for devouring me has she devised during the day? I stand under the dark-stained arch, an anxious thrill rising in me, and just wait, watching but not seeing the elephant chairs and my bloated old mother behind her paper. The room, stuffed with darkness day or night, any season, is a monochrome of immobility: heavy chairs, lame tables, parchment shades and curtains of ecru lace—all colorless as time, all under a layer of antediluvian silt.

Arrangement in gray and black—portrait of my mother profiled, soft and bulky in her sagging chair: a big Irishwoman "fulla life" with eyes ready to cry. For contrast, her white hair crimped in a prim Protestant roll seen against the walls (a deeper tone) papered in potato skins. A coat of yellow varnish, the years of our aboriginal love, over the entire picture. I have not long to wait, contemplating the classic scene of home, for she never misses a cue.

"Ag?" she says, not looking at me, and I don't answer. I entertain myself with the notion that one day it will be someone else come in the front door, a rapist or a mad killer, and she'll be caught there reading the obituaries or looking up her TV programs for the night.

"Ag, I bought snowsuits today for the children—downtown."

"In April? That's fine."

"On sale, Ag. Sometimes I don't think you use your head. There's been sales advertised downtown all week. I bought them big for next year." She smiles, puffy and red in the face, self-satisfied, imitating the well-to-do Irish.

"I don't read that paper. How much?"

"Well, that's it—only twenty dollars."

"Sixty dollars?"

"Yes, for *three* children. I guess I can multiply as well as you, Mary Agnes." Then she's had enough and pushes herself out of the chair, waddling off to get supper.

"Sixty dollars," I say after her, "and what's wrong with the ones you bought last year, not on sale. Can't they pass the clothes on? Can't Catherine wear Patrick's snowsuit? I didn't know a goddamn girl's coat buttoned from right to left when I was their age."

5

"I don't like to hear you talk that way, Mary Agnes." And then she says, hurt to wrench my heart—and it works every time; my heart *is* wrenched during her big scenes—the spectacle of her raw face, tears swelling, her blood pressure up: "Your father, rest his soul, was poor. It's a sad thing, Ag, when you've no more feeling left for your brother and his family way up there in Buffalo. It doesn't matter about me, but it's sad."

We never get more violent than that. I am cursed with gentility and can hardly do better than an occasional name-of-the-Lord-in-vain, but after each argument I like to look at myself in my own room or in the blue glass mirror in the dining room. There I can see what part of me she has picked at—her favorite soft flesh around the eyes, or my shamefully concave chest. I am gaunt—you might guess it, five foot eleven, one hundred and eighteen pounds.

But why do I start with such heightened drama when there are the usual tidbits: my mail opened, my bureau drawers "arranged." Clorox put in the wash with a new dress. Or: "Ag?" (Once again it is only me, not the sex maniac I dream of, and she goes on at me behind the paper.) "Christine Doyle called about the Sodality Tea and she said wouldn't you pour. Isn't that nice?"

"And you said yes?"

"Yes, isn't that nice." Then she is wise enough to hurry right on and read me something out of the paper: "Well poor Tom Heffernan died, that's a blessing. They say his body was full of it."

You will think now that I am stupid and incompetent, but you'd be surprised how I gnaw at my mother just by reading for hours, or not speaking, or muttering "Christ" in the direction of the television set as I pass through the front room. And, my choicest bone of contention, I take night courses instead of making myself one bit attractive to the gelded, balding boys that my mother finds in limitless supply.

"Tess Mueller is coming over with that nice son who works in the bank," she announces from behind her paper. I get a quick flash of Fred Mueller, a harmless pudding-beast caged at the People's Trust, counting out my money and saying, "Cold enough for you?" or "Long time no see."

"That's a shame," I tell my mother, "because tonight I'm going to the library in New Haven."

"The library, the *library!*"—shrieks of coronary outrage.

"The University library, Mother. Hundreds of men."

But she is gasping now and slaps her beloved *Evening American* against the brown velour chair. "That's what I'm to tell Tess when she brings that nice boy—that you've gone to the *library?*"

"Oh, you'd be surprised—hundreds of men . . ." But then never use even the simplest sarcasm on children, because they don't get it, and I wonder if I should illustrate my point for mother: maybe a story of a nun, a Sister of Mercy working on Cardinal Newman in the stacks; she meets up with an emeritus professor, a medievalist who has just been writing a piece on the clerical orgies at Cluny.

Scene: Sterling Memorial Library in the $9860.2n$'s.

Time: Four o'clock in the week of Septuagesima. It is a moment of transition. The lights have not yet been turned on. . . .

Mother smooths out the newspaper, folds it, tucks it under her arm with finality: she is finished, through with me.

"Ag, you are thirty-five years old." This is her master stroke.

What I should have written to begin with is that I am Mary Agnes Keely, a thirty-five-year-old virgin. Narrative should begin with essentials, not the oblique device—picture of a city, a house—that flirts with the truth in a maidenly way. I am called Ag, named Mary after guess who and Agnes after the child martyr who defended her virginity before it had even a literary value—I have never had much sympathy with her. At the age of thirteen can you honestly say there's a choice—I mean between a lion and a dirty, nasty man. I cannot believe in a world which honors that prissy little girl and dishonors me as one of a million social misfits—lets me be fed daily to my ravenous old mother.

"Ag," she will say, her mouth watering, "you are thirty-five years old."

As I write this I am at peace for the first time in years, sitting at my desk (an old dressing table) where I can look at myself often. I admire the freshness that has come to my cheeks this evening and what appears to be a new firmness to my throat. I have laid out a thick pad of yellow theme paper, and with a smooth, satisfying ball-point pen have begun to write. I can hear my mother at the telephone out in the kitchen. She is aggrieved, whining to the long-distance operator and asking again, the fifth time in the hour, if the girl will dial her son in Buffalo. My brother and his family don't seem to be home. That's the straw, she tells my Aunt Mae in a lengthy call, that broke the camel's back in her already broken heart. She has told her sad story to Aunt Mae and to her younger sister, Lil, and from what I can overhear, Aunt Lil will be over after supper, done up in her ranch mink stole, to reason with me and try to straighten things out—though nothing is tangled as far as I'm concerned: things are straighter than they have ever been, and I intend to set the whole scene down on this pleasant yellow pad.

It is spring now, but nine weeks ago tonight it was winter, the beginning of February. I came in from the wet gloom of the brown streets to the shriveled gloom of our house. There was mother with the *Evening American*, but she didn't ask who was standing under the arch; so at once I knew there was to be an announcement on a grand scale.

"Is it still raining, Ag?" she asked, sweetness itself.

"Yes," I said.

Then she put down the paper so I could see that she had been to the Edna-Lou Beauty Shop. Her hair had a fresh purple rinse and was kinked in to the head. She was wearing her best stylish-stout wine crepe with a surplice top and her new Enna Jettick shoes.

"Well, wouldn't you just know," my mother said with put-on petulance, "wouldn't you just know it would rain tonight." She waited, preening her fat bosom, but I wouldn't ask, so she heaved out of the chair. "Dinner is almost on the table. We have to eat early tonight, Ag, because of the novena."

"The novena!" I gasped. Her backside looked broader than ever as she hustled out to the kitchen. Ever since I was a girl, for over twenty years that would be, I have had to drag my mother to that novena in the winter, tugging her up the church steps like an impossible rolled mattress and stuffing her into a pew. Then the Rosary, the Aspirations, the Benediction, the Prayer for Peace . . . The whole thing started just before the war and was addressed to Our Lady of Fatima, who as I recall appeared to some pre-pubescent Portuguese and said the world was coming to an end—as though that were news.

So off to the novena, and afterwards from St. Augustine's to Friedman's Dairy with the Scanlon sisters, Aunt Mae, and a toothy schoolteacher named Louise Conroy—there to reap the reward: heavenly hot-fudge sundaes topped with whipped cream, and a symposium on every hysterectomy in town. Unfortunately, when the novena was four-ninths or five-ninths over it coincided with Lent, so my mother and her friends would stand in the back of the church and debate about going to Friedman's. But they always went, denying themselves nuts and whipped cream to commemorate the forty days and forty nights in the desert. Nine weeks ago tonight the novena began.

"I've put your dinner out," my mother called, and I walked slowly out to the kitchen, switching en route from the Spenser-Milton seminar, which was given on Friday evenings, to Modern French Poetry. She had already settled herself behind a dish of glutinous brown stew.

"I have my course tonight, Mother."

"You have what?" Poor Mother, she saw I was serious.

I sat down opposite her, just as loose and easy. "My French course. It comes on Thursdays."

"God knows"—she started the harangue right away— "you were brought up a good Catholic girl, that you should choose a lot of dirty French books over your religion. And thank the good Lord" (with a tremolo) "your father is not here to see you an ingrate to your mother . . . a woman the age of you, Mary Agnes, thirty-five years old . . . ," and on and on with a sad scum forming on her stew. She looked hateful with the veins jumping in her face, yet I almost cried, out of a perverse love for her ravings. I was consumed, ready to say yes I would go with her and try to stop the end of the world, until she said: "I will pray for you, Mary Agnes," with her lips all pursed up as though she were sucking the marrow out of my bones. That was new, and for eight weeks I have heard it—how she is praying for me, for a woman who would let her old mother climb the slippery hills and go up the church steps alone at night.

It must have been her praying for me that started me on the pastel houses. I had to have something to come back with after all. Three or four times a week when I came in from work, I talked about the Italian houses, the houses painted pink and pale green. I mentioned how gay they looked on a rainy day or remarked what a lovely aluminum curlicued "C" the Capizzolis had put on their front door, or how I admired the Riccios' empty urn, a cemetery urn painted red, standing in front of their peachy-pink house. And all the while I had no knowledge, I'll swear to it, that I was provoking her more than usual. Sure I was nibbling, and there were the expected retorts about foreigners: "They

weren't stupid. They knew how to improve their property."
But when I told her I liked the Italian houses it was only
partially true; I had come to love them. I left the house early
to hurry down my street and around the corner to the
first one, the Marcuccis', who had left corrugated metal
awnings up all winter long, waiting for sun, and then on to
the Riccios' splendid red urn that promised to have flowers,
and to the Capizzolis' with all the twisted aluminum and the
pressed stone that knew no geological limitations. A few
gray blocks on, near my office, was the last house—I don't
know the people—a three-family aqua wonder with glass
bricks set around the old frame windows to modernize, and
the front yard cemented up except for a small patch of dirt
the shape of an irrigation pan. There some hardy ivy grew
all winter—green. It was an oasis I rushed to, and one day
I walked into the cement yard and picked an ivy leaf. The
urn, the awnings, the ivy remembered another season, though
I suppose it was the future that I really admired in them,
because I had none.

One night I told my mother, "That's how I get to work
and back, from one bright house to the next. I think lots of
people go on that way, from one bowling night to the next
or even from meal to meal."

I thought she hadn't heard—she hardly ever did when I
took it upon myself to explain things—but later by the blue
light of the television set she remarked, "You used to be a
good, plain girl, Ag. I can't see what's changed you."

I bought a red silk dress at this time and let my hair grow.
At the office they all said how snappy Miss Ag was looking
—there I command respect for seventeen years as a cheerful drudge. I am secretary to the president of the Standard
Zipper Company. Everyone knows the type: a pinch-faced
lady who supports an old mother, can locate every paper
clip and advise her boss not to merge with Reddi-Zip, Inc.
It makes the salesmen laugh to say I know all the ups and

downs. Pathetic—I think of a million flies all over America, zip, zip, zip down the trolley—miners, truck drivers, farmers, junior executives, Hollywood stars—never an embarrassing moment, due to the efficiency and diligence of Miss Mary Agnes Keely. I think of harassed women catching their flesh (you must never hurry it, *I* know that), and tossing babies kept warm for the night, and the suitcases and tents and silver bags—everything closing and opening like breath going in and out, while I am sealed—as though our 72-inch model were stitched into me from the toes up, and the zipper stuck forever on a broken track under my hawk-Irish nose. It's pathetic, but funny.

I mentioned the dress, the novena naturally, and I shall want to write about my course. After my father died, my brother went to college anyway, but my mother sent me to work to pay off the mortgage on our wen-browed, dark house so we'd always have a roof over our empty heads. I started filing at Standard Zipper and taking courses at night, and I discovered that being a homely gawk I was smart. Well, I was smarter than anyone at the teachers' college and as smart as the Saturday morning crowd at Columbia. I have a world now, the size of a circle of light thrown by a desk lamp, that is mine, safe from my mother and the zipper company and my brother's children. It is the one space in which I am free of self-pity, and I hold it as sacred as some impossible belief in guardian angels, though when I am outside my circle of light I see that it is dim and small. Someone is always saying how fine it is and what a mark of maturity to be able to think, to read; but I am sure for most people it's cowardice. I mean, we should want to stand in an amphitheater with spotlights on us, like F.D.R. in a black cape, and say something significant:

"At last, my friends, we know the world can come to an end."

Well, the small circle of light thrown by the reading

lamp has been shining with special brightness since the beginning of February because of my course in the modern French poets—they speak to me. That happens now and again, though I fancy myself a sophisticated reader with all kinds of critical impedimenta: I read something so direct, so pertinent to exactly where I am—the way I feel, my precise frame of mind. That is the rapport I had—I still have—with Nerval, with Baudelaire, with Rimbaud. Not only what they say in brilliant, disparate images but with their diseased, eccentric lives. I feel pain where I have never been touched, dissipation in my early-to-bed soul. There now: have I written an illumination?

(My mother has got through to my brother in Buffalo. She has only to hear his voice to cry, so what must it be tonight—an endless keening, ancient, racially remembered. I wonder if she will ask me to talk to him, way up there in Buffalo. "Hello," I will say, "how are you? How are the kids? Yes," I will assure him, "everything is *fine* here. The weather is fine. I am going away." She is wailing. She will not give me the satisfaction of defending myself to Francis on the phone, but no matter where I may go I will get the bill—I always pay. If I were to steal out of my room and hidden in the murky nite-lite of the hallway spy on the succulent sight—my mother leaning heavily on the refrigerator, dabbing at her wet eyes and nose with a disintegrated Kleenex, weeping and weeping to the child she loves, my brother—then I could not go. I would offer myself to her, the last sweet bite, a soupçon airy and delicious to restore her, humanity fudge. Warriors did that—not as long ago as we like to think—ate the heart of the enemy. I will stay in my room.)

Now let me tell what has happened:

I have told about the red dress, the novena, the pastel houses, and the French poets. Tonight I came home, a Thursday, and turned up the hill to my house. The scene was wrong: the weather had been fine all day from the window of the zipper factory, and the sun still glowed, low and late on my dirty brown street, but now I saw a flash of electric blue—intense Immigrant Blue. And I ran up the hill to my house, because it was *my* house with that blue all over the front and halfway down the side, and I ran up the steps ignoring the luminous sign of warning, my feet sticking to the gluey wet paint. Inside, there she was with the newspaper held up higher than usual, waiting—

"Ag, is that you?"

"You know it's me," I shouted. "You know that." I tore the *Evening American* from her face. The smile she had prepared to greet me with was plastered on her speechless mouth.

"You have gone out of your mind," I said evenly, "*out of your mind!*"

"Now, Mary Agnes, the painters came today . . ."

"The house is blue."

". . . the painters came today, Mary Agnes, and I had it in mind for a while with the house so run down, and I wanted to do something for you, something to please you, Ag."

"The house is blue."

"Well, that's it." Her voice rose an octave—her face was flushed. "For weeks now you've been talking up those houses the Italians own, every day it seems you're at me about the colors and the decoration." Now she got up and began to gather the torn newspaper, stooping as best she could with the blood rushing to her head and those veins jumping faster than I've ever seen. "You've been plaguing me with those colored houses, but there is no pleasing you, Mary Agnes."

"In the first place we are not Italians," I said.

"Well you don't have to tell me," she screamed, "you're the big mixer, aren't you, with all your talk about those wops . . . It wasn't me wanted the house blue."

"We are not Italians." Then in a whisper: "We are withered brown people. Can't you see that? Can't you see one rotten thing?"

"No, I don't like the way you speak to your mother— out of dirty French books I've seen in your room. I bless the day your father died, not to see you like this, a heretic and a spiteful woman."

I grabbed her fat arm when she turned from me and held her. "Now tell me," I said, "how much does it cost to paint a house?"

But she only started to cry, so I had to answer. "It's my bank account, isn't it?—spread all over the front of this house."

"You'd go off and leave your mother to die, Mary Agnes." Then I saw the working of her voracious mind. Her words grated through the sobs, "You've no more feeling than stone; you'd go way off to the other side with the money and let me walk up to church in the winter, and go off on your summer vacation and leave me alone—all when I chose that color for you."

Then *I* began to cry, and it wasn't the Economy Flight I mourned. I had dreamed, indeed put my deposit down on seven magic lands in twenty days—too far away, unreal. I don't for a moment think it would have come off. Now I threw myself into an elephant chair. "For me. For *me*. That's the color for your Holy Mary. Must the whole street know, the whole city, that I am a virgin and thirty-five?" I pounded the bulky chair, thinking it was my mother's body. She must have felt I was wild—staring up at her with my ravaged face. Suddenly I was smiling and sure.

"All this," I said pleasantly, looking around the front room, "has no importance." My mother thought I meant our house. "I am going to play Bridgeport Bus, once and for all I am going to play Bridgeport Bus and go away." (It's a wonderful game, Bridgeport Bus: you line up the dining-room chairs in two rows and you collect fares and joggle along through the Naugatuck valley talking to all the passengers and then get off at Bridgeport.) Mother went out weeping into the kitchen, but I stayed there hugging the large bosom back of the chair.

Aunt Lil has come and gone. She stuck her head into my room and seeing that I was calm, writing on a yellow pad (school work no doubt), she went to comfort my mother, saying it was only one of our arguments like any other. Then I could hear Mother, loud and choking to Aunt Lil, that tonight was to end her novena and the girls would think it queer, waiting for her in the vestibule of the church. She is too ill from the exertion and all the shouting. O, M. Rimbaud, say it: "This can only be the end of the world, kept going." It is obvious that I will not finish my course . . . no matter.

I intend to travel light: only the red silk dress, some books, my cosmetics—though my face has a surprising fullness and the skin on my neck seems tight, like the skin on an out-of-season hothouse fruit. I am like that, maturing too late—will I be more valuable, that is one of the questions to be asked, still unplucked? My girlish head luxuriates in absurd decisions: I will take the Bridgeport Bus and joggle to the railroad station and choose between Boston and New York. I will wear my rhinestone earrings or leave them behind. I will call a taxi to take me to the bus depot, or I will walk so I can see for the last time my obscure, night-dark city with its hills rising—unlit funeral pyres, gray and brown, rising from the beach of industrial rubble . . . and the river used up, ashamed like a deserted woman.

"So long!" I will say, "you have loved me like a mother; I take nothing from you but bare necessities: one suitcase, the beginning of this story. So long, sweet Mother, good night, good night."

The wise boy Rimbaud writes: "The hour of flight will be the hour of death for me." Let me establish that I *know* this as concretely as I comprehend a world of zippers. So having cleared myself of some naïveté, I have only to put on my coat and go—through the living room where my mother is soothed at last by her television, watching lives much more professional than ours.

"Let's not say good-bye, only *Adieu, bon appetit. . . .*"

2

---◆◆◆◆---

For an instant the young woman saw her tired face reflected
in the glass door of the hotel, and quickly looked beyond,
past her own opaque eyes to the rain and the traffic. It was
difficult to get a taxi in bad weather, so she waited inside,
passive and dry, thinking she would see a cab with its light
on and then go out. After ten minutes she was still there,
expressionless, indifferent to the women who came in shaking umbrellas or those who hesitated before stepping out
into the rain as though on the brink of a small adventure.
She stood in her place like a dummy sentinel. Her anonymous black costume worn with a double strand of pearls

might have been chosen for her by the impersonal young men who had "done" the hotel lobby, a women's residence hotel: the foyer white and hung with expensively framed etchings of no value; there was a mock lavabo. The contrived niceness of the scene was disturbed only by Lydia Savaard's face, not made up, surprisingly bare and vacant. A face like Mrs. Savaard's—like many standard faces in this part of the city—evokes certain suburbs, certain schools, horses and sailboats. But there was a difference about her, an emptiness that was more than a surface, a social manner. She was young, indeed she might still pass for a college girl dressed up for some polite occasion in her dormitory, but her eyes were disengaged, weary with disappointment.

At last she turned to check the time on a gilt clock. She was not impatient, aware that she had five minutes to make a trip that would take twenty in good weather, and she showed no sign of relief when a taxi drew up in front of the hotel. A tall woman climbed out of the back seat.

"Now you stay here, Mr. Perez," the tall woman shouted above the noise of traffic. "Don't you go away." She stooped to grin at the cab driver, then hurried to the hotel, her long arms and legs swinging out. Pushing, she found that she had to pull the glass door, and in a comedienne's series of leaps, stumbles, and recoveries arrived at a delicate writing table. There was no one on duty.

"No one here?" the woman asked Mrs. Savaard.

Lydia Savaard sought the reflection of her own face in the door and did not answer. Behind her, yet beyond her—like a cinematic trick—the gangly, high-shouldered woman hovered in a dumb show over the unlikely registration desk and found a china bell to ring. But no one came. She stretched her long neck, peeking down as though by chance someone might be hiding, crouched there on the carpet. Stretching, she dropped first her soiled string gloves and then a large carryall, transparent except for a red rose captured in layers of plastic. The bag had nothing in it worth concealing: two paper books, a lipstick, compact, comb, lady's wallet, and a real red apple which fought with the color of the imprisoned rose. A moment later, perched on the edge of a *prie-dieu,* she coughed in the direction of Mrs. Savaard.

"Pardon—"

With an effort Lydia Savaard turned her head.

"Pardon—do you think there will be someone here soon?"

"I have no idea."

"That's a queer way to run a business."

Lydia found herself under attack: the woman came straight at her, affronted her with a direct smile that only children have. "Look, how long will you be here?"

"I don't know." Mrs. Savaard spoke from a constricted spot behind her nose.

"Do you know when they come back? I have Mr. Perez waiting in the taxi."

"I'm sorry . . ." Mrs. Savaard began.

"I only thought if you were going to be here . . ."

"Excuse me," and Mrs. Savaard walked out into the rain. She had seen a free taxi coming down the block, but it was taken by the time she raised her hand in a limp summons. When she came back into the lobby she allowed herself to smile at the tall woman before taking up her post, wondering without concern what possible good it would do if she *were* going to be there, what that had to do with Mr. Perez. It would soon be pointless to try to get downtown, Lydia thought; yes, soon she could indulge herself in that strange satisfying shame of having let another slowly spinning day pass by without so much as taking a swing at it. She could go back upstairs to the dead safety of her bed.

"Say," the tall woman said in another cheerful assault, "why don't you take my taxi?"

"Thank you, I couldn't do that." Mrs. Savaard's words were spread out with flat Midwestern vowels. She brushed dampness from the sleeve of her black suit. Through a half-open door she caught a glimpse of the chic motherly type who usually sat on duty in the mornings. It was clear to Lydia that she should speak up, call the woman from her cup of coffee—"Hello there, this odd, distressed person wants . . ." Once she could have cared—not in any bustling, helpful way—would have cared to be nice. She thought now of going upstairs to telephone and break the appointment with her lawyer, not difficult, only a word to his secretary saying she was unable . . .

A recently divorced school friend had recommended Mr. Godnick as completely detached, never embarrassing. Lydia had not found that true, though Godnick himself had said at their first brief meeting that these matters were easy.

"Listen, I know how you feel, believe me. Think of it like going to a doctor. We've heard it all before. You don't expect they give you anything in court just because you look like a nice girl?"

No, she hadn't expected that, or anything else.

". . . so I left my suitcase at the Pennsylvania Station," this amazing gawk was still talking, "and I thought since it was years ago my cousin put me up in this hotel and I could only remember where it was, you see, that I'd dash up and find out if they had a room." Lydia watched her twittering like a long-legged bird, ridiculous though somehow enchanting and original, swooping out the plastic carryall in a dangerous arc that just missed the glass door.

"You wouldn't know if they have a room? . . . Because then you could take Mr. Perez and go."

"I don't know."

"It *is* a queer way to run a business with no one here. Don't they usually have a room?"

What a bird, thought Lydia Savaard. She had not talked to anyone in days and did not want to now, but felt besieged. In a voice thin with disuse, she said: "Yes, usually they have rooms."

"I'll do my shopping, then I'll pick up my bag." Pulling,

finding she had to push, the tall woman went out, crashing into the glass door, uninjured, joyous, into a burst of rain; then she turned in the middle of the sidewalk and called back, "Where do you want to go?"

I want to go off the end of a flat earth, birdie, but I guess I go to Mr. Godnick instead. As she walked out to the taxi the rain fell lightly on Lydia Savaard, leaving her neat and nearly dry. "I'm going to Thirty-fourth Street." With her words she gave nothing of herself.

"I'm Mary Agnes Keely."

Drawing back into a corner of the cab, Lydia kept her eyes on the red light until it changed; then they drove out onto Fifth Avenue. Central Park was misty and cheerless with moody lumps of fog sticking to the rocks. She had seen it this way on afternoons when she walked out from the women's hotel, gazing in on the leafless trees and those terrible buildings, unable to enter the public paths, fearing a lonely slope or empty bench where the scalding tears might start again. She had looked in over a low damp wall and imagined the park whole, a rectangle on the map of Manhattan, set out in her mind like a country for children to play with—here the boats sail and the cars go crosstown, a theater, a restaurant. On one of her worst days she had decided to go live under a bridge, the madwoman of Central Park with snarled hair—and in time people would laugh at her clothes.

Now Lydia Savaard saw that Mary Agnes Keely was wearing red silk—wrong at this time in the morning, wrong at any time on her gaunt figure, wrong with an apple in a plastic bag, offensive with that sealed-in rose. Over the dress—it was more a lustrous cerise than true red—she wore a spring jacket of powder blue, the matted cottony stuff of a baby blanket. Though Lydia was not at all the sort to wonder about strangers, she supposed that with those books Miss Keely must be a schoolteacher. There was Baudelaire, etched like a statue with one eye bulged out of focus, seeing what no one else could see, next to the untasted apple which was bigger than his bald head, a dirty comb, and that rose, the cliché of beauty. Mrs. Savaard, who felt that her own life was a nightmare as arbitrary and disturbing as any painted dream, found no meaning in the woman's surrealistic kit.

Miss Keely jutted forward, talking to the cab driver. An ageless, unhealthy-looking man with a Brooklyn accent, Mr. Perez was involved in a scheme to sell Easter baskets and coconut cake in the shape of lambs to Spanish-American Clubs.

"They're *using* pink," she said with gay insistence as they drove past the Sherry-Netherland.

"It's just I thought purple and yellow . . ." said Mr. Perez.

"No. Look at the colors!" Turning to Lydia Savaard with arms flung wide, the odd woman presented her with all the windows on Fifth Avenue: flowered hats and paper gardens and bright chiffon, sapphires and emeralds dangling from egg beaters at Tiffany's. At Saks' the jaded dummies who had changed their pose a dozen times since Christmas were pretending to be little girls in sailor hats and Parisian blazers. They came to a dead stop in traffic, which gave Miss Keely time to admire these costumes extravagantly, and Mrs. Savaard was forced to admit that with such a presumptuous smile the woman would look fine in navy blue with brass buttons and a leghorn hat . . . though to herself Lydia thought, "She must have ten years on me, but such eager eyes . . . funny bird."

And she loved the white lilies laid out in Rockefeller Center—"silly heads, silly heads," Miss Keely laughed, bobbing as though she too were set out there in the soft shower, equally delighted with the purple swag in the doors of the Cathedral. The pageant, as always, was there, only in need of someone to proclaim it.

Through the stiff casing of her own sorrow, Lydia Savaard

began to sense the strangeness of things: sharing a cab with this skinny out-of-town schoolteacher, who was not repressed as one might expect but abandoned, reckless with gestures and words. Happy cadaver—Lydia thought she could see it: the cheek bones, the eye cavities, the disarming grin of a skeleton, directed now at the Library lions (obviously old friends), now at the candy in Barricini's window. Miss Keely prodded Mr. Perez—

"There are the big pink eggs."

Lydia, brooding continually on the ruins of her own life, thought, "Risen from the dead—"

"It's just I thought purple and yellow," Mr. Perez said. "Fix them with bows, and that grass."

He offered this plan over the shoulder of his leather jacket to the lady in black, who passed it on in a bewildered frown to Miss Keely.

The sun shone on the Avenue, surprising and decisive, and the daily shoppers with painted faces and dyed hair came forth at once to begin their grand tours. It was spring in New York, and Mrs. Savaard, except that she had the sad eyes of a discreet mourner, might have been any young wife searching for the good plain dress of next season. Mary Agnes Keely reached into her carryall, clawed around for her compact, then dabbed at her nose with powder the color of an Aztec queen.

"I've been up all night. First on the bus, then on the train."

"You don't look it"—the answer came to Lydia Savaard's mind, but she could not make herself speak.

"I get the lambs fresh-baked Friday night," Mr. Perez said.

Both women got out at Thirty-fourth Street.

"It's a glorious day. I must *walk* to Macy's." (Miss Mary Agnes Keely paid out of her lady's wallet.) "Thank you, Mr. Perez. Good luck with your chocolate bunnies, too."

The young woman in black, holding out a dollar bill let

something almost personal, an unguarded twitch, come to her eyes as she watched Miss Keely, beak up, wings fluttering, poised for flight.

"Breathe the air of this city!" said Miss Keely, ". . . and all the faces, so many different faces."

Which left Mrs. Savaard with her dollar bill, thinking for a moment of someone other than herself, a caricature more foolish than life, yet genuine, an honest performance—that was the woman's saving grace. Lydia put the money back in her purse, and withdrew across Fifth Avenue into the privacy of her sorrow.

Up in Mr. Godnick's office the fluorescent tube shone bright as sunlight, but dead, on the steel filing cabinets and the brass-haired, brass-tongued girl who snapped up a folder (SAVAARD *vs.* SAVAARD) and said, "Mistah Godnick will see yah now."

Lydia remembered the first time, led to an inner office, probably by this same girl. But seeing Godnick, the legal adviser for her divorce, she thought she would have passed him by in the street; it was only his eyes she recalled, expert Levantine eyes that had classified Mrs. Henry Savaard right off as cool suburban womanhood. She had not been able to look at him much after that. His eyes seemed to summarize her case: nothing had happened to her before this, she was a clean slate written on at last.

Lydia stood by a window contemplating the sinister back end of buildings while he gave the girl instructions not to disturb him and to call Mr. So-and-So.

Life is *merde*, she thought, for the uncomfortable truth was that Godnick had made her feel like one of the never-ending brides in the *New York Times*, a stiff-lipped girl in white satin wearing the veil of her maternal grandmother, lilies in her hands . . . only that when she looked down from a dreamy spot in the photographer's studio life turned out to be the scrawl of a dirty word learned at school.

Godnick's acceptance of her ruined marriage had annoyed Lydia: it implied that all she had suffered through with Henry was nothing extraordinary. The lawyer's desk was piled up with the outlines of unfortunate lives. She had seen names while Godnick talked on the phone—Wein, Hadak, Anguri, Brostler—but she could not believe that these men, these women had lived through scenes more degrading than she had known. Godnick treated her divorce as routine procedure, and that was supposed to be some comfort to her no doubt—"Often the situation is unavoidable"—but she had taken his condescension as belittling accusation; as though, suffering with a common cold, she had been naïve enough to come to a doctor claiming incurable malignancy. Her final defense, which she had come round to many times in the rumpled sleeplessness of her bed, was to assure herself that this lawyer and his clients—all those others—were coarse and insensitive.

"Please sit down . . ." Glancing at the folder his secretary brought to him, Godnick added, "Mrs. Savaard."

She waited. "Intolerable mental cruelty," he read. "You're still at the hotel on Sixty-ninth Street?"

"Yes."

"Your husband, Henry Savaard, is . . ."

"No," her thin voice spoke quickly behind the weary mask, "in a mental institution."

Godnick acknowledged this with a nod, and began to search for a pen. To Lydia he seemed archaic, a holy man, a rabbi out of a Testament unfamiliar to her—not her Old Testament of gently interpreted stories that lead up to *the* story in which everything turns out all right. She found hereditary sadness in the drooping discolored patches under Godnick's brilliant eyes; she read indictment in the superior pinch at the end of his downcast nose, of all her kind who have nothing more than personal sorrow—no, again she made it too pretty—nothing beyond personal problems.

"Your husband," said Godnick. "What hospital is he in?"

"I don't know."

"You don't know?" His eyes caught her smoothing the black stuff of her skirt, comforting her knees.

"He is somewhere upstate. His mother did not tell me."

"When did this happen to him?"

"Nine . . . ten days ago now."

"Have you spoken to anyone—a doctor, say, who can tell you how long he will be there?"

She didn't answer, and after Godnick wrote something in her folder, he asked, "Mrs. Savaard?"

"She, his mother, said it might be permanent this time: 'permanently institutionalized.'"

"You haven't signed anything? No one's approached you about commitment papers?"

"Commitment—" Any attitude she might have had she screened from her answer. "I know nothing about it."

At their first interview she had found herself speechless, without a tongue in her head when Godnick asked the simplest questions: How long married? Husband's occupation? She had felt weak and foolish when he had suggested that she make another appointment with the girl outside and come back—he had not actually said "prepared," but had dealt with her nicely—come back when she was "relaxed," another day.

"This sounds like your divorce case is over before it begins."

He took a turn around the desk, watching her closely as she stood up and pulled on a pair of black kid gloves.

"The law in the State of New York is explicit in cases of insanity and disappearance . . ."

"If you will send me your bill." At the extreme moment Lydia Savaard offered a tepid smile, *noblesse oblige*.

"Let me finish my job." Godnick was all business. "You would have to wait five years to file for the divorce you want, because your husband is incompetent now and cannot contest or . . ."

She waited politely for Mr. Godnick to explain, not listening to him, feeling it was easier to let him go on than to turn her back and walk away.

Insanity and disappearance . . . the combination had seemed bizarre when he said it, but now she thought it ingenious, because Henry, strapped down forever, had certainly gone off into another world, wandered, was missing except for his body upstate somewhere. She tried to confine all memory of her husband to that perfect body, to think of him like a cast statue all hollow inside—only the sculptured surface, the magnificent structure. Set him in the sun, or better, in a leafy place; observe the variety of light upon his monumental torso, in the scoop of his thighs. Set him in Central Park and I will grow flowers all around his feet and worship his body of bronze. People will say I live in the zoo with no keeper to comb my poor matted hair. It was less fantastic than the scene which she had never been able to envision: the trip to some unheard-of Southern town where she and Henry would plead friendly disaffection. Surely that had been the dream.

". . . your only possibility." Mr. Godnick touched her gloved hand, demanding contact. "An annulment, this is your only possibility."

Startled by some remnant of self-preservation, she looked directly at the lawyer for the first time.

He thought, "Poor girl, how it appeals to her. I have spoken the magic word."

"Give some evidence of your husband's condition having existed previous to your marriage and you have a case of misrepresentation."

"—evidence?"

"Some indication, no? You get signed medical reports, statements from his family, proof of previous mental illness."

"I have no proof."

Godnick's smile was arch. "You never saw anything strange? He never went to a doctor?"

"Before our marriage everything was—" she started to use a word, then flushed "—ordinary," she said. Now there was life in her plain face, the beginning of color, a trembling of interest.

"So tell me what you do know," said Godnick. (Oh, he'd seen it before: tears starting, a fumble for the handkerchief, collapse into that chair.)

"I can't," she said, snuffling back into her head, "I simply can't. You told me last time it was like going to a doctor. That's not true."

"Mrs. Savaard," Godnick said with patience, "how did he treat you? What is this mental condition? Take a few minutes, think about it."

She saw him open his attaché case with "Genuine Leather" stamped in gold near the handle. Godnick, the seven-day wonder, that's what her school friend had told her.

"We were in Alabama before we knew it . . ." But wasn't her friend the most brittle girl Lydia had ever known? A field-hockey type involved in a messy affair with some man who trained dogs in Bucks County. *She* hadn't seen the wise circles under the lawyer's eyes, or that long nose so easy to look down. Lydia had only wanted it to be easy, like confiding in a stranger on a train or a boat, someone you'll never see again. Now she had only to look at Godnick opening his mail, throwing letters in the waste basket, to realize that he understood her reasons for coming to him. He *knew* how she would go on about "a marvelous little man," "a hideous little man," "this little man who had us in Alabama before we knew it"!

There was the folder: LYDIA CLARK SAVAARD *vs.* HENRY BLAISE SAVAARD. The touching thing was the line which Mr. Godnick had drawn through Henry's address—*their* address. She pictured their small house, no one in it, only the

29

remnants of his final madness, splinters of china and glass, blood from his hands and feet, the green silk torn from the Biedermeier bench, the stinking stain on the bathroom rug. . . . What could she say? Mr. Godnick, my husband when taken in a rage, sir, sprayed the walls like an alley cat, killed the plants, smashed the china. I submit our cottage as Exhibit A—unless his mother has come to clean up for her boy, to smooth and patch and disinfect what was left after the naughty wife ran away.

That was it, of course, the mother: there was an old story (she had decided upon it countless times in the hotel room —the one way to speak her piece), an old story that Godnick, everyone, knew well. What better myth than the mother to explain the horror of her marriage?—and as true as anything she would be willing to say. A case history then, which told everything and admitted nothing, a man dominated by his mother, unfit, paranoid, increasingly manic.

"Shall I begin?"

"Yes," said Godnick looking at his watch, "we had better get started. Whatever you can say about this mental . . ."

"Henry was the most charming boy . . ." Lydia recited as though she had known all along what she must say; she sat straight in her chair with folded hands, a senior once more, delivering a report on *Romeo and Juliet*. A contemporary tale of crossed-up lovers confounded by the complex evil of the world: the Princeton boy gardening for his mother, the garden itself, spectacular once, still dazzling with its deep English borders to the trusting girl from Cleveland. She had felt a nuisance getting herself invited out to Long Island every weekend just to see Henry. Ah! but love, love makes bold, and she clinched the whole deal during a two-week vacation from her nice-girl job editing children's stories. By which she did not mean to imply to Mr. Godnick that Henry had not met every train and from Monday to Friday sent her witty, sardonic—oh, completely *crazy* notes, she saw that now. He said he would be starting to work in the fall with an oil company; we would travel to the Middle East, to Venezuela, to Brazil. . . .

"The mother is a widow?" Godnick asked.

"Yes." Somehow Lydia had lost track of Mrs. Savaard in her tale. Yes, the mother lived in that big summer house all year round and hated the idea of her son getting married—like the woman in some Greek drama, she would have liked to explain to the lawyer; the mother's warnings were mysterious, obscure riddles cried out—"Mrs. Savaard had reservations," Lydia said. And nothing would do after they *were* married and home from Nassau but they go out to see Henry's mother every weekend and fix up a little house on her property—more for her sake, Henry said, to please. . . . It must be understood that there was never any "adorable momsy" business between them. No, that would be too open and above board, that would be almost funny to the Savaards. It was all lies: "his job for instance was just ordinary."

"What do you mean 'ordinary'?" Godnick asked.

"He was a trainee in a junior executive program!" Lydia could still be scandalized by the thought. "Henry wasn't going to South America or anywhere. That was all made up. Mrs. Savaard blamed me. As far as she was concerned I deserved the abuse." Lydia stopped. She had said enough, but the boredom in Godnick's eyes told her that she was wrong again.

"What did he do, Mrs. Savaard?" he asked indulgently.

"He beat me."

"Some men beat their wives every week, but that doesn't put them in an asylum for the rest of their lives."

"I know." She felt trivial under his gaze. "I have no proof that he ever was sick; but I know that between Henry's graduation from Princeton and our first meeting a whole year of his life is not accounted for. His mother has never told . . ."

"First we contact the mother," said Godnick.

Lydia answered rationally, though she believed nothing would come of that. He paced the office floor, reciting legal possibilities and complications, his mournful eyes cast down on the dull broadloom. She followed his words attentively, but when he stopped, she said, "If there is nothing else?"

"This insanity, Mrs. Savaard—I still can't make a case," his clever, impatient eyes (she watched him) calculating all the angles: his smile showed him to be as sympathetic as possible, but the lawyer had no use for her delicacy. He wanted things spelled out, words on the city streets. Lydia stood for a moment like a plain schoolgirl.

"Henry ordered two-hundred-dollar suits one month and wore frayed collars with them the next. A pattern, isn't it? I have a scar which runs in a line—" she drew her gloved hand across the breast of her black suit "—quite by accident you might say. I did—I said it was quite by accident with a kitchen knife—to the doctor who sewed me up. I said I was naked—at midnight—peeling an avocado pear."

"I'm sorry—" Godnick said with respect, "I'm sorry."

It was windy outside, darkening, the scent of another shower in the air. Lydia took a cab back to the women's hotel, and when she paid the driver she thought of Mary Agnes Keely. It would be necessary to pay her back: put a dollar in an envelope and leave it at the desk. What was left of her sensibilities might demand that she be grateful if she met the loony-bird in the elevator, but she could not bear to see the spinster now, full of green hope, twittering like a ridiculous wind-up toy—and somehow demanding life even from Lydia's ruined world.

"Miss Keely, I believe I owe you a dollar." She printed her message in an anonymous hand on hotel stationery; then she felt free to dwell on every move, every word in God-nick's office—her legally satisfying story of Henry, his mother, and her own pathetic innocence.

In her dim room "charming" came to mind. A conversational word . . . he was the most charming boy at the Christmas party where we met. . . . Cheating to begin with: an easy, unthinking description of Henry's lost, self-approving smile, frightening in its power to cast a spell over a whole room. A golden boy with soft authoritative words. A reincarnation of the grown boy as he was before two world wars, upper-class American manhood, terribly dated, like drawings of magazine heroes with high collars, wavy hair, and faces narrow, feminine in their perfection—but what a cruel time she had spent figuring this about Henry, what a distance he had taken her from that idyllic band of Princeton boys and their smiling girls.

Now she knew: every one of them—shapeless yet conforming—wanted to believe in Henry Savaard that night. He seemed to arrive from another world, almost foreign in its intricacy and appeal. His desultory pride and air of self-destruction was stronger than anything they'd got hold of. Someone brought a present, a tiny Swedish crèche from Bonnier's, and when the bright wooden figures were set out on the table the Mary and Joseph were awfully cute, the baby a faceless bead, and those darling animals.

I told a boy that I found Henry Savaard charming and he said, "Yeah, but he turns it off."

In the summer someone went off to Europe and left him a sailboat. He told most of his lies playing the winds, sweeping the shore with such economy of gesture—I was only ballast. We idled off Montauk, sneering at the hired fishing boats with their cargo of pale, beer-bellied factory workers who would be given fish to take home. His body was frail but hard—not a false move in it. Too much would be lost in a statue.

She had owned up and told Mr. Godnick an honest, true story—but it failed to buoy her up. She sat listlessly in her slip at the foot of the bed.

The mother came out on the porch to ask where they had been, appeared in hallways, came sneaking to the kitchen door—gray-haired, with the same features that made Henry too pretty but gave Mrs. Savaard the face of an athlete. Where were we going? Who would we be with? Her questions were burdens upon them in the summer heat. The mystery had been easy to solve: a widow with nothing much to do, waiting for Henry to come in, stealing out onto the terrace of her big stucco house to call his name.

We walked out through the French doors down to the sunken garden where Mrs. Savaard waited, pretending to read without her glasses. She fell back, wounded, on her chaise longue, and told poor Henry not to marry. He stood helpless between his mother and me, appealing to us both. Mrs. Savaard drew herself up on one elbow and said, "A *sweet* girl!"—and then fell back stiffly on her chaise, twitching her man's face, her inspired gray eyes not hating *me*, because I wasn't even in it. She put a marker in her book, saying that we would have to excuse her: dear old friends were coming for a drink, and she walked past us, up into the dark living room. We could see her moving about in that vast room with blackened beams crossing over her head, and wing chairs, an ugly Queen Anne card table, Tudor windows of the twenties.

"How could anyone blame me?" Lydia wanted to shout it out. "He lied. I said that . . ." (Out of his twisted mind he had spun her castles on the sand of Nassau.) She counted out three aspirin and one sleeping pill.

"Mr. Godnick, we bought wildly expensive chairs covered in green silk, and delicate tables that later broke with one blow. . . . Our bed was false gold, brass that injured his hand. I didn't realize until his suntan faded to yellow that we were elegant children playing house." (She could not recall the number of times she tried to get him to a doctor.) "He said they all hated him in the office: the messenger boy conspired with the Board of Directors, the typists snubbed him in the elevator, executives plotted against him in the washroom." (Their love grew jaundiced, too.) "Henry wouldn't take a bath, but he stood white above me, beating and beating . . . remembering nothing after, he seemed to believe about the avocado."

"Annul"—it meant intact to her, and it would come to mean, she told herself as she huddled on the narrow bed, a recaptured virginity. In the pink-and-white hotel room her dreams of redemption through Mr. Godnick carried her into sleep. Still someone beat and beat again.

When she roused her half-drugged body to open the door, there was Mary Agnes Keely, an apparition in white terry cloth, her hair rolled into a crown of fat chocolate sausages.

"I owe you fifteen cents; it was only a dollar-fifty, and I gave Mr. Perez a quarter." She chewed at that apple. Lydia Savaard drew back with a dry smile which Miss Keely mistook for an invitation and swept into the room, there to perch on a lavender hassock (with bells on crocheted slippers she shall have music wherever she goes), hugging her bony knees to her bird-breast, ready for a chat.

To Lydia it was a scene in her college house. She sighed —that was where she wanted to be, wasn't it? Through the gauze curtains they could see the spring rain.

"Il pleut dans mon coeur comme il pleut sur la ville," Mary Agnes intoned. The chocolate sausages bobbed on her head.

"You wouldn't like to see a couple of old foreign movies later on? I missed them in New Haven."

"Well . . ." answered Mrs. Savaard, "perhaps." She allowed a dime and a nickel to be dropped into a cool yet receptive palm.

3

<hr/>

A Saturday, early June—

I am glutted for the moment with whatever I demand—
my cut of life—and as I write for the second time in my
yellow journal (I suppose the pad becomes my Journal), I
remember a story about soldiers in a concentration camp:
they shriveled—scurvy, rickets—bellies popped. When they
were freed their liberators handed out goodies: chocolate,
caramel, almonds. Many died. Death by Milky Way. Death
by pie.

And I think of old Duffy lived in the next block to us.
He went out to the pantry after Thanksgiving dinner, when

all the other Duffys were prostrate on their beds. Poor old Duffy was diabetic, and at dinner he denied himself all he craved: fruit cup in heavy syrup, gravy, stuffing, pie, even the puffed sugar mints; but later in a solitary passion the old man sat at the kitchen table and devoured an *entire* pumpkin pie. He was dead that very afternoon.

"He went happy," said Eileen Duffy at the wake, "always had a sweet tooth, God rest his soul."

So pity me, Mary Agnes Keely, after the bread-and-water existence I have led, tasting the fleshpots at last. Is it my own end I'm after? Will *I* be found one day on the pavement, after a good lunch, with my French poets in hand, surfeited with the smorgasbord of New York? I amuse myself by writing of food, but on a perfectly literal level I can still taste those boiled dinners of my mother's, with canned vegetables and soft manufactured bread. Now I devour wondrous cheese cakes, curries, omelets—and my dress pulls at the waist.

A Saturday morning, and going through the clutter at the side of my bed—I had meant to read on in the life of Verlaine—I discovered this yellow pad. Lydia has put away my books in some logical place—all to the good, for I shouldn't launch the weekend with a Frenchman's dissipation. Yet, Verlaine, *c'est moi*—the simple nostalgia for a domestic life, a weak and sentimental man trying to settle himself in a cozy way—heart of a poet, soul of a clerk. A fat disgrace of an uncle with advice: Absinthe thee from felicity awhile.

Well it *is* easy to be charmed by the sound of my own voice, the sight of my words on a page. I determine to put down in businesslike fashion thoughts on the new apartment—there's a hell of a stretch before I get into the bathroom: Lydia Savaard has just started her ritualistic ablutions.

To begin: when I came to the city I lived at a small hotel for women. The lobby inspired me with its black-and-white tiles marching in chaste precision to the golden elevator doors. I felt like a new person, *du monde*, walking and smiling differently. There, before we moved to this apartment, I had an identity: Miss Keely, 21A.

I do not move with ease in unfamiliar settings; only one place ever claimed me: my mother's dingy flat. Its dark rooms still imprison my memories: the scent of moth crystals burdening the air when I came in from the zipper factory, spoiling the earthy smell of spring: my mother rewrapping her stillborn baby's clothes in newspaper, brushing my father's worn fireman's uniform (he was buried in a new one), airing that dress of yellowed crepe de Chine, the dainty tea gown she was married in. I had to finger the transparent wings of that dress to believe in her story: a violet net bag of rose petals was pinned to the waist, defeated by thirty years of naphthalene.

"There's how small I was." My mother forms a circle with her coarse purple hands. "Years after Francis and you came I wore it to the Firemen's Ball—Easter Monday; they always held it at the Armory before the Knights of Columbus was built."

Year after year she preserves her unhappiness, brushing, spraying, wrapping it in the *Evening American* so she will have it to unpack and savor yet another ruined spring. Fondling my brother's Navy uniform, bawling: "Lost my son, lost my son—way up there in Buffalo, might as well be Japan . . ." and so on. Through the aerosol spray I see my own limp gown of blue tulle, *circa* 1941, intended for a high-school prom, worn by that jilted maid in the Living Rosary—another Hail Mary stuck at the end of a decade because of my height. An accumulation of my worn-once costumes: pink taffeta, teal velvet, beige lace—jeering: always a bridesmaid—never mind. I only meant that the mothball spring days back there are richer, penetrate more than anything here in New York. The feeling of being "at home" in the lobby of the Touch-Me-Not Hotel is thin—and anyway suffering is more valuable, more exquisite than comfort: the mutually destructive love of mother and daughter more substantial than tidy freedom. I too describe the color of vowels—in a murky spectroscope of unintentional evil— when the ba-ba-bloo of the night meets the ga-old of the day, someone waits for me-hee.

So I have to saturate this city, this neighborhood, this apartment, with sorrow, love, hate, happiness. My!—girlish My!—and will this bring me eventually to the same bondage? Yes—but the time and the scene of action will be mine. The exits will be mine. I will believe in my rooms as I have always believed in the golden-morning set of *Oklahoma*. There was corn and sunshine. Or in the Chekhovian garden (back street dump of a theater)—*that* was the end of summer, and *there* in a rustic arbor the bored lovely lady struck an attitude of grace.

I must get into the kitchen and start breakfast . . . I hear Lydia's slippers slapping on the bathroom floor, mid-point in the service . . .

"I will wash my hands among the innocent." She will eat nothing for breakfast but black coffee and dry toast, but I want to make the air rich with bacon smell and construct a layer of marmalade on thick English muffins.

While I have a minute, something more about having to make my own world, not accept one made for me in a disappointed woman's womb . . .

My poor old man, trained to put out fires. He sure did. My wretched mother burning to be more than a fireman's wife.

"The more fool I, Tim Keely"—struck dumb with shame, my cousin and I overheard them from our bedroom—"listening to your plans for a great career." My father was a shy man who bored her to chocolate cake in the evenings while he read Ring Lardner and Sherlock Holmes under the fringed lamp. Often they did not speak, not so much in anger, just without words for each other. The cruelest thing he ever said was, "Whatever happened to your painting on china and your water-color pictures?" My mother had been "artistic" before her marriage, and copied moose under pine trees and peonies dropped on a Spanish shawl from the illustrated ladies' magazines.

Why do I always come back to her? Because it's painful to write about this apartment, empty rooms which will always echo my foolishness. I'll allow myself one more dodge: listen to Lydia Savaard gargling with minty antiseptic down to the lesions in her heart. She is young, average height, average build, medium-colored eyes, hair neither blond nor brown worn in nondescript style. Her nose and mouth are set in the right place, well proportioned; in fact, the only thing worth mentioning about her face is the excess of injury and disappointment. We all play a game of musical chairs, and Lydia has been beaten out.

Let me try it this way: she lives in this apartment as if in a prison—no walls, no locks, but a prison nevertheless— tin trays and latrine duty. Her only emotion is moral indignation; she's gloomy, but not like the Irish, on top of the world then in despair: she comes out of her black moods only pretending she finds me the funniest clown on stilts she has ever seen, but then I can't help feeling she's only been to the slicked-up circus, never to the old down-and-out freak show. The cheap restaurants I search out, this apartment I stumbled upon, Lydia accepts them with the same wistful smile—life, she would have me believe, is quite finished. What does she intend to do with her suitcase full of emptiness? There are no costume changes, no false noses or transformations, nothing to disguise the dullness, and yet it fascinates me—an alien world, her genteel background and good education.

One day I asked this question: "Did you ever know anyone who wore nylon blouses, the sort they first made, sleazy, sheer, you saw all the bra straps and the slip?"

"No," Lydia replied, "I never did."
(Well, you do now.)

She enters from the bathroom. Her face and hands are red from washing. "What are you writing?"

"Nothing."

"I must get up to the laundromat."

"Wait till I eat and I'll go as far as Gristede's." I have decided to wear my canvas slacks and the burlap poncho.

"What are you writing?" She has ripped the dirty sheets off our beds with personal vengeance. She has put on her Saturday morning uniform, something Ida Lupino once wore in *Girls Behind Bars*. She has started the *Tribune* crossword puzzle:

"*A town in southern Spain? A tragic mother: lit.?*"

I am ready to go: "Duessa," I suggest absently.

"No, five letters."

"Medea."

"Of course." Lydia, gratified, hitches up her sack of soiled linen. "It fits with Malaga."

The next day: a warm Sunday has loped to 11 A.M.—

Nearly a month ago I left my room at the hotel to pass the day at the Museum of Modern Art. It was a brilliant day, verging on summer, and the air conditioning in the Museum was stimulating. For the first time I saw more than blobs and the smattering of objects and figures in organized compositions; I saw some pictures that were funny, others that were horrific. Delighted with myself, I bought lunch: an excellent cheese-and-jelly followed by a Napoleon ice-cream brick. Then I settled in the courtyard to decipher Baudelaire. It was pretty heady—a passage describing the sinister lady of his dreams, above me the noble family group of Henry Moore. A man came.

He said: "This is not occupied?"

41

"No," and I pretended to go back to my book. The man: forty-five, gray temples, gray suit, pale flecked eyes that changed from reserve to visionary wisdom. He was reading a French newspaper, and when I could contain myself no longer I asked, "Pardon me, do you know what *taudis* means?"

"*Pardon?*"

I pointed to the word in my book. And with amusement he exclaimed, "Ah, *taudis!*", pronouncing it properly.

"Baudelaire say . . . this hovel, this room of eternal boredom which is mine."

"Thanks."

We talked, and I let him lead me down the garden path, begged for it. Gracious! I can't believe myself, it all came so naturally—talking with M. Chatelaine, an art dealer. He showed me a cartoon in *L'Express*, after the card players of Cézanne but with faces of the political rulers who deal out the tricks to us all tired and joyless. I did not understand the caption, but, "Yes, yes," I felt the truth of it. M. Chatelaine accepted me: the wisdom of his eyes found a place for Mary Agnes. An extraordinary thing, sympathy in the eyes of a stranger who will be from that instant my friend: we will agree, we will understand. Our look said yes, yes, but there was a demure moment for me after "exposure."

We stepped across the little bridge which spans the garden pool.

M. Chatelaine: "You are fond of Baudelaire?"

"Yes, my, yes! This year I'm reading all the *symbolistes*. My French is rotten. I'll never catch up."

"Catch up? Mademoiselle, ees not a train, the great literaturrre."

"A *century* has gone by and I'm just finding out. I don't discover anything myself."

Alors—

(Flapping my arms, describing inaccurately a great hawk

flight): "It's an inferior mode. All my life I sit, I sit like a cripple and read, read, read—"

"Ah! In America you have such taste for running up."

We talked like this for a long while. Time was unimportant in a meeting like ours.

M. Chatelaine—how shall I describe him so that my future imaginings don't transform him into Hollywood's Continental hero? His temples were gray, it's true, and from where I looked down on him I could see his pink scalp with only a wiry black tuft to disguise its nakedness. His feet and hands were delicate, but those hands had strength to emphasize his words, and I sensed the control, the artfulness of M. Chatelaine's gestures. Here translucent fingers cupped the essence of beauty, the love of humankind, there they flattened downward in a mock blessing for *matérialisme*, swept out in a breast stroke that we might swim through the *banalité*. The thumb and forefinger held an invisible host —nothing, nothing any more in this world, holding that nothingness there, the only thing left to us.

He said: "Dry, empty—the prosperous persons of Paris are dry—and here too." Chatelaine was a *petit*, exuberant man with full mobile lips that suddenly thinned to a cut in his face asking, I thought, "What is this woman?"

As I record this it's too stilted, but we *did* talk like this about my reading, and about politics, travel, art. We were, after all, Mary Agnes Keely and M. Chatelaine—improbable people. Yes, I see myself, limp giraffe neck bending to *mon ami* as we walk around the garden dodging the statues. I wear my new Mexican skirt with the fringed border; silver fish (also Mexican and new) dangle from my ears. I have often caught sight of myself, my spine humped over, defining my hollowness, my head too heavy for my body, swinging like the oversized blossom of some cruelly bred plant; admiration for the world spread for the world to see on my gullible face—unlike my other face with the sour look of a starved peasant. Discover the *real* you, the girl

43

who's not shy of new smash-up pinks, the woman always soft as her cocoon-of-mohair stole who can be as sharp on the Market as she is on coffeehouse poetry—the lady in traditional black daringly cut who offers not the disturbing flush of youth but serenity and knowledge.

Me: Mary Agnes Keely in my would-be Bohemian dress, a novice in New York, unemployed, unmarried, unlovely, untouched.

Experience: limited.

Education: Hard Knocks High, English Award for "Not By Bread Alone," also study of literature as a substitute for life.

Position: vulnerable.

So I strolled round the courtyard of the Museum with M. Chatelaine, who, wise man, was too proud to look up at a woman. He contemplated the honest-to-goodness Métro entrance stuck against a wall and drew in to himself, deciding upon his *destination*, his lips in a taut line, pale eyes coated with reserve—not regretting our sudden friendship but making very little of it.

Last month, under the indifferent sky of New York, in Fifty-fourth Street's avant-garden of Modern Art, a small cynical dealer in *objets d'art*, meticulously buttoned into a dove-flannel suit, set out on a course that the world . . .

M. Chatelaine: dago-dazzler, urbane, self-employed.

Pressure: normal.

Blood: high.

Position: en garde toujours.

"*À neuf heures, Mademoiselle,*" he said as we parted.

"Yes," I chirped, "nine o'clock."

The streets changed to chill blue on my way back to the hotel and I wished I had brought my jacket. I stopped at Lydia Savaard's room and saw she had taken those pills to make her sleep the whole day. She threw a cotton wrapper over her pajamas, and attempted to hide the uneaten chicken sandwich on her dresser which I had brought up to her the night before.

After a long look at me, blinking the daze out of her eyes, she said, "Mary Agnes."

"Headache?" Every time I came upon Lydia still in her night clothes, the shades drawn, the day gone by, I asked after her health. Her room had the stale dimness of an invalid's last place on earth, nothing used but the pill bottles and a glass with a spoon in it. She was the only person I knew in New York at this time, besides the people I talked to in shops and parks, so I had taken to stopping by at her room, at first to make a friend and later to see that she was still among the living. My trick was to talk to Lydia Savaard as though she cared about my adventures.

"Well, I may have found an apartment."

"In the *Times*?"

"A man I met." I gave a sly wink that always made her laugh.

"That man with the coffee-energy candy?"

"No. M. Chatelaine." I said his name with pleasure. "A Frenchman."

"Really, Mary Agnes!"

"You sound like my mother."

"Well, it's none of my business . . ." She stepped into the bathroom and began to wash. I could see the side of her face as she rubbed at the lifeless skin in the ghastly fluorescent light—like washing a corpse, the eyes set, mouth dry. When she came back and stood in the dim room she seemed to be considering some remote metaphysical idea.

"I should imagine one would eventually get in a mess, picking up all these men."

"All talk—no action."

She went to the window, raised the shade and saw that it was night again. Then—for something to say—she asked: "How many rooms in this apartment?"

"I don't know."

"What's the rent?"

"I didn't ask."

"Really, Mary Agnes." Lydia Savaard turned to look up at me, her eyes filled with self-pity. "You could meet some crazy man that way."

"I have my dreams."

But no one was more rational than M. Chatelaine. He opened the door to me cautiously.

"Ah, Miss Kelly."

At first sight the apartment appealed to my overdeveloped sense of wonder. Crammed within the high narrow rooms of the last century were crude cupboards, settees, tables, all worn to a luster. My foot dumbly set a cradle rocking. Mixed with farmhouse furniture were large gilt chairs big enough for royalty to sit in, and a scattering of small tables with gold edges and porcelain pictures set in the wood.

"You will understand," M. Chatelaine explained, "that some things you see here now will ship with me to France." He hurried me down a dark hallway to a galley kitchen. I realized that we had passed the bedroom, and I could make out the glint of chairs against the bulk of heavy wood objects—more of the primitive stuff there.

"I have a client who is very entertained by your American antiques of the countryside," said M. Chatelaine, dancing back to the living room with dainty steps—like someone in a ballet, really, those articulate hands touching velvet drapes and cut-glass decanter. He poured me a glass of wine.

Mon ami opened a package of pistachio nuts, and I sat on a bench which was once a church pew. As soon as I hit the hard seat my spirits sank, as though I was with my mother at Mass. In his apartment on Ninth Street M. Chatelaine was disappointing—less masterful than he had been in the Museum garden. Here with his wares, I saw that he dealt in homely articles, and the ruby velvet which closed us in from the street, the glittering droplets of a chandelier over a milking stool, made the antique dealer ordinary, a buyer and seller of the used furniture of life.

How I must have looked to him, my shoulders drooped, my deflated dream in plain view.

"But it is commodious?" he asked.

"Oh, yes." I looked at the high ceiling, remembering that we had talked that afternoon of humanity, art, essentials— and so this, our second interview, seemed tainted. My questions were on too grand a scale, his answers inappropriate. Yes, the ceilings were high, and who was I, Queen of Zippers, to complain when he took my hand in his and drew me round the room to look at his pictures?

"See here, ees little girl with cat . . ."

I agreed—"so simple, so unaware," and began to enjoy myself once more. M. Chatelaine's paintings were American primitives, straightforward in their charm: a little girl with flat round face and Sunday-school eyes holding a cat more wild than she would ever know; two wooden horses out of a toy box pulling a red wagon along a narrow canvas on a road with no perspective; trees growing God's mottoes as well as his fruit; beasts and birds and men and angels joined in allegories of heaven on earth—right here on our earth—with barns and houses I have seen in Watertown and Branford.

"There is nothing to compare with this strength," said M. Chatelaine. "It was a great hope, and ees it not still, Miss Kelly?"

"No," I said, "I don't think naïvety can help anyone . . . ever again." Then we sat in gilded thrones and talked as we had in the garden that afternoon, about the simple ones who can see directly, and the *poseur primitif,* and oh, so many subjects to do with art, human beings, responsibility, and LIFE. The wine gulped hypnotically into my glass and the pistachio nuts compelled—soft-cracking and rosy-staining. Ah, and my Frenchman—

"*You* have the quality of early art *en Amérique* . . ."

"Golly, Monsieur!"

"Eef not of the artist themselves."

"But alas—"

Now if there is anything that makes you feel more like a saint, superior to the whole world, it's this kind of talk, all very high-minded, the eyes of a man and woman meeting. Yes, I must have looked come-hither with my cheeks the color of my red dress, a fateful combination of rouge and blushes, and my eyes gone seductive, looking straight into the man as though I wanted to see his soul. It is painful to write it down at all.

THE FOOLISH VIRGIN

After the people had gone home from work and all but the questionable shops had closed, the virgin arrived in the city. The sky was red with debauchery. The smoke of cooking fat and cigarettes drifted in the streets, and she thought it was beautiful to be so close to the clouds which before she had seen only up in the sky. Meeting a corpulent man in fine clothes she asked, "Please, sir, where can I get some oil for my lamp?" When he didn't answer, the virgin asked: "Where can I get a good steak?"

"That I know," said the fat man. "Manny Wolf's."

After she finished eating her steak and smoking her first cigarette, she looked at all the happy people who were husbands and wives and lovers and businessmen helping their business friends to relish and ketchup. The glow of satiety which she had often dreamed of lit the diners from secret and indirect places (part of the atmosphere). This clever lighting reminded the virgin of her duty, and she asked the waiter, "Where can I get some oil for my lamp?"

"We use only pure imported oil," he answered.

"It's getting late," she told the waiter, "and if I want to be wise, I better find the oil for my lamp."

"You want to speak to the manager, lady?"

"Where can I see a little life?" she asked.

"Depends," the waiter said. "Me, I like to walk around—Times Square."

She ran on tippy-toe to where there is no night and where a great monitor entertains the crowds with the happening news, where a Chinese midget lady draws all her subjects firm-jawed and alike, where heroes are foot-long phallic sandwiches and where everyone knew so much that the poor virgin felt that she and one blond sailor were alone. Wanting urgently to be wise, she went up to the kind policeman and said: "Where can I get some oil for my lamp?"

"Let me see that lamp," the policeman said, for it reminded him of one that was sold as a souvenir, but the virgin's had no decal of the Empire State.

"O.K., move along," he said, pointing down Broadway with his heavy wand.

She walked to the end of the city and prepared to leave by the *S.S. Cornelius Goffe*, knowing sadly that at that very moment up in the East Sixties the wise virgins were trimming their wicks for all the bridegrooms who were kissing them on their necks.

Hope faded as the city floated away, but turning up from the dark water the foolish virgin sighted a great lady with a glowing lamp and shouted out, "Say, where do you get the oil for your lamp?"

The big lady finished the chorus of her corny song.

"Oh, please," the virgin called, "where do you get the oil for your lamp?"

"No one uses oil any more," the big lady said. "You've been had."

"Goody," the foolish virgin cried, and felt very wised-up.

Sunday evening—

Yes, I paid M. Chatelaine two months in advance and a month to insure any damage to his irreplaceable furnishings, with his assurance that the apartment would be less like a shop when I moved in. He had his compatriot client, muchly entertained by Americana.

(Now then here is Lydia fresh from another soak. From a whiff I'd say she'd been into the geranium bath salts again.

"What did you do with the paper, Mary Agnes?"

"Here. I seem to be sitting on it."

"Oh dear"—she is more unhappy than ever—"you've got the print all over your pants."

"How grand. It's a big picture of the Shakespeare Festival I've been squatting on.")

No discipline. I should say that it was Lydia Savaard who exclaimed, "Mary Agnes, did you give that man money?"

"I gave him a check."

"You don't know anything about him, not even who he is." This was our great bond then: after all the weeks of my trying to wake the girl from her trance she now wanted to save me.

"You've no lease? Who owns the building?"

I could see that she argued from experience—a con man had sold her sour grapes for champagne. She changed that drawn old lady's face she wore for one remarkably similar, of a young matron who scouts out bargains at the supermarket and lavishes her care on some remote humanitarian cause: Save the Children and Miss Keely Committee.

It was on a Friday morning she sought me out for the first time, the night before I had committed myself to M. Chatelaine. Lydia wore a Puritan collar.

"I'm going to a lawyer today—" she looked blankly at the door "—about personal matters, and I fully intend to ask him what recourse you might possibly have."

I said, "Well," or "My!" Then I put one of the questions to her that had occupied me since last night: "What kind of furniture is it with fancy metal and painted china set into the top?"

"With ormolu?" she asked. I hadn't a clue.

"Whatever it is, Mary Agnes, that stuff is easy enough to imitate. No one is about to go off to Paris and leave a perfect stranger with . . ." Her clucking reminded me of my old mother. She marched off full of *vertu*, and I realized I had been intrigued by Lydia Savaard in the role of a mournful enigmatic woman prepared for a living death. Barely functioning from day to day she had made a mystery of her passive world. With each long sigh she seemed to proclaim, "I dare you to condescend," but as the efficient person cooling her clickety heels in front of the elevator she commanded little attention. With some regret I must add that she was motivated by a diabolical revenge on *man*kind, not by devotion to the indefensible Miss Keely.

When Christ raised Lazarus from the dead I wonder if He was disappointed in him? With the shroud off was he a boring type? Grateful, a little sleep in his eyes from the grave, all set to be tedious about his experience?

"All right," I said calmly over my egg-drop soup, "we have only to wait till Monday." The pork in sweet-and-sour sauce was extra delicious that Friday night, and even Lydia had to laugh when I chewed open my fortune cookie: "Your future will be realized soon."

She, of course, had ordered almond cakes, annoyed by fortune, though she did smile—not at my patsy performance this time, but at herself. The juices were running again: she'd put a touch of lipstick on her bloodless mouth. But still she bickered. "You can stop payment on the check, Mary Agnes."

I was obsessed with those inlaid tables at M. Chatelaine's. Whole scenes painted on those small insets no bigger than a saucer: ladies and gentlemen walking out in vast parks with classic colonnades; Venus displaying herself naked on rocks —the landscape of high romance stretching back as far as the eye could see. Fragile and meaningless—the decorative arts had never been part of my life except as I remember them with bitterness in the Doric capitals stuck below the

"Girls" entrance sign at my high school, or the tin plate with some bright scene captured in Kodachrome that covered a defunct flue high on the kitchen wall over our expensive electric range. And once my cousin Sherry, while she was still beautiful and live, had cohabited with lots of fancy furniture, fabrics, carpets and things . . .

Lovely things. "Don't you miss your lovely things?" I asked my cousin after she had moved to barren rooms designed for a divorcée.

"God, Ag! I never noticed—like they got thrown out with the potato peelings."

Now I held the key, literally, to the world of niceties where objects are chosen like jewels for a woman to adorn the regrettable fact of living. The key to M. Chatelaine's apartment slipped about at the bottom of my carryall, nuzzling the spine of *Paris Spleen*, lost for a terrifying moment in the wrapper of a Hershey bar.

O bright little Yale key, cut in the combination of my secret heart, open the world of pretty tables and artful scenes that I, too, may find craggy rocks of love as desirable as a foam-rubber mattress. Open with your sweet irregular teeth, o my key, rooms that will be mine, crammed with regrets, heated with responsibility, where happiness hangs like a cobwebbed chandelier, each crystal called a teardrop.

Pretty easy to run off at the mouth in that manner. Fantasy is easy—like my thoughts of the precious weekend before I moved to Ninth Street. A bit more difficult to admit that on Saturday morning I received a manila envelope full of bills: gas, electric, water, house painter, children's bathing suits, and a doctor's bill for a costly malady which seems to have been with my mother all spring.

"How did she ever find you?" asked Lydia.

"My brother, I imagine. He's with the FBI."

"Really, Mary Agnes!" Lydia said with familiar exasperation.

"Really."

My brother is one of those straight arrows who defend us against Internal Fraud and the Foreign Powers who roam through the world seeking the ruin of Our Government. He has always been like that—fine and upstanding, with a U. S. Navy medal his wife keeps in a drawer with the children's birth certificates and his B.S. from Fordham. Make no mistake—I am gentle and sincere—you just cannot write ironically about people like my brother, Francis X. Keely. After you're through with your jibes at their Foxcroft Estates and their subscriptions to *Time*, you have to reckon with the man. He bears arms for his country. He would act. In Francis is our hope and our despair, as they say—only it's a pity there's none of the poet in him at all, none of the other Francis they meant to name him for: there's no use trying to picture my brother emaciated with pretty birds on his head and beasts eating out of his hand.

"Will you pay the bills?" Lydia Savaard asked sensibly.

"Yes, there's no way out." Figure it this way: poverty is too good for my mother. How she would love to be pitied by the family and rescued by my brother in her hour of need! . . . "I'm glad her father's not alive, etc., etc." With the bills paid, she can only say, "Money is cool comfort"— not her style. After all the years I've watched her hunt I know the move she'll make, blowing out a screen of lies to hide behind. Of my father she said he never found his niche in the world—that was her burden. It was the courthouse he belonged in, not that firehouse over on Thorne Street. Tim had an extensive vocabulary. . . . Now maybe she would say I was wasting my time at the zipper factory, and what is a mother's sacrifice compared to the opportunity of a brilliant girl like Mary Agnes?

I told Lydia that I had to find a job.

"That Frenchman with all your money."

We were having *bœuf bourguignon* on West Forty-ninth Street, and Lydia cleaned her plate with bread like a good girl. "I must work too." How earnest she was—"I can't keep living on my family. Mr. Godnick will have his legal fees. I must pay for my mistake."

"Your divorce?" I asked.

"An annulment," said Lydia with an awful look of Christian virtue. "You have been so kind. I should tell you, Mary Agnes." Suddenly I felt vulgar for wanting to laugh at her across the cute little table for two—as if I had suppressed a Bronx cheer during the Passion Play.

"My husband is ill. I'm getting an annulment which will bring an end to our disastrous marriage."

"What's wrong with him?"

"Classic paranoia," said righteous Mrs. Savaard. "Violent, manic depressive."

Well, let me say here and now that as her story unfolded I felt more and more sorry for that poor nut Henry Savaard. Think of a handsome boy who everyone wants to be one of the more pathetic types out of Scott Fitzgerald: then he acts the part and they lock him up. Naturally this is a world I know nothing about—how could I, always having lived with the mad who are free to walk the streets?

There we sat, twisting lemon peel intimacies in our coffee —which is another way for friendship to begin (my first big fling having been with universal truths and M. Chatelaine).

And now Lydia, the sad girl I had jollied, rewarded me with her undernourished past: From Cleveland to Vassar, then to a job on children's story books. At last she found Henry. He touched her unspoiled face with eyes all for him. He smelled summer in her hair. Did she dote on his long aristocratic toes? Was there the taste of salt on his back after they went swimming in Nassau? I am moved by all that; I would cry with her—if I thought for one moment that she had ever cried for him.

"Don't you see?" Her serious pale face quickened with injury. "I am too ashamed of what I have done to keep

taking money from my parents. My friends—I'm supposed
to forget it and not depress them."

(*Just one minute, please, who the hell is in this hospital
anyway?*)

"I don't want to see a living soul until I am free."

"When will that be?"

"When Mr. Godnick gets my annulment," Lydia said,
sure of the way things come true.

We arrange to go live on Ninth Street and save money
to pay our debts. Little Lydia will find that lost girl in
sneakers and knee socks and be free. Mary Agnes will find
that sensuous full-blown Cleopatra and be free. Open
Sesame: on Monday morning with our suitcases still out on
the landing we enter the apartment: a narrow empty room
with dingy linoleum floor, one three-legged love seat
bravely standing, the velvet curtains—more puce than ruby
in the morning light—*naturellement* a bare light bulb, and
in the bedroom two army cots with stained mattresses. The
magic key was still in my hand. I laughed out loud.

"It's not funny." Lydia's whole body was stiff with
offense.

"Now, Mary Agnes, you must go to the landlord of this
building," she began in the patronizing manner of a kindergarten teacher, and I knew this was the tone she had taken
with dear Henry as he came toward her with some cock-
eyed notion passionately blooming in his head.

"When you lose your money learn to lose," I sang, and
my voice bounced off the walls of the empty room.

"There must be someone in charge." Off went Lydia with
a belligerent chin, and returned with a hefty Jewish woman
in orthopedic shoes and sundress. Mrs. Mertz, owner and
"super" of the building, had seen everything, including me.
I was sitting on the safe end of the three-legged love seat,
but I was no surprise.

"A new linoleum rug last January," said Mrs. Mertz.
"Wall-to-wall."

Mother of God, I can't get down on my yellow pad the act that ensued: righteous Lydia with her heritage of justice and the American Way backing Mrs. Mertz into a corner from which only Mrs. Mertz, with all her experience as the persecuted, could get out of—and even end up holding the whip and a broken chair in her hand.

"One month in advance I have, no security from Mr. Chattle-lain. This he paid to Mr. Mertz, saying a lady would move in for the remainder of the lease."

"She never signed," Lydia cried.

"A *lady?* Already I'm surprised," said Mrs. Mertz. "His boy friends you wouldn't know from ladies." She hiked the sundress back up to the tan line on her breasts. "You look like nice girls," she said pleasantly, "but you understand: I promise nothing until Mr. Mertz has consulted our attorney."

"Why can't I take the apartment?" I asked. "It's paid for the month."

"I never wanted a foreigner in the first place," said Mrs. Mertz, pointing downstairs where she lives. "He—the *New Republic*—says what am I, the immigration authority?"

"Miss Keely paid for a furnished apartment," said Lydia.

"I already told your friend," Mrs. Mertz said to me, "I had this funny feeling Friday afternoon. We left for Monticello. Leon Mertz says, 'What do you want me to do—stay and mind the store?'"

Her feet were encased in shoes of ox-blood red with roomy bunions molded on the joints. Her hair was tawny silver, styled in high fashion, a mad confection topping that world-worn face with hatchet nose.

"*Why* can't I take the apartment?" I pleaded. "*Why?*"

In the end I got the best of them. We have our place. Mrs. Mertz has given us a chrome dinette table from the basement and two canvas chairs which she and Leon once used on summer nights.

"You're welcome," she said, "they fall through the slats." Now as I look out the back bathroom window, I see that on these first warm nights Mr. and Mrs. Mertz enjoy the fire escape in new wicker tub chairs: barely covered, like some South Sea Island king and queen, between them a matching table with an ice bucket and a large bottle of cream soda.

Will it surprise anyone to hear that I am the new copy writer for Wunda-Clutch, manufacturers of the miracle grip which makes the zipper obsolete? No. Seventeen years of virtue rewarded: a knowledge of the market and a fine literary background won me the prize. Wunda-Clutch is the end of talons and tape—no jamming up your sewing machine—the end of unreliable snaps, buttons. So banish unsightly zipper bulge says the complaisant matron to her tortured daughter—and always put toilet paper on a public seat. The hundreds of little Wunda bristles on one side of the fastening clutch at the woven miracle hooks on the other side—like lovers long parted, like babies at their mothers' breasts. The famous burr-action—a rich world of possibilities for me to explore. But note how I am forced to build on the past, even as I pay the Connecticut Light and Power Company and Nick Del Maestro Exterior Decoration and Doctor Thomas Flynn, internist. Yes, yes, I lost my head like a girl at her first dance. M. Chatelaine, I want no part of your ormolu, or whatever. Fie on your Sèvres. Damn your witless girl with cat and all your unnatural animals. How green of me to demand my freedom and then accept M. Chatelaine's furnishings—emptiness, rather: or the anonymous dinette table and the discards of Mrs. Mertz.

What occurred to me so many yellow pages back when I began about this apartment is that I must make these rooms *claim* me; make this place rich with smells and noise so that one day when I am off—maybe just to Coney Island for the day, or perhaps gone forever to a fancy address or

57

to a Home for Catholic Gentlewomen—then just the mention of this place on Ninth Street will fill my throat with a flush of love, or hate, or pity and regret, like memories of home.

For me our apartment must exist as the first place on earth, a Paradise without Adam or as yet a snake; but I have learned patience, and I am waiting, waiting for them . . . not as I was taught to, for the Resurrection and the Life, because I know that with this sort of human epiphany they will come. Meanwhile I learn to cook the most extravagant dishes full of butter and cream and exotic herbs. My *velouté* is superb, my *crêpes* a bit heavy. Now that it is getting warm I will try vichyssoise—and move the buttons on my red silk dress. I wait in a canvas chair, after dinner, reading the life of Verlaine.

Lydia Savaard is waiting too, like a woman unjustly imprisoned expecting the governor to call at any minute with a parole for good behavior. Or are we in a convent here? Each with our chore, Lydia's to clean: I have never seen anything like it—scrub, wash, disinfect the whole weekend until our cells are sterile and her hands incarnadine. She has gone back to her job on children's books. They were glad to have her. (When a girl is young she toys with a job until she marries, is properly more valued as a divorcée or widow, having purged all the nonsense . . . the tough lady executive, our modern Prince Hal.) During the week Lydia brings home manuscripts to read: *Tales of India, The Book of Number Games, Ludwig the Great* (the drab adventures of a flea who wears yellow suspenders), but my favorite is *The Jolly Atom* accompanied by a portfolio of illustrations by the author of a romantic mushroom cloud and an ungodly striped carnation—mu-*tay*-shun caused by ray-dee-*ay*-shun. It explains all the splendid newness that can be because the world is such a routine script (the situation comedies my mother watches, with canned laughter), and we will need something different (meaning better).

Leaning in at the bathroom door, I asked, "Are you going to publish *The Jolly Atom*?"

"We already have our atom book for the intermediate list," she answered, and went back to washing her underwear viciously.

She breathes with a deep physical satisfaction as she hangs her underthings over the tub. Busy: tidying the compound, reading her fairy tales, keeping up with the *Tribune* puzzle. Before the light goes out at night, before she takes a shower in the morning, I recognize that lone, eviscerated girl I met in the hotel lobby. There is a strange scar on her body—I think of a smutty song the zipper salesmen sang at the Christmas party: "Oh, Lydia, Lydia, have you seen Lydia, Lydia, the tattooed lady . . ."—violated, marked forever.

I must write quickly—why labor over notes that should be a diversion?

Sunday night leaves all but the fatuous whimpering with unfulfillment: Lydia, who is sitting by the window for a breath of air, pushes her way through the "News of the Week in Review." Even my mother is expanded into her chair now, watching the Ed Sullivan show, complaining about the Borscht Belt comedian and the Harlem quartet— Fibber McGee could make you laugh. Whatever happened to the Moylan sisters?

Lydia in the window, framed by velvet drapes. The light fades, she folds the paper, sighs. The faded drapery becomes rich again in lamplight. "It's warm in here," she says, and then, shyly, "What are you writing?"

"Nothing." I have been short with her—after all my clowning I've refused to perform. But what makes me self-conscious? That I have written about her? Partially. That I have written about myself? Partially. That I have written things down at all.

My first entry gave balm to old wounds, but I don't know my own flesh now; I have a full covering for my bones, and with this human shape I can no longer diagnose.

"What's eating you, Mary Agnes?" (Well, I thought everything was beginning, and I'm still waiting, Doctor.) "Nothing. A kind of diary, I guess."

"Oh." She is laughing at me again, not overly interested. "If you go out later, Mary Agnes, will you get me a large Lustre Creme shampoo?"

Lydia framed in the window is guessing at gnus, mongooses, prepositions, and generals. The drapery made rich by lamplight is a theater curtain pulled back before the play is ready, before the actress knows her part . . .

"I thought you were going out, Mary Agnes."

"Right now. This minute."

Note: Monday morning I will suggest the use of Wunda-Clutch for space suits, fallout coveralls, etc. "No old-fashioned metal but the safe closing of the future, the sure opening of tomorrow."

"I'm going, I'm going."

And I meant to write so much about the city: pageantry of the garment district, a daiquiri in the Rainbow Room, snubbed by the clerks at Bergdorf's, accepted at Bloomingdale's cheese counter—which makes me yearn for the delicatessen right now.

Framed by the velvet drapes, Mrs. Savaard sits in the window hoping for a cool breeze to erase words which do not fit. The drapery, faded to puce by day, gains color by lamplight. It is a theater curtain drawn back to reveal a plain woman with no role in the play.

To be completely honest, I should get rid of those heavy drapes and let more sun into the apartment, but they remind me of the curtain at the Rialto-Poli back home, the movie house I went to with my cousin every Saturday afternoon. We sat through the serial, the cartoons, the newsreel, the coming attractions, and the double feature, because my mother wanted us to carry the groceries home from Ryan's and go to confession. Except for its opulent curtain I didn't really like that theater, and once I got spider bites on my legs. Still, I took my allowance and went to Poli's every Saturday afternoon to cross my rubicund mother.

Then Grandma Walsh—who lived over at Mae's until she died, who wore black sateen aprons, drank beer and spoke with a brogue, crocheted through her cataracts and remembered where she came from, County Mayo—then Grandma Walsh said, taunting, "And how was your show, Ag?"

"Not so good."

"Well, Fool-eye's got your dime."

4

"To beard the lioness in her den," Lydia thought, "or maybe the mountain is going to Mohammed." She sat next to Mr. Godnick on the Long Island Rail Road. When she met him on the lower level in Penn Station she was fresh, full of their purpose, but now the wilt was setting in, the creases forming in her skirt. Her white gloves, clean this morning, were gray at the seams from the city and blotchy red from an old copy of *Henny Penny Sees the World*. For conversation she told Mr. Godnick that nowadays children's books did not bleed.

She had plotted the trip for Thursday, after lunch, hop-

ing she would avoid Henry's friends (her friends, she supposed they were) who might be going out for the weekend
on a later train. Not her luck—she encountered a boy
named Lovell on the platform; he used to drink a lot, she
remembered, the beginning of a skinny drunk; now he was
fat, with a healthy tan and dull, settled eyes. He looked
closely at Godnick, memorizing his suit, his tie, his hat, his
nose, and uncomfortably touched his skimmer to Lydia.

"Hello." She said it as a terminal remark. Lovell was the
one who started them on grapefruit juice and gin, Tiger
Piss, that summer. She had called it T.P. It wasn't her fault;
she tried and couldn't get the word out of her mouth.

"Something's gone wrong with the air conditioning,"
Godnick observed. He gave her legal papers to read, sentences that doubled back on each other, claiming Henry's
insanity, knowledge thereof, condition existing previous,
before the fact, on unspecified date. At the end there were
several dotted lines.

"We all sign?" Lydia asked.

"Look, I don't expect . . ."

"Here on these lines?"

"If *she* signs, we all sign with a notary," Godnick said.
He wiped the heat from his face, swiping at the indelible
circles under his eyes. To Lydia he was impressive, a man
from the city in a dark suit and good tie going out on
business. His hat was a Panama with a black grosgrain band,
the kind her father wore after Memorial Day. It was more
than acceptable: that hat had distinguished her father in
Cleveland. Easy to imagine it on the long table next to the
empty silver card tray in the Savaards' front hall. Godnick
would go right to work on Mrs. Savaard, he would (to
use his constant phrase) "lay things on the line." A mountain, he looked a mountain beside Lydia on the train, his sad
marmoreal face turned to the scenery which passed him by.

"What if she doesn't sign?"

"I don't expect her to. We want to feel the situation out, leave a copy of the papers . . . lay things on the line."

"What's the use if she doesn't sign?"

Godnick's idea was that she must be kidding: no one can be that dumb. In all his years of wrenching man and wife asunder he never found this simple a girl. She wanted to put the past away, shut the door and walk off—no hate, no love, just mild regrets about the fun life had once been, an itchy memory of how nasty things could be. His women clients all had *some* idea, if only in fantasy—a new man, or a desire to be by themselves, develop thwarted personalities, fondle their children, preserve their dignity, or make a man suffer. But this one wanted to shake off a sick man for no reason at all, and wanted nothing for herself except to go back to the beginning, stand in the first Garden and say, "I don't care for apples, thank you."

Her open mouth still asked the question.

"His mother has refused to answer letters. Hangs up the phone in my face," Godnick said. "Finally I threaten to bring her to court. At least now we get to stand in front of her and let her see we mean business."

"Even if she doesn't sign?"

"That's right."

"*Can* you bring her to court?"

He laughed, "That's another long story," and took the annulment papers away from her.

Lydia thought, "Why all this duplicity?" but kept her peace. She contented herself with Godnick's strength and his reassuring Panama—like her father's. That mattered. Slowly she read through *Henny Penny Sees the World*, each page dealing its sweet-sad ecstasy of recognition. It was the exact same book she had loved as a little girl. That morning she discovered it in the storeroom, down behind the metal supply shelves, a dusty red cloth cover and oh— slightly nicked, set in a band of gold—that unforgettable picture of Henny Penny in her calico apron and sunbonnet

64

with her shopping basket over her wing. All the bright little cuts of Henny's tidy cottage with the plate rack and the table set for a cozy meal, fresh muffins and jam. And, oh God, that wicked fox lurking outside Henny's window with his sack and his brazen plumed hat. The book must be reissued; it was absolutely a classic which had shaped the imaginations of a generation at least, and, oh no, too much —look at that golden labrador, prototype of all the good dogs in the wide world.

"Do you remember," she asked Mr. Godnick, holding out the book, ". . . when you were a child—this wonderful dog?"

"What?" He looked up from his newspaper, "No, at present we have a purebred Siamese. My wife prefers it to the children."

When they arrived he ushered her off the train and into a taxi with the air of a man who has not come to a summer town for sport. They drove past the white frame shops on the main street, which staged the look of a village square in spite of foreign cars, boys in shorts, and the expensive dress shop with a carrousel horse in the window. They drove out toward the shore where all the greenness of lawns and hedges rose up from the road like waves rolling over them in their city clothes and hired cab, and the smell of the sea, unseen, was there for them to breathe.

"This is a beautiful spot," Godnick said.

Her father and mother had said that, when they first came to meet Henry—though wasn't it usually the other way around: the young man presenting himself in the girl's living room? But she had pointed out these houses and roads to her parents; "Magnificent," the Clarks had exclaimed: they had nothing like this to show.

Henry, driving his mother's old Chrysler, was strangely silent until he turned in at the gate. "Here. Here!" His word broke upon them with force, as though he had described the ridiculously large house before them in adjectives freshly minted in the heart. In the dark hallway china asters were stuffed in heavy crystal vases which the Savaards had bought by the dozen years ago, another proof that they could indulge in bad taste. Henry's mother, like a house-keeper in faded seersucker, appeared on the staircase with arms held out in welcome. She took the straggly line of people to her—the timid Clarks from Shaker Heights, her silent son with his smile set by panic. She knew her duty—once upon a time her parties had been reported in *Town and Country* down to the last waxy camellia floating in a finger bowl. At dinner her large face was alive with intimate attention.

"More wine? More lobster?"

They demurred.

"More love?"

"A touch, thank you."

Henry performed like a well-trained horse, stepping high and handsome, coming to his mother with an affectionate nudge for a lump of sugar; the show was on.

Mrs. Savaard was a revelation to Lydia that weekend. All she had ever seen was an austere woman with heavy fea-tures; now Henry's mother led them into the garden, giving them sunlight or shade or a breeze from the sea, giving her own volatile beauty and her own easy way of doing things best. She moved swiftly to close the windows against a thundershower and posed before the French doors in an ancient linen skirt which swept the floor: one of Sargent's great ladies—while Mrs. Clark in a new cocktail dress ram-bled through an anecdote about friends of theirs who had recently returned "brown as berries" from a Sunline Cruise. And her father, Lydia noticed, was unfamiliar too, a portly businessman who let his wife do the talking—with Mrs. Savaard his manners were noticeably fine though somewhat antique. Not really as he had been at the officers' club in

Neuilly, but as he remembered himself in a sentimental haze, the forgotten glory.

"Your mother is great," Lydia said to Henry. She was upstairs, dawdling in his room, going through his shell collection, playing "the girl in love." Next, she tucked a blue foulard scarf in at the neck of her dress, unconsciously imitating the mannish style of Mrs. Savaard.

"She's spied on us all summer, but don't you think she's perfect with my parents?"

"You don't know how she is." She turned and caught his contempt like a blow.

"She's great—I said."

"How the hell would you know what it is for my mother to live like a pauper and stay out here all winter pitied by her friends. For her to be without my father . . . my father . . ." One side of his face twitched, seemed to catch up the words with a horrifying wink. He drew back from her and sat on the edge of the bed, waiting for it to pass, all his fine young looks distorted, until gradually the jumping nerves gave way to a stricken moody stare.

"Henry?" she whispered. Wrongly and simply she thought they had argued, that this was the way men and women fought. He rested his cheek against the smooth turning of the bedpost and looked at the photo of his mother and father which stood on the bureau in a tarnished silver frame.

Lydia had first come to his room one day at the beginning of summer, when Mrs. Savaard had driven off in the old Chrysler. It had seemed a marvelous place, with the sailing cups, the Lawrenceville and Princeton banners, a bookcase full of college texts set beside the Tom Swift and Henty books. They had come up at secret times and lay on the bed in their clothes like children taking a nap—until one afternoon in mid-July when they both stripped before Mrs. Savaard was even out of the gate. Then the whiteness of

67

their private bodies was startling: her breasts, his loins, were soft and pale compared to the lean brown limbs they had known. They hesitated, fondly, drawing apart, but the only strangeness was that they had held off, walking along the beach hand in hand like innocents. Henry's infamous charm had led to more than the usual number of college affairs, but it was part of his game with Lydia to be fresh, unknowing. Now she gave herself without thinking, and like the sailboat lent to him for the summer, she was privileged to be handled by Henry Savaard.

And after, when she came to his room she felt that all his books and banners, the photograph of Henry's parents, were marvelous, had been told in fact that things were special. "One day they were cleaning out some bookcases in the Union Club and my grandfather asked Herman, 'What do you plan to do with Tom Swift, Herman?' and tied them up in his overcoat and walked right out onto Park Avenue. . . ."

Much later, Lydia would say, "So what!"

But the first time round she was enchanted—the second, the third, were lovely too. She could have listened forever when Henry spoke of aunts and uncles, grandparents and aged cousins. He conveyed his own sense of wonder at the self-importance of their lives, and even the grotesque episodes read like Scripture. In the Savaard family there were financiers and ambassadors and grand ladies who had Berenson buy pictures for them and who did not "know" Mrs. Potter Palmer; there was a Titian ceiling, gold serving plates for a hundred, an arboretum, a Philippine girl to embroider the linen, a pavilion by Stanford White, two Jesuits, a leper, one Madame de Sacré-Cœur, a bigamist, and a marchioness. There were old cousins who bred Sealyhams, or classified the seaweed of Long Island Sound, or collected clavichords, or wrote letters to the *Yale Alumni Magazine* about the Old Fence. Savaards had died in all the places worth dying in: Vicksburg, San Juan Hill, the Ardennes, North Africa.

For Lydia his tales had the fascination of a gossipy family novel—Galsworthy or Marquand: richness, panorama, variety, the wildly revealing past that never existed in Shaker Heights with its planned streets and suburban scandal.

On that day when Henry twitched, she said, touching his shoulder lightly, "I know what you mean. Your mother must have been beautiful."

But she never could convert to Henry's private religion, not even during the sickening months of her marriage when she wanted to believe any mumbo-jumbo to make the world reasonable again. It was out of her scope—worshiping eccentric aunts and almighty grandparents, houses sold to embassies and religious orders, paintings in public museums. And there were the young Savaards: brokers, lawyers, a balding civil servant in the Pentagon, society housewives—all ordinary, like the people Lydia had known all her life, with an extra dash of smart-alecky confidence lent by the Savaard name. Henry despised the lot of them for being common—the great tragedy that failed to move her: the humiliation, the disgrace of being no one in particular.

"My parents are waiting," Lydia said.

Henry saw his mother and father in the silver frame, and physical exhaustion drained him, his body filled with aching hollowness. It was the afternoon of the golf tournament and Lilli Briggs's wedding. On a bet, his father played and won in patent-leather dancing pumps worn with plus fours. His mother, in blue silk draped low at her neck, held the large silver trophy and a champagne glass from the wedding. He saw them standing in the best of worlds, against the shingle side of the Club, as he faced them with his first box camera. With a click he captured that day's sunlight, that summer's lawn—brighter and greener in his mind than they had ever been.

His mother said: "Not another. The sun is in my eyes."

His father took off the dancing pumps and walked through

the circle cleared for the local photographer and for the boy. A magnum of champagne was poured into the trophy cup, shared by the Savaards' coterie.

"One sip," his mother warned.

His father said, "Turn your camera to the next number. Slowly when the dots come up." He bent down to the boy. "Did you get one of the boat?" There was the implication that people didn't matter. They would leave together and drive over the green hump of land to the basin and take pictures of the sailboat. The blue folds of his mother's skirt fell in front of his eyes like a curtain.

"So rude," she said, "not to get back to Lilli's wedding."

His father straightened up, and said by way of proclamation, "Only an ass like Lilli Briggs would get married on the day of the golf tournament." People laughed, but to Henry his father's voice was deep with final authority. From that day Lilli Briggs was the girl who had her dumb wedding while his father won the tournament in dancing shoes; and after, when she turned into a divorced and leathery blonde, like many others, he found her an unnatural figure, decadent, a symbol of fallen standards.

"Go back to the beach," his mother commanded, and then, less sharply, "Where are the MacIntyres today? Where's Angus?"

In the summer her hair, skin, eyebrows were all the same shade of honey; her large face, soft and tranquil, seemed washed with golden light. A cluster of ladies in pastel dresses waited for him to go away.

Henry dragged his fingernail around the red celluloid circle in his camera. The group of golfers had started off, led by his father in stocking feet, and then his mother whirled across the lawn, blue silk caught in the air, the empty champagne glass dangling in her hand, and without stopping she grabbed the trophy and ran back to her little boy: a dance, graceful and spontaneous—not one of the pretty, tanned young women waiting for her could have done it—only Julia Savaard. The men watched her. Though nothing surprised them much any more, Julia got at them in some new way—sprinkling the last drops of warm champagne onto the grass, presenting the bright silver cup to Henry.

"Take care of this for Daddy." Her breathless words fluttered about him like wings.

He did not go back to the beach where the children played but way to the end of the wooden porch, where he sat up on a rush-bottom chair—a small, solemn monarch checking the nursemaids and little people who amused themselves in the sand. It was low tide, and his beach extended out in a dark rippling flatland to the turgid sound. Far out in the water boats skitted about. No one *he* knew was out today (ass Briggs's wedding), and the sky was clean of all but perfect sugar clouds. Clutching the trophy (Angus MacIntyre would want to handle it with damp sandy fingers) Henry was high and special above the whole world, until the colored chauffeur came round on the lawn, much later, and whistled to the kid through his front teeth.

"My parents are waiting."

The girl who sat on the bed with Henry was talking—saying with her flat, trusting voice ". . . there's nothing more stupid than taking people at face value. . . ." Her eyes wandered over the room: his books, his ties hung on the mirror, his school banners, his model ships; her eyes, large with belief, accepted his things completely. She had listened with that same open look—no doubts, no laughter —to the stories of his family which rolled over the blankness of his own days like soothing waves.

He picked up Lydia's hand to see the oval ruby set in diamonds, which had been taken from a depleted safety box for their engagement. They were joined in the same creed: Henry felt it, the Lesson of their love; there were fine instructions of independence and power in the old parables which others had discarded as useless and quaint. One girl he had grown up with, slept with, loved slightly, had said that his "Savaard talk" was boring, boring like listening to her grandmother when the old dames paid a call.

"If you still feel jumpy—" Lydia said.

"For Christ's sake, I'm not jumpy."

She always fell for his calm superiority, and nothing was shattered by those few nervous minutes in his boyish room: this was the way a woman gave herself. Lydia imagined they were closer, there was something deeper between them now than making love in the summer.

"Come, have some nice cool T.P.," she whispered.

Mrs. Savaard appeared in the doorway. "You both look a bit sour."

"Oh, no!" Lydia sounded as though she had been stealing cookies, and noticing Mrs. Savaard's dress, the shade of lemons, she said, "That's a nice color."

"It improves with age."

Now, in time of a different nature, Lydia and Mr. God-nick, stiff figures in the back of a taxi, drove in at the Savaards' gate. Pointing back, behind a screen of bushes, she said, "That was our house."

The size of the cottage, miniature Tudor to match the big house, makes it more desolate, Lydia thought. The narrow casement windows screwed shut, the Alice-in-Wonderland door shut too, an empty flowerpot blown over and broken on the diminutive front step. Air should be let in and the curtains drawn until the sun goes down. It was so pretty she imagined that Henry's twisted mouth, full of curses on her, had been far crueler here than if he had gone to pieces in the city, in their rented apartment. Seeing the cottage after so many months brought her back to the hope-less long nights in the hotel when she constructed in elab-orate detail the story of how things should be for them, how they *would* be when Henry wasn't sick any more. . . .

The back door should be open to encourage a breeze from the garden. Nuts to the Savaards; she would set the table with the Italian pottery her mother had sent from the gift shop in Shaker Square.

As she walked up the steps to the big house with Mr. Godnick, Lydia's knees were unsure and her fingers scrambled after the red book which whacked down on the bricks. Henry's mother was at the screen door to meet them with an entirely social manner. The lawyer in his wash-and-wear suit, Lydia in her career-girl dress, waited for their orders, while Mrs. Savaard, who wore sneakers and a shirt of faded sailing blue, took Mr. Godnick's hat and put it on the table with exaggerated care. Once the hat was placed between vases of prize bearded iris, Lydia recognized it as a copy of a Panama—not floppy enough, not creamy enough: the newest thing from Wallach's.

In the living room, prominent and forbidding, sat a tray with gin and tonic, ice, a saucer of lemon slices. Mrs. Savaard talked amiably—the defeating train schedules, the dirty cars—while she made Mr. Godnick a drink. Nothing for me, said Lydia, taking up her position on the edge of a straight chair with her gloves still on. Mrs. Savaard spoke of the heat, how they must suffer in the city, and went right on making another drink. Her voice was hypnotic with a rich womanly charm coming from her large face. To Lydia she was more than ever an aged version of Henry, yet like a poor sharecropper's wife, too. In that ragged shirt she was stringy and indomitable, only a feminine voice left in a sexless body. Bringing the drink across the room to Lydia she said, "That unnatural air-conditioned climate!"

"Things are slower." Godnick settled into the couch. "Of course my wife and children are out in Westport."

"Well, how nice," said Mrs. Savaard, sitting back, far away, on the other end of the couch.

"Yes," Godnick was nonchalant; "about five years ago we got fed up with this summer camp business. . . ."

Lydia put down her drink with a disapproving thump. Mr. Godnick was clay, putty in this woman's hands, trying to prove himself—children's camps, the house in Westport, the something-or-other beach club—as though old Julia gave a damn! Often she had listened to people rattle on in front of Henry (*she* had done it, her father and mother had been guilty)—a pitiful compulsion to mention clubs, schools, European cities, or even Abercrombie's and Plummer's, and if you were smart at all you could have killed yourself the minute the words were out of your mouth, because Henry was supremely indifferent. They made you feel—the Savaards—stuck with a thousand nettles, caught in some horrible mire: social tags—did people still carry on about that sort of thing? Well, if you thought *that* was their world, you were mistaken. What they intended was highly personal, not a validity or a presence—not quite definable—perhaps . . . ; you listened, you listened. but the secret never came. And Lydia knew it wasn't good rugs in a vast house, or pictures, or piecrust tables that had prompted Mr. Godnick to pull out his credentials; it was that square-shouldered woman intoning like a sorceress, parading the tattery shirt of a gypsy.

Now Lydia saw Godnick the domestic creature, weighted with the school problem, vacation expenses, and the transportation of a cat from the city to Westport. Everyone turned out pathetic and small in front of the Savaards. Well, *she* knew what they were: an old widow, a madman—lunatics, out of touch with anything that was real and happening. She lived in an empty barn and went to work every day to free herself from them; and, by God, she was not going to let her scars and hard-earned money be washed away with gin and pleasantries! She was paying for Godnick's time as if he were a plumber and determined to be as hard as Henry's mother, who was offering at that moment to show him the garden.

"We don't have time," Lydia said weakly. "I have to get

a train back to New York. I must be in the office tomorrow."

"You're working?" Mrs. Savaard asked.

"I have my old job back."

"Ah, with the children's books."

"Mr. Godnick wanted to know if you had read his letters?" Perched on the chair, Lydia looked as though she might fly at the first warning. "He brought some papers which he would like you to sign today."

One glance from Godnick put her back in her place. "We're getting to that, believe me. You understand the difficulties of coming out here, Mrs. Savaard. However, I got no answer to my letters about the proposed annulment . . ."

"Wasn't I quite ready for you today?" Mrs. Savaard pointed to the gin, the ice, the lemon. She had gone to the trouble. She did not drink herself—one poor woman, alone. Suddenly their being in the room seemed a coarse intrusion.

"I suggested you might want to have your lawyer here." Godnick held out his legal statement. She did not take it. He let it drop between them on the couch. "These things are fairly technical." Godnick nudged the papers on the worn linen slip cover.

"They are only complicated if we make them so? Don't you agree, Lydia?"

Lydia slumped back into her chair.

"Mrs. Savaard," said Godnick, "I'm going to lay things on the line. This girl married your son and within a few months he was completely out of control. We have every reason to believe this mental condition doesn't come on overnight."

"I have no way of knowing."

"Naturally, we have consulted a psychiatrist."

"Naturally," countered Mrs. Savaard with a cool smile.

Mr. Godnick got up to pace the floor, trying for the mastery he could always manage in his office. His knee caught the tray, a disastrous quaking of bottles: slosh and fizzle of tonic water. Well, this was it, thought Lydia, this was the Marx Brothers Mary Agnes took her up to the Museum to see—two zanies come to visit Mrs. Rich-Bitch, crashing the china, snagged in a rope of pearls. If she had the courage to slip a piece of ice down the dowager bosom —only there was no bosom. With one long finger Mrs. Savaard steadied the tray. Lydia and Godnick were the only fools.

"The point is," he said, dabbing at the rug with his handkerchief, "why should you make this girl suffer when all you have to say is that you knew your son was disturbed at some time prior to the marriage. It can't do him any harm now."

Mocking the lawyer's words, she spoke tenderly to herself, "The point is that my son suffers, too, more than this girl." She turned to Lydia, "You never went to visit him in that place."

"You've never told me where he is."

"You never asked."

"Well," Lydia said, about to cry, "I'm sorry about that."

"The point is you wouldn't have gone there in any case."

"No." Lydia propped herself up again to seem rigid, unyielding. The tears dribbled down her cheeks. "No, I wouldn't have gone. I couldn't. And what about that year?" This was her big scene, the hidden trump that would reveal her power. Her throat was clogged with pain, but she shouted out, "What about that year after college and after Europe? Where was Henry then? Where is that whole year if he wasn't in a hospital then?"

"Henry was in the army, like everyone else."

"Jesus," Godnick murmured. He did not attempt to hide his exasperation. All the way out here to discover her husband was in the army, and the old woman, he might have told the minute she opened the door—she wasn't handing out prizes.

76

Lydia cried out, "He never, never, mentioned the army. I can't remember—"

"I can't remember," Mrs. Savaard carefully picked up her own thread of memory, "how many months. It seemed forever to him. It's a great disappointment to these boys without a war."

"All right, all right." Godnick, cheerful, enthusiastic, tried to recapture a reasonable mood. Once he had seen women go at each other physically; that was understandable, but this—this was too tony for him.

"The point is that if at *any* time your son was upset and received treatment, if there is any way that you could indicate this for us, Mrs. Savaard . . ."

"I don't imagine I can." Mrs. Savaard abandoned them, walked over to her desk at the far end of the room. In a haze Lydia studied the beams which crossed on the ceiling and noted for the first time that really they were flat boards. They didn't support anything, were no more structural than the salt-box overhang on her parents' house. She thought how the Savaards *would* live in an imitation Hampton Court, and her father and mother in a glorified farmhouse. Mrs. Savaard stood above her, planted firmly in sneakers.

"I have a proposal of my own which I'd like to discuss with Mr. Godnick." ("*Your* Mr. Godnick," she might well have said.)

"Lydia, being Henry's wife, is legally responsible for his debts and his doctor's bills. Doesn't that appear to be in order?" And she handed the letter to Godnick, who read the name of an almost legendary legal firm who acted for the Savaards. She was within her rights.

"I don't have any money," Lydia whined, "I don't have a cent. I can hardly pay *him*, and I'm not asking my parents again."

Mrs. Savaard did not listen to the weeping girl. "I wanted the best of care and chose a 'home,' quite a nice farm once."

"I'll call a taxi." Lydia made a dash down the long room.

"Aren't you interested?" Mrs. Savaard commanded her to turn back. "Henry wants to see you."

"Oh—"

"He's not in a strait jacket." All the space around them, all that could be seen—floors, walls, hollow beams, the dead drinks, the distorted bits of terrace and garden that glowed through the pocked and tinted glass—more than ever belonged to Mrs. Savaard. This day was hers. Lydia could not remember why she had come here, and her lawyer was stuffing papers into his attaché case like a sidewalk salesman without a license. She found the number of the cab company in its old place on a list by the kitchen phone.

"There," said Mrs. Savaard when she returned, "I felt it an obligation to tell you." Her lovely woman's voice, the voice of an old actress, an old empress, gave her final control of the scene.

"What's that?" Lydia asked.

"To tell you that Henry wanted to see you."

"Oh—" The envelope printed in smart modern type read "Shady Acres."

"Not much—as much as he wants anything." Mrs. Savaard closed her eyes, let the distance grow between them, shutting them out.

"He is building a boat in a bottle."

"I'll walk out to the road and wait for the taxi."

Mr. Godnick, Panama in hand, found her sitting on a rock with her feet stretched into clumps of plantain. He saw she was crying again, a silent, rhythmic sobbing that threatened to go on. "I had a few words with her after you left."

This time it was not Henry's mother who had brought on the tears. Lydia, knowing her own folly, had walked straight to the little gatehouse and put her nose against the window. Everything was as she remembered, but as dead as a room in a furniture department—even the tables, splintered before her flight, stood delicate and proper. The lifeless room was overwhelming, as though, in comparison, the resentment of months and the raging at Mrs. Savaard were mechanical reactions. *Here* was the only place she had ever lived, this room made with her stupidity and Henry's madness and their invalid love. Now it was lost. What was the point in gluing things back together again? Suppose he were to come back whole; they could not use these stained silk chairs, these maimed tables, the white pot with the beheaded Dieffenbachia. That would be climbing back into a bed where the smell of death lingered. She looked closely, as people do when they are about to leave a house, checking the past and future at once.

"The stairs were on the left . . . the doors on the cabinet got off their track . . . the ropes were broken in the kitchen window." As she turned and walked out the gate, Lydia cried. It wasn't that she wanted to be attacked again, was it? She didn't know.

"Oh, it's not her," she sobbed to Godnick, accepting his dirty handkerchief. The taxi came, and they were quiet, letting the lawns and the trees and the high hedges swell over them. The driver cut down a little street to avoid a gang of men who were hauling a dead elm across the road; it brought them to a great vista—a sight of the sea. The world was exposed again: sand and water, sky, houses. The sun was still high.

"We'll get the five-thirty," Mr. Godnick said.

"Good." Then with a doubtful smile Lydia sighed, "The water looks wonderful." It was not for her.

"Yes, this is a beautiful spot." He pushed his hat back on his head, opened the top button of his shirt, and pulled his tie loose. Lydia Savaard could see the thick mat of black hair which grew up to his neck. Her blurred red eyes shifted with embarrassment to the man's face. "You didn't believe me, did you? About Henry's mother."

79

"No," Godnick admitted, "but then I never met anyone like her."

"She's got us about the annulment, hasn't she?"

"About the annulment—about everything."

Mr. Godnick and Lydia talked to each other all the way into the city. Not that it mattered or changed things, she thought, but rotten times did bring people together. Their defeat made them both want to prove, at least to each other, that Mrs. Savaard had not killed them both with one stone. Lydia described the empty apartment that she rented with Mary Agnes Keely—a wild woman, a complete clown. Godnick was effusive about his house, his wife, his children —still always critical, unsatisfied. Lydia was a little girl from Shaker Heights who never made it; he was a smart kid from Jersey City.

In the station she held out her hand, a shocking crimson from *Henny Penny Sees the World*. "Thank you for trying, Morton, anyway."

"Look, we're not through with this yet," he told her, but his sad eyes already accepted a loss.

"Oh, I know, I know," she said in eager disbelief.

5

October 29, Chalk Night—

Back at the sweltering end of summer I took a cab up
to the agency. When I tiptoed into the artists' workroom
with the paste-up of our mail-order brochure (Wunda-
Clutch invites you to its miracle opening) Stanley said,
"Built like a brick shithouse."

"Miss Keely!" a warm flush rose in his cheeks as he
swiveled round from his drawing board.

What a love Stanley is! Say it is all hemoglobin and
nerves that makes for blushes, but I'll show you a man who
has not grown calluses on his heart. He was describing the

blonde from billing, not me, for though I have a prouder front these days I don't get judged a sturdy outbuilding, not even by Stanley.

His cliché can never be mine—for the same reason that cloistered within a woman's mind I'll never fully get a war novel. Sure, I read Stephen Crane and Norman Mailer, not to forget the Punic Wars, as literary exercise, but the barracks and the battlefield don't touch me directly. Maybe girl guerrillas in belted khaki and rifles know a bit more, *maybe.* . . .

Say I were to ask Stanley (red in the face) what does it mean exactly, about the brick house or what's it like in the men's room, and say he explicated the graffiti and described each urinal with the tongues of men and of angels, it would still be tinkling brass, as I have not . . . but I don't envy. What I haven't got is hunky-dory with me. And a sexual scrambling doesn't give any answers: who hasn't seen them sashaying up Eighth Street, who doesn't know the wife who wears the pants, the boy tangled in his mother's apron strings, gestures and attitudes in all of us. Muddy waters there. Since the beginning of *L'affaire Stanley* I am struck by all the things he will never know of me, that I cannot know of him. *Vive la différence* is a melancholy phrase.

I am alone in the apartment now. It is less difficult to write—not easy—with Lydia off for the weekend visit with her husband at the funny farm. Stanley has gone home to his family in Brooklyn, leaving me awash in desire.

Saturday morning—an empty apartment. I cannot imagine any more desolate landscape, the first hours after a lover has gone . . . Caught in another convention: I cannot imagine the horizon, that line where the earth finally meets the sky.

Eight o'clock. On a weekday one might get ready to go to work. *One* might. One *might.* Baking a chocolate cake seems an absurdity, pleasuring myself with yet another bonbon, different color foil, different tint of sugar dip—looking for the same nut inside, don't you forget it. My yellow pad, however, makes demands that are as real (nearly) as those of my lover. I see I called it a journal, that I turned an image of the *un*written play one way, then another. It was early summer then—June—she sat in the window: now, on Ninth Street the frost is on the pumpkin. The children do not play after supper. Leon Mertz tends the thermostat. The Woolworth's up at Broadway is *flambé* with vinyl autumn leaves and jars of corn candy. So I have let the months escape—July, August, September, up to Chalk Night —without holding to my modest plan: record life around you, Mary Agnes. Chart your painful journey to freedom. Here you are—alone in the hollow sand pit which lies at the center of the Isle of Carnal Delight, situated in the windswept, turbulent lake of Worldly Knowledge . . .

Oh Christ, why do I make sport even of my love! Because I am afraid to write down: Stanley Sarnicki I love you.

He is an artist. The copy I write, mere words on a sheet of paper approved by Sigal, the authority, is sent to the advertising agency where he works. There, in a room filled with men on high stools, Stanley breathes life into my seeming nonsense. He sets it to sketches.

WUNDA-CLUTCH
makes *you* perform like Houdini

Close the back of your dress without that pretzel twist? The gentlest touch—one finger tip—secures the gripping bristles and they *stay* closed

Well, madam! If you're going to saw yourself in half . . .
At your favorite sewing shop   *59¢ and up*
or write:

Wunda-Clutch, Inc.
230 7th Avenue
New York, N.Y. 10001

These bread-and-butter words, sometimes clever, always cheap, made to sell, come back to me in a variety of types.

83

Stanley's design gives them substance: a proof—glossy sheet wanting only petty corrections; the paste-up—line, size, proportion. A cartoon of a frenetic lady (satiric machine-part squiggles grow in place of limbs) busily hacking herself in two. It is like Paul Klee, perhaps, and a little too good for Mr. Bert (Sigal), but if I say this to Stanley he turns moody and defensive: I've got fancy notions and spend too much time in museums. It's just his work.

"I'm lucky, that's all. I still have ideas."

"Yes, but Stanley, dear . . . it is very close to something . . . something big, more than finding a Mondrian label on your vitamin capsules."

But let me reconstruct the scene of my romance. Let me put in the trees and background figures, unroll this length of grass. Here a mirror will do for the lake, and over there let us have a trunk with the stuff we need: the bottle of wine, two glasses, sheets, cooking smells, the TV noise. We will get them out ourselves. We are not helpless.

It was—it *is* Labor Day weekend. For the first time Lydia has gone to visit Henry. I am left to myself; empty apartment, refrigerator full, two new paperbacks: Baudelaire's *Mirror of Art* and *The Art of Italian Cooking*. I make up my cot on Saturday morning as a tribute to Lydia, pull up the Indian spread and stuff the pillow into the cotton sham. Then I settle to my accounts: rent, telephone, electricity, back home my mother's alimentary canal still being X-rayed —but as I make out the check to the medical laboratory I feel nothing more than the slightest loss, as for a glove already gone at the seams. Yet, my memory of her gall bladder attacks is clear. Long nights with the unpredictable heating pad and the foxy hot-water bottles, lifting her into the bathroom, scraping around under the bed for her rosary. Beef broth and saltines in the morning "kept up her strength" but they never stayed down. Such details no longer drive me to excesses of pity, anxiety, and love. I am empty of all feeling except the cool remembrance of how things must be back there, back then . . . Aunt Mae comes with the little dishes of waxy custard ("Nothing but eggs and milk. I usually put a sprinkle of nutmeg, but I thought with her stones . . ."). Aunt Lil comes with the flowers from Bladgies (a costly spray) and Mother moans aren't those flowers lovely, if only she was well enough to enjoy them, and "the custard tastes like nothing in your mouth— then Mae never was good in the kitchen." After a few days *in extremis* she will crawl out to the telephone to tell them all, the Conroys and Mae, the Scanlons and Mrs. Duffy, how the pain came sharp as a knife, no letup. In a few more days she'll be ordering up sugar buns on the sly from the Dugan's deliveryman and be mumbling, inarticulate, slack-jawed, eyelids drooped: "You nah . . . nah goin' out tha' class, Ag?"

"I guess not."

"Well I should think not. I'm alone here all day and so weak at night."

She was well again, ready for the fray, and then I let my scrawny heart fill with relief—which was my only notion of joy.

Ninth Street. Labor Day weekend—

I remember the sequence of these events, and others, and the way it will all go. My brother, if not on an assignment for Old Glory, will load up the station wagon with the folding crib, the favorite toys, the toilet-training seat, the squabbling kids, and Joan the put-upon wife. They will drive the whole way down from Buffalo to grouse at Grandma. They will present themselves in their best clothes at Lil's on Sunday, and on *the* day, Monday, they will eat, no matter what the temperature, a hot roast-beef dinner— the lot of them crowded around the dining-room table laden with two enervating dishes of mashed potatoes, with shriv-eled string beans and peas, coarse late corn that sticks to the teeth, and the good gravy boat dumping its lumpy cargo on the linen cloth. Before the lemon pie—loose when cut, beads of sweat on the meringue ("I turned the oven to three-seventy-five," Mother says, spooning it up, "and with Patrick screaming it's a wonder we have anything comes out right at all")—before the pie is sloshed at us, Francis will speak his line about getting an early start to avoid the holiday traffic. He will load up for the long journey home; grim Joan will be quickly in the car, telling us to "take care." Mother wipes her eyes and they are on their way, bye-bye, with stops all the way for the children to throw up by the side of the road.

I feel nothing but distance, separateness from the way it will go: it does not matter. Now I am free. I no longer have the tenderness in my hands to give that gross old woman an alcohol rub. I no longer delight in the life of Francis with three plump kids coming up the front steps—oh, but I used to adore them, squealing with them in their games. And I didn't despise Aunt Lil's pretentious bouquets, nor ache with the sense of waste, of lives wasted, when I flushed Aunt Mae's custard down the toilet.

On this lonesome Saturday at the end of August, another summer slipped away forever and what have I got? A numb, clean life; a numb, clean roommate. I sense that I may become one of those all-right-looking girls you see at their daiquiri lunches or skimming through the dress racks on the budget floor. Sometimes they're at the theater or in let's pretend foreign restaurants with all-right-looking men, wearing new clothes and their made-up lives. But if you watch them as they look at a painting you can tell by their shoes or their eyes—there is always something that gives them away—that they live in clean apartments where nothing goes on. They look at the painting as though they want to *remember* it, for God's sake! They have a reason for going to the ballet: it's on the laundry list to be checked off.

I pay a bill at Macy's for a rattan rug and a sleek lamp

with no family background. I sit for hours in the void of Labor Day weekend: I have this barren time, this inoffensive place, and nothing more. When the phone rings I am hardly curious . . . maybe Henry Savaard has bludgeoned Lydia with his model of Old Ironsides . . . maybe Mother has passed a priceless gem from the depths of her outraged bladder. . . .

"Miss Keely?"

"Yes."

"This is Stanley Sarnicki."

(Pause)

". . . from the art room at the agency. Stanley."

"*Stanley!*" (Had I forgotten to hand in my copy for *Synthetics Journal*? "Wunda-Clutch, the natural fastener, speeds inset production 50%!" Carmen Rodriguez, dark and experienced, of Queen Mab Loungewear, allows me to put the words in her mouth: "Now my work goes fast with Wunda-Clutch.")

"I'm in your neck of the woods, and I thought maybe you'd want to have a beer."

Stanley Sarnicki I Love You.

All afternoon the sun was bright, shining on Stanley and me and the children splashing in the fountain in Washington Square, and the old woman with the sunken mouth who sits on the same bench protecting dirty mystery bags, sewing her different little scrappy cloth hats. She wore purple spots as we dollsied to the bar and had changed to dotted swiss when we returned hand in hand through the hot yellow twilight. Did she know? Did anyone see—the hairy young man at the chess table, perhaps, or the Village mammas gathering up the last of their uninhibited babes? Did they see that we had changed after two beers? No longer wandering, not entertaining each other with quips about the shop windows or quick analyses of the people at the agency, we knew where we were going—to Ninth

Street with a prop copy of the *New York Post* and a bottle of Chianti. Our steps grew fast, for we were late—fifteen years at least—for our appointment.

"Come back and I'll cook dinner."

"I should be heading out to Brooklyn." On Stanley's part a boyish flush.

"I've all this food in the house."

". . . a lot of trouble."

"I love to cook, honestly." Teen talk. Oh, the children we like to believe still exist in us, when actually Stanley said to me, "You know why I called you, baby." And I replied, "Indeedy me, yes."

The verbal game of love as much a revelation as any act. Preserve that always presumed innocence one more time with words. Imagine the satisfaction of squatting down right now with a piece of soft pink chalk, printing in capital letters on the sidewalk: STANLEY SARNICKI I LOVE YOU.

He's as tall as I am, but that's not so remarkable in a man. Then, of course, he's portly—rather an old-fashioned word, but Stanley is an old-fashioned boy. There is a largeness to Stanley, a solidity: his hands and feet are broad, his body well-nourished, not fat to be laughed at, not dumpy, not pot-bellied, but the comfortable square frame of a man who goes to business each day in a fresh shirt. Stanley's shoulders are wide enough . . . That looks hedging on the page. Say instead that he is not athletic, not like one of my mother's fancied-up cowboys who seem pumped out in the chest and strapped in at the buttocks. Nothing is narrow about Stanley. His face, as though to confirm my judgment and insure my love, is wide open: wide cheekbones, wide jaw. Maybe I have gone wrong again and made Stanley simple, the man with the hoe, but actually he is a burgher, neither weakness nor malice in his features. His high coloring, his fair hair and blue eyes, make Stanley Sarnicki a model of American prosperity.

(Polack, yes, Hunky—they were interchangeable as far

as my mother was concerned—"I see that Polack lawyer is going to run for office over in the East Side, that was Tim Kiernan's ward always, from St. Mary's to the Brass Company.") He lives with his mother and sister in Brooklyn and next week he is bringing Mary Agnes Keely home—in the grand tradition. I expect a delicious kielbasa and a picture of Kosciuszko in the front room.

When we went back to the apartment I said, as though it were useless information—there are only 2,594 kangaroos extant in Australia—"The girl who lives with me has gone off for the weekend."

I began to pound the veal cutlets in the galley kitchen, but I didn't get far because Stanley was there, the two of us squeezing past each other to the knife drawer and the refrigerator, careful not to touch, and then reckless with flour, intimate with salt until we kissed awkwardly, and with practice became good, wedged in between the cabinets; Stanley's hand was at my breast fumbling with the embroidery on my Peruvian blouse.

"How do you get at this damn thing?" he said.

"In the back. That's not real in the front."

"Real?"

"For heaven's sake!" That's what I exclaimed to any man who joshed me in the zipper factory six months ago when nothing was for real under my sweaters. "For heaven's sake! I must get back to work."

"I'm not that hungry."

When we came back to the kitchen the cutlets were dry.

That's how a thirty-five-year-old virgin would write it—the easy dodge and a genteel fade-out: again—

Wunda-clutched together, we moved in a staggering two-step away from the light into the dim bedroom where the early September heat let us lie uncovered, stretched in nakedness against each other. Poor starved body, late for the feast. I saw everything of Stanley, everything that was necessary for the moment, and he found all he wanted in me. His strong hand upon the flat of my stomach and down across hips, thighs. "God, you're smooth," he said. "That's a nice appendix thing there, kind of sweet. You're a sweet girl."

"No, I'm not. I'm not very sweet. Anyway I'm missing my appendix."

"Well, you aren't missing anything else, are you?" and he rolled away from me.

I felt the tightness in his shoulder. "That's O.K. Stanley. That's more than O.K."

"I knew it," he said apologetically, "I knew it and I didn't care."

"Can you tell from looking at me? Can you tell I'm a virgin?" He didn't answer. "Stop blushing," I said, kissing my way up his back. "Well, I know you blush. You blush in the office. You blush over the phone."

"Ag—"

"Come on, Stanley, come on . . . it's purely vestigial, I mean it. Why do you care, if I don't?" But it took some work. "Aw, come on, honey. . . ." And we did, while below the guns saluted from the Mertz television set, violent crime enacted in front of their tired bodies: kisses, car door slams, sirens, screams of a starlet in a night-club set. As the patrol car screeched towards the warehouse . . . we did.

"Well, who's sorry?" I sat up, leaning on that magnificent mound of flesh, Stanley.

He said, "Nobody's sorry."

I'm not sure about that either. Perhaps that's the scene done by a thirty-five-year-old lady *writer* who fancies herself a woman of experience when really there will always be something too delicate about her sensibility.

Now, Chalk Night, this nervous time. Stanley gone back to Brooklyn. Easy to embroider the memory of "our first night" for my journal. So many blank pages, the rest of this day and tomorrow . . . until Lydia comes sighing in the door with her overnight case and the double-crostic finished.

October 31—

A laborious Sunday. Thinking about Stanley still. Why is he in Brooklyn? What do his mother and sister imagine when he stays with me all night? How can he deceive with the uncontrollable color rising in his face? What can he say?

"I have been to the apartment on Ninth Street where I shack up with Mary Agnes."

Oh, there is nothing here but a few chairs and tables and a devil's-food cake in the oven. Perhaps they don't question. Perhaps his mother and sister turn from him as he lets himself in—not to see, not to ask—or have they been told it's his business? Like that, he can end it: two women hopelessly shut off. And so I stood with my mother as she asked, "Well, Francis, did you go to the show last night? Is that it, till two in the morning?"

Francis didn't answer. He was eighteen, always a good boy, going off to Fordham at the end of the summer. He slouched across the living room to the front windows and watched Mr. Dunn back out of his driveway into one of the ash cans that lined our hill on Saturday mornings.

"Boy, some jerk," Francis said.

"Some jerk, all right," I said.

"That's enough from you," my mother yelled at me. I stood against the archway, squirming on one leg, chewing a long straggle-end of hair. I wanted to die with shame for what she was doing to Francis. I wanted to run into my bedroom and lock the door for hours, but there was a fascination that kept me there, for she was never quivering-at-the-lips mad at my precious brother.

"I'd like to know the movies that don't get out till two in the morning?"

My brother gave a hollow laugh at fat old Dunn beating white ashes out of his pants.

"That girl was never any good. I told your Aunt Lil to get her out of the house, and I'd just like to know what movie you took her to that gets out at three in the morning?"

"You want to know the plot?" Francis said, edging closer to the window.

Her mouth trembled, still she was fierce. "Don't you be flip with me, mister."

Then there was an end to it. Francis turned on us with an unmanly look of humiliation. "Take that filthy hair out of your mouth," he cried at me.

What do they know in Brooklyn—his mother and sister? They are as distant from Stanley as I am here (a mean consolation). The part we play is not as we want it, but as we are made—with the genitals God gave us.

Last night at the theater, as always, it was easy to buy a single. All alone by the telephone. It must be today. It feels like a Sunday. Hours until Lydia comes back bringing the everyday week to a beginning with the sudsing of soiled undergarments and her great faith in a new puzzle left on the doorstep in the morning. She will figure it patiently. Once I knew a dumb girl in the office at the zipper factory who filled in all the four letter words of the easy home-town puzzle. *S h i t* she wrote when she could not guess the answer. Such happiness as that I wish for Lydia. I would like to stop prying and picking at the facts of her life and present her with a big dictionary full of all the answers. Perhaps it is Monday she comes. The entire cake frosted with dazzling white cream, a sugary membrane over my black devil. (Stanley Sarnicki I love you.) I will write that down —of course it is *tonight* she comes back, Sunday, and last night I went to the theater to kill time again. That was good, people on the stage saying things, actors in costume playing at being people saying things, women and men, mothers and sons, servants and masters, and on the streets it was Halloween, boys and girls who were dogs and cats and queens and gypsies. Only one small girl in man's clothing, rolled-up trousers, hair pinned under her father's old hat, a hobo—and it was a cold night to cut holes in your shoes. Which makes this All Souls . . . unusual it falls on a Sunday, such a small thing to look forward to—if I still did —only the one church day instead of two.

It seems to me I must use everything on the yellow pads: Lydia with her cheese-paring story, my brother's life, almost a great big zero in any fast play, almost but not quite, others gone, but not forgotten, all the modes which I pick up quickly around me, perhaps too quickly. *Mary Agnes loves Stanley*. I will write that down for sure. And a scene maybe free, maybe plotless, only the condition described of all the souls, the ladies' and the gents'.

THE CHEESE STANDS ALONE
A Piece of Chic in One Act

Scene: A long, narrow room which the audience looks into. Shelves on all sides—empty, except for an old New York telephone directory and back issues of *Look* and *Life*. A conference table takes up most of the stage, but the room still looks vacant. On the left are four high-back chairs which look like carved thrones at first, but on closer inspection prove to be stiff cardboard imitations which a set designer has painted in muddy swirls. On the right are four swivel stools, old-fashioned bar stools screwed to the floor.

To the left, behind the thrones, is a door with a small lighted sign—"Girls"—like the sign for the ladies' rest room in a bad restaurant. To the right, behind the stools, a sign above an identical door, "Boys."

The women:

MRS. TIMOTHY KEELY, fat old mother of Mary Agnes Keely

and Francis Keely. She wears a faded Hoover dress and a paper crown. Also wife of Timothy Keely.

SHERRY HENDERSON, tall, redheaded, luscious, desirable, theatrical. A dark mink coat is thrown over her shoulders, and underneath she wears a dancer's costume: sparkly black sequins, net stockings. Cousin of Mary Agnes and Francis.

LYDIA SAVAARD, medium, ordinary girl (plaid skirt and pullover). She carries a suitcase plastered with college stickers —Vassar, Yale, Princeton—not in keeping with her black veil and the pleated wimple of a Sister of Mercy.

MARY AGNES KEELY, long, camel-humped creature, winningly animated. She wears a black dress, double strand of pearls, discreet gold pin, white gloves and a large black handbag like working girls carry to give themselves importance. She wears her First Holy Communion headdress, netting secured by a lace sweatband with two satin rosettes, à la mode 1933.

The men:

TIMOTHY KEELY, father of Mary Agnes and Francis. Also husband of Mrs. Keely.

FRANCIS X. KEELY, brother of Mary Agnes and son of Mrs. Keely. Also son of Timothy Keely.

HENRY SAVAARD, husband of Lydia Savaard.

STANLEY SARNICKI, lover of Mary Agnes.

(*As the lights come up, the women enter from the door at the left in a solemn march, their hands folded in prayer, heads bowed. They take up positions behind the make-believe thrones and wait in silence. The men enter from the door at the right. They sit on the swivel stools, laughing and talking down the table to each other like regulars at the neighborhood bar. They wear standard evening dress which gives them, as a group, dignity—gentlemen at the Rotary Club banquet or male models assembled for a whiskey ad. They talk before the play begins, and then* FRANCIS KEELY (*unexceptionally thirty-seven*) *goes out through the Boys'*

*door and comes back with party hats which the men put on
with coarse male laughter.* TIMOTHY KEELY (*pale, bloodless,
fifty*) *wears a red paper fireman's hat.* HENRY SAVAARD (*handsome, snotty, twenty-five*) *puts on a pointed dunce's cap
decorated with streamers and ruching.* STANLEY SARNICKI
(*solid, fair, forty*), *pleased and embarrassed, adjusts his
floppy artist's beret. Suddenly all are quiet while* FRANCIS
*dons a red-white-and-blue top hat—Uncle Sam's—with rev-
erence.*

*The silence settles. Nothing happens. The silence persists.
Nothing happens.* MRS. KEELY *clears her throat, once, twice;
and to forestall her mother,* MARY AGNES *takes a step into the
spotlight. She is weak, faltering at first, but speaks out with
obvious enthusiasm as an idea grows.*)

MARY AGNES: If . . . well . . . yes, if you think about it,
that is, if you look around . . . we are a mixed lot . . .
here in this place, this . . . room, and one should never
. . . always you are warned against the assorted pack for
then you're stuck with a lot of cheap peanuts. From this
we learn that these men and women are nothing to each
other . . . for the most part and in various combinations.
There exist only the bonds of family . . . meaningless
now, or the bonds of matrimony which they have forged
with each hour into chains. Look then for the one possible
excuse for us to assemble in this chamber: each man's fate
has been inextricably woven to one of these women, each
woman has been passionately involved. . . .

MRS. KEELY: I haven't been so much as introduced yet.

MARY AGNES: Mother, I'd like you to meet Henry Savaard.
Henry, this is my mother. (*She stuffs her mother onto a
throne.*)

HENRY: I've heard so much about you, Mrs. Keely. (*He gets
up and offers his hand, but cannot reach* MRS. KEELY,
which suits him just as well.) You don't disappoint me at
all . . . your dropped breasts merge downward into your
ample stomach, your turkey-gobbler neck, the roll of

95

flesh there under the arm where your corset leaves off, your frigid-frizz hair—it's all absolutely correct, and my standards are high, extremely high for mothers in particular.

MRS. KEELY: Well, that's nice to hear I'm sure, these days. Of course, I've no way of knowing what she's told you but I'll say this, she was brought up a good girl so it's no skin off my backside . . .

SHERRY: Does anyone have the time?

STANLEY: Why, yes, it's ten after six, but then I'm often slow.

MRS. KEELY (*to Henry Savaard*): Who's that fella?

HENRY: No one I'd know.

MRS. KEELY: Some artist, do you suppose? Or painter or something of that kind? He'd do well to stay clear of her: *Sherreee*—that's not her real name—was never anything but trouble.

SHERRY: The time doesn't matter. I don't know why I ask. But I used to be so hipped about getting to the theater early. You see, sweetie, I had a compulsion: I always had to be the first girl in the dressing room every night, every matinee, even during a long run. It was my attempt to compensate, you see sweetie, for basic insecurities even during a long run (*she smiles to herself, comes around her throne and sits down, slipping out of the mink coat*) . . . and let's face the problem, sweetheart, there was only *one* long run: OK-LA-HO-MA!

STANLEY: *Oklahoma!* Hey, I saw that show. That was quite a while . . . quite a while on Broadway.

SHERRY: You know, you're a cutie.

MARY AGNES: They do not know each other, this man and this woman. I do not think they will get on together, not that it's necessary, and then, too, I should never have said "passionately involved" when what I meant was "morally committed," one man to one woman, here in this . . . *salon*, has cleaved . . . cloven. So there is no reason why he must listen to her, her to him, she to he, Daddy to dumpling, for there is much else to think of, memories and mental obsessions to keep us busy, there are fantasies which *girls*, I happen to know, are clever with (*she closes her eyes and begins to see with her hands and body*). . . . Stanley comes in at my door, wearing a thick fur coat and hoof-clumpy boots. I am in black lace on the sofa, the sofa is white silk, the window is behind, New York is out the window. *He* approaches. There are hard metal buttons that cannot be seen through the fur. I do not move, but lie there as though wood, as though dead. I am thirty-five . . . O.K., thirty-six. He is forty. . . .

SHERRY: Forty-three. The spring of nineteen-forty-three we opened. All the kids in the show had the world's best poker game backstage and we knew to the second when to throw in a hand and run upstairs, never missed an entrance . . . never goofed up. . . . (*The men and women, especially the men, have been intrigued by* SHERRY, *and as she realizes that she has an audience, she begins to perform, pulling the mink up around her shoulders for effect, consciously projecting beyond the people on stage.*) Except one night I went on in my practice shoes and with the King of Spades in my apron pocket, and once I had a full house, so I held on and on, and held on through the second chorus of "Kansas City," that was how you played the game, and then one of the kids said, "Ya-ha, Sherry, YOU ARE THROUGH." Of course, if you had a lousy hand you'd try and throw in early, but some tricky kid would listen and say, "NO DEAL, DUCHESS!" And you had to sit it out, fake it out, for the whole boring—it never ended—ballad.

STANLEY: Say that *is* something, being able to go out on a stage night after night—but to run out of a poker game, cold . . .

SHERRY: It was never like that, even after a year. It was always warm and exciting. Then I went on the road.

MRS. KEELY: I imagine she did.

SHERRY: And that's the story of how I got my first billing.

97

God, it was warm and exciting, and temporarily obscured the frustrations of my personal life. The big dance number, the dream sequence—Paris Postcard Girls: my name featured—of course they don't much go for the big dream ballet any more . . . (*She begins to hum some music from the show and sweeps her arms up and around through the air.*) My name first in the third billing: Sherry Henderson.

MRS. KEELY: Her name is Mary Elizabeth Hurley. I took her first after my sister died, then she went over to Lil's, but I had her for seven years in the house.

HENRY: Christ!—there is hardly any doubt that she intends to dance for us.

MRS. KEELY: It wouldn't surprise me.

SHERRY (*takes a few turns at the side of her throne, knocks her hipbone*): Boy am I out of it!

HENRY (*An announcement*): Her thighs are heavy. Stomach muscles gone.

MRS. KEELY: That's right. Nothing that girl could do would surprise me any more. We did everything for her, everything, but she was dancing around, displaying herself to anyone came in the house since she was six years old. I used to say to my husband, "Don't encourage her," still he'd take her down the firehouse on a nice day, and she'd jog away in the driveway for them . . . it was only *after* she went to live with Lil. Just the other day I said, "I did everything for Mary Elizabeth, sent her to the nuns, but she was disrespectful, Lil, she was an ingrate, Mae."

SHERRY: This isn't my sort of routine. (*To Stanley*): Sweetheart, what's the gouge? Is this one of those workshops, an "evening in the theater"?

STANLEY (*touching his artist's beret*): I work for a living. I do layouts, hand-lettering. Mary Agnes will know.

SHERRY: She's a good kid, Ag, always ready with an answer so long as it's poems.

STANLEY (*coloring*): I wouldn't say that.

SHERRY: Sorry, darling. Listen, as far as I'm concerned, Mary Agnes and her father were two sweeties in a barrel of sour apples.

MARY AGNES: Daddy, hi!

TIMOTHY KEELY: Ag, such a nice dress. Turn around, that's it. Who picked that one? Not your mother. (*He motions her to sit down.*) Take the load off your feet. (*They both laugh.*)

MARY AGNES: Gee, did she get mad when you said that!

TIM KEELY: Now, Mother, it's just an expression.

MRS. KEELY: Money was very tight.

HENRY: We all know that.

MRS. KEELY: —and I said, "You know, Mary Elizabeth, we could as easy send you to the public school as St. Augustine's with all the extras"—there was always books and mission money.

HENRY: Sub-mission. Ad-mission. Re-mission. E-mission.

MRS. KEELY: For Chinese babies—and Africans. Five dollars you bought a baby and could choose a name. "Kathleen," I said, "that's a pretty name." Well suppose it's a boy? "Kevin," I said, "that's a lovely name." Fridays they brought in their mission money. Lil paid for the dancing lessons, tap and ballet. We did everything.

HENRY: Yes, at dancing school we sat like this, boys on one side of the room, girls on the other. I never worked it over: I was, in fact, aloof—no punches in the receiving line, no chewing gum on the white gloves. It is fairly goddamn difficult if you have a preconceived notion about yourself, and by preconceived I mean at least one civilization before the womb, to enter that whole fox-trotting world . . . though I don't intend to bore you with a lot of social history, when, in fact, we were allowed one passé jitterbug number per tea dance. There was this child, Daphne Trueblood, a girl, straight blond hair, velvet band, lace collar, black velvet dress, patent-leather pumps and a pale, still face that told of notions grander, if possible, than mine. I spent my entire week caressing the idea of Daphne Above-the-throng Trueblood. It was first love— love of the picture we presented turning with childish grace through the last waltz, cool little people, turning on superior toes, me and Daphne Regatta Trueblood, who has, in fact, ended in the interior-decorating business, turning and turning in this tender tableau which my mother found not unpleasant. I told my wife this once and she said . . .

LYDIA SAVAARD (*still waiting dumbly behind her throne; she speaks out to the audience*): I don't know who I pity more, you or me. I've told so much of my pitiable life to Mary Agnes, but she does not understand, because when I told her about Henry at dancing school she said . . .

MARY AGNES (*to her father*): I don't know who I pity more, you or me.

TIM KEELY: Now, Ag, don't come on serious with me.

MARY AGNES: Well *you* figure the years. My term with her was longer than yours.

TIM KEELY: Your mother was lovely, though you won't believe me. The prettiest of the Walsh tribe—full of life. She had a knack for painting little cups and saucers, views of the river. I don't know what happens to people. She turned . . .

MARY AGNES: Like a quart of milk left on the back stoop.

TIM KEELY: No, she had blondish hair, little white feet, and maybe blue eyes, that was all the fashion then, but you don't want to understand.

MARY AGNES: There will be personal disclosures, confessions, a confrontation with the truth . . . it is unavoidable in this bedroom, with these men and these women who will blabber on with studious intent, the kind of thing they feel they must, given the chance, say, or be forced to say, all of which is known and a bore— (*Clapping and jiggling in her place*) To market, to market to buy a fat pig,/ Home again, home again, jiggety-jig./ To market, to mar-

ket to buy a fat hog,/ Home again, home again, jiggety-
jog.

TIM KEELY: That's what your mother said, but I'm not sure
it wasn't something else she wanted. I saw her that day in
the butcher's buying a piece of suet from that big Kraut,
Furster. I won't say what it looked like to see them laughing together. I walked away from the store window but
little Francis spotted me, "There's Daddy!" Your mother
was furious on the way home and she said, "I forgot they
stuck you with the night duty again this week." "It's a
cold day, isn't it," I asked, "to come out for a penny's
worth of suet?" She never answered at all.

MARY AGNES: Come on, Papa, don't let it get you. Here we
are in the dining room, line up the chairs and we'll play
Bridgeport Bus.

TIM KEELY: My stool's screwed to the floor.

MARY AGNES: Face out, in position, men! (*She is determined
to make the game.*) That's right, turn your ass to the
Methodist church. (*The others watch as she rides along
on her throne, and soon they begin to travel with her.*)
Look there! The filthy river. Look! Look at all those tires
in a mountain, heaped high as a mountain.

TIM KEELY (*glum, but under pressure*): The rubber company.

MARY AGNES: What ever do they do with *all* those tires?

TIM KEELY: Why, they melt them down and make rubber
boots.

MARY AGNES: Like my arctics?

TIM KEELY: Yes.

MARY AGNES: Like your fireman's boots?

TIM KEELY: Boots, boots, boots, joggin' over Africa,
There's no discharge in the war.

MARY AGNES: How do you do. I'm going to Bridgeport.

TIM KEELY: Why, so am I!

MARY AGNES: Then I'm going on, far, far, far away to the
Dark Continent.

TIM KEELY: Why, so am I . . . oh, it's no use, Ag, this stool is screwed down for good. (*The game sags and all resume their former positions.* LYDIA SAVAARD *is still standing by her throne.*)

LYDIA: Mary Agnes didn't understand. It meant *everything* to Henry, everything to hope for in the chance that his mother would see him waltzing with Daphne-on-Hudson Trueblood, and I was just some girl he got stuck with in an unfortunate Paul Jones.

FRANCIS KEELY: John Paul Jones?

LYDIA: I suppose.

FRANCIS: And your name?

LYDIA: Mrs. Savaard.

FRANCIS KEELY (*showing his badge*): Francis X. Keely, Federal Bureau of Investigation. Now, if you will take that chair, Mrs. Savaard. No, don't open the suitcase, put it up on the table and slide it down to me, Mrs. Savaard.

LYDIA: I don't understand—

FRANCIS: You said that Mary Agnes did not understand.

LYDIA: That was different—

FRANCIS: In what way different, Mrs. Savaard? (*She looks about her for help, but the women are touching up their make-up; the men are reading old magazines.*) Now then, you are married to a crazy man?

LYDIA: How do you know that?

FRANCIS: Severe depressions.

LYDIA: Oh, why? That is the question I ask. Why? We had everything, everything. I had my Senior Life-Saving Badge. I did so well on my College Boards. Oh why? (*She sings this heartfelt little song:*)

> Te-ell me wh-y the stars do shine?
> Te-ell me wh-y the ivy twine?
> Te-ell me wh-y the sky's so blue?
> Te-ell me, dear Girlie-School,
>   just why we love you.

We had our little cottage. We had a pretty pot. We had house plants. He learned to put the cap back on the toothpaste. I learned to drain the grease off the bacon. We were both Episcopalian; I was Low and he was High, but even that did not seem insurmountable to us . . . oh, tell me why?

FRANCIS: Well now, if we knew that, Mrs. Savaard, we'd know everything.

LYDIA: And why are you holding me here? I want to call my lawyer. (FRANCIS *opens her suitcase and begins to look through the clothes.*) There's nothing in there. I want to call Morton Godnick 1-2345.

FRANCIS: They only call lawyers in the movies, Mrs. Savaard. Clean underwear, soap, astringent, talcum, mouthwash . . . and what have we here?

LYDIA (*ashamed*): Crossword puzzles.

FRANCIS: I'll send this to our decoding section at once.

LYDIA: The answers are there in the back. Please, sir . . . Officer?

FRANCIS: Mister Keely, F. X., FBI.

LYDIA: Mr. Keely, let me call Godnick 1-2345.

FRANCIS: In the movies, Mrs. Savaard, in the movies there are many effects which we can not achieve here. Long shot of the city from a distance, camera zooming in to one dark window, close-up . . . We might even hear the telephone ring with maddening urgency and see your Mr. Godnick groping for the night light by his bed.

LYDIA (*docile*): I think I studied this once in French. It was called closet drama.

SHERRY: I always like a little plot between the numbers, though once I was in a review—oh, poor, really poor, not my sort of work.

STANLEY: Television?

SHERRY: Ah no, that was one more flop. This was in a cabaret, invented by some witty kids. I supplied the money and they gave me a couple of songs to do and we pretended I was one of the gang. I was pushing thirty, see—*had* pushed—and this was my "comeback," see—

STANLEY: Don't . . . please.

SHERRY (*fondling herself in the mink coat*): —only there was nothing to come back to—

STANLEY: Can't you see I'm blushing? You stop this. It's pointless.

MRS. KEELY (*to Henry Savaard*): Did I tell you what that fella would get from her?

HENRY: Chalk it up, Mom.

SHERRY: I hadn't been any place, if you get what I mean, only around—

STANLEY: You're determined to go on with this.

SHERRY: Sure, I'd been around—

MARY AGNES: And on and on until she comes to the end of her story, actually one of the sadder testimonies we shall hear in this court. "Look. I am bad, I am a whore, I am beautiful. No one has ever touched my soul, that's left for you on this one last go-round." They have come, these gents and their ladies, to demonstrate the various methods of displaying the merchandise. "Ah, look," she says, "now that I've got your shoe off I see you've a hole in your sock. Poor smelly sock, poor punky toe, and is there no one in the world, then, to kiss this poor horny heel?"

SHERRY (*slipping the coat off her shoulders, not about to give up her big scene*): Oh yeah, I'd been around—

STANLEY: Say, I'll bet you were great in some of those big Rodgers and Hammerstein numbers!

MARY AGNES (*loud and lewd*): We've been around the mulberry bush, mulberry bush, mulberry bush. We've been around the mulberry bush, so early in the morning.

(*The women play the game, singing and going through the pantomime led by* MARY AGNES, *but the domestic chores do not interest the men, who are soon absorbed in batting averages. The women carry on*):

This is the way we wash your clothes,
So early Monday morning.
. . . . scrub your floor,
. . . . mend your clothes,
. . . . sweep your house,
. . . . bake your bread,
And skiddle-ree-do we go to church,
So early Sunday morning.

SHERRY: I had been around. Yes, I went so far as to get married: the husband, the house, the money, the psychiatrist—the works. The decorator: he recommended a lot of Louis—"It's a very nice period, Mrs. Leavit." What you need is a good massage, Mrs. Leavit, or a matching purse, or a vermeil pot, or a *truite amandine*, or pelmets, or avocados, or avocado pelmets, or personal freedom, or fish forks, or port strainers, or a feeling of security, Mrs. Leavit.

MRS. KEELY: She married a Jew. I said, "The Lord can judge us, Lil, we sent her to the nuns." Well, Mary Agnes laughed at me and I said, "That's all right, but what have you got, Miss, if you've not got your religion?"

HENRY (*singing to himself*):
Lloyd George knows my father, My father knows Lloyd George,
Lloyd George knows my father, My father . . .

MRS. KEELY: I was speaking!

HENRY: And I was just a little kid crouching by the Stromberg Carlson, perhaps ten minutes after bedtime, that's all, when that fat Irish nurse came down the back stairs . . .

MRS. KEELY: Have you said your prayers, such as they are?

HENRY: It was Gangbusters on the Air (that was the one boyish pursuit I allowed myself)—the bandits are of a dark complexion wearing silk-stocking masks. If they are in your area notify the police immediately. They are armed and dangerous.

MRS. KEELY: Stop that foolish talk.

HENRY: You're not my mother, Molly Macree. (*He begins to tear the decorations from his clown hat, and machine-guns* MRS. KEELY—*"ak-ak-ak-ak"—before he settles down.*)

MRS. KEELY: I was on the point of calling Mae in any case. (*She dials on a nonexistent telephone, and nods and talks to herself.*) Well, I wouldn't trust veal, a nice piece of pork cooked through . . .

HENRY: I'm on this team forever, like some monastery—(*he pulls at the bar stool*)—like some up-your-ass monastery.

LYDIA (*dreamily*): Like a rest home, the chairs nailed to the floor and the sweet curtains drawn so you can't see the bars.

FRANCIS: Would you repeat that, please, Mrs. Savaard?

LYDIA: I was only saying that when I go to visit my husband I think . . . I feel it's like going to a prison.

FRANCIS: Why is that, Mrs. Savaard?

LYDIA: I suppose because we sit across from each other and pretend we are in a living room and that we could— either one of us—get up at any moment and walk out, walk out on the whole messy business, back to our weak, nice, colorless lives that have no interest for you, but we choose to sit in that snake pit of a tearoom.

FRANCIS: Then why do you go there, Mrs. Savaard?

LYDIA: I must.

FRANCIS: Why *must* you?

LYDIA: He is my husband. It is my duty.

FRANCIS: Ah!

LYDIA: Why did you make me say that?

FRANCIS: Mrs. Savaard, we never "make" anyone.

LYDIA: —and because there is no place else to go.

FRANCIS: Only the madhouse?

LYDIA: Yes.

FRANCIS (*starts on her again*): We know that you have

been away, Mrs. Savaard. We know where you have been, Mrs. Savaard. Now, why do you go?

LYDIA: To see Henry.

FRANCIS: And why do you visit Henry, Mrs. Savaard?

LYDIA: I must.

FRANCIS: Why must you, Mrs. Savaard?

LYDIA: Because he is finishing his ship in the bottle.

FRANCIS: *Why* must you, Mrs. Savaard?

LYDIA (*cries out*): Because I loved him once.

FRANCIS: That will be all.

STANLEY (*to Sherry*): Why is that guy so nasty?

SHERRY: He's my cousin Francis. That's his job.

STANLEY: He sounds like a prize . . .

SHERRY: No, sweetie, he is very good.

STANLEY: That poor kid . . .

SHERRY: They have always said how good Francis is, the aunts and the teachers. I have proof that Sister Mary Redemptor had the hots for him in the fifth grade. He got to carry the cross in the big processions.

STANLEY: He's a rat.

SHERRY: It's not his fault. Francis is never to blame. They have given him a little niche in the home-town hall of fame . . . O.K., let me put it this way: what do they think of you at home, Stoshie?

STANLEY: What does who think?

SHERRY: At home? What do they think of you at home, Stanley boy?

STANLEY: My mother and sister?

SHERRY: Exactly, sweetie. (STANLEY, *pink with shame, gets himself the New York telephone directory to sulk with.*)

MARY AGNES: Swing your partner, do-si-do,
　　　　　　Back him in a corner, yo-ho-ho.

　　Now we see that each guy has fought with his gal as we might have expected at this roller derby. (*She directs the men to turn away on their stools.*) See how the gentlemen withdraw from us, while the ladies are left in the rising dawn of guilt and unfulfillment. It can get nasty, waiting for the silence to break: "Shall I lay my body down once more," she says, and there is no reply. "There, I've fixed you a little soup the way you like it," she says, and the soup grows cold. But we must not always look on the gloomy side, there is as a last resort the sport of emasculation—why call it by a lesser name—and it falls upon us, the brave women, to keep the balls rolling.

(*She takes a pair of horn-rimmed glasses, terribly smart and aggressive, from her big black bag and reads from a typed script*):

I have a letter here from Mrs. G. W. of Tacoma, Washington. She writes: "My son is a lovely lad of sixteen who does not reveal himself in the locker room or go out with girls. He makes up the loveliest hats for me in all his spare time and fixes lovely tasty-trays to bring up when I have one of my headaches, but he is afflicted with one unlovely habit which will drive me to distraction. He leaves his underwear on the floor. Please help before things are less lovely!"

(*A sharp buzzer sounds and* MRS. KEELY *gives her answer; it will sound every time a member of the panel answers.*)

MRS. KEELY: She could sneak ice cubes into his clean drawers, so that when he puts them on it would serve as a little reminder. I've found that very satisfactory.

LYDIA: Sometimes the old ways are best.

MRS. KEELY: Or a hot poker.

LYDIA and SHERRY: Wonderful!

MARY AGNES (*taking off the glasses, to emphasize the solemnity of the moment*): This is a cry from the heart. We have a telegram from St. Paul, and this problem, girls, is the major difficulty in many homes today. The telegram reads: HUSBAND LEAVES SEAT UP ON TOILET AFTER USE STOP FAST HELP NEEDED STOP, and it's signed, RECENTLY MARRIED.

MRS. KEELY: That's a hard nut to crack.

MARY AGNES: If I may be allowed—I suggest that she rig up the seat to a long invisible string and when he is through with his business she could yank it down quick—WHAM!

SHERRY: That'll take the air out of his tires.

ALL: Good enough! Swell! Grand!

(*The men turn around abruptly and face the women with contempt. The women hang their heads in shame.*)

MARY AGNES (*to her father*): Yes—I know. All right. It was an attempt anyway. It was something. You can't just give up like this, Daddy, we've got to do something.

TIM KEELY: I almost did once. It was the night the old ice house burnt down—a rotting landmark, not worth saving. I broke out a window with my ax, and there from a stupendous height was the waterfall and behind me the fires of hell coming through the door. Now, I said, it will be quick and an easy thing to do. I began to cough, breathing the smoke, and for one holy moment I knew it would be a sin to go back to the firehouse and wash up and then go on home to my family. For all the years I lived it would be a sin even more than if I was "boarding" with that schoolteacher, like Ned McCormick. And all I needed to do was breathe the black air until I went. (*Shaking his head, laughing at his story.*) Well, Ag, you'll never guess what happened. I stood there, engulfed in my own finality if you will, and remembered that I hadn't paid Dowd when he came for the life insurance that previous week. Your mother had said, "Put him off till we finish with Francis' teeth," and Dowd, the smiling gentleman, marked us behind in his little book. I thought, there'd be only the pension and not enough to bury me, and walked straight for the door.

MARY AGNES: What door? Where were those fires of hell?

TIM KEELY: Ah, that's what I neglected to say—there *was* a door, I neglected to see it until the moment I walked straight out, for the other door opened onto an outside staircase and all I had to do was chop at it a bit and walk straight out to the world.

MARY AGNES: Were you sorry after?

TIM KEELY: I didn't think of it often, but when I did, then I'd say to myself—there'll be another time. There'll be a day when you're paid up with Dowd, but I was never on call for the big ones again, only small fires—stoves, mattresses, and the like.

MRS. KEELY: Your father died still a young man.

HENRY: We know that.

MRS. KEELY: Ah, button your lip.

MARY AGNES: There we are—it's that sort of constant bickering. I was only trying to do something, Daddy, waiting for the silence to break, waiting for someone to knuckle under and say the first sweet word.

STANLEY: Sherry—give us a song, Sherry.

SHERRY (*cynical, out of tune*):

> I'm wearing second-hand things,
> second-hand clothes,
> That's why they call me
> Second-Hand Rose

STANLEY: Awww, come on.

SHERRY: I couldn't any more.

STANLEY: A number from *Oklahoma*—you'll be sensational.

SHERRY (*soft and sultry*): Sweetie—you know you're a *real* sweetie.

MARY AGNES (*annoyed*): Pin the tail on the donkey, anyone? Play musical chairs?

TIM KEELY: I don't see the use, Ag.

STANLEY: You'll kill 'em, Sherry.

SHERRY: —or kill myself trying, sweetheart.

(*She gets up from her chair, slipping out of the mink coat, and tries a few tap steps. The music starts, low at first, "It Had to Be You." SHERRY comes downstage in a hazy blue spot and, looking straight at the audience, speaks with great, true sentiment, all choked up. Reappearance of Much-loved Star at Carnegie Hall.*)

It's . . . it's thrilling to be back . . . here, to know . . . that you want me, because I've always wanted you. When they tack up a star on my door there's the warmest feeling comes to me . . . just to know you're waiting and that I can come out here and make you laugh a little, or maybe we'll cry together. Yes, it's lonely up here! Oh, yes . . . I can only see the blinding light and the blackness, so until I win you, until I have you, this is the emptiest place in the world.

(*She comes farther downstage and sits with her legs dangling into the orchestra pit. The glistening tears in her eyes are large enough for all to see.*)

"All the world's a stage!" Listen, Hon, I was never much at school, but I know that one—"All the world's . . . a stage!"—and I'm just an actress put up here to give body and soul, because I love ya, and it's crazy, I know. . . . Once, after an opening—it was in a roadhouse outside of Erie, P. A.—my agent rushed backstage and said, "They loved you, Sherry. Did you hear them? They loved you." And I said, "Not as much as I loved them."

(*She gets up, the spot grows brighter.*) I want to sing all the songs, all the songs you remember. (*Doing a few steps in place.*) I want to sing to you.

(*As she begins her dance, the men get up from their stools, take off their funny hats and form a male chorus for* SHERRY'S *act, like the flunkeys who twirled Eleanor Powell and Ginger Rogers. Indeed, what style* SHERRY *has is an imitation of these dancers plus a shade of Dietrich in the voice. She is not wholly bad or incompetent, but she is pathetically weak. Her voice is thin. At the end of her routine she gets winded twirling, and the whole act cranks down.*)

> O, that she was pure
> Of that we can be sure

Her future was secure
And long may she endure . . . Ma Mère.
 Hey, Hey, Hey—and shimmied around
 And presently found
 That anyone new, anyone now
 With the breath of a cow
 Could take me to bed,
 Could make me see red,
 If I showed him how,
  With all thy dough
  I love you so—
(*Repeat*) O, that she was pure, *etc.*

 (*When the attempt dies out* SHERRY *goes back to her seat and draws the fur coat over her like a blanket. Suddenly, to escape the silence,* STANLEY *starts to applaud, and all the men join in as they return to their stools and again put on the funny hats.*)

TIM KEELY: That's grand, Sherry! That's my girl!

FRANCIS: You're great, Mary Elizabeth!

STANLEY: Gosh, that was marvelous!

SHERRY: Save it boys. Sherry is marvelous. You can always manage that as a lead-in. Well, I guess I know what I'm marvelous at.

HENRY: What's this lady of the evening after? (*The men turn on him and he makes a madman face.*) Therapy? Ah, see here is Henry the unbalanced little boy. He has put a crown on his mother's head. There's his wife. He's given her the vows—Poverty, Chastity until death do us part.

MRS. KEELY: Mercy! It's the Mercies we have over at St. Augustine's.

HENRY: Enough red herrings, Mum. Note well: I have selected a fool's cap. I am building a boat in a bottle.

LYDIA: Mr. Keely? You understand that he doesn't mean it—actually the boat is built outside of the bottle and arranged in collapsible parts. You understand that, sir?

HENRY: I am building a fucking boat in a kiss-me-ass bottle.

MRS. KEELY: Naturally, I was pleasant. He reminded me of my son, but may I say that Francis is a good boy. The other day I said, "Mae, he's been a wonderful boy to his mother."

HENRY: For the record, I can take Mother now and again for old times' sake, and my wife is an inoffensive version of a standard product. It's the other two, the lady executive and the *actrice,* who steal my material without so much as a program note.

STANLEY: All right, buddy.

HENRY (*at Sherry*): Deanna Durbin
                 Wears a Turban
                 And she is a Star
                 S-T-A-R Star.

STANLEY: That's enough!

HENRY: Diana Dors
        Wears no ———

STANLEY: I said that was enough.

HENRY: And she is a Star
        S-T-A-R Star.

STANLEY: You crackpot—

SHERRY: Stanley! Stanley, darling, I can take care of myself. (*She has pulled herself together and is ready to go on.*) Well, hi—I'm back at the party! Stanley, hey, Stoshie Sarnicki, did anyone ever tell you that you were a sweetie? I mean it . . . a real Teddy-bear man. . . . (STANLEY *blushes.*)

MARY AGNES: O.K., O.K. Everybody up. When the music starts we all march around. (*A searingly nostalgic tune comes from the pit—heavy on the sax.*) Play and Play and Play and . . . (*She claps her hands like a schoolteacher.*) That's right—all the boys up, and one and, all the girls up too, and two and three and . . .

LYDIA (*calling out a sharp command*): I don't have time for games! (*The music and the marching stop.*)

113

FRANCIS: Then we'd like an explanation of the puzzles in your suitcase, Mrs. Savaard.

LYDIA: I made that one mistake. I thought you wouldn't mind.

FRANCIS (*gently now*): I'm sorry about this. You see it's my duty.

LYDIA: I understand that—perfectly. I was wrong to expect. I simply thought that loving him once—you could speak to the warden and change the plot.

FRANCIS: We would like to help in any way *possible*.

LYDIA: It seems so terribly long.

FRANCIS: It is long, lady.

LYDIA: What do you do? What do you do when it itches and aches?

FRANCIS: I pray.

MRS. KEELY: Blessed Be God.

FRANCIS: I drive on the turnpike.

MRS. KEELY: Blessed Be His Holy Name.

FRANCIS: I eat.

MRS. KEELY: Pray for us.

FRANCIS: Very late at night.

MRS. KEELY: Pray for us.

FRANCIS: I kneel down to darkness.

MRS. KEELY: Amen.

MARY AGNES: Da dee da dee dum dum—everyone's got to have his lyric moment though it may be inappropriate— (*Clapping out the beat of a Sousa march*) Da dee da dee and in line Hen-ree and da dee da dee eyes front Mo-ther.

MRS. KEELY (*marching, but yelling out her complaints above the noise*): I got a bunion doesn't take to this. I'm supposed to call Lil. She says it's Mae's turn for Thanksgiving and I'm sick to death of them dried-up birds. Well you know I had my attack right after she did Christmas last year. I said, "Mae, what's in this stuffing makes it so wet?" "Just a little cut-up onion," she says. "Well onion never made anything runny like that," I says, and I saw the neck and gizzard all boiled up in a greasy pan and it was that night the pain started, worse than labor it is, coming in sharp thrusts. . . .

MARY AGNES (*Stops everything*): O.K., there we are. It took a while to get that one. (*She begins in the mother's voice*): "Oh, the pain I had with you, glory-be-to-God was it worth it, Miss, what I went through when I look at you now. Francis was no trouble at all, just twenty minutes and I had him—a beautiful boy."

MARY AGNES (*clapping furiously, determined that her game will not be fripped away by silly chatter*): Da Dee Da Dum Da Dee and Stan-lee take a chair away Da Dee Da Dum.

(STANLEY *comes around to the ladies' side and tips one of the mock thrones up against the table. He goes back to the marching line on the boys' side. After a suspenseful minute the music stops and everyone gets a seat except* SHERRY, *who gathers up her mink coat with a sporting smile.*)

SHERRY: It's a pleasure. I've wanted out for so long . . . to let the roots show, to let my voice crack, to eat a piece of coconut cake, not to feel obliged, sweetie, to love all the kids backstage and the cute doorman and the delivery boy and the darling little sweetie navy beans . . .

TIM KEELY: She took her own life, Lord Have Mercy on her.

FRANCIS: The night I read about Sherry I was supposed to pick up an agent coming in from Syracuse. The railroad station was full of people going places with magazines and candy bars. I couldn't stand the sight of a living person and I went into the men's room and locked the door on a pay toilet. That was all, to be somewhere with her as dim as my Aunt Lil's couch, to feel all that lust again with no hope now. I knew exactly what to do—my heart told me, I guess you could say that—and I took out my Dick Tracy pen with the invisible ink and wrote on the wall: Mary

Elizabeth Hurley, I love you. There was nothing wrong in that, nothing that wasn't as shameful as anything else I had done in my life. Then I touched her name with spit and it brought the secret message out. I thought that I might have changed things for her, that *she* might have changed things for me.

SHERRY: That's more like it, isn't it, sweetie? Well, never you mind.

STANLEY: Don't go, Sherry. Take my stool.

SHERRY (*obviously moved*): That is honestly the nicest thing a man's ever said to me, Stanley. Thanks all the same.

(*The music begins—a swing tune, and* SHERRY *moves with professional grace toward the Girls' door. She is smiling a true smile, twinkling at the toes, and seems for half a minute to be superb onstage.*)

STANLEY: Don't go, Sherry.

SHERRY: So long, sweeties. (*Throwing kisses*) I'm off . . . I'm off to that big chorus line in the sky.

TIM KEELY: Give us one more song, Sherry. One more song.
(*All the men clamor for one more song.*)

SHERRY (*turns back, smiles consent, waits for her cue, and belts out a final rousing number*):

> Our Lady of Mercy, to you we're singing
> Mother of Sorrows, our voices ringing,
>> We will never find your equal,
>> Ho-Holy Mary, here's to you,
>>> Say it does not end—
>>> Say it does not end—
>>> Say it does not end here.
> Patron of virgins, to you we're singing,
> Star of the Sea, our voices ringing,
> We will never find your equal,
> Ho-Holy Mary, here's to you.
>>> Say it does not end—
>>> Say it does not end—
>>> Say it does not end now.

(*She exits to wild applause, leaving the happy, excited crowd to their marching, which they resume to the tune of "When the Lights Go on Again All Over the World."* MARY AGNES *goes to the men's side, unscrews the seat of a stool and puts it on the table. When the music stops* TIM KEELY *stands back, his fireman's hat in his hand.*)

MARY AGNES: You didn't even *try.*

TIM KEELY: That's all right, Ag.

MARY AGNES: It's not fair. There's not a cavity in Francis' head now.

TIM KEELY: I've been contemplating this for a long while, Ag. It's been eating at me night and day.

MRS. KEELY: He went so peaceful—in his sleep. I called Lil first, "Tim's gone," I said, "right off in his sleep. The heart."

HENRY: Something was wrong that whole week before: agony, torture, disappointment around his ears. He never went to the office—there was nothing to work for, I heard him say that to you one night. Later, I thought it strange that he held together during the worst years. The coroner's report said he died of a broken heart.

MRS. KEELY: It's a lovely way to go. I said then, "When my time comes, I pray to God I go in my own bed as peaceful."

HENRY: Who's kidding who? He died at the Central Park Zoo. His heart failed in the monkey house and I had to run out and find a policeman, a big Paddy who thought I was pulling his leg.

TIM KEELY: Good-by, now, Ag . . . you'll remember me to your mother. She had small white feet . . . The prettiest one. Ag? I'll say good-by now.

MARY AGNES: Farewell, dear Mother.

TIM KEELY: Thy loving father, Ag. (*He moves away.*)

MARY AGNES: Yes, yes—oh, Daddy look, look at the mountain of tires! Think of the miles they've rolled! (TIM KEELY *puts on his hat solemnly and goes out the Boys' door; while* MARY AGNES *continues to call him back, the music begins: "Bright College Years."*) I'm going to Bridgeport, where are you going, Daddy? Will you go to Boston? Daddy, come to Africa—come on the bus—come on the train.

(*Again* STANLEY *has tipped one of the ladies' thrones against the table, and when they rush for seats* LYDIA SAVAARD *is left out.*)

FRANCIS: You may go now, Mrs. Savaard. (*She hesitates.*) You are perfectly free to go.

LYDIA: My puzzles? (FRANCIS *hands her the suitcase after gluing on several customs stickers: Amherst, Smith, Cornell.*) I thought I might interest Henry in the puzzles. (*She goes toward the door, but lingers, picking up an old picture magazine.*)

FRANCIS: We won't detain you any longer, Mrs. Savaard.

LYDIA: Thank you so much. It's been perfectly lovely.

FRANCIS: Shall I call a taxi for you?

LYDIA: You're too kind, really, but I have my bicycle right outside. I have to be running along. (*Patting her suitcase*) All my things to wash out, and the apartment will be simply *affreuse* after three whole days of Mary Agnes. Thank you again for the delightful weekend. It is such a pleasure to get out of the city in this beautiful autumn weather and I always think that the leaves in New England are the prettiest of all. We have decided to put some serious work in on our bridge game so that we can be a challenge to you next time. We look forward to you and Boozie calling when you come into town shopping, and perhaps we can have dinner and see a show. Until then we will remember our heavenly weekend and your excellent currant buns. Our love in trumps, Lydia Savaard. (*She arranges her wimple, checks the pleats in her skirt, and finding everything in order goes out with a sincere smile of gratitude for Francis and a schoolgirl's wave to us all.*)

(MARY AGNES *goes to the men's side and removes the top of another stool. A circus tune, high and insistent, begins on a calliope. They march in a quick trot and all are running when the music ends. The men rush for the two remaining seats and Henry loses out.*)

HENRY: You mother-fucking creeps.

MRS. KEELY: It was the shape of his face reminded me of my son, but there's no resemblance.

HENRY: I would like to know who you people think you are. Jesus! That would be of interest.

MRS. KEELY: Someone should have washed your mouth out with soap, young man.

MARY AGNES: Jaysus, Grandma Walsh always said: Jaysus, Mither and Joosuff!

MRS. KEELY: A little prayer, that was.

HENRY (*trying to pull* STANLEY *off the stool*): This is my rightful seat, my good man.

STANLEY: Look here, kid, I got this seat and I'm not about to give it up for any crazy . . .

HENRY: Crazy what, Mister? Crazy who?

MRS. KEELY: Be a good sport now, Henry. That's the way. Smile when you lose. I know we were always happy we could afford that scout uniform for Francis.

HENRY (*pushing his guards off, he assumes a supercilious air of composure*): Sorry about that, but I'm told these seizures are on the decline. (*He takes off his dunce's cap and sits down in Stanley's place again, twirling, insolent.*) It's something of a laugh anyway because I have no interest in this club and certainly not in these people.

MRS. KEELY: You needn't be rude.

HENRY: Shall I tell you that I am sailing in the Bermuda race?

MRS. KEELY: Isn't that fine.

HENRY: No, I'll say that I'm going off tomorrow to the south of France.

MRS. KEELY: Isn't that fine.

HENRY: You will have the great blue dress, Mummykins, and champagne for breakfast.

MRS. KEELY: Oh, that's nice, Henry.

HENRY: I'd like to make it easy for you spooks to patronize me. You should love *this poor boy*. (FRANCIS *comes toward him looking officially austere*.) Do you imagine that I'm going to keep your stool, Mister? (*He twirls around, taunting*.) No, no, no, no . . . I am a very busy boy. Yes, yes, Mr. Creep. I'm building . . . myself—in a bottle. And if you think I'm about to tell you how it's done, you're crazy.

FRANCIS: This stool belongs to this gentleman.

HENRY: That's right, gentleman. (*He twirls*.) It's done with extremely delicate, long pincers. That's the clue. You look so decidedly . . . uncomfy. Ah, but you should love *this poor boy*. I mean in the way we love those forlorn, feeble hemophilic princelings. Gentleman, have a seat. (*He twirls the stool just before* STANLEY's *bottom hits the seat*.) It is difficult, you see, and requires hours of concentration, especially if one is obsessed by detail, all the nerve filaments to be put in place . . . the skin to be sewn on . . . each little hair to be glued to the chest and under the arm. The miracle of creation!

MRS. KEELY: My Francis was no trouble at all. He came just as easy on the kitchen table and I never had the heartburn with him I had with Agnes . . .

MARY AGNES: Music! Let's get this show on the road.

HENRY: Don't worry, lady. I'm a busy boy. (*He is almost to the door when he swings around and comes at* STANLEY *again as though to attack him but then laughs. He turns the punch into an obvious caress and, at this, both* STANLEY *and* FRANCIS *draw back*.) Oh no, no, no—but I do have you poor foops scared. Don't you worry. I have to carve my privates this afternoon. It requires a steady hand. Good-by, Mother dear. (*He leaves with a champion smirk on his face as the music, "Pack Up Your Troubles in Your Old Kit Bag," begins.)*

MRS. KEELY: Didn't I tell you? O, Mary conceived without sin, pray for us who have recourse to thee.

(They march, and when the music stops MRS. KEELY *and* MARY AGNES *both sit on the last chair left for the ladies. They push for possession with their fannies until* MARY AGNES *shoves her mother off onto the floor.)*

MRS. KEELY: She used to be a good girl, God knows. I said it doesn't matter, Ag, you don't look like much, you take after your father's side, so long as you're a nice girl. I said you'll catch more flies with sugar than you ever will with vinegar.

MARY AGNES *(sarcastically)*: I said the way to a man's heart is through his stomach.

MRS. KEELY: I said, Lil, the way she's gone is not my fault. I did everything, everything. Why it was *you* brought her that lovely *peau de soie* she was confirmed in. Many nights I go to sleep thinking what's wrong with that girl. Was I to blame? And truthfully I . . . *(The music has started again, a simple old-fashioned fox trot.)* Don't bother about me. I know when I'm not wanted by my children. Francis way up in Buffalo. I know you'd leave me to die, Mary Agnes, go way off there to the other side . . . Well, I told Mae I'd meet her for confession, so you needn't worry about me. *(She gets herself up off the floor and starts to the door.)* Don't worry about your sick old mother. No, I couldn't touch a thing with my stones coming on. I said it. Clean the wax out of your ears, I said, Bless me, Father, for I have sinned. It has been no time at all since my last confession. I stole a cookie once. I answered my mother and my father back twice. I used a swear word three times. I had an impure thought four times. I wished I had a mink like Mary Elizabeth five times.

*(*MARY AGNES, FRANCIS, *and* STANLEY *look at one another*

*—guilty, confused—after she has gone, and the music—
"Let's Remember Pearl Harbor"—sets them to moving
once again.* MARY AGNES *circles the one chair left on her
side, while* STANLEY *and* FRANCIS *circle the stool left to
them. When the music stops* STANLEY *easily slips onto the
seat.*)

FRANCIS: Many are called, but few are chosen.

STANLEY: I'm sorry about this—

FRANCIS: The early bird catches the worm.

STANLEY: Sometimes things seem to happen out of our control.

FRANCIS: Ask the man who owns one.

STANLEY: I don't see that I can do anything—and be honest.

FRANCIS: Sister Susie sewing shirts for soldiers.

STANLEY: That's a hard one.

FRANCIS: Yes. (*Walking resolutely toward the door.*) The
Big Black Bug Bit the Big Brown Bear.

STANLEY: You're off, then?

FRANCIS (*reciting as he goes*): Lives of great men all remind
us/ We can make our lives sublime,/ And departing leave
behind us/ Footprints on the sands of time.

(*The lights dim and* STANLEY *and* MARY AGNES *come and
stand on either side of the one remaining throne in a romantic spot.*)

MARY AGNES: This is the way I always imagined it.

STANLEY: With you, Ag, with you.

(*He throws his beret on the table and* MARY AGNES *pulls
off her Communion veil. They face each other unadorned
and come back to the chair, leaning over it in a tender
kiss. Cool, subtle jazz begins to play in the background as
they hold hands high in a London Bridge and circle the
single chair.*)

STANLEY: Hi there!

MARY AGNES: Alone at last.

STANLEY: We forgot. There's still the one stool.

MARY AGNES: Oh, Stoshie, I don't play games with you.

(*They stop marching, and during the following scene the chair is used as a prop on which they kneel, lean, stand, but never sit.*)

STANLEY: I thought they'd never go.

MARY AGNES: You weren't exactly showing the door to Sherry.

STANLEY: What am I supposed to do with a girl like that?

MARY AGNES: Don't ask me.

STANLEY: She was desperate . . . I couldn't let her go off.

MARY AGNES: Mmm, of course . . . but it's automatic with Sherry. She's been able to get any man she wants since age seven—pull a lever.

STANLEY: Automatic the hell. (*He turns away.*)

MARY AGNES: Stosh (*peeking around the back of the chair*), Stoshie, I'm sorry.

STANLEY: I thought you liked Sherry.

MARY AGNES: I *love* Sherry. I think she's one of the best.

STANLEY: That sounds fine.

MARY AGNES: No, I mean that. And I never minded that she had my father, my brother, my uncles and all the rest—but you!

STANLEY: She didn't *have* me, Ag. What gripes me is this "automatic" business. That poor girl feels, really feels.

MARY AGNES: Some of it's acting, now. It has to be.

STANLEY: She throws herself into the part, by God.

MARY AGNES: Yes, it doesn't make it any less . . . What did you think of my mother and Henry?

STANLEY: Not bad.

MARY AGNES: Pretty bad at the end. There's your amateur dramatics.

STANLEY: I don't know. I feel sorry for that poor bastard.

MARY AGNES: Gracious! Everyone's a poor bastard.

STANLEY: Maybe so. (*She kneels on the chair and holds him close around the middle of his comfortable body. This softens him considerably. He blushes.*) Your brother and Lydia went fairly well.

MARY AGNES: A little shaky at first.

STANLEY: There was a common meeting ground, though. All that about loving in the toilet.

MARY AGNES: Absolutely.

STANLEY: I hope your father had a good time.

MARY AGNES: He didn't really fit, but it's hard to figure. The table only sits eight and even then I have to use some of the kitchen plates.

STANLEY: Didn't your mother carry on about the dressing!

MARY AGNES: I've had that gallstone up to here.

STANLEY: Perhaps we should have played something else— spin-the-bottle, post office.

MARY AGNES: People get nasty about kissing games.

STANLEY: The chairs were all right. (*He yawns.*)

MARY AGNES: Going to Jerusalem?

STANLEY (*tired, leaning on her throne*): Ag?

MARY AGNES: I'm not sure I get it. Pilgrims, maybe . . . holy wars?

STANLEY: Ag? (*He looks at his watch.*)

MARY AGNES: Christ. He always fits. You know what I read the other day?

STANLEY: Listen, Ag.

MARY AGNES: Some actress said Jesus was the first angry young man. No kidding, in a publicity release.

STANLEY: Mary Agnes, love? Aren't you sleepy?

MARY AGNES: No, turn the record over, Stosh, and we'll dance. (*The jazz starts from the beginning again, low and insistent.*)

STANLEY: You don't dance to this music.

MARY AGNES: Why not? Why not dance to this music? I mean I'm not trying to win any prize for knowing what niggers and artists don't do.

STANLEY: That's enough. That's fine.

MARY AGNES: Or girls in black dresses or guys in little button-down collars.

STANLEY: Let's not get upset, Mary Agnes. You know I have

to go home. Now let's not go through this all over again, sweetheart. (*He leads her gently to the chair and sits her down.*) I have to go to Brooklyn.

MARY AGNES: Don't go. Oh, look at that funny line the hat made on your head, a red silly-line. Stosh, let's go out, see, and get the Sunday paper . . . O.K.? We'll go over to Fifth Avenue . . .

STANLEY: I may have to wait for half an hour in the subway now. (*She turns from him and puts her head down on the arm of the chair.*) Monday . . . Monday I'll take you to lunch.

MARY AGNES (*cross and sniffy*): I have to meet the man from the plant with the new samples. (*She looks around and smiles faintly.*) Tuesday?

STANLEY: Dear, you know Tuesday is the schedules with Sammy.

MARY AGNES: Wednesday?

STANLEY: Wednesday we'll go to the Armenian place and have grape leaves and lamb ka-stuff and stay out all afternoon.

MARY AGNES (*childishly*): And honey and white wine?

STANLEY (*kissing her lightly*): Honey and white wine and asphalt coffee. (*He turns, and is nearly out of the spotlight when she jumps up, defiant and foolish, to do a clownish dance on the seat of the chair.*)

MARY AGNES: The cheese stands alone, the cheese stands alone, heigh-ho the dairy-o, the cheese stands alone.

STANLEY (*coming back*): Let's not start, Mary Agnes—darling.

MARY AGNES (*she is suddenly ashamed and sits quietly in her chair*): I'm sorry. Good night. (*He kisses her quickly on the forehead.*)

STANLEY: Night-night, sweetie. (*He leaves the spotlight behind and we can hear the Boys' door open and swing shut.*)

MARY AGNES (*sharply*): Sweet dreams! (*She joggles along in her chair.*) Alone at last. Do dee da dum, baby. Left to my own resources . . . da dee dum, baby. (*She gets up and wanders.*) I'll just write in the sand with my stumps: Stanley Sarnicki I love you. (*First, she picks up the telephone book; next, in the bottom of her big purse, which has been left under the table, she finds a cigarette and lights it.*) I don't smoke. I'm going to leave the dishes till morning. Let them soak overnight. (*She sings a little, wanders again, consciously evading the audience, and then with a shrug and a sigh gives in, comes back to her chair, and faces straight out across the footlights.*) What do you want? One more trick, is that it? You feel all queasy without a climax—without a proper end that you can look back to. I know, it's not been enough. Not enough—these men and these women loved and fought and begat and wept and played and sang and died and danced . . . gone now, every last one of them, but it's not enough. You want to suck in your breath as you recall the final startling act; it's not enough for the lights to come down, the curtain to close. . . . You stumble out into the night still wanting. What is it you want? Mmm, well-ll . . . more than one actress just sitting up there on the stage . . . alone . . . sitting. . . . (*She pretends that she is weary, stretching her arms wide, and then the idea comes to her. She gets up and walks jauntily to the stool which is left, on the men's side of the table. She sits on it: proud, defiant, and amused with herself.*) Shall I snuggle into a tricky coffin and let one of you come up here and saw through the secret panels? No? Go over Niagara in a barrel? Not enough? (*She is pleading with her audience now, all the sport in her solitary predicament faded.*) A hole-in-one? Kick the extra point? Run for home? Nothing in this jerry-built crate-wood world is enough. I, Mary Agnes Keely, famous illusionist and escape artist, will now attempt THE ONE MORE as performed before the crowned heads of Europe, the late Dalai Lama of Tibet, and in the glittering Red Room of the

White House, Ladies and Gentlemen: THE LAST! (*Solemnly, with a broad stagy gesture, she makes the sign of the cross upon herself:*) In the name of the Fa-ther and of the Daugh-ter and of the Ho-ly Ghost. Amen. (*Now, to some soft, sad Chopin mazurka,* MARY AGNES *in a quivering fright exits through the Boys' door, and the darkness comes.*)

6

————◆●◆————

December 24—

Don't let the miserable season get you. A few drinks at the office under a paper bell, a bonus with greetings: "Thanks to our swell new copywriter and good wishes for the New Year, Bert Sigal." A young man wearing a wedding band vomits on the subway, his striped tie carefully tucked out of range. Console yourself, Ag, with the world that lives in Lord & Taylor's Christmas windows, minuscule perfection—tiny princess, wee prince, how real your dance seems to us frozen stiff in the outer world of unreality. You run and jump and play (and copulate under the drawbridge)

in such a chic Yuletide Eden. Pretty ass, sweet Teddy—
little lamb, who made thee?

Lydia had misgivings, laying the presents for Henry in
with her pajamas: a diverting book, a harmless sweater, my
fruit cake the weight of a man's shoe. (Would the doctor
approve?) Then the happy-holiday call from her parents in
Cleveland and the exchange of lies all round—"He's doing
fine, Mother, just fine. Did you get his boat in the bottle?
They're starting him on water colors now." Though we in
New York know that only last week (after a visit from his
mother—ha!) Henry ripped the felt off a pool table. Season's
Greetings: it's a strain on us all, and for Lydia I was an
extra burden: Mary Agnes all by herself tonight, sad and
unnatural.

"We should have had a tree or something," Lydia said,
handing me a large box. "Isn't Stanley coming?"

"Not till tomorrow."

She tilted her head at me, disapproving.

"But Christmas Eve is big with the Poles. He has to take
his mother and sister to church, you heard him."

She gave me a big earthenware pot to stew in—oh, just
what I needed; and my present to her: a silk contraption to
wear in the evening, scarlet, to wrap her pale shoulders—
probably never, but at least a pleasant fiction of music,
frivolity, excesses to be tucked away on a top shelf. She
swished it around her body and paraded to the window and
back, to the rubber plant and back—once pretty enough,
once blonde, once warm—but her spine was rigid as she
folded the flaming silk neatly and put it away. The party
was over, Lydia recalled to the front line. "What about Mrs.
Mertz?"

"I bought the five-pound nut-and-fruit assortment. She
doesn't look cream centers to me."

Wondering how far she was obliged, Lydia asked, "Mary
Agnes, would you?"

"Sure. I'll go down with them later. You go ahead. It'll be

hard getting a taxi tonight. The trains will be crowded."

"I hope Henry's better this week—easier." She cradled the Christmas box in her arms for the dream of a second. Next, an appropriate Dickensian bustle as I wrapped the Mertz candy, then Lydia leapt into her Visiting Nurse's garb for a holiday romp at the asylum. Before leaving she ran through her distress, sincerely felt, at poor old Ag alone on Christmas Eve.

"Now don't just sit around, Mary Agnes. You do something. Work on your dinner for Stanley."

"I can't stuff that goose until morning."

"Well, do *something*. Work on your play."

"That's over now, finished." Well, do something, something—I found myself with this in mind after she had gone. Something in the bedroom, a piece of paper that missed the wastebasket. Sit on the toilet and read the back of the aspirin bottle. Something: like building a ship inside. Flush the toilet twice and listen to the hissing hot steam of the leaking radiator. Then in the front room I let the light fade, watching people out the window—all of them going into snug-lit houses where trees hung with baubles reflected babies in Doctor Dentons, plates of fresh cookies shaped like stars, the crescent moon . . . candlelight . . . eggnog . . . the voices of the great oratorio. Like hell: they are all going to white apartments to watch the Trapp family on the Christmas Extravaganza and eat chemically mated, cheese-dyed grease-rings out of plastic snack bowls. Already the green tree is rare: "Remember how Aunt Maud always had those dear old polyethylene bags of Rancidos for the children."

As I cried in the window, it seemed that Stoshie could have called at least, Polack festivities or not. He could damn well have stopped off on his way to Brooklyn—that forbidding borough. I have had two psycho headaches and an attack of self-induced ptomaine avoiding the episode in which I stand before Stanley's mother with a red "A" flashing on my breast—but that's a ruse—my fear of a wise old woman in a black babushka spitting on the hearthstone as a curse upon me. No, I think she will ask . . . what? "What are you?" Pardon . . . I didn't hear. Maybe it was your accent, Mamma Sarnicki. "Are you animal, vegetable, or mineral?" And I will have no answer to satisfy her. Sin to tell a lie, I tremble and quake to imagine the cozy room, the friendly cup of coffee, the sucking little noises that would come from my mouth, the premonition that I would not *do* at all. I am terrorized by anything that might come between Stanley and me entwined on the rusty army cot in my back room, something that will remind us it is not the marriage bed or embroidered linen and precious ciderdown . . . our bodies tilted out of whack by some fusty old Brooklynish geegaw.

Lydia gone with the same old coat and wool socks for the trip. You think she would have put on *something* a bit more in the spirit of things. The same turnip-brown sweater, the same dead skirt. Oh, if only I could be there to hear her as she greets Henry, the voice subdued, holding back from joy. The faintest movement of her bloodless lips suggests a smile. "Merry Christmas, dear." That "dear" a gift to them both.

What did she mean anyway: cook something or write something. Like Henry with his therapeutic crafts. She's finished her little play. Next week they're starting her on villanelles. I am not ashamed of my yellow pads—a stack of them under the bed now—that's something. Still, I refuse to strike a false defiant note—all that crock-full about the alienation of the artist from her society. Suppose you don't have Brooklyn with a big-nosed Polish sister and a fat mamma in a cotton house dress or a Princeton sweetheart gone mad. Suppose you have yourself crying in the window . . . then try a holly-berry red on your toes or a little figure of Baby Jesus on a bed of parsley or write a sketch of some-one you have known, a teacher or a relative who has impressed you or perhaps changed the way in which you think or see the world around you. In your sketch include a physical description of your subject and remember to develop and restate the theme which is set in your introductory paragraph. Hard sauce, Ag, you might at least have sent toys to Francis' kids or something.

Mrs. Mertz, when I went down, opened the door as far as a short brass-color chain would allow. Seeing our present, she unhitched her fright of the intruder, a dark shape lingering in the hall, an evil presence forcing himself upon suspecting ladies, making off with their diamonds, their furs, their jars of chicken fat. Sensing a lighter mood, Mrs. Mertz threw her portal wide.

"Shut it down!" she yelled to the unseen corner of the room. "All night, all day, a perfectly healthy man sixty-seven years. Retired." Stooping to knead a bad foot, twisting her head up, Mrs. Mertz said, "Happy Holiday."

"Merry Christmas, and to Mr. Mertz, too."

She took the box of chocolates demurely. "For me and Leon? Such a nice girl, Miss Keely."

"From Mrs. Savaard, too."

"Such a nice person. Divorced?"

The Mertzes had been divided about Lydia: Leon had said a widow—but Mrs. Mertz, more attuned to the modern world, had said, "That nervous? A divorcée."

"Such a nice, clean person—divorced?"

"Well, no—" I saw beyond her into the front half of their living room: lustrous rayon drapes, Italian provincial suite, glass tops on the end tables, plastic covers on the cushions, cellophane on the lampshades, everything new for their triumphal years of dynamic repose.

"Come in. Leon, shut it off."

"I couldn't disturb you."

"Come, sit. A cup of tea?"

"No, thank you. I just wanted to say—"

"That's a nice young man *you've* got." Mrs. Mertz's eyes

gleamed: "You don't mind my mentioning. He reminds me a little of Chester Morris."

"Oh?" A wee convulsion of embarrassment shot through me.

"None of my business, but that's a very nice guy. Always pleasant in the hall."

"Well, Merry Christmas."

After too many smiles and waves as I went up the stairs, Mrs. Mertz shouted, "Everything all right with the apartment?"

"Actually, there's that valve broken on the bathroom radiator. It drips brown fluid."

"Monday morning I'll have him up."

You stand up remarkably well under the tear splats, my jaundiced yellow tablet.

Joyeux Noël.

SHERRY

During the war, when I wasn't quite twenty, I began to come to New York two or three times a year to visit my cousin Sherry. New York as I knew it with Sherry has nothing to do with my life now; returning years later, I am still a novice in the city. Her world was constructed of distorted pieces of time: workaday nights, supper at dawn, dreams in the afternoon—toast, coffee, and a quick shower in the evening.

The only way my cousin and her friends ever let on that they knew the moon still drew the tides, that the stars still moved in the heavens—not on Forty-fifth Street—was in their devotion to the big aluminum sun lamp under which they "took five." When the girls came back to Sherry's after the last show in whatever club or chorus line they were working, they all—except Sally, the Negro singer—had a go at the big bulb. As I watched, hunched and happy in my corner, there was always a lovely body smeared with oil turning under the ultraviolet rays. Aside from the uniform orange pallor which the show girls imagined was natural, nothing in their routine acknowledged the day, or allowed that there were other places in the city besides all-night automats, late subways, blue-lit bars, and bright swinging rooms at four o'clock in the morning.

I used to arrive in New York in the late afternoon on Saturday and find my way to the newest address I had for Sherry, for in those days she was never with the same friends or in the same apartment. Back home it took hours of cajoling my mother and the aunts before I could get away to the bus station and make the train in Bridgeport. I was told I had no business with Mary Elizabeth in New York when they didn't know where she lived, or with what kind—and Mary Elizabeth (last seen in one of those dirty little news sheets with her bum bare to the world) had no business with me. I promised myself to get to the city early to see the Metropolitan Museum or a play, or to walk in the busy streets, but they got the best of me: I was always late. I would come from the everlasting darkness of the platform in Grand Central into a radiant palace, the main waiting room. There in an antechamber I would clean up and apply the "Raven Red" lipstick I dared not wear at home. With my mouth the color of dried blood I'd saunter down to the Oyster Bar for a bowl of chowder, a black coffee, and a puff on whatever cigarette came in the fanciest package. Outside, New York was not the movieland of flashing neon, blinding marquees, and bright windows I now expect; it seemed all office buildings—thick, high, menacing—blacked out for the duration. The time was right; Sherry would be getting up.

To greet me she wore a silk dressing gown of a confused oriental design—mandarin neck, kimono sleeves—and her eyes, slits puffed with sleep, were fittingly exotic. As soon as I arrived, the rush to the chorus line began. There was only one uncluttered moment, time enough for one of the changing cast of characters to say, "You must be Sherry's

134

cousin!"—not that I resembled Mary Elizabeth in any way; I looked such a hick, bumbling through the hall with my suitcase.

"Something to eat, Ag? A cup of coffee?" Sherry displayed her hostess smile, and I'm sure she thought there was a tasty sugar plum somewhere. She *wanted* one for me, but I knew there was only the stale metallic coffee, the bleak icebox with a quart of skimmed milk and a few forgotten apples.

"No, I've eaten."

"I tell you what—" Sherry said, inspired in the old way— "I tell you what, Mary Agnes, we'll go over to Aunt Lil's and ask for ice cream and she'll come through with enough money for the movies . . ." "I tell you what, Mary Agnes, after we do the dishes we'll go down to the drugstore and buy a *Silver Screen*; we'll work on my Ginger Rogers routine, we'll play pinochle . . ." "I tell you what, Mary Agnes, we'll send out for sandwiches at the theater and you can have a big milk shake." So it was at all times for Sherry: life might seem a little makeshift right now—no parents, crabby aunts, hand-me-down clothes; but it was only a matter of making it through a single gray moment into the bright future. And I must say she escaped the dingy days of our childhood. If in the end things didn't turn out right it wasn't her fault. She tried; she made it; it was just that the big world was not what she imagined.

In those days when I visited Mary Elizabeth I found myself waiting on the edge of a bed while her friends threw stockings and slips from their jumbled bureaus and spidery drying racks. I remember trying to tuck my big feet out of the way, scrunching myself to the wall, but if I suggested waiting outside Sherry would turn to me in surprise: "You just came, honey. When can I see you?" And the girls agreed I was no trouble at all. It was years before I sensed that they created the confusion of mismatched hose, tipped-over cologne bottles, and make-up stains on the dresser—

the scene lit by an infuriating fifteen-watt bulb over the mirror. To have me sitting around the house at breakfast time would have disrupted an ordinary household, but none of Sherry's friends wanted to be mistaken for ordinary Betty Boops who ate cereal in the morning. They all practiced wackiness as a religion: they worked hard and long on outlandish pompadours and upsweeps, silver eyelids and glistening talons. Then, coated with ideal artificiality, they went forth into the unsuspecting street, onto a shocked bus, into the glare of the dressing room, where they started all over again to defeat the bit of nature that *would* show through on their pretty faces. They were all simple girls— like Mary Elizabeth—with simple names. Once she shared an apartment with singing sisters from Milwaukee: Jean, Jane, and Joan—I never sorted them out.

No matter how ardently Sherry tried for the bizarre effect with pitch mascara and false fingernails, she had a natural beauty which the most extreme maculations could not destroy. Her hair was red, not at all that Irish-red that brings the obvious stare, but the color of black roses, a mysterious shade that women try to imitate without success. With Sherry all was real: her hair, her height, the bones of her cheeks, the cleft in her chin—and her smile was as fresh the last time I saw her as it was the night years and years ago when her mother, old, finished at thirty, carried her up the back steps into our kitchen. My mother and Francis and I stood weighted with sleep while this child we had never laid eyes on, Mary Elizabeth Hurley in an outgrown coat, smiled at us as though we had invited her to a grand birthday party, right then, that minute.

"We'll give her some warm milk," Mary Elizabeth's mother said, "and put her to bed." But the child—almost a year older than me, almost seven—had to show us her pretty, impractical shoes with T-straps. Her baby girl legs, without leggings, were red from the cold night air; her dress was taffeta with a sash, the sort I wore only for Sunday. Soon we were all having ginger ale and cookies—at three o'clock in the morning.

"Where's Jack, then?" my mother asked.

"Off. He's gone off." Mary Elizabeth's mother took off her close felt hat, and then we could see her hair, the same depth of red she had given her child, hanging in dead broken strands over her ears.

"Gone for good this time," she said. "We'll not see him again."

"You've no such luck," my mother said gently. And she was right; he did come back soon—to watch his young wife die.

He was Black Irish, handsome Jack Hurley; he sat in our front room during that awful week, sobered up in a cloud of cigar smoke, waiting for God to be merciful—until the very last hour, after the priest had gone; then, cursing himself, he knelt by the bed, where the woman who grew beautiful again as she died put out her frail hand with great effort—to comfort him.

Mary Elizabeth told us her father could sing and play the banjo and the mandolin and slide a quarter into his cuff and make the fifty-cent piece in his hand disappear.

"Nobody will contradict that," my mother told her crossly if she was within hearing, and soon our pretty cousin understood it was best to tell me—Francis didn't believe—her marvelous stories about Jack Hurley and other imaginary princes, in secret, behind the couch or up on the attic stairs. Sometimes at Christmas Jack Hurley sent cheap jewelry which Mary Elizabeth raised from the cotton wadding with reverence—like St. Thérèse pictured on a holy card accepting the rosary from the Virgin's hand—and she would wear the little necklace or bracelet until her neck or wrist was ringed with green and the green turned black. Then my mother scrubbed her skin raw, and tears hung on her dark lashes. One ring her father sent, with a yellow stone set in golden prongs, tore her face in the night, and Aunt Mae, helping my mother bathe the sores with lysol solution, said he must have got that one out of a Cracker Jack box. Jack Hurley never remembered his daughter's birthday—none of the grownups did, for I suppose though they had to take her in as a child of seven they didn't want to celebrate her clouded birth. I don't know actually when or where she came to be, but Sherry told me once in New York that her parents had run off together to Providence—much in love, so happy that all those fat hens couldn't hold them. From bits I overheard I presume she was born in a charity ward to a frightened girl with another fake ring on her finger while Jack Hurley disported himself (that was the word they used) in a barroom.

It didn't take long for the sweet sadness of her mother's death to wear off and the edginess to come back in the aunts' voices. Mary Elizabeth was another mouth to feed, another body to dress, and we heard that often enough. It didn't take long for her to learn that she was lovelier than other girls, even in faded dresses and cut-down coats, so she smiled and helped with the dishes to get ten cents for her dancing lessons or for the piano lesson with the music Sister after school. No, it never occurred to me, towering on spindle legs above the children my own age, gaping down at the top of their heads through steel-rimmed glasses (which finally uncrossed my eyes), to be affronted by her beauty.

"She has Catherine's hair," they said fondly. "She has his eyes." That was all she did have, after all: the remarkable smile, the glorious red hair, the chin dented with the shadow of her father. Later, after Sherry had used her looks to get other treats: furs and checkbooks—a free ride beyond anything her aunts could imagine—I often thought that was all she had and nothing more.

My Uncle Peter would take her on his knee, and poor Jim, Mae's silent asthmatic husband, would chase her around the table with a wheezy laugh. My father, who never could manage my long limbs, took Sherry under his arm and swung her easily, almost dropping her to the floor, then catching her; and up she flew again through the stuffy living room with giggles and shrieks of delight. They forgot for a minute where they were and made that close brown room a wild, dangerous ring for their acrobatic feats. The truth was that her uncles loved to play with her; such feminine grace, though only in a child, recalled their own lost charm of manhood which had been nicely put aside by the scrubbing, cooking, endlessly talking women they had married. And Sherry (Mary Elizabeth to them, of course) knew instinctively how to wink at her admirers, how to toss her head of bouncing ringlets and arch her black eyebrows in surprise at every kiss.

If I make her sound like a detestable coy child, a baby movie star, I give the wrong impression. She had a talent for loving men, for giving herself freely, which she did not defile till years later, long after most women have deceived even themselves. The lonely kid throwing her arms around our Uncle Peter's neck was no different than the nervous woman in the best restaurant smiling at some man over the corpse of an extravagant fish: Sherry meant it every time.

In eighth grade her legs suddenly grew long and sleek, and she could tap the whole length of the auditorium platform in twirls—and did for the class one afternoon, her skirt twirling up too, exposing pink garters, until the frenzied rapping of Sister Edmond called a halt. Mary Elizabeth would not dance for graduation—let Lou Magee recite the funny piece where she took off a lady going to the dentist.

"But I can sing," Mary Elizabeth said, and began "Mexicali Rose" with all her heart. Then we were transported from that damp school basement with the water running in the toilets down the hall to an unfamiliar place of yearning flesh and sad withdrawal. Hers was a thin voice, high, forced into the low lusty throbs of the blues—a poor imitation to be sure, but how did the eighth grade of St. Augustine's know, how did Sister Mary Edmond know? Sherry wailed, a woman before us, of the disasters that would come upon us soon enough; and she sang at graduation finally, bound into a white organdy dress meant for a child. She sang out for everyone else's parents: "Hark, hark, the lark at heav'n's gate sings, and Phoebus 'gins arise."

In the Freshman Talent Show at high school there was no holding her back. A whole new audience of boys from all over town whistled and stamped for more after she exhausted her two dance routines. There was her shape, undeniable now, and her hair brushed back into waves blending into the red velvet curtain on the stage. She was admired in Pappadoulous' Sweet Shop all afternoon while I did the Latin homework for us both on the dining-room table. If I envied her, it was only for a moment, when one of the perfect boys in saddle shoes and a pork-pie hat came, breaking the terrible dullness of our house with lively shuffling and patronizing good will until the queen made her entrance. And she was, without seeking the title, the queen of Central High, gracious in the corridors, stately in class, a presence in the girls' lunchroom—never with unseemly pride but with the inherent simplicity of royalty in her plain clothes.

"Come along, Ag," she would say on a sunny afternoon when a carload of boys waited in front of our house, and she would lure some poor sap who wanted to gaze at her into asking me. I was vulnerable on different grounds then, and couldn't stand the contempt in their eyes, the gagging politeness in their mouths, so I preferred to stay at home with my library books. Later on, when Sherry wanted me to come to New York, it didn't matter: I had accepted myself, an ugly cousin, my sharp nose pressed against the sweet-shop window.

There are many girls who come to flower at the silly age of fifteen or sixteen and hold their loveliness like perishable blooms. I am shocked to meet them in the stores downtown and discover them wilted at twenty, bodies already turning to hard pods, closed to possibility and change. It might have happened to my cousin if she had fallen in love with one of her high-school beaux; but she never really had a chance even for that deadening solution; she was too spectacular for our factory town.

I can't come up with the answer to Mary Elizabeth, any more than *she* could, though a Park Avenue psychiatrist furnished her with long plausible stories to tell. There was the rootlessness of Jack Hurley in her that wanted nothing to do with two-family houses and supper at six o'clock; and like her father she was always performing just a little—her walk, her smile, the inventions that brightened the evenings when we sat together at algebra and French. Being no one at home but an orphan with a name that was bad cess and a burden to my mother who was looking for crosses to bear, Mary Elizabeth hoped in her adolescent fantasy to be someone even grander than Aunt Lil, who had married a lawyer, to dwell in a land more magical than the one green hill across the river where rich people lived. For years, while I learned to accept a hall-bedroom and the lonely oblong of my face, I told that incredible person in the mirror, substance of myself, that it was her beauty that set her free. Such nonsense: that perfection of form trapped her; she became a rare animal, a spirit caged within her own body.

Mr. Garafano, the used-car dealer, gave us a ride home after Glee Club one day in a Packard convertible the color of heavy cream with caramel leather seats. It was spring and anyone could see us, including my mother on her way to the second-day bread store. We thought it odd that Mr. Garafano complimented Mary Elizabeth (he called her "Red") on her height when I was three inches taller, and though she never took a ride again he was not discouraged: when we came around his corner on the way to school

Mr. Garafano lingered at the front of his lot. He was fat and forty and smelled of cigars—a big laugh—quite a different matter from the young druggist, Mr. Shea, who began to pay for our sodas and give Mary Elizabeth perfume samples. He was handsome in a lanky way and kidded around with us about boys, but when summer came he spent an indecent amount of time watching out the window to see Mary Elizabeth come down the street, and he ran out and wound the awnings up and down, talking to her about serious matters: movies, dancing, love, her family, his family. When he came to the boiling point Tom Shea would ask her to come into the cool dark store where fans blew the air and the smooth marble counter took the heat out of your hands. He would fix her a cherry Coke. Such innocence is touching, but she was still a little girl and he was a man, I suppose, so one Saturday night in August we all woke up to the noise of glass breaking and found that young Shea had dropped his bottle on our front walk. My father helped him out of the barberry, and with lovesick eyes going all over Mary Elizabeth's pajamas, Tom said, "I must have lost my way."

That fall when she would have been a cheerleader and the Princess of Transylvania in *Sweethearts*, Aunt Lil came up with the money to send Mary Elizabeth away to the Sisters of Mercy. There she played field hockey and girls' basketball and went through a religious period (with the same fervor she called forth for her analysis). It was novel for Sherry to be holy and calm, to conjure emotions from the depths of an inexperienced heart—to exist on guilt, self-abnegation, humility. The demands of the role were great; I'm glad I missed the performance. She came home at Christmas ten pounds lighter from the spiritual indulgence, more shapely than ever; she paraded all the way up the center aisle to Communion in her blue serge uniform, a small black mantilla draped over her head—more enchanting than any bride in white.

All our bells rang—the phone and the front door—but Mary Elizabeth turned her suitors away with a saintly sigh and the secret smile of one who has the higher calling. Then, invited to the golf club across the river she went out on New Year's Eve and danced till morning. I was waiting in the hall for her, listening for the sound of a car, but she came walking up our hill alone, and when I let her in she ran down the hall to the bathroom.

"Come in, Ag," she whispered. Under the borrowed evening wrap her dress was torn; a gardenia, crushed and brown, hung from the tattered ruffle. We spent an hour washing the mud spots out of the skirt, but the dress was ruined.

"Silly old fool!" Mary Elizabeth wailed, despairing over the limp net. "Silly old fool!"

I didn't know what to ask. "How was the party?"

"Dreamy. A big band—I got to sing two numbers in front of a real mike, and the leader said any time he needed a girl . . . Oh, that silly old fool," she cried again, finding another rip where her heel had caught the underskirt.

"Who?"

"Dr. Morrisey." (She had gone to the golf club with young Jim Morrisey: I had watched from a dark corner in the hall when he came to the door with a corsage.)

"Well, Jimmy put rye in his ginger ale to prove he's a man. He passed out, and his father gave me a ride home."

"How awful!" I said, not having the slightest idea what could have happened. "Are you all right?"

"Oh, sure." Mary Elizabeth laughed. "He didn't mean anything." Then she sat down on the side of the bathtub. "Oh, Ag," her voice was young and bewildered, "why does it always have to be me?" The question seemed easy enough to answer.

Back at school, she taught the cancan to the Senior Sodality, smoked in the cellar, and got herself dismissed before Easter. Aunt Lil, whose colored girl had left to have a baby, took her in for the housework and didn't allow Mary Elizabeth out of the yard. In May my father went to bed one night and never woke up. My mind was so full of him laid out in Conley's funeral parlor that I never noticed how my brother Francis was making himself useful in Aunt Lil's garden. Francis used to wait for me after school and we'd go visit Mary Elizabeth in her respectable prison. I sat on the slatestone porch, which was one of the features of Lil's house and which she had learned to call a terrace. The only time Lil gave us a thought, when she was home at all and not out playing bridge, was when she stuck her head out the sun-parlor door and said, "Don't sit on the cold stone, Agnes, you'll catch cold in your bowels."

No doubt there were buds on the rambler roses—held within delicate tendrils until their time came—and surely the apple tree snowed down on us, promising so much more than the stunted wormy fruit it bore each fall, but I saw only the throbbing heart of red carnations (chosen because they hold up so well) trailing the golden motto "Beloved Husband" into the magnificent box in which Mr. Conley set my father stiffly to rest. In the murky funeral home, which seemed to me a vestibule of fitting horror for the grave, clots of flowers blocked my vision: gladiolas and snapdragons wired and puttied into wreaths, sweetheart roses in a baby cross—"Our Dear Father"—and bouquets big enough to open a bank. Tributes to the florist's art appeared on every page of my Gallic Wars; I wore a black skirt, and the sight of this might bring to mind, between the successive *gaucheries* of M. and Mme. Perichon on their imbecilic voyage, other arrangements for death: the hasty purchase of our mourning; the warehouse of caskets down in New Haven, a dazzling display of varnished boxes lined with velvets and silks in pale colors to complement the morbid tones of the embalmer's palette. Then I saw again the dresses, rose and pale green like the slabs I sat on, dresses banked by the rentable palms, dresses of lace and crepe, unwearable garments of no size, slit all the way down the back to "fit" a woman wasted or bloated in death.

In my aunt's yard the sun was bright and warm. Along each side was a strip of garden neglected since the old Yankee schoolteacher sold the house to my Uncle Peter, though the tulip and daffodil bulbs still yielded up a few weak blossoms, and forgotten plants pushed up out of habit through years of dry stalks and a blanket of leaves. No one in our family had any use for gardening: they had heard enough of poor potato crops and pitiful Mayo squashes to ever want to kneel to the earth again. Indeed, I heard Lil tell a neighbor that her family had been "in agriculture," as though my grandfather was a gentleman farmer, breeding fancy apples or prize cows. Childless, bustling woman that she was, Aunt Lil had developed a sharp eye for clutter of any kind, and I suppose that looking out beyond the sterile tidiness of her kitchen one day she saw her back yard and thought Francis might clean it up.

Neither my brother nor Mary Elizabeth had the slightest notion of what they were about when they went out together in that spring sunshine. One of them would rake as the other hacked at the rubble, and then they would sit together on the grass and talk till supper time. It was a slow business, clearing away the brittle stems and matted leaves, and Francis carried off the debris in a peach basket and dumped it to rot behind the garage. They scratched at the ground with metal claws, uprooting what they thought were weeds, until they drew an ugly rim of black soil around the grass and only the obvious flowers were left—naked and humiliated. Aunt Lil was pleased, for now the yard looked like one of her pantry shelves, stark and irreproachable before the world—and she believed that the world saw and cared about the state of shelves and closets and fingernails.

What's worth telling?

When they asked me, "What were you up to, Miss, that you couldn't see?" I didn't have an answer—then. There was nothing to see: on my lap a geometry book, black perimeters defining truths within range of a sophomore—each day a new proposition, another proof. The yard, inscribed around us in a black line of earth, holds the three of us, Francis and Mary Elizabeth and me, forever, the last of our childhood dumped behind the garage. We are circumscribed by one another and by the knowledge of what would become of us as sure as my father is by his damp-proof box.

"What kind of fool were you then?" The same kind I am now. They dug in the ground; they sat on the grass. Sometimes, not often, they came to be with me on the stone porch.

Francis wore his mourning tie still and looked a likely candidate for the seminary. My mother had always wanted it for him and claimed on occasion that she had heard his call (an unnatural voice whispering of the power of the rectory). My brother was handsome and about to graduate from high school with his clubs and teams set down next to his picture in the yearbook: History, Junior Service, French, Thespians, Glee Club, Swimming, Basketball, Cross Country—and Class Secretary. It's a wonder Francis turned into such a dull man—but maybe the tribute under his name summed him up too well: he was voted "Most Affable." Active and happy—taking showers, training his hair, studying, serving Mass—too important to mope with me and Mary Elizabeth in our projections of black lucite and smoked mirrors, marabou and Leslie Howard. It kept him busy the whole time to be the most affable Francis X. Keely.

What *did* I think then when he didn't go to graduation practice and missed the Senior Prom? Why, that his life, like mine, had stopped on the edge of our father's grave. And "that one," as my mother called Mary Elizabeth forever after, as if her name would bring the Devil back to live among us, "that one" shuffled off to Buffalo on the porch, her breasts bouncing, her red hair beating her back in a rhythm of life. She costumed herself in an old cotton dress of Aunt Lil's which she drew tight at the waist with a belt —pathetic, a ravaged heroine of postwar *realismo* breathing desperation and desire. Well, the hell with that: this was still the Depression for us and I was fifteen years old. The hell with that and other afterthoughts.

I drooped my head down between my high shoulders and sucked sadness from the air. We were studying *Hamlet* in English. It's hard to imagine a more personal reading of the play than mine.

" 'Tis not alone this inky cloak, good mother . . ." I stalked the misty cemetery where the sod was not yet settled over my father, and appeared in a nurse's cape behind Conley's blessed candles (which were not lit until we arrived at the funeral "home"). I swept away the sickening floral arrangements—"What?" I said with a cynical laugh, "these for a man to whom you gave not the tribute of one flower while he lived." Or, switching roles, I tripped, maddened, down the altar steps in a dance modeled on Mary Elizabeth's Fred Astaire number and confronted my mother and aunts in their black hats with fennel and rue tied in packets like the sachets they gave each other on birthdays. "Hey non, nonny," I sang, for I could see this much: that they were bitter women with empty complaints who at last had gained a terrible dignity in their widow's weeds and their ceremonious weeping; their fragile minds shattered, they moaned lunatic sentiments: "He went peaceful," "A beautiful death," "Never a word," "It's those behind who suffer"—and by the time it was over they came to believe that my father was a sneaky fellow who slipped off without warning.

One Friday night the mad world became real, and like other tragic figures I was left alone: my father, my brother, my cousin Sherry, all the people I loved, had been taken from me—in the normal course of affairs, I might say, because death, shame, a boy going off to college seem like childhood diseases compared to the larger plague. It was coming to the summer of 1939. There was nothing left but report cards and the pomp of Francis' graduation ceremony —nothing but the joyless procession of hot days and wasted hours. Summer idleness had settled upon us already, and with the garden work finished we three sat on the porch every afternoon, our only project to get ten cents out of Aunt Lil for the Good Humor man. We might have been inmates of a hospital set out to get some warmth in our bones, so it was difficult to tell them why God gave me eyes.

"There's a lot went on under your nose, young lady. You just better come down to earth, Ag."

It had been a Friday; perhaps I know that only because Lil still tells the story: "It was a Friday night," she says. "I remember Mary Elizabeth wouldn't eat the haddock. Nice fillets I got to poach in milk, but she never would eat half the perfectly good food we put in front of her . . . I did everything for that girl."

It seems Mary Elizabeth got up in the middle of the meal to make it to the movies; I know it was one of the first times she was let out of the house. I went down to church with my mother that night to pay for the Month's Mind Mass for my father—so Francis went to Poli's with Mary Elizabeth, and on Saturday morning "the whole thing was clear." I've always wondered at that phrase, because to me there's never been anything about it that wasn't muddy. Aunt Lil got up to take a seltzer because the coconut pie was a little heavy, and hearing a noise like breathing below, she went downstairs to find them "at it" on her couch. "The blouse open," she says. "I thought it was an animal, and I told her, you are no better than a *low* creature. . . ." And the story goes on—Francis seduced while carrying incense up the center aisle, Sherry doing a belly dance on her mother's deathbed while Jack Hurley strums the ukulele at the foot of the Cross.

On Sunday Sherry was gone, with the mayonnaise jar full

of pennies off the pantry shelf and all the money she could filch from Lil's purse. She was sixteen and they never tried to find her, never saw her again except in the newspapers, smiling over her shoulder with her rump bared. We stood in the bus station together, knocking our shins into the suitcase Lil had bought for her to go to the nuns.

"Oh boy," she said, "I'm finally getting out of this rotten town."

"It wasn't your fault."

"Sure it was," Mary Elizabeth said looking down at her flesh as though it were separate from her, the embodiment of an impossible child. "For weeks I told old Francis to chase his tail; but it's always my fault."

I handed over her winter coat, wet from the heat of my arm, and at least five men rushed up to help with her suitcase. When she turned on the step of the bus to wave good-bye her gesture was big; her smile dramatized the moment: she was already on stage and she hadn't even left home. In her high-heeled shoes, bright with Shinola, and with a brave Carmen mouth, she was gone from us. The crowd of strange men who looked up at her seemed a chorus of male dancers ready to follow her with whatever grace they could muster into the stinking hot recesses of the Bridgeport Bus.

The summer heat settled into the rooms of our downstairs flat, never to leave; even during thunderstorms when the air blew the curtains it never got inside to us. Days moved slowly—Francis went off to mow lawns in Lil's neighborhood and I read stacks of library books with sticky red and green covers: mysteries and novels and everything of Eugene O'Neill that was in print—and behind each uneventful day was the figure of my mother, a mound of lard melting on the kitchen stool, fingering the bankbooks until their pages were transparent with grease, tucking them in and out of their snug envelopes with a trembling that tensed us all. Where was the money to come from? It was certainly unfortunate (by this she meant unfair) of my father—Lord have mercy on him—to die when Francis was ready to go to college.

"May he rest in peace," she said with an unforgiving edge to her voice that echoed across town toward St. Michael's cemetery. May he rest in peace while she goes begging to her sisters.

Nights I lay on my bed and wondered where Mary Elizabeth was, now that she wasn't sharing my room, now that I no longer listened for her admirers coming up the hill on hot nights: the shy smitten druggist, the butcher, the baker, the candlestick maker ensnared with passion in the barberry.

"Rich man, poor man, beggar man, thief . . . Count your buttons, Aggie." I could hear the promise in her voice as if she was sitting on the other bed brushing out her hair, sparks crackling in the dark—my nightdress *tied* at the neck; I didn't have a button to my name.

Where is she now? Where is all that spring sadness I felt in Aunt Lil's garden? Faded at the end of summer, burned out, like my father, like the patch of grass in our yard. By now Lil's penny jar was empty; where would the money come from? There was never any real doubt that Francis would go off to Fordham in the fall, and it seems now that other events didn't surprise us. We stopped only for a moment (as the aunts did when that girl ran off) to cluck at the war—not at the enemy—and went on with the bedlam of our lives: years that went by like the pages of a calendar flipping over on Poli's screen to the swelling strains of "Tipperary."

But the days were long. "Another day, another dollar," my mother said jauntily—she thought it was a happy phrase —and hustled me off each morning—not to school, for I was sixteen and could be put on as extra help in the zipper factory, where I sat sorting government orders stamped RUSH. I had to finish paying for our happy home. I had to pay for Francis to study 16th-century logic and rhetoric

with the Jesuits. I thought of Mary Elizabeth, and stole a
fifty-cent piece out of my pay envelope each week and put
it in a candy box, which was hers. Francis walked among
the righteous. He found himself in the NROTC and at a
desk and on a ship and with a war. He was thrown against a
gangway. Mamma pin a rose on me.

Something was going to happen. I felt that for a couple
of years, saw the expectancy somewhere between my bird-
beak nose and the slope-off of my chin—in my mouth to
be exact. I thought there might be words that mattered, like
the song of a Chinese maiden perhaps, stark and elliptic, or
the street cry of a French whore, *symbolique* and endear-
ing in its shrillness, but my tongue went dry, my lips
cracked, and when the words came they were cheap sar-
castic replies to my mother, invective without wit, without
meter, without imagery. Nothing was going to happen. I had
nothing to say.

At home the months went by. We were two fish in a
bowl, my mother and I, drowsing in mid-water, suspended
in liquid slime, chasing specks, darting at each other in
pecking motions, sustaining ourselves automatically in the
staleness with some low-grade will to go on for no reason.
Francis wrote in navy lingo from the Good Ship Lollipop
about a matey life on board a secret ocean. My mother
prayed for him—a jumbledy gurgling:

"Lite uv adjuz prayfruz, lilisuv fiel prayfruz, Virgin mose
pure prayfruz—prayfruz who have recoursa Thee." She
started, never to end, a series of novenas, fretted about
ration books and got slipped an occasional bag of sugar by
a Democratic committeeman who had always been sure of
the Keelys' vote. In the zipper factory I sorted, stapled,
filed, then was put to typing routine letters for the president—Dear Major Spoolfiddle: Your contract (USQMC/
100257z/42m) for 150,000 total-slide khaki tapes, as acknowledged in our letter of March 14th, etc. . . . I pasted
defense stamps in books with the Minute Man on the cover,

wore a snood and flappy slacks, carried Spam sandwiches in a black tin box, grew nearly six feet tall, and earned a First Aid certificate by wheezing the air out of my coworkers (drowning victims), bandaging their head wounds, and cutting off their flow of blood. I ran around our block in an air-raid helmet carrying a blank piece of paper from Mr. Dunn to Mike Ford in three minutes. History made up the meaningless games I would have learned to play in any case.

It took a while to figure out: a postcard with a fat lady in bloomers running out of a Chick Sales. A printed caption, *Let's get to the bottom of this, cutie!*, and written on the other side: "Will be in New London with USO Sunday. Love, Sherry." Among other things I learned that day was the story of Mary Elizabeth's new name. A flamenco dancer claimed that in a spotlight her hair was the color of aged sherry—blood of his native land—and so he had named her that, Sherry, during a two-week run at a Newark night club. She never used her real name again. In a few years when she blithely ordered Tio Pepe at the best bars in New York, Sherry said, "He was a Frenchman—you know, *haute monde* with a title—and he insisted upon 'Chérie.' " Then she repeated something which had been said to her: "Well, it became Sherry—corrupted like everything else, I guess." But in the full sun of an April afternoon with the Thames River dazzling and the air full of music and the roaring, whistling sailors, the name Sherry Henderson seemed as natural to her as Mary Agnes Keely was to me.

"How did you manage it, Ag?" she asked. "I never thought you'd be able to get away from them."

"I told them I was doing a Sunday shift at the plant."

"That's the ticket!" She sounded as if we were still in league and had escaped from the house for an afternoon show. As nearly as I can remember she never mentioned any of the family again, and when I spoke of my mother, of Francis, of Aunt Mae or Uncle Peter—as I had to since there was no one else to make up my scenes—she listened with little comment. From that day on I might have been any friend she had shared a room with in one of those many apartments. I might as well have brought her up to date on the ailments of a family she had never seen.

We sat on the grass under the crisscross of two-by-fours supporting the temporary stage at the submarine base in New London. There was bunting with stars and stripes tacked up around us, and the sun shone through the gaps. Near us three little dogs, two poodles and a mutt, strutted and yapped through a rehearsal of their act—sitting up, praying, playing dead, and jumping through imaginary hoops—and for a minute it looked like the Hawaiian girls in hula skirts with long tangles of hair and paper hibiscus blossoms were going to outnumber the rhumba dancers in wedgies and fruited turbans; but then another cluster of banana heads and ruffled breasts scurried out of the barracks across the way and there were more rhumbas than hulas. We talked about the places she had been: Pensacola, Fort Benning, Camp Kilmer. You were always singing and dancing—you never knew whether there'd be a stage and a mike or whether you'd have to sing off the back of a truck.

"Gee!" I said, fascinated by the dots of flaming rouge at the inner corner of her eyes, the streaks of white grease on her eyelids, her cherry lips coated with oil, and the pink shading on the lobes of her ears. White birds fluttered in a cage, white rabbits nibbled the air, impatient for false bottoms and secret pockets—all of this, though magic to Sherry too, was yet natural. And so I felt that Sunday, with the band booming, the M.C. warming up the boys with jokes about their officers, the gray warships lolling like harmless zoo mammals, that she danced through strangeness as most of us stumble through houses we know, accepting an irrational arrangement of doors and hallways, getting on with the business of the day. The notion persisted in my head for years that she was at home in the marvels of her world; but of course there are mornings when you can't find your way down the hall to the bathroom, when passages are sealed: then midgets and amplifiers, klieg lights and diamonds in the navel are freakish distortions in a macabre scene—gothic, unmanageable, disordered.

A heavy-set man with talcum powder on his beard and a rose in the buttonhole of his uniform came over to Sherry when he had nothing else on his mind.

"How's it going, kid?"

"Pretty good, Stu."

He wandered off in the direction of his comic cigar, and came upon us again through a slit in the bunting.

"How's it going, kid?"

"Just fine, Stu," Sherry said with a smile. "This heat is murder on the make-up."

"Powder it down again, kid, before you go on." Stu took her head in his manicured hands, examined her mouth and eyes with professional interest. He flicked a swarm of gnats away with a green silk handkerchief.

"A coming talent," he said. "Remarkable girl."

At last Sherry explained, rather defensively I thought, "This is my cousin."

"Is that so?" He bit the tip of a new cigar, moistened it with a sucking of his lips and tongue and went off to see about the line of hulas filing up the steps to the whooping of sailors and the twanging undulation of guitars. The dog trainer threw bits of biscuit in the air and the poodles leapt high—one, then another, in perfect time, with the little mutt in a paper ruff and clown hat popping up on the fifth beat and tumbling down in a sorry heap.

"Stu's the manager of our outfit," Sherry said. In a moment he came back.

"You've got five minutes, baby." We stood up and shook our skirts, and I looked at my shoe while Stu fastened the hooks at the back of Sherry's dress. Then—unbelievable to me—he ran his fingers up her legs, straightening the seams of her stockings—soft fingers with clear nail polish and a chunky onyx ring.

"Don't give them any more than two numbers," he said, "I want to be in the buses by seven o'clock."

"Shiny face—I know, honey." Sherry twisted her mouth in a grimace that recalled her answers to the nuns.

Stu—foppish, middle-aged, blatantly handling the beautiful girl—was the first of many agents, managers, patrons: Mert, Sol, Jerry, Tonkey, the Colonel. I came to take them pretty much for granted, and towards the end I always expected some stocky gent to show up when I visited Sherry in New York. The man would enter her apartment, or be in his place already, a Scotch and soda in hand, wearing a blue cashmere suit, white-on-white shirt, initialed silk tie, cuff links, ring, cologne—all the appurtenances of control. Like all the rest of them, Stu took particular notice of her clothes, her hair, her figure. Like no other breed of men, they were concerned with fabrics and style, and I even got used to chatting with Sol about the length of her skirts and agreeing with the Colonel that she should avoid anything but dramatic hats.

"A simple cotton is all Sherry needs," said Stu, "nothing fancy, a little sweetheart neck like the girl back home. That's what the boys want, see—" He spit cigar juice.

I took a seat out front, on the end of a bench next to a sailor with a long face the color of oatmeal, and tried to imagine his girl back home. Sherry, smiling big enough for all the boys in the world, sang "Don't sit under the apple tree with anyone else but me . . ." and it didn't matter that the lyrics were supposedly sung by a man—on the battlefield, say, or in the bowels of a submarine—all that existed was the sea of male voices cheering, rising in waves to her. Sherry spread her arms wide to welcome them all—oatmeal face, baby lieutenant, weathered old commander. It didn't matter to the USO that her voice was thin, untrained, and rasped on the high notes as she sang the third number.

"Stu will give me hell," she said, afterward, blotting her tears, "but I can't help it . . . they were all so darling to me. See, Ag, here's the picture I send them for a pin-up." Mary Elizabeth in another simple cotton blown up over the knees, on a swing all twined with blossoms—apple blossoms, back yards, girl's hair massed on shoulders, fuzzed sunlight —the pay-off.

"Well, Sherry," I said, "Sherry!"

I left her at the door of a gray barracks. A man's voice called, and she hurried up the steps into her wonderland of yapping dogs, sweat, cold cream, rabbit pellets, and Stu with a bottle of Kentucky Moon come to the door to find her.

Mert said, "I see her as the exotic type, black jersey and an upsweep."

"How's that . . . ?" I hadn't been listening. We were standing outside the theater waiting for Sherry and some of her friends to come out after a performance of *Oklahoma!* The crowd was more interesting than Mert, her agent, who I'd been telling yes, oh fine, all evening.

"Sherry should come to the theater in a cab."

"Yes."

"Get a press agent."

"Oh fine."

"Shouldn't waste her time on some two-bit band player."

"Yes." Sherry could do worse than show up at the clubs around town with a certain star, all to be arranged by him, Mert.

"Oh fine."

"I see it this way," Mert said. "Columbia Pictures may take an interest in the girl, but I happen to know they're loaded with All-American kids . . . besides, she could get typed, bad idea at this stage in her career. As I see it, *Oklahoma!* is a springboard, but she's no comic, see—a natural yes, but what she needs is to show a versatility—an exotic quality for the switch: black jersey halter, furs, upsweep."

"Fine," I said. "Fine."

"This Columbia Pictures deal could be very big." Sherry came out in a raincoat and saddle shoes, her cheeks scrubbed, her hair held back by an elastic band. This started Mert again: "If you want to stay in the chorus the rest of your life that's all right with me too, you know. I could very easily arrange for you to make the columns next week, but I mean if you go around looking like Miss Nobody . . ."

"Jesus, I'm only going back to my place with the kids."

Mert pointed out the whole disaster with one finger brutally jabbed into my shoulder.

"That's just it, that's just the angle with this baby. She thinks she's working in Kresge's—going to have a few beers with the girls." He turned, hacked in the gutter, and one sweet act suggested another:

"Thumb your nose at Columbia Pictures, sweetheart—it's no skin off my back."

"This is my cousin," Sherry said with exaggerated patience, "we are going to have a little fun."

"A lousy sax player," he growled.

"Some two-bit sax player," Mert heckled, and scurried off toward war-dim Times Square: clickety click click clickety—that one wore taps on his shoes.

Some two-bit sax player was Tony De Angelo, the big handsome product of an Italian father and an Irish mother out on Staten Island—though I'm not sure how Sherry ever found this out, because more than any of her show-biz friends Tony created the impression of having always lived in midtown Manhattan. For him there was no harking back, no hatred for a crowded house with oilcloth on the table and cooking smells in your clothes. He existed now, only now, at the moment he stood before you: tall, jazzy, self-

157

absorbed, product of the whole yearning American psyche with its Jack Armstrong heart cut out.

During the run of *Oklahoma!* Sherry lived at some good addresses, old places on the West Side with doormen and mahogany elevators; and Tony always had his key. As I talked to her at three in the morning her eyes seldom left the door. Tony would be coming in half an hour—in ten minutes, in five seconds.

"Well, you know how it is with late subways if you miss one, kid . . . don't crump on me now, Ag"; Sherry would brighten with her stage smile, "Tony's going to be here in a minute."

So I nursed another can of beer until it was warm in my hands and flat. The girls in the show came in and gossiped for a while, timing themselves under the sun lamp. They assumed that Sherry was waiting for Tony, like a housewife with dinner on the stove. They thought it was kind of cute, and I remember one storybook blonde who was inspired to write long letters to her guy in the Marines on pages and pages of blue stationery while we waited for Tony.

"So tell me," Sherry said, and I talked. Her face was full of anxious devotion, the injured beauty of her mother, and she blinked at the closed door through which he would come.

"So tell me," she said.

I told her all the goddamn nonsense on my mind, talking to the four walls in a drowsy monologue. I wondered if I could absent myself from the nausea of daily life, from the factory with its everrunning day—put a net on my mind so it wouldn't get caught in the gears. Then I wouldn't have to address myself to the cafeteria slop or the Red Cross collection or the damn figures on the time sheet. They could be made natural functions of the body, and I would have control over all that was stupid and necessary.

"Why, Ag, I thought you liked your job."

"I am giving myself to eight hours a day at a zipper factory, and if you count the overtime there's nothing left but supper and a bath."

"Look, honey, this show's been running for nearly a year, and all I know is I get on that stage every night and put out."

"But then," I said, "safety guards presume you have two arms and all your fingers to begin with . . ."

"Ag, do you think Tony'll want coffee when he comes in?"

Those nights waiting for Tony became my favorite times. I recall them as triumphant, and if Sherry didn't understand, Jean and Jane and Dolly and Peg never got it at all: they had learned to sit and smile at oddities, and I was just another mad thing, like the bum who picked theater programs out of the gutter every night on Forty-fifth Street, the fat lady in the delicatessen who had been Miss Binghamton of 1932, and the men who spoke the gibberish of army maneuvers or Wall Street while they waited to be taken off and fondled in a taxi. I was Sherry's skinny high-toothed "little cousin" (tall as a man). Three or four times a year I made it to New York at dusk, ate my chowder at Grand Central, stood through the whole of *Oklahoma!* with its bright days and blue love-song nights: good snared by evil with "adult" touches.

"Suppose a man" (I didn't mention Francis) "were to follow the expected road without any hitches, become nothing more, nothing less than his training and his character dictated . . . it'd be like the life of a larva moth."

Sherry was on the floor, going through her dance exercises, stretching toward the door.

"He could be a very nice guy."

"But of course," I said, "I only talk like this while we're waiting for Tony."

"He's working a small club downtown." She arched her back, her arms working overhead in a graceful plucking— "and that's why Tony's late." She was Mary Elizabeth justifying some shamefully cheap trinket Jack Hurley sent to our house with the postage half paid.

Tony De Angelo was worth waiting for, I suppose— and then again he wasn't worth the tip of her little finger. He let himself into the apartment whenever he pleased, and usually stopped to light a cigarette or run a comb through his hair before he gave her so much as an insolent smile. He stood before us for a moment to be admired, which wasn't hard for me after months of doughfaces at the factory. He was grand and big and stuck in your eye. Sherry feasted: his thick black hair grew in waves close to his head, except for a forelock which flopped boyishly. His face was heavy, square at the temples, square at the chin, with a frankly Italian nose, almost Roman but ever so slightly askew— busted once, a miracle considering how often Tony enraged people. His eyes—I don't think they were brown or black, but a dark color of his own—private, skimming over the objects before him (people were objects to Tony) as though nothing commanded his attention. At last he settled on Sherry, and his gaze was a benediction. There was damn little that Tony could appreciate without a sneer, but Sherry was on the list with the world's greatest trumpet player, Harry James, the big radio networks, and custom-made suits.

"Tony has bedroom eyes," a model said one night—but that was wishful thinking. He looked through your clothes all right, but it wasn't your body that interested him, it was whatever crippled thing hid inside: the nasal Brooklyn accent of an actress trying to sound like Katharine Cornell, the parrot mind of a script writer, the fear in a tough Master Sergeant. I was not a member of their beautiful-bodies club and when Tony De Angelo looked at me, I like to think I puzzled him. There was no deception in my hungry adolescent form: I was the cynical clown, the sensitive spinster, the hell-of-a-good kid.

"Mary Agnes, how's the girl?" His words sounded like a joke, and I can imagine him thinking:

"You have no secrets, do you, sweetheart? You plan to make that a way of life."

If Sherry made coffee Tony would say, "Not right now. I'll have that Canadian Club." And when she poured him the best liquor she could buy, he flicked it away.

"What have you got in the house? Fruit? Maybe I'll have some scrambled eggs to start."

Then she watched him eat, and asked (as if the management had sent her), "Is everything O.K.?"

"Great," Tony said, but in some small way—his finger tapping on the burned edge of toast, his fork held to let the egg dribble through the tines—he let her know how hopeless she was as the Little Woman.

I never set eyes on Tony De Angelo before three o'clock in the morning, but he was always perfectly dressed, often in a tuxedo with wide glossy lapels, so if he hadn't come in with his bulbous sax case he might have been arriving from one of those prewar parties I had seen in the movies, with frozen-faced extras fox-trotting around the pillars. I was to understand, and so were the kids who lived with Sherry —she told us with misty eyes—that Tony "could not fight for his country." They wouldn't even have him in the U.S. Marine Corps band. There was something damaged (a vague internal organ which she described on different occasions as the kidney, the liver, the pancreas)—just something that made him unfit.

It was true: there were many sad stories during the war, but when I think of it now I can't imagine that Tony De Angelo would have been any less bitter if he had sweated out his days in glory on a Pacific island. Sherry and her friends had big enough hearts to accept his tragedy, and so that covered the situation nicely. Injustice for Tony was so much bigger than a lousy medical fact—it was the whole deal that brought him into the world in a four-family house on Staten Island, that gave him a musical facility but no original talent, that made him expect because he was one gorgeous kid he could have something besides hard luck—and by the time Sherry met him he was not even angry, just using one setup after another for whatever it was worth: a drink, a few dollars, a woman.

Maybe his style was unfamiliar then: we were involved in a spiritual renaissance, and we hoped, we cared, while Tony, convinced of personal destruction, played his own game. He was a prophet: youth turned silent, moody, and selfish—sick because it knows that nobody wins. What mattered to Tony was lonely nervous grace—his nighttime body beating to the rhythm of the band, shut off from the dancers, finding its momentary salvation in a note that came off—as good as sex. Once at the Palladium I saw him in his ecstasy—but only once, because Sherry did not like to watch him play. If Tony were around now, exactly as he was twenty years ago, he would be a cliché—but then, ah then, he was a remarkable bastard.

"A terrible bastard," Little Dot said in her ladylike drawl, ". . . and Sherry could have a lead in the road show, but she's sitting around for him . . . it's one handout after another." Little Dot was wiry and resilient, the only one of Sherry's friends who ever made a name for herself. She had worked hard training a sweet lyric soprano voice for years, and when her first big chance came on the Major Bowes Amateur Hour she lost to a quadruple amputee who played (with a spoon held in his teeth) "God Bless America" on nails stuck into a cigarette carton.

"You wouldn't catch me jumpin' through a hoop for that bastard."

Little Dot went right on with her scales. I took up going to night school to learn whatever useless pleasantries existed in poems and stories—to learn something apart from the zippers which evolved each year like a Darwinian species: grew longer, smarter, more durable, only to be killed off by superior models with better teeth, more adaptable bindings. My mother, praying for Francis, who was in Washington and later got that piece of gangway in the thigh, was inspired to return to the arts. She created a cake made without butter or sugar and only one egg. It stuck like paste on the teeth. She made a display of weeny figures for her Civil Defense class with peanut shells for bodies and pipe cleaners for limbs, and set them in cigar boxes: peanuts straddled peanuts, performing (one hoped) artificial respiration; healthy peanuts carried sick peanuts on a snip of old blanket; there were peanuts in tourniquets and arm slings, peanuts with concussions and complex fractures, and one old peanut (modeled after the bedridden ancient of our block) being evacuated in an Indian handclasp seat by two sturdy peanut wardens to the cellar of the Congregational Church. Sherry continued her chorus-girl role in *Oklahoma!*

Sherry Henderson's career was a child's dream—that was the maimed thing Tony De Angelo saw. There were at least three screen tests maneuvered for her by a bull-neck named Jerry, and she was content to come back from the Coast and pretend she was interested in her future; but she would have chucked the whole business in one minute if Tony had agreed to teach dance and music with her—which was, of course, Sherry's idea. We were hiding the liquor in the bottom of a closet, because of his kidney or liver or pancreas, and I was delivering a facetious sermon to myself on the advantage of developing my given peculiarities—no chest, long nose, sunken eyes—into full-fledged eccentricities.

"Do something with what God gives you," I said, "for His mercy is unbounded. We have only to look around us to discover there is a Great Intelligence behind the intricate patterns of the Universe, and it is our duty to discover further the purpose for which the Good Lord put us here . . . for He moves in strange and mysterious ways."

"Put that pint in the shoe box, Ag."

"It is our duty to discover ourselves as part of the Divine System; for surely with this body I am meant to carry a burden on my back, and these eyes must see deep into the machinery of souls—yes, even into my own faltering soul; and the nose . . . the nose must smell out corruption and decay."

"Oh, stop it," Sherry cried. Her hair was all crazy from stooping in the closet. "You're always laughing lately, never serious for a moment. We do what we must. We do what we can. I could give tap lessons, you know, and teach ballroom dancing. Tony could teach the sax and probably the accordion if he would only settle down."

"You must be kidding," I said.

"Yes." Big tears washed the mascara down her cheeks. This was wilder than any of the mad schemes for fame and fortune she ever had back home. She actually conceived of rented rooms up over a drugstore in some sizable outpost, "The De Angelos" painted on the window and rows of kiddy legs wriggling around on highly polished floors— "with my foot I tap, tap, tap, with my hands I clap, clap, clap"—while Tony listened to farts exploded out of a cheap instrument by an unwilling boy. I saw the curtain of faded chintz that separated the "studio" from the little room with the sink and hot plate. I saw Tony and Sherry (thought to be a little on the flashy side) grown to forty, still holding tight to a New York concept of themselves, eating out in bad restaurants, playing the accordion and singing at weddings in the BPOE Hall.

Tony came in and said, "How about a drink."

"I don't have a thing in the house."

"Look around, baby . . ." and she went directly to the closet and brought out the bottle.

So the next time I came to New York Tony was unable to work, though he still came in at four o'clock in his tux. Sherry had set him to song writing, where the real money was. On top of a Steinway she had rented for him there were three songs penciled out—notes, lyrics, titles and all— "Why So Bitter, My Sweet?," "When Bonnie Comes Marching Home" (about a WAC who left her love behind), and "Love Letters in the Sky" (a pilot who is afraid to declare his feelings except when he is gunning Japs in a B-47). Tony's socks and underwear were all over the bedroom, his razor on the sink, and he slept in the bed where I had last seen Little Dot propped up with pillows memorizing the score of *Cosí fan tutte*; I can't say that I was shocked, for I don't suppose that even *I* thought they had been playing post office all this time. That night Tony was snarly, got drunk, passed out on the living-room floor, and we had to drag him to bed. Sherry loosened his shirt collar, took off his shoes, and smoothed that wild forelock back out of his eyes.

"Poor Tony . . ." she said looking at me, and we both knew that things weren't going to improve.

When he left her she went on the road with a second company of the show, singing those bright songs all over the country, dancing and whooping, shouting out about the beautiful morning. She made a movie which I saw eight times. When Dane Clark entered a small night club she said, "Good evening," and tried to check his hat.

"Where's the boss?" Dane asked.

"Over at the bar," Sherry answered. Later she screamed when the shots went off, an unconvincing shriek, and she wouldn't answer the hard old detective.

"I only work here, Mister"—Sherry was never good at repartee. Her features, blown up on the screen, were not the common dollface the role called for: her high cheekbones and cleft chin were too powerful facing the perceptive camera; she looked as if she had wandered into this contrived piece out of a drama on the Irish Revolution— moving close-ups of faces with "character," damp, darkness, and meaningful death.

My mother and the aunts weren't much for movies, and I never let on that Mary Elizabeth could be seen down at Poli's because I knew that all they'd go for was the net stockings, the cleavage, the "low types" wished into existence by their literal minds. I cut my class in Great Thinkers of the Western World to study what I saw in Sherry's eyes—the crease of doubt forming on her brow, the air of acceptance in the droop of her bare shoulders. Though she was only twenty-three she had gone through one life already; I could see that, and I walked out of the theater while Dane Clark was still dying, while the lights were still on in the night classes at the high school, illuminating the sophistries of Mr. Ruggiero and Miss Flynn as they argued free will and determinism. The two-bit sax player was gone forever, and I hated him for the years he had taken from Sherry. Later, during her "mature" phase, she told me he had married a neighborhood girl out on Staten Island and had two kids and worked in a shoe store.

Sol was a loudmouthed puffed eunuch who had great success in shaping the careers of female comics, and he was sure that what Sherry had was a flair for dancing, a kind of rag-doll in a Baby Snooks routine he had devised, the surprise being that when she pulled off the Harpo Marx wig and the Harold Lloyd glasses there was a real pretty girl who sang a couple of sweet ballads. It was blistering hot the night Sol and Sherry and I went down to the Village to show the act to a very big man who was opening a new club. Sol advised Sherry on her costume in a lilting falsetto.

"The simple backless number, dear . . . no jewels . . . ruins your neck," and he pursed his lips in disgust at me, done up in my best Bemberg sheer:

"Why don't you go to a newsreel?"

But I went along, paid the cab driver, and watched from a leopard-skin booth while Sol and Sherry dealt with the very big man. The club was to be a jungle with a lot of African masks, bamboo tables that caught the stockings, and a ceiling weighted with oppressive greenery. A pair of caged monkeys chattered over the bar.

"Zow, *some* people!" Sherry cried out in an effeminate voice, an imitation of *Maître* Sol. She slid onto the dance floor as if kicked in the seat of the pants and attempted to get up on rubber legs; she pulled a great big Times Square funny comb from no place and further mucked up her blonde wig.

"I'm gonna sing a little song," she said with a croak in her throat.

"Why don't you Voo-Do-Do what you did did did before . . ."

I walked out to the street where a gang of little children in filthy underpants were working to unscrew a fire hydrant. I thought I could watch anything as long as it wasn't Sherry clowning in the veldt, but the sight of the screaming kids—sweaty, no doubt tired, for it was past ten—nauseated me and brought to mind the six gray mollusks (the color of their dirty hands) I had swallowed whole at the Oyster Bar. Sad they seemed, those oysters, exposed on their icy bed and wanting nothing more than to contract into the known darkness. Slowly I went to the hydrant and we pulled together: the straining little fingers and my own scrawny hands; we pulled in a hush of effort until the geyser shot into the sleepless night-city. Squealing with relief, the children performed a frantic dance; shiny bare limbs, freshened, made clean.

The audition—that's what they called it—was over when I went back. Sol and the very big man sat on rattan stools at the bar celebrating their mutual distrust. They toasted

Sherry with cuba libres. I watched from behind the glistening leaves of a paper tree.

"I'm glad you like the act," Sherry said—that good face full of hope once more.

"We'll talk about the act, honey," the big man reassured her with several pats on the fleshy part of her back.

"Oooo, you naughty boys," Sol chided the monkeys, who were very busy in their cage; and then they saw me in the mirror, my dress shrunk up over my knees, my hair soaked into kinks, an untamed freak of nature after a tropical storm.

After the war there were two musicals; one closed in Boston, the other petered out in the city before I got to see her. Then Sherry sang, restrained, intimate, in supper clubs—which was less embarrassing than most of her ventures—and it was in this role of sophisticated *chanteuse* that the Colonel discovered her. Beneath the show-biz patina and the undercoat of spoiled innocence he detected the expansive, natural girl. The Colonel had had wives; oh yes, but no woman challenged him like Mary Elizabeth. That was his trade: he had rebuilt a European city from the ruins of war and occupation, restored its dignity with a fine respect for history, set it to live and grow once again. Now he was revitalizing a great newspaper that was sick unto death. He was rich and bright and powerful.

The marriage came as a surprise, a telegram I found opened on the hall table when I returned from work one day. My mother's voice called out to me with a tremble of excitement:

"Ag—Ag, is that you?" She was on the phone, and it must have been a difficult moment for her, not knowing whether to continue her damnation of Mary Elizabeth—satisfying in the mouth like chocolate creams—or to come hustling through the dining room to exact testimony from me of Sherry's depravity. The verdict she had already reached.

"Don't you tell me you never saw the man on one of your sneaky 'visits,' Ag Keely."

"I never even has heard of him," I said in my grandmother's jibing brogue.

"Throw insults on the grave—that's good, Miss."

"I don't know who he is."

My mother plumped herself out like a proud fat pigeon. "That name," she said with malicious pleasure, "he's a Jew!"

The Colonel was a Jew, but all that was left was a story now and again with a Yiddish expression and a dreamy painting by Chagall hanging in the dining room over a fine carved cabinet (which I was expected to admire).

Was Sherry Catholic any more? The question was irrelevant. Her new mode was ultimately enlightened, free of the limitations of any simple identity. The first time I saw Sherry and Colonel Leavit together I tried to understand the cosmopolitan perfection he aimed at, but in minutes my head was fuzzed by Martinis and I felt the three of us floating in a soft white room to a melody plucked from a fragile box.

He was fifty, Colonel Harry, Daddy of All the Ages; he wanted the best for his little orphan girl (even *that* was in a literary tradition), and he never failed to have something in his pocket for me too—the ragpicker cousin.

"We can't use our tickets to the Philharmonic, Mary Agnes," he'd tell me. "I want you to come down here and enjoy yourself. Bring a friend."

"Oh, Harry, she can't just hop a train," Sherry said.

She was right. Still, the offer was like a crisp five-dollar bill.

He was fifty. That didn't seem old: it seemed right. His head was a phrenologist's dream, bare and gleaming, with bumps that I read—without even knowing the science—as intelligence, creativity, success. And since he had no hair,

169

one looked hard at his face: lean, composed, a model of a commander whose kindly eyes made the people around him want to perform in style. His whole body was lean, and I never knew until Sherry told me—oh, much later—that he worked out at a gym every day.

I don't know why I found that disappointing; he worked damn hard at an "image" of himself, as hard as he now worked on the ailing newspaper or had worked over the demolished city. Those quiet evenings I was invited to share —they were carefully conceived. His scheme for Sherry was delicate, but its process was superhuman, and of all his plans the only one she took to was the study of music: she learned to play the harpsichord.

"Tasteful beginners' pieces," he said, "nicely done all the same." He knew her voice was good only for a few songs after dinner, so we listened to her in a white drawing room sing sad short *lieder* in memorized German. To me it was all strange and perfect, and like the thick herbaceous liqueur I rolled on my tongue I believed in it; but surely the Colonel knew that their life came out of bad historical novels.

"Tomorrow let us ride over to the Manor House in the pony cart."

"Oh yes, that will be gay," Miss Agnes said, letting drop her needlework that she might dream a while of her new bonnet, looking very pretty indeed in the orangery.

Gold flowers blooming in gold pots, Sherry in a green velvet gown covering her arms to the wrists, open at the throat. Her look says, "Ain't it the berries, Ag!" And the Colonel, in a smoking jacket, talks of pleasure: *his*, in having me with them—"one of the people Sherry loves."

Other treasures: a frieze of saints given by a grateful city —part of itself—to take away with him; the edition of *Parnasse contemporain* bound in pearly leather—"of particular interest to you . . ." The wine I couldn't possibly know . . . everything real in the way heaven must be: softly lit, with one all-caring God.

Their bed (I see it when led off to wash the Château Lafite-Rothschild out of my sweater) is big enough for a host of lovers, high up on a dais—a throne, yes, but to me more like the altar in my parish church, its canopy hung with starched lace, thick embroidered initials on the spread: His and Hers intertwined, scrambled. I saw IHS: Harry, Sherry, Leavit, the bottom nodule of the "L" strangely shortened for the sake of the design. "To God who giveth joy to my life." Maybe it was that: ascending those green (for hope) carpeted steps onto the consecrated king-size mattress—was that what became impossible?

At the table Sherry, now learned in sauces and salads, had to be followed closely as to which fork—and that peculiar small knife for a russet pear with the leaves left on, or a platinum-blond apple; and grapes (Lord, they must be fake), frosty, purply. But no!—she cuts them apart with a scissors! The salt sits in open silver shells with midget spoons, and the coffee cups are doll-size.

Sherry *tried* with all that food and wine business, but she never could make herself eat the special smelly cheeses—or brains or kidneys or sweetbreads. I could tell just the way she ate—not seeing the elaborate entrees the Colonel ordered —veal and chicken and tongue: larded, farced, and truffled in glossy gelatin—that she might as well be eating Mae's overcooked meat loaf swimming in canned tomatoes. She hid peanut butter in a jar labeled Queen Bee Hormone Jelly, and Ritz crackers under her lingerie.

"It's a terrible sign of a regression, Ag . . ." The Colonel had sent her to a Park Avenue psychiatrist so she'd know all about herself—as well as George III teapots and pre-Colombian sculpture. She wasn't always happy—Colonel Harry knew that, admired it even—and no doubt he expected the analyst to tap a vein of hidden meanings and obscure desires in his beautiful girl. But Sherry was still a "C" student: she took to the idea in her own way, began to read inspirational literature, do-it-yourself salvation kits. Harry was infuriated; he had given her Kierkegaard and Nietzsche.

He staged a quiet evening of Camus—I was included—and she bubbled over about "inner resources" and "building toward personal maturity."

"I'm going to send you this book, Mary Agnes, by this woman . . ."

"Now, my darling," the Colonel said, "Mary Agnes knows she can charge any book she wants on my account at Brentano's."

"Yes, Harry . . . by this woman, Ag, this wonderful woman whose child died of leukemia."

Her recommended readings arrived at our house, and I found the books opened on the hall table—the Overstreets and Norman Vincent Peale—and I heard my mother behind her evening paper.

"Protestant . . ." and, making what was to her a logical connection, "Jew." I put the books, which seemed sticky with childish optimism, under my bed; my mother never dusted there because her heart started racing. "Jesus, Mary, and Joseph . . . no one to help an old woman."

At night after I had escaped into my homework from the endless days of my life at the zipper factory, I fell asleep under my student lamp and I heard Sherry call from her stack of goodness-readings under the bed (where as a girl she used to hide her contraband movie magazines):

"Say, Mr. and Mrs. North are over at the Rialto, Ag. Let's go; I'll get twenty cents easy if I sing down at the firehouse."

". . . just because a person has been disturbed by a difficult family situation doesn't mean that they have to react to a relationship without commitment. . . ." Sherry was on her favorite theme, and I could see the Colonel's disappointment as he suffered the obvious phrases she had picked up on the couch. He was bewildered by defeat.

"Well, what did you expect," I thought; "there's nothing in my cousin for a doctor to heal. Sherry is all surface.

That's what's great about her: if she's sad there are tears, a black mood that clears at the first dose of peanut butter. And she is happy every time she puts on that big mink coat you gave her. You know the smile."

We were both wrong: the Colonel for wanting her complex, and I was a fool to think that she was simple.

For five years I journeyed to the City when I could get loose, partook of their hospitable dream, became one of the mottled images reflected in that ancient mirror which Colonel Leavit hung at the end of his palatial salon. Thirty, I was thirty years old (which would have made her thirty-one), and by then the Colonel had built up several anemic industries. Projecting into the future, he saw the growth potential in fiberglas, in prefab houses, in tranquilizers, in television; and he began to take a lady painter—Bryn Mawr and boring to Sherry—out to fashionable restaurants while his wife went to bed with headaches. He escorted Little Dot to the opening night of the Metropolitan Opera. And then, when he flew out to the Coast to buy old Academy Award pictures, Sherry produced the grand finale.

"What will I say to Harry?" she asked, and turned the question into a tipsy song, "What'll I tell Harry, Harry . . ." She stumbled through forgotten dance routines.

"Nothing, I guess."

She wouldn't have to say a thing: all the kids were there, even Little Dot, who didn't stay long because she was much too fine for them now, but all the lamp-tanned chorus girls and all the dainty men who had not aged a minute, and Sol and Jerry and some of the way-back USO girls who were married now and brought their husbands in from the suburbs for free eats, and lots of people no one had ever seen before. Sandwiches ground into the Aubusson carpets, club soda spilled into the harpsichord, and all those wines were pulled out of the carved cabinet from their tilted mellowing sleep and drunk like gallons of *paesano*. On one side of the bed there was a blind man who played the electric organ in night clubs. He sat up stiffly, laughing and drinking, his white cane stuck through the lace. Someone had tied a brassière on his head, and behind him on a pile of coats a girl was cruelly used. I didn't want to see more, so I left my good coat and walked out in the rain.

How did Sherry look? Desiccated, hard, a hearty bitch? Not at all. She looked frail from the trying years of a fraudulent marriage, stretched in the neck and arms—bones and veins, without much flesh, but with hair the color of red maples, and her song, "Tell Harry, Harry . . ." was gay.

She had walked out, way beyond his control, away from the elaborate parlor game he had made into the good life. The act was over for me too, and I regretted that mutation of reality which had made our evenings together a séance —on my part a dabbling in the mysterious and occult. For a while there had been no factory, no zippers, no dinners at Sticky-Bun Inn where you presented Therese Sielinski with an orchid corsage and a Mirro-Matic Pressure Cooker and wishes for many sunny days of married life. With no mother, no Lil, no Mae with a breast removed; without them you are sinking into a white softness, your body suspended in a million goose feathers sewn in sacks of sky-blue silk. Think now of what you learn and what you read: Blake in night school, Villon in translation. Then speak through them to us, misty-footed angel: in your mouth are the phonemes of a strange mellifluous language. You will transform the ugliness of our landscape; you will tell us what it means . . . Speak, monkey, speak—and I moaned from my horrifying past.

"Love is like the lion's tooth." It ended so. No more artichokes, no more golden apples; only the reality of Florence Flynn and Mr. Ruggiero—my intellectual milieu—squabbling in the high school, this time about D. H. Lawrence in Modern British Lit.

"One individual has a responsibility not to destroy the

core of another individual," Sherry explained after the divorce. "Harry wanted me to look his way, act his way, but he didn't care anything about me inside."

"No," I said. We were having lunch at Stouffer's on Fifth Avenue after my morning with Shakespeare at Columbia. I had the distinct impression that all around us the ladies were talking about their lives in the same way, or about their clothes—as important as their lives.

"He never understood that he must respect me as a person." She wore a floppy brown hat that covered up her hair, and the mink coat was thrown over the back of her chair. I had not seen her out in the daylight in many years, and on the avenue the winter sun had caught every line; the girl that Colonel Leavit had preserved in candlelight was gone. Sherry could have been any faded beauty; the spectacle was over.

"Yes," I said.

"I feel I can breathe again, Ag, and dance. Listen, I have this wonderful voice coach, a sweetheart who says he can get me right back to work; not that I have to, but it's my old compulsion—Harry never touched it—of having to give myself . . ."

"Yes," I said. We must have looked a sight, me hunched over a parfait, skinny and dry, probably in one of those sexy knit suits I wore to fool the public, and Sherry wiping the floor with mink, wearing the biggest diamond in the world —third finger right hand.

"The Colonel never had friends. They were always business connections pretending to be buddies. It wasn't all Boccherini and Belgian endive, I'll tell you, Ag."

"Gosh!"

Her new apartment was in a shining glass building on Sutton Place, as friendly as a hospital, with the instruments for living laid out about the white walls: plastic wood tables at the end of the couch, a deep Naugahyde chair with a stand big enough for an ash tray and a drink. Here the portly men sat with Scotch-and-soda, bourbon-on-the-rocks, gin-and-bitters. They were all "sweethearts," "real cuties," who wanted to help a girl out. She went to Acapulco for rest and sunshine with an advertising man who put her in a detergent commercial.

I left my books to watch my mother as she watched Sherry (she never recognized her) as a worried housewife in a laundromat, a pleasant woman aging fast with the problems of sink stain and bathroom odor. Soil and deep-down grime drove her nearly to tears.

"I just can't seem to get things *clean* any more." Then up came a snappy dish with a pile of whiter-than-white towels and laughed right in Sherry's face.

"Why don't you use the new miracle tablet, a combination of gentle bleach and power-plus detergents that makes laundry day the happiest day in the week?"

"A tablet? Not on *these* filthy collars!" Sherry held up a shirt ringed with greasy body dirt.

My mother heaved herself out of her chair and hurried to the kitchen. Now that she had grown so *very* big her walk was labored and she put out her hand for support, first on the back of a dining-room chair and then on the buffet.

"Want anything, Ag?"

How delighted Mary Elizabeth looked, and she chuckled with Mrs. Goody Two-Shoes, right there in our front room with the *filet* curtains and the furniture the same as when she left.

"I guess my troubles are over," Sherry said, but she was a bad actress and the line didn't ring true. I felt when she left the laundromat she was doomed to droopy tresses or nasal congestion; and what's more, she knew it.

Mother was having a run on jelly doughnuts in the months Sherry's commercial was shown, and she would come back with two soft clumps oozing scarlet tapioca jelly.

"Have one, Ag."

"I couldn't."

"Aren't you going to hear the weather?" she asked as I went back to my studies. "Well, I'm sure I'm privileged to have got a look at you at all."

I wasn't a girl any more and nighttime visits to New York had lost their charm. After a few expense-account dinners with Sherry and one of her "sweethearts" I gave it up. Should I say I gave her up? Anything I had to say to her would sound preachy, the envious moralizing of an old maid, and why should I accuse her when she could still riffle through the bottom drawer of used emotions and come up with that best of smiles meaning jolly days, tomorrow, just around the corner? Her personal psychology was as out of date as the Depression song she used to sing about a pocket full of dreams. The world had changed on her. There was an insatiable lust for things: great-assed cars, freezing chests like coffins, magic boxes; love play in the supermarket, sexual poking at sealed meats and cake mixes, the thrill of climax as the register rings—the check-out counter. She didn't know what was happening, and I closed my door, unable and unwilling to cope with her life or mine. I had something of a problem at this time: Jim Neary, son of one of my mother's cronies, went so far as to declare an interest in stumping into the future with me. He had a limp and taught the fifth grade. He gave me a bottle of Blue Grass cologne and a little collie dog, but that is another story of misplaced trust and self-destruction, a melodrama starring my brother Francis (now an FBI agent) and my mother who breaks her hip in a cemetery outside of Buffalo.

To be honest, I had not talked to Sherry in years. Waiting for Tony I had talked *at* her, I had talked *around* her with the Colonel, but all I had said directly to my cousin was "Gee Whiz!"—a line straight out of the funny papers delivered with a look of bug-eyed amazement long after she ceased to amaze. I discovered more of the city in daylight after my Saturday-morning class at Columbia than I had in all the years of her night life, which now seemed trite for both of us. I'm sure it was as hard for Sherry to go on with the show—pulling out new wonders for the relative from out of town—as it was for me to come on all incredulous at outsized menus and happy-pills. What she had in mind now that she was free was a comeback, this time off-Broadway, the real theater—Art. The last time I saw her she was sitting on the floor surrounded by piles of new paperbacks: Brecht, Ionesco, Genet, and the plays of Yeats. The man in the Naugahyde chair (Scotch Manhattans and ladies' sportswear) smirked indulgently, said his daughter was interested in all that up at Sarah Lawrence. I said I had to get my train, but Sherry with her brand-new smile asked, "What do you think, Ag? Now that I won't have to play the ingénue?"

Almost a year later the Christmas card came with a drawing of a parrot in a golden cage. "Season's Greetings from Sherry Leavit and Jamie."

Since I never envisioned her cleaning a cage and setting out parrot food, I presumed there was a new "sweetheart" in her life—until she telephoned late one January night.

"Glory be to God!" My mother held her hand where she imagined her heart was. "I thought it was something wrong with Francis or one of the children."

". . . Wonderful," I said.

"This is the break I've been waiting for." Sherry used the same old words the same old way. "You'll see it in the papers, but the show isn't announced yet. It's got everyone: Merman, Leonard Bernstein."

"Gee!"

"It's tremendous, exciting. Listen to Jamie. Listen to beautiful baby; he was so happy for me I cried; honest, he *knows* that something great has happened. Listen to Jamie." I listened to Jamie's guttural squawks, which grew louder and soared to a piercing crescendo.

"Are you going to sing?" I asked, turning my back on my bird of prey, who was pretending to watch the Late Show. There was a flapping and scratching at the other end.

"It's not quite set, Ag. *The Gershwin Years* is a whole ninety minutes, a spectacular, and of course they need lots of kids."

"Wonderful!"

"He's right here on my shoulder, my baby Jamie."

She had given her heart for the last time.

"Lord forgive me," Mother said, "I thought it was Francis."

Sherry was right, I couldn't have missed *The Gershwin Years*, one of those cultural gestures on behalf of the network and a paternalistic oil company. I didn't say a word at home, and—small wonder—my mother went over to Mae's, lured by fudgy brownies. Alone in the darkness I waited for Sherry; girls swayed and sang, girls with giant Ziegfeld plumes wafted down the glittering stairs of our M-G-M dreams; girls drifted through arty mobiles in leotards. They were all young—Sherry fifteen years ago—with painted inexpressive faces and elastic bodies, a lifetime removed from the beautiful woman with a past, weighted with mink and diamonds in Stouffer's, picking her way through the days with a man or a parrot or another hope.

"George Gershwin came up from the Lower East Side, from a confining study of the classics to the restless jazzy world of discordant newness . . ."

It went on like that, a man's voice giving me all this about the American dream, the search, fulfillment; but the first half hour was over and I had not seen Sherry. Then the scenes from *Porgy and Bess*—nothing doing there unless they put her in blackface. I looked at the screen so damn hard—more young girls swooping about the Eiffel Tower. I thought I had missed her, perhaps unrecognizable behind a feathery fan, disguised by a boa—and then I thought, my

God, she never made it—all these kids jumping around and Sherry out of the business for so many years.

Ten minutes left, and my solemn commentator grew more lugubrious as he spoke again of Paris in the twenties: Gershwin had wanted much more than success. . . . O.K., O.K., yes, Fitzgerald, Picasso, Hemingway, Joyce, and as our own greatest spokesman for the expatriates, Gertrude Stein, said: "Everybody was twenty-six. Hemingway was twenty-six. I was twenty-six. The world was twenty-six." It was Mary Elizabeth reading the words out in a high faltering voice, toneless, uncomprehending. It was so bad, but I counted on Sherry not knowing.

Come to think of it, I counted on a lot: on an unbroken line that I followed, like a child's puzzle in which you draw your pencil from 1 to 2 to 3, through a maze of numbers and come out with the not so very hidden picture of our pig-eyed house snuggled in nightmare juxtaposition up to the zipper factory—Mother supporting the whole teetering works, old Atlas of the daily continuum. I counted on some freshly shaven gent with a Sulka tie to tell Sherry how talented she was, though maybe her style was more in the Arlene Francis line: wit and chiffon. I counted on getting up and going to work and coming home to Henry James. I counted on Sherry slipping into her mink coat and eating a peanut butter sandwich. I counted on the only death being inside me, an increasing numbness of some mysterious vital organ, like Tony De Angelo's kidney or liver or pancreas. But Sherry didn't even bother to switch off the set. She went straight to the medicine cabinet of her luxury bathroom, and when the woman who ran the vacuum over the wall-to-wall carpet came in she found the daytime "Price Is Right" blaring and thought that strange because usually if Mrs. Leavit was up she liked the old movies.

They notified the Colonel, who was in Washington about a contract for nose cones, and by the time her show-biz friends remembered my name she was buried in a nonsectarian cemetery on Long Island. A man I'd never heard of called me at the office and I took the next bus to Bridgeport and changed to a midmorning train to New York—as if something could be done. When the superintendent let me into Sherry's apartment he drew back the curtains, and there was the bright spring East River, sunlight on the water, green branches along the embankment. A toy tug fitted out with little men hauled a flat black freighter out to the sea—gay flags, a pretty world from this height, like the magic blackness embroidered with stars and strings of electric lights which had been Sherry's.

In a while the Colonel came with Little Dot. She was anxious about a rehearsal of *Traviata* at City Center.

"Harry dear," she said, "perhaps Miss Keely would like something of Sherry's." They offered a brooch I had never seen her wear, but then there were demanding screams from the bedroom, and we ran in to find Jamie—yellow and red and green with glassy eyes. He was in a flap and repeated again and again words we had not been trained to understand. Little Dot, always the prima donna, glanced at her watch:

"We called the ASPCA and I thought somehow that we should be here. Harry or someone . . ." Then she looked at me with a wan smile, perfect for the last act, the final brave aria.

"Would you like him? Would you like the bird?"

I said I found him disgusting. Colonel Leavit, full of understanding, brought me out to the living room again. He picked up his topcoat of some rich wonderful material, and said by way of consolation, "She was beautiful, beautiful."

"Yes."

We looked around at her plain room before we left, for Little Dot had decided that, after all, the doorman could deal with the parrot.

"Terrible place," the Colonel said, "no character."

I telephoned Francis from Grand Central, and as soon as I

heard his voice I knew I would not have to tell him about Mary Elizabeth. He had read it in the paper.

"Don't say anything to them at home—please, Francis, that's just what they'd like."

He said yes, and then, "Tell me Ag, was there time—did she have a priest?"

7

--◄◄◆►►--

March 21—

My life takes on a pattern. Now that can give me pleasure—the familiarity of the scrubbed kitchen as Lydia keeps it, every pot hung in place, her "tea towels" ironed and folded in the top drawer; Stanley climbing the stairs each Saturday night with a different wine to sample; my midmorning Danish from the coffee wagon that comes around in the office. The circumstances are given, so I am free to perform the automatic gesture gracefully. Soon there will be nothing left of the blundering phantom Ag, except what I want to hold onto for the sake of style. Now I can write

183

at night—as I have written about Sherry—or take up this journal again. I think I may now be pretentious enough to call it a notebook: last week I told Mordecai and Flo I was engulfed in the traditions of the anti-novel; next morning I excused myself to the bathroom mirror—after all, these artists make one talk rubbish.

The Wunda-Clutch ads are under control, too, though it is God's own hassle to introduce anything new to people. Ah, they're pig-crazy for the next new gimmick and insatiable about the flight to the moon, but the unknown, the untried, is not for them—"not personally, I mean *I* personally wouldn't. . . ." They are content to zip themselves in, year after year, the old comfortable way—the sure thing when there is nothing sure left; a sheet of metal bent in a fantasy, an added flip to the chrome, but underneath the same engine takes them over the road to grandmother's house Sunday after Sunday after Sunday after church. Big ad for the Spring Season: a Gay Nineties girl laced into an excruciating corset:

"Why suffer, Matilda?"
Please get Wunda-Clutch!
Same girl: calm Modern Miss, sealing herself painlessly into an airy girdle. All of this designed by Stanley with exquisite Victorian squirls that sweep into one necessary, definitive line of today. The job is routine, not unpleasant, demands nothing from me but eight hours each day toying with the dead-end possibilities of clutch-tape fibers—which is not at all "where I live," as Flo says.

A change of pace is called for, a walloping good yarn, new faces, plenty of action as I hit my stride. I live with Stanley (Saturday nights) and share a place to live with Lydia Savaard and live with the words I write. Late on Fridays I live it up with Mordecai and Flo, who are painters that came across me in a jangling *bar bohème* on University Place. They think Stanley and I are artists.

We said: "We are only in advertising."

Mordecai Schwartz, many beers under, screeched, "No, No!" We thought he was in his last agony; "Naa," he gasped, "I mean what you *do*."

Stoshie and I, speaking at once, tried to justify ourselves —the copy I write sent over to the agency by messenger . . . commercial art courses at Cooper Union, formerly associated with zippers—but Mordecai ticked on: "Sarnicki," he said, "I want to tell you that to the world I am a salad boy at Horn and Hardart's."

Flo, who is strong and ageless, with lots of black hair falling straight about her face and sunken expressive eyes, said, "I do not speak about my work," and told us at some length about the fertilizing complex of irrationality.

They came back to my place that first night with two pale boys from *The Catholic Worker* and finished off the bourbon I keep for Stanley. Now Flo comes every Friday, marching grandly up the stairs with Mordecai dragging after and the group they assemble during the first half of their evening. She does not ring the bell: she loves to hear the sound of her knuckles on wood. Sweeping into the living room she commands the linoleum floor, where she has begun to knick out a patch, three feet by six, with a razor blade and my good kitchen knife—digging and scratching in the "terrifying gummy density." Her panel is to be called "Confinement," a mysteriously depressing pattern of egg shapes dominated by the marbleized design of the linoleum. Flo never lets up—she is in fact developing a theme, for her full-time project is building a great screen of egg cartons, a study in the refraction of light, clipping off the "tits" (Mordecai's word) at various angles. He takes over the love seat and does all the talking to me and to the sculptors, musicians, photographers they bring along. I have a notion there is something going between Mordecai and the young girl-poet Ginny. Flo makes no comment; at the most she declaims two or three times an evening.

"The texture of macaroni gives pleasure," she said last

night. I had to cook up four pounds of rigatoni to go around.

"Ma Keely," Mordecai slurped, enjoying his dish, "has this extraordinary quality of a woman who can give herself in this way, with food, yah, with wine, yah, with a sauce—the basic thing."

Ginny and the other poets, boys of nineteen or twenty, drone on, reliving a flaming loft party, absorbed in a world I could never enter. They do not try to explain their presence in my house or to make me like them . . . they go on with the dead earnestness of young lives.

"Wasn't kerosene on the bed a bit much?" I asked.

Boy with the beard said: "He hated that chick."

"Was she unfaithful?"

Boy without the beard answered: "He wanted her to burn in hell-fire, Ma."

The fire apparently took place above a toy warehouse. Only the dolls burned up. Ginny and the boys see no significance in this apotheosis of brutal child's play; they see the world straight on, without amazement, like old people who have survived Dachau—but of course they haven't. It seems a feeble pose, their claim to identities: Ginny the poet, Boy the poet, Beard the poet. They might as well be wearing gang jackets like high-school hoods. Their verses run in thin directionless dribbles, like their lives—*always* the subject of their song. They have more of nothing than anyone else; they are arrogant about it, jealous of their holdings.

Ginny reads us a poem: it is all grit to begin with, the gray city and her gray body (quite accurate) swinging to some grit Caribe cha-cha, and then she eats some sausage and then she goes with this man and then she sees a pregnant woman and then she meets an Italian saint and goes up to Grant's Tomb, which is beautiful like at five o'clock in the morning and where she wants to be buried. Her face is dishrag gray and full of belief in her poem; she reads without delight, without rhythm, without any idea other than herself, in a dirty old sweater squatting on the floor: dingy ankles, filthy neck, sticky hair chopped like a boy's—one of those workhouse kids in Dickens.

"In the gray stone I want to screw with General Grant."

She comes to an end, and Mordecai remarks, "Yah-yah," which from the look of Beard and Boy is the wrong thing to say, though he claims to understand what these kids are about, and tells them a long story, punctuated with Yahs, about an art class he taught in a home for aged Chinese gentlemen and how the old men would die just as they learned to make something, yah.

I am intrigued by dropsical Lin Fang and palsied Mr. Wong. Ginny, Beard, and Boy turn to each other to share a studied vacuity. The great butcher knife of Charlie Lee, three hundred years old, means nothing to them. All the strange and wonderful turns common under their hostile gaze: we must allow them to find their own joy in a dish of cherry Jell-O eaten up on Forty-second Street.

"Mr. Lee, they said one morning, has gone to his ancestors—yah, and he left you this package. Done up in silk brocade was his knife, wasn't it, Flo? Yah. And listen, I can cut tissue paper with that blade of Charlie Lee's."

"Objects that are used are holy," Flo said, and gouged the floor—salmon roe in a clump—with my kitchen knife.

After they had gone Beard-poet stayed on—loitering in the kitchen doorway as I cleaned up, mute and unfathomable. Under the tight jeans, the workman's shirt, his body was not yet developed: a boy's hips, slight shoulders, and under the proud growth of hair on his face, a child's soft skin. He ate cookies out of a bakery bag and spoke at last, "Ma?"

"Yes?" (I don't mind the Ma—it is Mordecai's, taken from the M. A. Keely on my mailbox.)

"You write, Ma?"

(I was off guard. It was two o'clock. I had cooked a meal for the Schwartzes and their gang.) "Each day I go to an office. I write about the modern fastener. My work is in the trade journals: in sewing magazines, pattern books, *Simplicity* itself . . . and then there are throw-aways, don't you know: 'Place Wunda fabric A so that the million miracle grips are facing Wunda B.' "

"Crazy," the young poet with the beard said, meaning he found it another nothing in all the nothings he came across each day.

"I think it's O.K. to push something new, obsolescence being so fashionable and all."

"But I thought you wrote, Ma."

Seeing that I still had the pots and pans to wash, I took a maternal tone. "I write things down, just on a yellow pad—what happens. And then a little play, stories. I don't know . . . what I see in things that have happened, what they grow to in my mind. The shape of my failure, I suppose that's what I describe—personal disaster and whatever you make of that." I expected to see more nothingness in the boy's face—not disappointment, that would be too fine; but the nothing he found in me and all the pages I had written, blank for him and for his young friends.

Instead, he brightened and said with an ingratiating smile, "May I have more cookies, Ma?"

"Yes, and take some nice sugar buns." I tucked them into a bag. He went, without speaking, into the living room and put on his duffel coat, slowly drawing each wooden button through its rope loop, then pulling the gray hood over his head so that he was an El Greco boy, saintly and awful in the weird light of my paper lantern. Then I believed in everything he saw with his burning eyes, the beard moving as he spoke like a small mountain upended in his quest.

"Ten dollars and I can live for a month, Ma. It buys me a space."

"Apartment?"

"Yeah, yeah," he said with the detachment of an apprentice mystic, accepting "apartment" for my sake; more likely a cold-water flat, a dark cellar, the back of a store.

"Then how do you eat?" Already I had gone to the closet and taken my purse off the hook. "Not with the same ten dollars?"

"I have a place to eat." Before he puts the money in his jeans, he reaches out, gives the flesh of my upper arm a squeeze. He's off leaping downstairs. "Thanks, Ma," he shouts happily up the hallway, forgetting his pose, "Thanks, Ma!" At two-thirty in the morning. I shudder to think of the Mertzes . . .

My arm plump there where the boy touched me, a comforting roundness. My breasts heavy. Indeed, I look like somebody's mother. Better watch it—I'm getting fat.

Flo's linoleum carving put Lydia Savaard into a rage the first week, a tempered rage to be sure, all "damn nonsense" muttered under her breath as she went at egg inscriptions with Mr. Clean, full strength. Now I have a straw mat which covers Flo's Friday night Work-in-Progress and we do not speak of it.

Stanley slides the mat off with his toe each Saturday to see how it's coming. He laughs, "How are your artist friends?"

I'll never grow tired of the intimacy of his laugh, full of our assumptions about each other. Didn't I say that I would get on with things? But it's not so easy. Here I dawdle over a worthless idealization: the sturdy look of him in his favorite sweater, starting through the Sunday *Times* late Saturday night after we have eaten at home and decided to go no farther than the newsstand—man-mountain of tranquillity. I do not wish to disclose the trick which he plays against a receding hairline, or betray his indifference to the theater I so love. Stanley is poetry for me now, my *symbolistes* abandoned in the corner, the Everlasting Yes I feel watching him. I would lay with him in Grant's tomb or Washington's square, in Lincoln's tunnel or Pulaski's skyway.

"Ten dollars is ten dollars, Mary Agnes," Stanley said without rancor—as a matter of fact, with his hand on the broad of my back—"and you pay the bills for your mother."

"I wanted to give the boy ten dollars."

"Of course you did."

"Stoshie, that kid has such dedication . . . and the Schwartzes too . . . and it makes me feel good, giving them a meal, a few drinks—as though I know what it meant, as though I had a right to speak with them . . ."

"I'll tell you the truth, Ag." Stanley's voice was serious and low: this was an encounter, not one of our homely chats. "I would say just from talking to Schwartz in a bar that I use more technique in my Wunda layouts and sketches for Queen Mab lingerie. I mean Schwartz yapping that night about the weight of lead he soldered on canvas and the whole thing sagged; well, you have to build a thing, that's all, Ag, you have to build a simple flat with sky and clouds for one sitting with the models so it will *hold*."

"But they are different."

"And I'll tell you something else—" He stomped across the floor and took his stand on the straw mat, my Stanley, the color rising in his face. (I never meant to bring this on.) "I'll tell you something else: you know more about poems and all from your studying than any of them. I can tell, even *I* can tell from listening to you that they are stupid kids. You have more knowledge in your little finger than they have in all their unwashed bodies." He paused, one substantial finger raised to heaven. "There are a lot of freeloaders around, don't you forget it."

I sat there in a sick lump and didn't say what I should have: that permanence and knowledge may not be the perfectly grand keystones of Western Civilization we have always believed; we hold on sentimentally when we should push forward disastrously; but I never can feature anyone saying such things outside the Sunday Magazine section of the *New York Times*. Even the *crème brûlé* couldn't pull us together after this . . . There was a shameful feeling not far back in my mind that I was protecting Stanley from what I thought, and he petted me in a dozen polite, apologetic gestures until he left early—kiss on the cheek, beginning of a virus. . . .

Sunday—

Chill bright March morning. Supposedly vernal. I am up early and unable to cry. Not really a fight. These incidents pass, and what remains is our exhilarating passion and life and the sea and Walt Whitman.

The closet door stands open, full of color on my side, and on the other the drab garments of Lydia Savaard, further dimmed by protective coatings of plastic. In the full-length mirror, myself: one-hundred-and-sixty-eight pounds, which I carry well enough. An imposing figure—good long nose complemented by fat cheeks—bosom and behind no little wonders. Not a day over thirty-two when my face is painted; quite the lady when my hair is set at the Village shop which has also been honored by Mrs. Roosevelt and Flora Robson. It's nothing as pure and simple as narcissism which finds me in this study of myself and, what's more, writing it down (the yellow pads have given out and I allow myself the self-regard of white bond)—but the desire to see myself as others will see me when, next Sunday, Stanley takes me to his mother and sister in Brooklyn. At long last—Brooklyn, after God only knows what squabbles in Polish about nice Polish girls.

I must present myself as a model of womanly virtue; I can't have lost the touch: I must remember white gloves, church talk; I must straighten my stocking seams (a pleasantly dated detail to prove me simple). I must recapture my old humility—the hesitant laugh, the unworldly smile. What I write today will be the final word for the week. When Lydia comes back, spent with good works, and draws the death X on the page of last week's Museum calendar, I will start my devotions: the *Daily News* for conversational tidbits, a Jane Austen novel to bring marriage into focus, and *My Ántonia* for the *sine qua non* of the immigrant scene.

Enough: I will do no more than propose, outline in my head, what I should like to write about Lydia Savaard. Oh, all the stuff that she has told me is accurate, but diffuse. The sorriest tale needs focus: we must take a long, satisfying look in, as through the window of a German Easter egg, on the sane world pasted together in perfect proportion, in which no chick or fence or dairymaid looms too large for our belief. So when we take our eye away and see the gross torn cuticle of our thumbnail, the enormity of flesh that pads our fingers, we feel that though quaint and old, the pretty world exists. We pray that it still goes on.

8

After Christmas Lydia Savaard started wearing an old polo coat when she went up to Connecticut to visit her husband. It was long, for the styles had changed since her college days, but she could huddle under the coat on the train without caring. In any case Lydia had stopped thinking about her looks, except for a general effort to be respectable and unobtrusive when she went to work.

One Friday night in March Mary Agnes came in with the groceries and announced that it was snowing, so Lydia pulled her boots out of the closet and tied a woolen scarf on her head as she left the apartment, more downhearted than usual. A wet snow fell, turned to slush underfoot but settled in deceptive airiness along the curbs—reminding her of a budget pudding that had been served in her house at Vassar on weekends, the final insult, after whitefish or baked beans, to the manless girls who would make up a petulant group to go downtown to the movies. Waiting for the Fifth Avenue bus with her overnight case, it occurred to Lydia with sophomoric bitterness that now she was one of the lucky ones, going to Connecticut; all she had to do was stay on the train till New Haven and find a good party.

To Lydia the weather seemed one more evidence that life was out of her control: heavy flakes that turned to water on her sleeves and slurped down the side of her bag meant that Henry, euphoric in winter sunshine, would be caged the whole weekend. So they would sit in the overheated living room of Shady Acres and flip through the magazines or attempt a game of bridge with the artsy woman who picked her nose and rubbed the gummy discovery into her embroidered smock, and any other nut they could find for a fourth: one of the haunted girls, one of the haunted boys, one of the patriarchal gentlemen. The comfy chairs and tables would be arranged casually in the hopeless expectation of social groups, arranged once and for all: screwed to the green tile floor, which for all its friendly scuffs and the water rings from the geranium pots at the low window showed the big swirling marks of an industrial waxing machine.

A sense of meaningless duty closed in on the Savaards when the weather was bad. Henry's strong legs were set in paralytic heaviness and his eyes seemed like two drained vessels reflecting the polished emptiness of his wife's chatter. He waited for her sigh of relief, barely converted to a little chirp when the lunch bell rang. The half-hour session Henry had with Dr. Wishengrad became a special treat for them both, and when he returned, Lydia, refreshed, would do all the talking: about her office, the apartment, a movie (full plot), Mary Agnes (complete menus), a recap of *Time* magazine. At last she would look out at the snow or rain that kept them bound together in this purgatory, leaning back into the bright cushions in a posture to indicate utter relaxation. In a few minutes she would press her talk button again—a letter from her mother with the full description of St. John's Episcopal bake sale in Shaker Heights. Henry would place a magazine on his stiff legs and look at nothing in particular.

On the train Lydia could not forget the two of them confined in that room—all of Saturday, most of Sunday, until she could glance up, surprised, at the undisguised hospital clock boldly stating the time in the midst of gimcrack Americana. "Gosh," she would say, "I'd better run if I'm going to catch my train." Now she worked ahead in her book of double-crostics but managed only the simple fill-ins; the nerves in her body seemed to stretch out beyond reason, stretching her mind through the horrors foreseen. Her jaw was clamped tight. Her face ached: it was all pain, rising to her temples, burrowing behind her eyes.

The same wet snow fell in Connecticut. At the Inn she couldn't face the idea of a long dinner by herself at one of the side tables. Mr. Merton, the manager, understood perfectly: his bald head and half-rim glasses glowed with New England coziness, but tonight she was not amused by references to *your* room and *our* Chicken Pot Pie. Up three flights, under the eaves was her room, all little blue flowers and cast-off furniture painted white, bath down the hall—the cheapest thing they had. She ate a package of Lorna Doones which she had bought from the vendor on the train, took a scalding bath, turned out the light, and lay grinding her teeth, listening to the whoosh of tires driving through the slush, and after what seemed like hours fell asleep.

She awoke in dread when it was still dark, and turned her face into the pillow, breathing the muffled hot air of herself, until, sensing the day, she made the effort, got up, and stumbled out down the frigid hall with worn carpet into the dribble of an unsatisfying shower. She did what she had to: clean underwear, an ancient skirt, a mended sweater. The polo coat had dried stiff over the radiator.

Down in the lobby Mr. Merton was flapping about in a big show of cheerful beginning—coffee smell, fresh post-cards, the gift-shop door already open to lure the first two ladies toddling into the rich array of glass and scarves and earrings. Mr. Merton, ordering the boy to bring in wood, setting all the room to a Grandma Moses quaintness, dashed at Lydia before she got to the front door. She was halted by the gleam of his dentured face.

"Ah, Mrs. Savaard," he sang out, "we can't let you escape *this* morning." He dropped his voice to an insinuating whisper, "*Mister* Savaard is in the dining room."

"Oh—"

"I persuaded him to try *our* French-roast Coffee."

"Yes," Lydia replied, wondering if they knew at the farm that Henry had gone off by himself so early in the morning.

"I would have sent him up, but we have our rules about Shady Acres, you understand." Mr. Merton nodded his shiny head, showing he understood all things perfectly. "Once burned, you know . . ."

"Of course." She left Merton on obliging tiptoes in the doorway. At the far end of the dining room Henry sat in a bay window surrounded by white sunlit curtains and African violets. He wore the sweater she had given him for Christmas, and there he was: the perfect playboy again, the confusing sardonic smile, blond Mr. Princeton.

"Good morning," he said. "I've ordered *our* Famous Walnut Waffles. What will you have?"

"Nothing . . ."

"You can't ski on an empty stomach."

"Toast and coffee then." She looked down at his ski boots with a fearful grin. "Where did you get them?"

Henry said nothing.

"I've never been on skis in my *life!*" Lydia cried in mock hysteria and blundered on to a pointless story about a girl she had once met with a broken collarbone.

"The boots," Henry Savaard said in a steady voice, "belong to Dr. Wishengrad. His wife has a pair of skis you can try."

Lydia set her silverware straight, smoothed the tablecloth and fixed the spoons again—an eighth of an inch out of line. It was the most natural thing in the world to look up from the spotless cloth to Henry having a good time with the maple syrup; then she turned to the window, not wanting to betray her pleasure. There was the miracle: cold sunshine on drifts of weightless snow.

"Oh, God, it's beautiful!" Squealing with wonder, forgetting to go easy with Henry, who had launched the day by looking his old self.

"It's been like this for hours," he said with a friendly, drawling sarcasm. "It snowed all night."

"Not when I got off the train, ducky. It was nothing but thick slush and I thought we'd be in all weekend."

Henry Savaard thought about that, and he saw the sadness, long and unbearable, of their hours together in the living room.

The cow barn was built between two hillocks, and like all the buildings at Shady Acres appeared to be in perfect repair, as though to put one's house in order might impress the deranged and devious minds within. All arrangements were reasonable: had there been cows they would have felt safe and warm in the barn, nestled down in a nice valley of security; had there been farm hands instead of patients they would have felt independent in the cottages set off from the big house, comfortable around the family tables in the dining room. The idea at Shady Acres was to come and go as you pleased, almost . . . so when the Savaards came to the farm they were seen at a distance first, walking up the road and in at the gate and trudging through snow-drifts to the side entrance where the Wishengrads lived.

They carried off the skis in silence, printing the first tracks behind the house and up the little hill that sheltered the barn. When they reached the top and overlooked the remarkable quiet, Henry said, "You should have borrowed the jacket."

Lydia looked down at the strange boots on her feet, at the slim, correct pants which she had found in Mrs. Wishengrad's hall. Her worn coat trailed wretchedly, far below her knees. "Oh, well—"

"It doesn't look right."

"Oh, well," she said again. "I don't think I'll be able to ski." Her skin grew bright in the wind and her hair was blown on her cheeks, soft strands blown free from the tight under-roll which was meant to do for the rest of her life. "What's the matter?" she asked Henry, who looked at her and then out at the rolling dunes of snow.

"I was thinking."

She was afraid to ask what.

"It looks like the sea," he said.

They tried the slope together and Lydia was a failure. Then she waited while Henry went down by himself, bending his body easily, rising with the strength of his legs, swerving with the few contours of the hill. She wanted it to be a mountain for him. Again she tried, without success, and so they went through the morning. Watching the grim intent deepen on his face as he climbed towards her, she worried and asked if they might rest awhile, so they went down and took off the skis and pushed in the door of the cow barn.

It was still a barn at the back where they came in; two stalls remained; above, a loft with scraps of hay stuck through as if for atmosphere. Otherwise it was surprisingly slick: a hardwood floor, an empty stage at the far end shining with acoustical screens of polished wood.

"I never knew," she cried. "You never *told* me." And she could have bitten her tongue, because her words implied that he had told her something, some one small item during all the everlasting weekends, besides a difficult mumble about boat, balsa wood, bottle.

"Wishengrad had some idea about concerts and plays in the barn, but he never finished the job."

"You don't have to go back for anything?" Lydia asked.

"I'm not . . ." Henry began. He was on his knees, unlacing her boots, and she could not see his face. "Your socks are wet," he said.

"It doesn't matter."

"They . . . are cutting out my Saturday morning session and one on Wednesday."

"Wonderful!" She estimated that it would clip an easy hundred off the monthly bill, and hated herself for coming up with that point first, but it seemed that her life was overdrawn in a checking account, that all her feelings—loyalty, guilt, emptiness—were as impersonal as debits and credits, allowed to her only as financial problems that she must balance to go on at all. She thought, too, that she had become sharp with money: bargaining for a better salary than children's books paid as a rule, living on the cheap, selling her rings, investing like a veteran. It was fine to know she could write to her parents and say that Henry was somewhat better. She would not even be depressed by the maudlin yet accusing letter she would receive in return—"You have done too much, our brave little girl. . . ." Her parents never mentioned money any more. She had told them that Mrs. Savaard paid for Henry. Mrs. Savaard presumed that checks were sent to her from Cleveland.

Henry ran a few steps on the polished floor, then slid along in his stocking feet. Even at this sport he was accomplished—could use his weight to turn, jump, and slide again. Lydia noticed that he held his head high; his eyes were blazing, his cheeks flushed, and she knew that he was exhilarated by the snow, the liberation from his half-hour with Dr. Wishengrad; still, she feared when this lively mood was on him that it might spill over into violence. They had told her to "control the area of possible response" if her weekend visits were to "build a structure," and she had even been called aside and complimented by Wishengrad one Sunday afternoon—in the strange language he spoke which she never understood: balm and psychic wounds, emotional scar tissue.

Lydia sat on the stairs which led to the stage, and with a joyless knowledge women have, decided she must put an end to his game. "Have you ever been in a play?" she asked, stopping Henry in full flight.

He hoisted himself onto the stage, "No." He thought about her question as though the doctor had put it to him, strained to remember; "I never did that sort of thing in school. They weren't the people I knew . . . though we put on a scene from Molière in French class."

Shyly Lydia said, "Once I played the milk in a Girl Scout nutrition show."

"A bottle of milk?"

"Yes, and I was pasteurized; I had a bigger part than the lamb chop or any of the vegetables."

She looked up at Henry: his face, overly delicate or beautiful, or whatever it had once been, was crossed with shadows, hollowed by pain, destroyed; yet the charm remained, perhaps stronger now. What was the difference? She watched as he assumed an artificial stance; well, of course he never was an actor, he was an athlete.

"*Ronsard m'a célébré*," he recited, "*du temps que j'étais belle*." And the barn echoed the final poetic "e." "But I can't remember a line from the *Bourgeois Gentilhomme*." Henry danced back and forth, his eyes brilliant, two steps and a last daredevil slide done with grace for her alone. "My pasteurized baby," he began in a deep affected tone, and Lydia thought he was so bad on the stage because his whole life was an act so there was nothing left over to pretend. What was the difference in him now? He was somehow—a man.

"I can't," she protested pulling at the toes of her wet socks. "You do some more."

"Tiger, tiger burning bright," Henry called out.

"Right," the barn answered.

"Night," the barn answered.

Suddenly she wanted to be up there on the stage with him, trying her voice against the ghostly sound. And it was odd to her that she wanted it so much, to take her place on the stage and call out *her* words. Listening was not enough: like a child with neither racquet nor bat who strikes out with the flat of his hand, determined to play, she ran up the steps and onto the stage—"Hello! Hello!" she sang out, and she might have been a great lady of the theater, her deceptively ordinary body turned at a commanding angle, her head flung back to display an elegant throat. Like the ball perfectly struck her voice rang out: "I am a quart of pasteurized milk. Drink me every day and I will make you healthy; I will make you strong."

The barn whispered, "-rong," and she sighed—not at the contradiction, but at the cow bell that clattered for lunch, reaching out over the peaceful snow and into the empty barn where they played.

As they walked back to the house Lydia said, "Every time I tell Mary Agnes about eating meals here she says, 'Oh, Thomas Mann' and makes me list what was served and describe the fresh tablecloths."

"Yeh," Henry said, "how is Mary Agnes?"

"Just as nutsy as ever," his wife replied, and knew she should have said as funny, as amusing as ever. The Thomas Mann *faux pas* had slipped by, she hadn't caught it—disease and death—until Mary Agnes explained. Lydia had not read much outside of class, but she did what was put to her; she was clever at editing children's stories, the most valuable person in her office—and a good thing, too: Shady Acres charged her three-fifty for every meal she ate in their luxurious bedlam.

Henry tapped the back of her hand. "Tired?"

Her feet were damp and chill under the table. "No. No. We can try again this afternoon if you'd like."

The dining room was full of strange people eating in strange ways: secretive squirrels, lofty giraffes, indiscriminate baboons, and Dr. Wishengrad himself, observant as an old mother cat. Lydia could never stomach much in this zoo, but she liked to watch Henry filling his plate for the second time. Their morning on the hill, as he described it, might have been enacted in a glamorous winter playground of the international set. Still, she was satisfied: her husband herded all the creatures to the safety of his pack—snorting, ferreting, scratching, they looked to Henry to get them through the meal. Under the table Lydia's feet had turned to ice. Next to her a blank girl stared at an empty plate.

"May I help you to some vegetables?"

Dr. Wishengrad watched with amber cat eyes: the girl's daze turned to sickly horror as Lydia spooned beans and potatoes onto her plate. Without a word the girl rose and walked out of the room.

"This afternoon," Dr. Wishengrad said to Lydia, "if you have a minute . . ."

Waiting in the dark upper passage outside of Wishengrad's office, Lydia felt that she had been summoned again before a minister of God: nothing was private inside her any more. Everything that was hers had already been dragged out for Godnick last year, for Mary Agnes when they talked late at night, for the psychiatrists here at Shady Acres. Even to Mr. Merton at the Inn she was a known quantity: the threadbare, sacrificing little wife. It did not make it easier to have lost her personal life, though now she realized it hadn't been much to start with—indeed, she often thought it was more difficult for her with the tender keepsakes of a happy childhood and the delayed discovery of sorrow than it was for her husband with many lives, all mysterious and hallucinatory, rich with saints and hosts of wicked angels in pursuit of one small rich boy.

From Wishengrad's office a ceaseless rhythm of muffled words came to her in the dark passage where she waited. She was cold, tired in all her limbs, and wanted to go back to the Inn and rest. How she hated Wishengrad's paradoxical language, always something on the one hand, something on the other. It was less painful to be with Henry than to talk about him: the doctor's insoluble terms compounded the injury. A striking figure appeared in Wishengrad's doorway, a man she had never seen in the public rooms of Shady Acres—tall, gray-haired; he wore a suit with a vest and slapped his thighs with a pair of formal gray suède gloves. He turned his wild eyes directly on her in the dimness, "Good morning, Eleanore," he said with confident good will as Lydia squeezed past him into the doctor's office.

They sat at the window which faced out to the back stretch of farm land. Boundaries were defined by the snow: fences, walls, the brook; she saw that the wood which they had walked in was not very large, no more than a strip of trees left along the foot of a hill which rose to another old farmhouse with a bending barn. In the foreground Henry made his way up the slope. They waved to him, but the late sun against the window blacked them out.

"I'm sorry about the girl at lunch," Lydia said.

Dr. Wishengrad, a fat, easy man, dismissed the apology with a shrug.

"I'm stupid to think that because I can manage with Henry I can help someone else."

"You're all right," Wishengrad said.

"Does the girl eat anything?"

"She eats in her room. You and I can't imagine the agony it is for her to sit at the table."

Lydia said she knew this, pulling the sleeve of her sweater down—there at the elbow the wool had worn thin as lace, and she said, "I know this"—but wasn't the point that they should try to *imagine* the girl's physical revulsion brought on by beans and potatoes? The doctor thought certainly not, was even amused—"That way lies madness, Mrs. Savaard."

Out on the hill Henry swooped around imaginary slalom poles and came to a stop spraying the air with a glittering arc of snow. Dr. Wishengrad narrowed his eyes in appreciation. "He's doing pretty well."

"Of course. He can master any sport in half an hour."

"Oh, the skiing," said Wishengrad and slumped in his chair, resigned to his comfortable indoor body. "My wife and I have been skiing for ten years and we'll never look like that."

"I know what you mean."

"I see you gave up and went into the barn this morning."

"We thought it was beautiful."

"I had a patient here, a young architect . . . he never finished it." Nothing in Wishengrad's smooth manner told her why the building was left half-theater, half-cowshed. "And I'm not sure what the boy had in mind."

Lydia was muddled by a cold coming on, yet suspected that she was being dealt with in some way. Surely this idle talk only seemed easier than the bewildering problems Wishengrad usually set for her. "Did he die, then?" she asked.

"No, he didn't die." The sun was dramatic on the snow, flaming orange streaked over the land, swept up into the sky. Henry Savaard began his herringbone climb up the hill for the last time. "Yes, your husband is much better, Mrs. Savaard. You've done a fine job."

She sneezed, and the doctor, moving out of his chair softly, with experience, came to her with a handkerchief and a glass of sherry. The quiet wondering thread between them remained unbroken. "Was it cold out there this morning?"

"Terribly cold."

"Did you have a good time?" His question meant something; no matter how much he curled himself back into the chair, tried almost to be one with the chair, the question led out to something else.

"I suppose I did."

"You had a wonderful time." The doctor's warm yellow eyes, without a glimmer of irony, settled the fact. He was a gentle man. The softness of his body, the curves worn into his chair from years of listening, the nearly passive, melting smoothness of his voice all proclaimed a generous and gentle man. And the surface hardness, that shell of stark terminology and evasive metaphor, cracked easily, was intended to dissolve, to flake away, layer by layer like a continuous-action capsule, leaving in the end a large laughable figure of a Scout Master or a flabby coach. Confronted with Wishengrad's ultimate simplicity the tightest spirits opened up: it was pointless to deceive him.

Now, with careless lucidity he laid open the case of Henry Savaard. A turn that was "not uninteresting"—Henry wanted specific details: How much did it cost to keep him? Where did his wife get the money?

"This happens with some patients: when their delusions fade they are almost bored. We take this as encouraging; after all, why shouldn't we?"

"I don't know," Lydia said doubtfully, "you're the doctor."

"It's a guessing game," he said.

She had been told that till her head ached, and then told that it wasn't a guessing game at all but a science. There were drugs—new, still in process. What actually happened to the young architect that was worse than death? And would the girl at lunch perhaps be suffocated out of her agony one day by a string bean? Meanwhile Henry was in dollars and cents. "I've never said a word to him about money," Lydia said despondently.

It appeared that Henry knew the price of her room at the Inn, the cost of a round-trip ticket from New York. He had discovered her refuge in the fifty-cent ham 'n egg platter down at an unspeakably garish diner in the town. He could not remember seeing her in a decent coat.

Outside, the light was blue and cold. The day had come to an end with its sad sense of change, and no one expected it—not the Doctor, padding about to turn on the lamps; nor Lydia, caught in a series of bewildering sneezes; not Henry Savaard, a dark shape with the burden of his borrowed skis crossed up to the first stars.

Tugging at her sheer, bedraggled sweater, Lydia said, "All that I ever say to Henry is Peter Poppit books and Mary Agnes made a sauerbraten. That must seem pretty foolish to a man."

Dr. Wishengrad smiled at her, his fleshy cheeks blown into a large cat face, "Yes, there's no point in patronizing an intelligent man." There was a comfort in his directness which she had not known before. He saw with uncluttered vision, beyond the dragging days of washing and weekly waxing of the floors. "I don't say that your husband is going to walk out of here all pieced together next week or next month, Mrs. Savaard . . ."

"Walk out of here?" She heard the panic in her voice . . . "Walk out?"

Wishengrad reverted to those psychiatric phrases that would always elude her; in a medical croon he spoke of "cure" as an "operative level." There was so much to learn

—the newness, the uncertainty. He frowned; it was clear that Henry could go away from this controlled environment into a restricted but more natural situation.

"Natural—" said Lydia with a sigh. She heard the grinding of a snow plow straining around the side of the house up to the garage of Shady Acres. Wasn't it late for them to be plowed out, this place, a hospital? She thought of her divorce which had become an annulment by some sleight of hand until that hope dissolved in thin air; but she decided to keep it to herself and merely said, "I always find out things I should have known."

Doctor Wishengrad studied her with true concern. He is this way with his patients, Lydia thought; my injury is his, that's the power he has. She moved forward so that the lamplight caught her face; a flush of touching bitterness rose in her innocent cheeks. "The rules keep changing on me in the middle of the game."

"There are no rules. Think of the good you do coming up here each week." Dr. Wishengrad pushed his fat body out of the chair and stole round the desk for the sherry bottle. "Just think what you put out," he said.

"I tried to divorce Henry."

He disregarded that. "Think of the devotion. I'm not used to dealing with such stability."

"But his mother *told* me to come see Henry. I was *sent* here." There was nothing for Lydia to hold in place; it was all changing again, specks floating in the eye, facts shifting. She wondered if she should ask Wishengrad, "He did try to kill me once. That *did* happen?"

"Oh, you might have come here once a month because you were sent—"

"A duty," Lydia said. "The woman I live with in New York spent years taking care of her terrible old mother until she turned into a frenzied spinster. *She* told me to come to Henry; it's rotten—but, by God, you put in your time unless you want to be a big cipher."

"Her mother died?" Wishengrad suggested.

"No," said Lydia in triumph. "My friend walked out!"

Henry came in without knocking. He stood above them, stomping his boots. Lydia looked anxiously to the doctor, but he only puffed himself out and yawned.

"Take your wife back in the jeep." He sounded more exhausted than sleepy. "Get her to bed. She's running a temperature."

It was freezing in her garret room. Henry Savaard turned back the bedclothes, and Lydia took her pajamas from the drawer of a monstrous dresser caked with white paint. They looked at each other, man and wife. She was seized with a fit of coughing.

"It's gone to your chest." Henry blamed himself—dragging her out in the snow for a lot of nonsense. Lydia would not take her clothes off in front of him, reveal herself naked and scarred, the shrill truth. He picked up her cotton pajamas. "These aren't warm." She wouldn't argue: he stood with firm agility, not to be challenged, as though he were about to whack a ball or bring his ketch to shore against the wind. "Put on dry socks. Wear your sweater over these silly pajamas." Then he touched her forehead, let his hand trail down her cheek.

"Go downstairs, Henry, and get some dinner. You must be hungry after your day on the slopes." Only a little mound on the hospital grounds—brought out in the open the truth did not hurt.

When the door closed behind him—it was the cold in her head—she began to weep, taking off her clothes, tucking her underwear out of sight. Then opening her book of crossword puzzles, she remembered that things had been worse: solitary confinement in the stale hotel room: she had already been to the very end of existence. There would come another moment when Henry saw the mark he had cut into her, and another not dreamed of, and another, and so they would go on—scoring against each other for the rest of their lives. And oh, what if Mr. Merton discovered Henry coming down the stairs and went on in that oozing manner —once burned, you know. She wanted to run after him, protect him, but gently so he wouldn't know, cleverly so he couldn't guess. Closing her eyes, she thought that by now it would be all right: no one has bothered him; he has gone out into the new falling snow.

My friend walked out on her mother . . . what a great feeling to be one up on dear old Wishengrad; but then a flickering suspicion crossed her mind and she felt oddly undercut, as though she had to erase a word out of a puzzle which had fit too easily. Why that fat puss—he had known about Mary Agnes all along. And Lydia didn't care in the least that she'd been used: now Henry would be eating a sandwich downstairs or driving back through the soft winter night. . . .

But he came back to her with tea and chicken soup, tucked her in as though she were his sick child. Beginning from somewhere years ago, a nice girl with a young man at a good party, she said, "Gosh, Hen, you really are divine."

9

—◄◄►►—

The end of March—

I need only list my follies of the past weekend, a mounting horror of improbability, to elicit in my reader an exquisite surprise by massive accumulation: given second wind all things become possible again, one big belly-laugh that started as a smirk at slight excess. I have sold my mother, betrayed my lover, denied my friends. I have offended my landlady, my roommate, and an old Polish woman, one Mrs. Stanley Sarnicki, Sr., of Canarsie. I have eaten myself into a stupor and drunk myself into a vomiting rage, accused my brother long distance of moral perversion. I have costumed myself as a Novice to go whoring, created a public nuisance, pretended I had commerce with Christ and his entourage, insulted an officer, and curdled a Mornay sauce (meant to be as delicate as air on the first spring day) into foul water and ill-flavored cheese turdlets. Sing heigh-ho the ninny oh.

A bitter Monday: soot in your eye as the wind brings the gutter-stuff of the city up—all the scraps we usually ignore churned up to show the filth we live in and pretend not to, pretending too that the wind means nothing by it, is senseless, without direction, each gust not plotted somewhere in the past like a diagram in our science text, a pattern of swirling arrows charting air currents, factual, like the product of four nines. Or, What is an angel? An angel is a heavenly spirit without a body who serves and adores God.

Monday, and I am at home, though the captions must be written for the new retail package. Imagine, after all the crucial events . . . to go on writing that nonsense, one copy to the printer, another to Stanley for his design: Wunda-Clutch, "The Miracle Gripper!," as though someone cried it out in the old dark night of the soul; or maybe those hedging quotation marks hint it's not a true statement, is better ascribed to an anonymous party—*You* said it, kid, not me.

"The Miracle Gripper!" Bert Sigal named it my first day on the job with the authority of a meticulous scholar.

Early this morning Lydia Savaard stood at the foot of my bed in her dark work clothes: "Shall I call your office and say you won't be in?" A black hat had grown on her head like a natural appendage, cultivated for the picture she has of herself on the bus going uptown: a Lady Editor, a Nice Lady. "I'll phone and say that you're sick."

"Going to be all right," I moaned. Sitting up to look bright, the pain bounced in my head.

"Of course you'll be all right." How solicitous—the brisk tucking of the blanket, the lilting upbeat so effective with coo-coos.

"I'll go in at noon." I slumped back into the smell of sour wine and the purple stain of it which had run out of my mouth onto the pillowcase.

"Rest up. Take a warm bath," said the nice lady, resisting a dab at her tender nose like a well-behaved child. All weekend she had been trapped here with a bad cold, missing her visit to Henry, missing it like a birthday party. She coughed still, a deep bronchial rumbling. Poor woman, poor man. But I thought from the depth of my fouled bed that she looked grand without question in her somber outfit, her head set bravely on shoulders unbowed, her features shaped precisely by the strain of half-hopes—on to the poster of Victory. All that she doesn't know is paraded now, and the little she has learned is carried as high as the pale flag which signals not defeat but magnificent surrender. Ah, don't belittle her—she's all right. Myself, I am conscious of the different eternities of men, and other sonorous phrases. She's all right. She knows what she's doing: marching uptown with sterile bandages and a good heart to make Easy-Readers build up the basic vocabulary of forty thousand words so they'll all know what each other's talking about in the better world to come.

"Say to them at 'Wunda' that I cannot (pause for a moment) go in swimming today. They will understand."

I have gathered myself together with instant espresso. Here—I'll write it all down:

Mirabile Dictu: When the Sky Fell in on Chicken Little, or How Our Lady's Juggler Lost His Balls

All the long week I had misgivings about the proposed Sunday dinner with Stanley's family. No worse than meals at home, I assured myself: the roast beef my brother brought his fiancée home to chew, a birthday turkey over at Lil's.

It's like riding a bike: one does not forget. The beast will be devoured. A pie will be sliced. We will face each other in a ritualistic tension of politeness: the old mother and the unmarried sister, the woman who's taking the son away, the son who would have us sign a treaty before we survey boundaries and lay claim to our possession. We will speak and eat—their house will be all around me, unfamiliar: *their* chairs, *their* lamps. My pocketbook is a foreign concept to them. I remembered that when Francis brought home Joan-the-betrothed, she wore baby-doll shoes with ankle straps, and my mother thought she was a strumpet, despite the miraculous medal poking out of her blouse . . . and I had hidden the antimacassars off the living-room set out of shame—which made my mother curse me and cry, until, out of shame, I stuck all the starched lace scraps back again.

I called Stanley at his office. "What's so important about me going to Brooklyn?"

"You're upset over nothing," Stanley said. "And you know we didn't argue about those artist people, Ag."

"No?"

"No," he said with gruff male authority, "you're afraid of Brooklyn. You've backed down three times and it's beginning to look fishy."

"Oh? Well, does your mother like candy?"

"I'm paying eight hundred dollars to have every tooth in her head stuffed with gold."

I could not touch any of the episodes in the Lydia Savaard story. It made me feel a cheat to look in on her sane world and move the figures about, contemplate conclusions for their esthetic merit. So on Tuesday night I fiddled with a love poem—easy as song lyrics is what I had in mind: And if time tell on us/ We shall tell time/ Our dictates as our pulse grows fast . . . and I set the paper on fire in the bottom of the metal waste basket. By the time Lydia arrived with a pot of water it was ashes.

"Mary Agnes! What's got *in*-to you?"

A close call, for I might have found solace in academic doodling.

And on Wednesday while Lydia watched from her sickbed I flung open the closet door and tried on every piece of clothing I owned. Her cold had come back, to spite the miracle drug prescribed by Henry's doctor, and she coughed herself into fits, then lay wheezing, deflated, with the mock-up of *Pip the Poodle* sliding off the blankets to the floor.

"What's wrong with that one, Ag?"—referring to the black dress I wear to the office.

"A hard career woman. Imagine what Mrs. Sarnicki has in mind for her son—the demure girl, wife and mother, and in comes this big bruiser with the black dress, simulated pearls, executive shoes." One by one I threw my New York clothes into the reject pile.

Lydia spoke through the clog of mucus in her head: "I thought you liked those hand-loomed dresses."

"I do, but not for Canarsie. Not one button that says I am different from you, Momma Sarnicki, or different from your daughter there, Helen with her secretarial girdle and orlon goodness, because I am not different (if I can lure your attention from that nasal spray): I, too, would give my very life for your dear boy."

"Aren't you serious about this, Mary Agnes?"

I didn't give her an answer.

My red silk dress, lonely rag it seemed, though it was only a year since I bought it at the local Bon Ton, back home on the one street of shops in our town. As I pulled that dress on, for the first time I caught sight of a little paper label stitched into its seam: "Rayon and Acetate." *Comme on dit:* screwed again. With the front buttoned the dress would not zip up past my thick middle. With the zipper forced the buttons popped at the breast. Lydia recommended a gusset, but the costume doesn't become me now. I see myself, falsely gay, free as a kindergarten teacher in red rayon acetate, with, perhaps, an ankle bracelet under a seductive film of nylon hose, promising the touch of metal and fussy little catches that do not open.

Thursday I leave the office early and dash up to the good store, famous, expensive, self-conscious. I find my way through nostalgia-land of Victorian Easter eggs and gilt Italian cocks so desirable they would make a simple soul deny Christ, three, six, a dozen times. I am sucked up express to the floor which specializes in Lydia Savaard dresses; something that covers the body, not complicated in any way: just a dress that shows the world a possible creature, not male, but incidentally the other sex, a creature that can be dealt with—like the clean tabby next door. A saleswoman who does not like me because my face is made of skin comes around the velvet rotunda. "What are you looking for?" (Say you are after an androgynous toga that will not unsettle your lover's family, for they are all unaware.)

"You look about an eighteen . . ."

The saleswoman is runtish; no manner of life or breeding has raised her up, yet she is not servile.

"Maybe even a twenty." And she leads me contemptuously to the fat rack. (Tell her you are the size of a woman who can support the weight of a large man but prefers to disguise this accomplishment with an arrangement of pockets and pleats suggesting horsehair cushions as harmless as the old settee.)

"There's this in black."

"No black." I fix the small woman with a mysterious smile.

"Black is always good. You can dress it up or dress it down." (Let her know that you are not a widow, but a girl to be presented for the first time, pushing thirty-six —having pushed—and somehow traditional white seems wrong, strains even the old queen's credulity, and she so used to the costume balls at court.)

"No black."

"We have that also in a green."

"Nothing Irish."

"Any pah-*tic*ular color?" the little woman snarls at me thinking I've come merely to keep her on her feet. "Navy is very popular for spring." She snaps out a dress—ideal: a navy-blue uniform, white collar and cuffs, grosgrain tie, nice deep hem—oh, it's a well-made garment. (Ask if the Mother Superior buys the material by the bolt from a firm in Boston.)

"That's a very excellent fit on you," the saleslady says, alluding to my hips. "You can dress that up or dress it down."

At home, Lydia Savaard peeped out of her croup tent and smiled her approval. She would have bought the very dress. Presuming I was on the right track, I started a chicken soup and whipped up a blanc mange to tempt her queasy stomach. At last I could take on Brooklyn; I celebrated with a quart of ice cream drenched in fudge sauce, and tried to read one of the books that had been waiting for a month or more: Nerval's *Sylvie*. It was too thin for my taste now; I took it personally that his crazed love was for an elusive virgin and that his dreams held more reality than life. I went to bed but didn't sleep, thinking I might write a deceptively uneventful story in which dreams fade into the bitter past as reality makes demands that are more fantastic—here might be the focus for my work on Lydia Savaard. She coughed hard during the night in her corner of the room.

On Friday Bert Sigal said that Wunda-Clutch needed a new package for the big retail push. We conferred; our image would be friendly and familiar, not sniggling anti-zipper but largess, dignity—an established product on the American scene. Sigal was excited about a Wunda Fairy, an eviscerated blonde he had in mind, who would fly about our future advertising pointing out secret-safe closures with a magic wand. I saw her as a gadfly—tricky, bitchy, deceitful

—and was told to come up with something better by Monday if I was so wise, because he, Bert, and the salesmen were on the move. And he moved fast out of my office, a hard tight-built little fellow, forever calling to mind a bad impersonation of Jimmy Cagney. The retail aspect was exceptional—his cocky head popped back in the door—and that was one gravy train he was not going to miss.

And on the same day, Friday, I met Stanley for lunch in an Italian restaurant. He kissed me on the cheek and said "dear," the way men do when they are thinking about their work.

"I bought a dress to meet your mother."

"Great." He wore a stubby tie clip I had not seen, with his initial, a squat golden S. I hated it. I told myself that if every sock and pajama pattern wasn't to my taste I could go live under a glass bell.

Though we ordered different meals our plates came awash in the same red sauce. We smiled at each other.

"I'll wear the dress tomorrow night."

He didn't answer. We went on to iceberg lettuce and tasteless winter tomatoes. Stanley asked if I had watched a certain courtroom drama last night.

"I don't have a television set."

"Yeah, that's right!"

I found myself telling him a lie: "I went to the theater."

"Again?"

I let that pass. "It was an early Chekhov . . . have you seen much Chekhov?"

"Lydia still sick?"

"Yes. She can't possibly pack up and trot off to the nut house this week. A martyr—when I see her with the suitcase and the mature, 'Once more into the breach . . .'"

"Mary Agnes—the poor girl!"

"I know, the poor girl, Stoshie," and I knew the awful things that were coming out of my mouth; "but we've all put in our time."

"They sure murdered this eggplant."

"What do you think about tomorrow?" I asked. "Shall we go to a movie?"

"I can't make it," Stanley said, looking at his watch.

"Tomorrow is Saturday."

"I'll see you on Sunday, dear."

"What is this, Stoshie? Do you put in a certain number of hours with me, dear, so Sunday afternoon makes up for Saturday night?" I was shrill and cheap like the possessive women who make scenes in public places.

"Look, Ag." He touched me, his large forgiving hand. "I promised Helen and my mother I'd take them to this wedding."

"I don't give a damn where you're going . . ."

"It's Helen's girl friend who is getting married. Her girl friend from about the fifth grade."

"Good luck to her." I was sick of the whole Italian restaurant with placemats of Pan Am flight schedules covering dirty linen.

"How do you think it looks anyway, Ag, if I come into Manhattan on Saturday and stay late, and then on Sunday, in a few hours, I get up and go to bring you home for dinner? Let's go easy, that's all."

"It looks like I'm a whore."

"Aw, come on now!"

"That's perfectly all right." I sprang up and grabbed my coat, which he put on my shoulders with an excess of gentle patty-cakes. We dashed out of the restaurant, the money for our lunch shoved at the gangster who owns the place and thinks I don't know what food tastes like.

Out on the street I degraded myself by laughing at a midget who was rocking heroically across the pavement toward the waiting stream of mammoth cars.

"I have to get back early," I said, "for the big retail push."

"Can't you listen, Ag?" He led me along Ninth Avenue,

bleak land of marginal dry-good stores and kitchen-supply warehouses. Here a frump walked a smart-looking lap dog to the gutter. "You wouldn't be acting this way if you weren't all nerved up about Sunday."

"I love you. Oh, I love you." I flung myself crazily at him, my mouth against his suggesting any pleasure I could give. "Don't go back to the office. Listen, I know how we can recover this whole desperate lunch hour."

Stanley had a lot of hand-lettering to do that afternoon. Sensibly he put me in a cab for Wunda-Clutch. I was bad, but I might have been worse. I might have said that since Lydia would be home steaming her head and putting drops up her nose we would not even have found a place to rut in.

What seems shocking now is that I went ahead with the whole shooting match. After work on Friday I betook myself to the cute man at the beauty salon and had myself set in suburban curls instead of the usual vixen peaks and kiss-me-quicks. I stopped for groceries too, so it was late—nine, nine-thirty—when I arrived at the apartment to find Lydia drifting about the empty rooms.

"I can't go to Connecticut," she sighed, settling uselessly in the center of the love seat. Then she remembered. "Ag, someone has been trying to get you long distance."

"My family. There's no one else long distance."

Nevertheless, when the phone rang it was for Lydia, Henry calling with his own change, for he had sold a frigate in a Johnny Walker bottle. She spoke to him in a low caress of a teen-age tease, and then came dreaming in the kitchen door and watched me put a roast and potatoes in the oven.

"Who's that for?"

"The Schwartzes drop in on Friday nights—unless you'd rather not—"

"The linoleum lady!" Lydia said with a pretty laugh. She was ever so happy after her talk with Henry, and came over to show me the secret smile on her dry cracked lips. "I'll go to bed early, don't you think?" Behind this lay the notion, amusing re Mordecai, Flo, and their family of bang-around babies, that she really should put on her Junior League frill and pass the cookies.

"You need your rest," I said.

"Henry is sweet. He's better, Ag, so much better." She tittered and sobbed with relief. Then we were absolutely delighted about Henry Savaard, who I haven't set eyes on yet. Look at all those crutches and canes and steel braces, she exclaimed, look—abandoned the artificial limbs and rubber breasts. Oh, see! Here is a dish of discarded glass eyes. "Oh, see Jane. See the dog," said Dick. "Oh, see Dick. See. See the dog," said Jane. But Doctor, things like this don't happen in medical science. Yes, my boy, we make mistakes. You see, we're learning all the time. That is why we never give up hope: Miracles Do Happen . . . and some-where in a remote laboratory is a man no one has heard of yet, a quiet creep with frayed cuffs who's asking impossible questions to find a possible answer. Truth is elusive, son, but today we have found one answer, one small truth for you, and tomorrow, who knows, tomorrow all the pain and sick-ness of the human race . . . Music up as Lydia Savaard skips off to her cot.

I know what she is thinking, from one or two words spilled like pearls from a broken strand: I know she is dream-ing of a vine-covered cottage, woolly dogs, drinks before dinner. It's more to be pitied than my wild shenanigans, for she is being courted by a deranged man who sliced her up, and now wonders if she hasn't been wrong emasculat-ing our fairy tales, because sometimes even the most wicked old witch eating up the sweetest child-meat regurgitates at happy-ending time to make it the happiest time of all.

Then, Ladies and Gentlemen: I started my Sauce Mornay for the frozen broccoli, feeling that Flo, Mordecai, Ginny, Beard Poet, et al., might be slighted by meat and potatoes without the gourmet touch which says "Ma Keely loves ya." Take two tablespoons of flour and two of butter. Make a *roux* and add your stock (1 cup). Good stock, mind you, made up during the week out of veal bones, ground meat, onion studded with cloves, and your *bouquet garni*. Grate the imported Gruyère (½ cup) and add slowly, stirring constantly with a wire whisk and answer the phone.

A morbid voice said: "Your mother" (an insidious phrase used by Francis throughout the conversation), "your mother is a sick woman."

"Yes."

"What do you mean, 'Yes'?" he asked.

"What's wrong?" To myself I said, this is it, Ag. Hitch up, honey—they want you back in the disaster area.

"They don't know what's wrong yet. She goes into the hospital for tests on Monday. . . ." Francis let that sink in. I could see him, the manly type breaking the news, "and for an operation."

"What are they operating *on?*" I demanded. God help me, I had forgotten some details of the *mystique* of sickness: two steps back and three forward, right into the center of a rotted kidney or a malignant womb. Softens the blow —"Oh, Kate—she's had a time of it," my mother would say. "My, she's had a lot of difficulty. Oh, she's had her troubles, yes . . . well, They Took A Polyp Out Of Her Bowel The Size Of Your Fist."

"They are going to open her up," said Francis, "to see what's there . . . and to start with, what's wrong is your nonsense in New York. That's what's wrong. A woman your age . . . I tell you, Joan has had it, dragging the kids down on weekends to try and get your mother to a doctor. You know what Mae and Lil are. They work on each other's nerves . . ."

He went on. Francis, my big brother who pinned up my pants in the schoolyard when the elastic broke and gave me two Walnettos out of his pack; there were no surprises here, and yet each time it's news. In the hallway where Lydia and I have the phone there is no chair or table. The instrument is set on the floor, where we trip over it, and there I squatted listening to Francis' high-minded lecture and my own thumping heart. I said, "Any time but this weekend, Francis. I *would* go to her. But not *this* weekend."

"Your mother is all alone," he said. "I'll have to tell Aunt Mae to go and stay with her until the ambulance comes Monday morning. And another thing, your mother has precious little to live on. Mae is on Social Security . . ."

"I'll pay," I cried eagerly, "don't think I won't pay. I'll send a check special delivery to Mae for her trouble."

"You do that." Francis hung up.

I was crouched in the hall with my thought, I suppose she is going to die, when the knock came: Flo's textural excitement with wood. In they marched: Flo carrying a basket of jelly jars, Mordecai hailing me with a demonic Yah, Ginny girl-poet, bearded boy-poet, two flip-wrist "designers," and Chutney.

Chutney was sex all up and down, the big beautiful Negro man we are told not to dream of, but the myth is in our reactionary thighs: Listen, girls! He wore a guitar and that's all I can remember, and he never spoke, but sang —only sang moaning music; each mounting note held desire, and it would get faster, you know, and breathe off into whispers. Ginny, who claimed she would make it in Grant's tomb, had found Chutney for herself. I should have known she wouldn't bother to run uptown to any cold mausoleum —she was ready for the next dark corner she could drag her black god into.

"Yah," yelled Mordecai, "oh yah," setting up competition for Chutney's erotic strumming, while the rest of us were still settling our haunches in a campfire circle round the room.

"Jazz in the real days—what we had you could feel like a shot. It turned you right on, didn't it, Flo? It jagged you in a group, and not family-style either, punks."

"Syncopation is the essence of contemporary thought."
Flo stood apart from the fray, her straight Indian hair
whipping her cheeks like two coarse tails.

"Yah." Mordecai looked to her for assurance, nudging
Ginny's drab hand away from Chutney's ankle, a conspicu-
ously un-socked, delectable flare of bone. Flo flipped back
the straw mat and shut us all out. There in the linoleum
was her vision: decent, containable like cells seen through a
microscope, lacking the sweep of color, the great gesture
of life. With nervous speed she unscrewed the little jelly
jars blazing with bright dye.

The sauce is ruined. (Dump it. Have another drink.)

"What you writing, Ma?" jibed the bearded boy.

"Bread-and-butter things."

"You got something to eat?"

"The roast isn't done."

"Pecky cypress!" screamed one designer.

"Wormy chestnut!" screamed the other.

"Quiet, please. My friend is sick and trying to sleep."

Ginny writhed and Chutney built down to the cool silence
of a pantomime strum, while Flo with the determination of
twenty years' hard work splashed her dyes on my linoleum.

"Yah. Once there was a fat lady got on the subway,
Fifty-ninth and Lexington—we are nasty people. This fat
lady . . ."

"The drop of blood in a fertile egg touches deep to the
self," Flo pronounced.

"My mother always threw those eggs away," I said, "even
when we couldn't afford it, she threw them in the garbage.
They turned her sick."

"Nasty, yah, once there was another fat lady came in the
Automat every day for the egg-salad plate. Shoveled it in
while she talked to herself about how her old man arranged
her upside down, only one of the fellas working there finds
out she is a maiden lady lives with her sister. Yah—" Mordecai got himself into a choking fit on this one, ". . . and

the wipe-ups lingered, see, pushing the slop trolleys near her table, scraping softly to hear the details—collector's items—yah—of the fat lady and the phantom."

I poured a drink for Flo and one for myself, so when I remembered the roast and potatoes I'd missed the succulent, rare moment. Still I did not move.

"Pongee!" said one.

"*Toile de Jouy!*" the other.

"Sh-sh . . . she's trying to rest. She is not well." And my mother sick in an empty house, making her way to the bathroom and back with no one to play to, except Mae, who was not one to pick up dirty Kleenex without commenting on the dust rats under the bed—nor would the state of the toilet bowl be to her liking.

"One day she took the salad plate, O.K., everything as usual, but loaded up on the sweets: rice pudding, cheese blintz, cherry pie à la mode. Yah, so we all started moving in, see, with our sponges, our rags dripping . . ."

"No one cares," I said. Flo was in her color pots. The bearded boy was reading, Ginny twitching, Chutney singing:

> Glaudiamus figitur,
> Figitur est Rigitur—

"Tiger pelting," cried the one.

"Self-welting," the other.

"What do you want to tell us these foul things for?" And I went out to the kitchen steady as I could, where, as predicted, the dinner was spoiled, and served it anyway—for who can disappoint the hungry? Two young spooks with electric guitars had arrived and Flo berated them for stomping on her linoleum.

They all eat, everything but the plants, heh-heh, and drink my good liquor and their own gallon of upstate Tokay. Once, in a moment of fearful clarity, the Mornay curds stopping up the drain, I turn and see Lydia Savaard in her glen plaid bathrobe standing in the kitchen door as though at the gates of hell.

And Stanley by this time must be well on his way at the bachelor party for Helen's friend-from-the-fifth-grade's boy friend. I suppose he was laughing at those jokes men tell, and drinking blended whiskey, like they say, while at home his mother and sister, hair wound in curlers, press their finery. Knowing how the trivial rituals are performed sucks me under while the new people dance and sing, fight and splatter my floor, lick the beef bones right before my eyes. Ginny is hot now, rocking with Chutney while he sings. Now I hear his words—"I got the Coca-Cola"—in the plum lovely voice of a West Indian:

> I got the Coca-Cola
> I got the Pepsi too
> I got the Orange Soda—
> > Man, buy it in the fa-ma-lee,
> > Buy it in the fa-ma-lee size.

Pale, flat girl—an obscenity dancing—while he is first-rate, sex the way it should be, not the way they think it up. Mordecai describes his most inspired work. "Nothing like the classics. Right, Flo? Maraschino cherry on cottage cheese ball on pineapple ring on lettuce leaf."

"Who reads French, Ma?" The boy with the beard, posturing over my books.

"I do."

"It's been a long time since I read any Baudelaire." He looks at me with memories in hand sweet as old-fashioned peppermints that he wants to bring up and show me.

"And how long ago could that be?"

"I went to France in the summer with my mother and read all the books lying around the villa."

"Say, that is dandy."

"The Deli-Delite. Yah! Parsley on chopped chicken liver.

The lemon wedge, gherkin, two black olives—on curly endive."

"Could you lower your voice?"

Thanks for nothing. Aunt Mae will never be able to find the bed pan . . . kept in the back of the linen closet under a pile of new sheets that we could never touch because we were forever using up the mended gray ones and because my mother never liked to admit that the apparatus for sickness was on hand (the syringe was buried there and the glass urinal from the time my father had scarlet fever). There would be a terrible scramble about respectable nightgowns for going to the hospital.

"The arbor hung over the Mediterranean, like being inside of greenness, the earth, my hands on the book of poems, the lizards were green, the air smelled green."

"Cerulean!"

"Flamingo!"

Flo swirled blood, egg, black-caviar juices on my floor in the midst of the rising music. Oblivious? No, she heard Mordecai through her back. For years she had listened to his Yah climb to a psychotic pitch, and she knew the moment he would need tending to as surely as another wife knew when to put a glycerine tablet under the stricken man's tongue. I poured us another drink.

"You read this French, Ma?"

"Not any more I don't."

"You're too busy with The Job."

"Listen, son, I don't think a dog and a whore and a piece of paper in the street is all that special to look at any more. We've been there in every art film. Why don't you break new ground, my boy, write your poems in grunts, static sounds, transistor babble—it's not available to me—but you, you can write hilarious verses without language about small blond children who die of obsolete diseases and leave lonely toys behind, melting snowmen, half-played games."

The music stopped—a hush in the room. I was center

stage, delivering my sottish discourse: *"Fertilisante douleur?* Who needs to be told? Why not dispense? Why not dispense with the message?" They sat in my parlor silent as strangers observing each other on a subway; surely my great moment was at hand.

But a rank amateur upstaged me: a woman screamed out in agony from the bedroom. Then Ginny's voice in the hall —a terrible word, scuffling bodies. Mordecai showed himself first, cuckolded little fellow in corduroy, dragging Ginny by the scruff of her dirt-ringed neck, she with her head down like a daughter who's come in late and messed-up to a fierce father.

"Leave the girl alone," Flo commanded. "Get your coat."

"I saw her making for him all night, didn't I, Flo? Yah, she needs a wallop."

"Put the coat on," Flo directed in a hard voice, packing up the jelly jars, and yah, said Mordecai once more, a weak catch in the throat.

Chutney appeared, his shirt unbuttoned: the startling darkness of his smooth chest. I would have liked to touch him, but I was sober then. I watched him pull on his sweater, hitch the guitar string round his neck.

Mordecai flew at him, but Chutney held him at length, simply held him up and out for us to see, the puny pretender to art and sex and *la vie bohème*. I should have been on the end of that black arm, I should have been there too, a midget in his hand.

Mordecai screeched, "Jig, yah, jig!"

"Boss," Chutney smiled his high pearly teeth on us, "try being a nigger one Saturday night, you never want to be a white man again." He set Mordecai down, and said slow and tranquil: "There is a lady weeping in the other room."

Exit Chutney with the guitar, Ginny hot in pursuit.

"Trompe l'œil!"

"Faux bambou!"

Then they turned goosey goodkins, tutting and thanking

227

me for a delicious dinner. How was I to know they were not stock tweedledum characters? Out of place in the scene? Certainly not. They purchased all Flo's materials, a third off to the trade. Mordecai, crumpled over a stairpost in the hallway, waited for Flo, who said: "Don't turn that rug back over my composition until the stains are thoroughly dry."

I slammed the door in her face and turned to find the bearded boy lingering, my books tucked under his arm. "Can I borrow these, Ma?"

"Sure," I said, handing him the last coat left on the floor. "They're yours. Take them. Take the paper off the walls if you can get it."

"Seriously, Ma—" he put on his coat, flipped the saint's hood over his head—"give me ten bucks."

"Get out of here." I shoved him out the door. I should never have put my hands on the boy, for I felt more than his frail shoulder, more than spare bones under a thin coat—I felt yet another body torturing itself for some mad notion.

"Suppose I starve, Ma?" he called through the door. "Suppose I get the malnutrition and starve, lady?"

"Then starve." I cried softly, "then starve," for I was aware of Lydia Savaard, an off-stage presence. I thought the music must have kept her awake to begin with, and she would have heard the beating, sighing bodies in my bed, so close to hers in that small back room. What had she seen? Enough to make a lady weep, but she never said a word, only gazed down on me in the morning with shock hidden by pity and pity overlaid with gauzy wisdom. She did not chastise, but started to build again—order in the kitchen, ammonia in the bathroom; and even the night before, when I finally put myself to bed, I could not help but notice that she had already changed the sheets.

My town was medium in size, a small city, so I knew people. The names and faces went together, and some faces, in a casual glance, displayed long histories to me, for I knew the wife, the brother of a man; had, most likely, gone to school with his children, entered the rooms of his house and seen his clothes hung out to dry upon the line. I'd heard what ailed his body and detected the care with which he dealt a dollar to the corner grocer, or, penniless, called out with bravado to cover fear, "Put this on my account, will you, Louie?" as he stole out the shame-tinkling door with a nickel pie. Sometimes—as with the drunken postman or the cruel woman gym teacher—I felt it was this public knowledge, more than any personal complaint, that troubled their souls.

Al Esposito was one nice guy who I met when I took my first course at the Waterbury extension of the New Haven State Teachers' College (an institution that now goes by a grander name). We came to know each other in a big schoolroom meant for little children, jammed into junior seats with the penetrating odor of orange peel, graphite, Vicks cough drops, and goodness knows what daytime misfortunes lingering in the air. On the windows the paper cutouts changed from turkeys to bells to cherry trees to bunnies to American flags as Al despairingly pursued the intricacies of the English language. He was a big ape of a man—low forehead, long arms—and he worked himself into awful sweats in the little school seat, blotting his thick neck, honking his flat nose behind an immaculate handkerchief.

Why Esposito now? Why Esposito on this Monday morning of self-abuse? It will take time to do justice to this moral tale while the strands—Stanley Sarnicki, Lydia Savaard, Wunda-Clutch—lie tangled on the workshop floor, while my mother lies stretched out against the sky. Still, it is worth any risk to command a history, whether you (those who sort my pages) like it or not. Now that you—let me slip into the familiar second person—have come into being at the ends of the jump rope there are new rules. I must skip to the most diverting rhymes, and list, so as to keep you constantly turning, five cars, ten actresses, soaps, fruits, cigarettes. The art will not be in my breath lasting longer than your arm, but in my artful persistence: the antic demands will deceive you into thinking that you turn with some skill; and that will give you pleasure, so that at the end when I falter or just stand and let the rope beat at my ankles, O diligent reader, you will not see that I mean to stop the game. And if the whole thing comes off, then *you* in the retelling of your part can say with a proud self-effacing shrug, "Yes, I am not bad at turning double-dutch," when in fact *I* have no mind for that sort of serious Queen of the Block accomplishment at all.

When Al Esposito copied the answers from my workbook he did not think he was cribbing, he was ah jus see'n if he got it ah right. I could not help but respect the passionate desire for self-improvement which had brought this strong man to such a humble seat, and soon I was printing my answers in black ink with a thick nubbed pen so they would be easy to read across the aisle. But alas, the workbook itself was too complex, and he watched with envy as our master, Dr. McNulty, drew his bloodless hands expertly down the flapping oversized page. We filled in blanks, checked boxes, overscored egregious grammar *gaffes,* commaed and coloned and capitalized indecent paragraphs all nude and open on pages that creased from left to right, or folded back with the answers on the reverse side: 1d, 2a, 3e. Upon occasion we were directed to tear whole pages out and check our partner's test against Dr. McNulty's indisputable answers chalked in fancy backhand on the blackboard: gerund, whose, ly, Tues., participle, Dear Senator Monroe. Esposito had copied my paper exactly except that the blanks to be filled in were all off by one number—ly became the abbreviation for Tuesday, and, most touching, the informal epistolary address of the Senator was dropped to the bottom margin where the words sat like three uncomprehending savages on the rim of a civilized world.

One night in the middle of the school year when we had turned the last page of the workbook in some tricky fashion, Dr. McNulty announced in his ladylike voice that seemed to sit behind the ugly oak desk, behind the double-breasted suit, behind the boring tie and rimless glasses: "We are now prepared to write themes, or at least to try ourselves in the art of English composition; for it is an art, ladies and gentlemen, and if we bear this fact in mind perhaps the goal itself will elevate the effort of our strivings." From that point on each evening class was launched by five minutes of ministerial gibberish which even then, in this my first escape from the Zipper-Momma syndrome, I suspected was the prattling of a semiliterate whose veins coursed with some thin distasteful liquid—celery water or birch beer. But to Al Esposito, McNulty was the wise man, the articulate man he could never be.

"This is risible," Dr. McNulty sang out to us each week in his distant cultured tones as he fluttered Esposito's paper in the air, "that we should assemble to learn the fine art of composition and have no thoughts beyond the mundane, the commonplace machinations of our workaday world. I will give no names, to spare the sensibility" (here we were let in on a girlish irony), "the sensibility, ladies and gentlemen, of our *Author*."

"My Role in American Democracy" was our first attack upon the written word. Al had met it straight on. His theme was titled "Western Beef," though our teacher pointed out that he had been kind enough to give us the ideal heading for our papers. "I am a meat cutter," Al began. "I work down Western Beef on Housatonic Street beginning since the army and know all different cuts like Chuck Bone and Newport Roast." My attempt to reproduce Al Esposito's true American prose will only turn his style into parody, and that would strike the wrong note; for what he revealed in his themes was all that he knew about himself, eloquent details of love, folly, and the terrible doom of self-betrayal which he saw would come upon him.

He knew all the cuts and was the proudest butcher at the wholesale meat company, so proud that he never left his block like the others who delighted in unloading the refrigerated cars or riding around the city in delivery trucks. In his army jacket and bloodstained apron he stayed all day in the icebox cutting up the noble steer, the delicate calf, the shorn lamb, the hulk of hog—whacking and slitting and slicing dead animal flesh with the *finesse* of a surgeon. Al, with *his* knives, *his* cleaver, could get every pound to pay out of a pig better than any of them, and he dared us to match his rolled crown of lamb on special order. The spirit of democracy was forgotten: it was his arrogant boast that he was not only the best cutter but the fastest, though he allowed that only in the United States of America was the Board of Health working for all its people in making every man, even the "hacker"—a lousy kid butcher who didn't deserve to touch a side of beef—wash his hands each time in the lavatory.

When we were asked to describe an object—Dr. McNulty had a vase or an oil painting in mind—Al Esposito wrote a theme about veal cutlets which was so beautifully explicit I shall always seek and never find in the cheating world that ideal slab of pink springy calf-flesh, cut exactly across the grain, its bone ring set with marrow shading from ruby to garnet, slightly off center in a perfection of asymmetry which we take for granted in nature and praise in art. The tender transparent sinews must trisect the cutlet to form a bold composition that is not visible at first but comes to one slowly as the pattern of bone circle within flesh circle emerges. Oh, the tenses, connectives, clauses, and such, were not to McNulty's liking, but that cutlet was honestly admired and fully seen; *I* see it still, and where is my perfectly written page and a half of faked-up enthusiasm for *Blue Boy* or Venus de Milo? As dead in memory as a rule of grammar.

"We must widen our vistas," Dr. McNulty exhorted; "in this modern age of travel and communication, we must open our minds to new experience available to us through the miracles of science, and yet I see that one in our midst was inspired by our topic, "My Most Unforgettable Experience," to tell us about a . . . a . . ."—at this point he decided to be at a loss for words— ". . . a personal failure almost too ludicrous to read to the assembled class; and yet it affords such plentiful examples of the English language twisted and tortured into vulgar phrases that we will find it, if you can bear with me, richly rewarding."

Al creaked and sweated in his seat, dangled his gorilla arms between bowed legs with no more protest than an occasional grunt of pain. He might have flattened that anemic reflection of a man, McNulty, with one big cleaver fist, but our teacher was protected by his desk, by his glimmering eyeglasses, by his title, by his empty claims to the finer way of life.

It was unforgettable, indeed, the day that Al Esposito went down to Western Beef and found the "hacker" at his block defiling a spring lamb so the bones chipped into the choice chops, and for another joke all the guys had done something else which was not so nice, which he could not tell in his theme, and he was so enraged, for it was only two weeks till his wedding (and the joke had something to do with that). He took a hind quarter of beef off the hook and smacked into the shank so blind with anger that he chopped the index and middle fingers off his left hand. There were the stumps for all to see, tied off at the first joint like hideous white sausages, emblems of his trade that would go with him always to remind Al of a disgraceful performance, to remind us that too much love and care can make a man foolish in the eyes of his fellow men who simply take their pay checks and go away.

After that "*most* risible" paper, Esposito's work improved in the colorless eyes of Dr. McNulty. Where did he get the stuff?—correct sentences that did not hang together at all —out of encyclopedias and magazines, I suppose. "Keep this up!," "Good Work!," Dr. McNulty wrote on his papers, which Al, hurt and perplexed, showed me after class. "The Two-Party System," "Our Natural Resources," "The Pleasures of Reading"—only once did Al backtrack and give us a peep into the now secret world of his obsession. The words were a part of himself: on the page they sparkled like bright fillets—fresh, tender, rare, surrounded by the tired canned prose of the *National Geographic*.

"Truly, Peru is a land of contrasts," Al Esposito had written out in his large hand; "the rich and the poor, the fine and the crude . . ." and so on, until, thinking about McNulty's proposal for the week—"The Wonderful World of Travel"—he said that though it wasn't much to be a meat cutter he sure would like to go to Italy, where his mother told him animals hung in the shop windows so you could see the whole beast in his hide when you bought your dinner. His wife, Gloria, had come into the refrigerator down at Western Beef one day and said how disgusting, and made like she was going to be sick, but Al thought it was natural to want to see what you were eating before you got it on a plate with a mess of potatoes. "The tin industry alone," Al's paper went on, "constitutes over eighty per cent of the gross national income and employs nearly three-fourths of all unskilled Peruvian workers."

Dr. McNulty cleared his throat. "How many times, since the inception of this course, have I stressed the benefits of an outline in order that we may not fall into the pit of disorganization. If ever we hope to express ourselves in the written word we must—this is the last time I intend to stress the point—we must employ the outline as the framework of our thoughts."

It was clear sailing for Al after this reprimand; though he no longer squirmed in his seat, he developed an unhappy blinking of the eyes during class as though trying to see a distant fading light. "You've come a long way," McNulty wrote on his last theme at the end of May. "Three cheers!"

That summer I found myself over a display of liver slopped in plastic bags. I rang the service bell in our first supermarket to beg for the specially indigestible chunk of mutton my mother insists on for her Irish stew, and Al appeared over the freezer from behind a mirrored panel, dressed in a starched white coat with name tag: Meat Manager, Mr. Esposito. We smiled in happy recognition. I would like to report some sign of shame in his face, but no—only a feigned embarrassment at his own good fortune and a blinking suspicion of the whole foggy world. The cold counter between us exhibited bits and pieces of animals, all phonied into promiscuous attitudes, with lumps of grizzle, sinew, and bone hidden underneath. Al's hamburg was as fat as you'll find anywhere, sprinkled with paprika to give it the meaty look.

Now he wears a Tyrolean hat: he travels around in a small foreign car as a general factotum of the frozen-food trade. About a year ago in the parking lot out at the Mid-State Mall I caught him talking to ancient Dr. McNulty, and I drew back into the doorway of a shoe store to watch them, man to man—exchange of risible guff, Mr. Esposito's gloved hand upon the old man's stooped shoulder in a patronizing gesture of camaraderie. Knowing I would never be heard over the din of a stupefying Strauss waltz piped out of the discount store, I cried out, "Hip, hip, hooray!" three cheerless times.

At least in the big city we are strangers one to another. We carry our faces like masks which betray only the abstract of an emotion. What I imagine about a mouth drawn on in an eternal smile may be better, or worse, much worse, than what I knew for fact about faces with names in the fairy-tale town where I spent too much of my life. But not for real. Still, God help me, think what the world may conjure up from a look at me. . . . The rope is wearing out against the pavement, I am stalling, stalling for time. We've been through the fifty states and are up to Y my name is Yolanda, my husband's names is Yves. We come from Yemen and on our ship we bring back Yoghurt. What? Have I patronized you, *mon hypocrite lecteur?* That was surely tasteless enough, so I won't add: Don't you know I didn't mean it? Don't you know it's all a front, like my face now to the strangers on the city streets—full fat face of a funny lady.

My story goes on: Saturday morning after the Chutney rumpus, I'm sick at heart watching Lydia go about the housecleaning with her runny nose. She discovers the ruined linoleum. It could make a lady weep. Stoically, she begins to pull the mat over Flo's work without a tear, and then: "Why, Mary Agnes! Look, isn't it beautiful with these colors?"

At my feet a great sweep of life, or, rather, the promise of life in the golden crimson fertility, dropped like a joyful scrim over the stultifying, always menacing pattern of marble linoleum.

She asks, "Can't we leave the mat off so that we can look at it?"

"Why not?"

Thinking of the big trip to Canarsie, I eat a lot: toast and jam, a bag of peanuts; but it hardly touches my hunger. Unable to settle, I ask Lydia, "Want anything at the drugstore?"

"No, thank you." She is writing a long letter to Henry that makes her bite her pen coyly and hum an old love tune.

Outside it drizzles. The presentable curls fall flat. I ride uptown, vaguely on my way to the Guggenheim, but get out to see the shop where they are pushing gaudy orange beach clothes for the last simple souls who want to escape south. This is no more fantastic than the Easter business they have started already in other windows: chicks, duckies

with eggs too big to be mauve, to be pink—laid by pre-
historic eagles.

> Madam, do not put that bonnet on.
> Still our world is lavender and weeping.
> Your winter hat of felt is more in keeping. . . .

With a criminal headache I wander over to Broadway
and buy a ticket to the matinee of a play I never intended
to see. Things are less jangly in the red plush seat, only the
actress who has the second lead reminds me of Sherry—
how she was at about thirty, not so pretty as Sherry but
trying nearly as hard. The play is about people coming in
and out of an American living room, very nice room with a
marble coffee table, pots of flowers, and a lot of dummy
books. Some woman is infatuated with a well-preserved
boulevardier until her husband invites the girl like Sherry
to come for the weekend. They keep changing their clothes.
They all keep coming in and out of the room: sometimes
they have to go to the bathroom and other times they have
to get ice for their drinks. The wife discovers her husband
with that wench (it is innocent we know) and says well,
pardon her, she only wanted to use the phone. Once a man
comes in to look for a book—not very likely—and carries
it up a pleasant staircase, stage left. The audience laughs a
lot with some effort. The end of a long run, perhaps the
end of this sort of thing altogether. After the second act I
go to a restaurant which has Muzak issuing from the walls
at no customers. I want a straight whiskey, but fear the
waitress.

"What'll you have?"

"I think I'll try one of those Manhattans." And I have
another; I eat, knowing the food is left over from lunch on
the steam tables. Little Whiskers—is he hungry? Will Mae
sleep the night for a price? I forgot to put the check in the
mail, and it seems I'll never do anything right again. I buy
two bottles of Beaujolais, not to go empty-handed to Brook-

lyn. Back at the apartment I know one thing I can do right: Lydia is asleep, and I cook a large, nourishing meal; but when she wakes up she prefers bouillon. I devour it all myself: liver and bacon, baked potatoes, first California asparagus of the season and Kadota figs—with wine. Indeed, they will think I am too fat and old for Stanley—I open one of the Brooklyn bottles and drink too much.

Suppose the bearded boy is starving—there's nothing to him at all. I try on my new dress to get the feel of it—constricting in the upper sleeves if I want to make a run for home. Lydia is remote, much professional marking of the poodle book; and so, with the last ten-dollar bill in my purse I go out to the bar on University Place. The boy with the beard is not there. A child with braids of clean blond hair and a milky mustache of Löwenbrau tells me where he lives—not far, near the Public Baths. Isn't that strange, I never heard about the Public Baths. I am curious to see.

He lives down in a cellar. The bell does not work. No one answers my call. I fold the ten dollars and stick it under the door. But the happenstance way these kids live— somebody else will grab it, and then what? I would not have done the one thing right. On all fours, my face down to the smelly cement areaway—part musk odor, part—I send my pinky in, but the money slides away. A nail file will do the trick. Heave ho, there goes the knee of the stocking. Stink. This is the relief-station for every cat and kiddy in the neighborhood. Once more, scraping against maybe a hairy mat or frayed carpet and I have the money in hand. The door flies open and there is the boy staring down at me, a big animal scratching to get in.

"What's the matter, Ma? You change your mind again?"

"Help me up." He turns the switch of an old desk lamp which dangles upside down from a gash in the wall. "What are you doing here in the dark?" In all directions such filth, such rubble.

"Sleeping," he answers, and sits on the edge of his disgusting bed. Still the young mouth sullen and the eyes burning up our scene. "I had a big night."

"Didn't we all."

"We went up to Flo's."

"Gracious! After my place!"

"*Gracious?*" He laughs at me, like he always has, only deigning to come for one of my Friday-night meals. "Where do you get that," he says, "gracious?"

Slowly, as though I am not right in the head, he explains that Flo is now under tremendous pressure to find another girl for Mordecai since he has washed his hands of dirty Ginny. I sit on the boy's bed. Our feet are delicately placed not to disturb the unwashed dishes on the floor, a cup with coffee evaporated to a gummy solid, end of a rubbery hot dog, glass of soured milk, bread crusts, egg shells . . . he's watching me to see if I'll comment on the garbage. I'll be damned if I'll play Ma Perkins.

"What does she do? Pass Mordecai around?"

"That's nothing." He leans back with the shaggy little beard up to the ceiling. The hairs are brittle auburn in half-light. "Pass Mordecai around is a nothing. Flo has this big show in a couple of months. She doesn't have time for his craziness."

"Big show?"

"Uptown in a gallery, Ma. *Uptown.*"

"Fancy?"

"Pretty fancy."

"Can't she work during the day when Mordecai's out?"

The boy twists his legs in a holy contortion. "That foop hasn't worked in twenty years."

"Mordecai works in the Automat. Now why would anyone want to make all that up about the fat lady and the salads?"

"Twenty years—" the boy raises his voice, from the dull, no pitch, no expression level of his pose—"Flo keeps that operation running by painting the faces on dolls every day."

"The faces on dolls!" I kick a beer can . . . "Like my zippers, my non-zippers!"

"Whaat?" He is upside down, coiled around himself.

"It's like my job writing about the wonder tape."

He's laughin' and laughin' at me (impossible position), the lovely little striations on the roof of his mouth, inside arc of his teeth all visible, until he chokes and I lift him right end up, slap him on the back. There I go again, handling him—no muscle, no weight of flesh. Now Stanley —there's a hunk, but this young man quivers under a gentle tap. I don't know my own strength, that's the truth, and I think I've almost hurt the boy, for he's blistering me now with a look of rage.

"What did you come here for? To prove you're a nice lady who likes to distribute bread to the poor?"

"I'm sorry, I can't follow your moods."

"Don't *you* think it's pretty funny—to compare yourself to Flo?" He aims at me with the protesting goatee, "Too wild. Presumptuous, Ma."

I begin, "What you don't know won't hurt you . . ." and stay there for five hours proving to the young man (and to myself) that I am a serious person. For once in my life no joking. No dodges. No attitudes loitering outside the shop, balanced (ingenious footwork) on a Chaplinesque cane.

The boy talks, too, disjointed phrases that are hard to follow, almost unendurable for him to utter. He speaks in mathematics which have been growing inside his frail head for a long time. His sunken temples appear burnished, throb: his voice flares with intensity and fades, trying to catch fire. His propositions are of the physical universe which *he* sees as a metaphysical system. (Dim cellar room): describes a medieval astrolabe, a magic wheel charting the movement of life. (Dirty mound of sheets form the contours of our earth): fallacious, beautiful. I don't understand about it—any more than the answer lies in the problem itself. To have the big puzzle laid out in his mind, to figure one law against another, phases and stars, new planets, to keep working out the system—always. In a blaze Joyce is invoked. Da Vinci. Here I find my leg asleep, shift, slap the life back into it. Blake. Yeats. Now I can't help myself: suppose it's the key to all mythologies he's after, or no more than inscribing the Lord's Prayer on the head of a pin. But the boy doesn't seem any crazier than I do.

We share epiphanies.

We are accustomed to believing something will happen, someone will come. Now we must think nothing will happen: a tremendous loss of will is indicated, loss of the meaning of will. Destruction appears to be the last creative act. What I wrote about this cousin, this girl, this beautiful girl Sherry, was meant to display all the hopes, like old clothes, tried on again, altered, fussed with; but they were silly and wrong. They won't get you through. And I destroy myself in the telling, though I survive to tell the tale: it isn't the lady and the tiger—more like kids playing cops and robbers, bang, bang, you're dead; no, you're dead. Who calls it?

Only this may be the funeral oration for what is no more than the story of a show girl.

"I write bad poems," the boy says. There is always that danger, too. He's no dope, but a young man who has walked out of college and grown a beard. Now he has come to a calm rest beside me, the insolence which he has picked up at bars and all-night parties sighed out of him—long, deep breathing of a boy needing sleep. Here we rise and put out the light, take off our clothes—wipe that smile off your face!—and as an extension of our confidences, in the fresh bloom of our belief, we lie down together, a bit exhausted, I'm afraid, but we manage the final tribute.

"Mary," he calls me. No one has ever called me that. Suddenly it seems as though it might be the name of a living person. The boy sleeps and I lift him out of my arms easily, steal around to find my clothes. I tuck ten dollars under an immensely white eggshell. I am doing the one right thing now.

"Where you going?" comes from his dream politely.

"I'm tired. This has been my first date with a college boy."

"Cut the comedy."

"Well—good night."

The city does not sleep but goes on as an assurance that Saturday Night still means something to all the relentless adolescents—middle-aged people who have been on-the-town in party clothes and are heading toward the bridges and the tunnels. Skinny Puerto Ricans come up out of the subway at Astor Place. An experienced bum settles into his newspapers. A dachshund is brought out for its last trickle after the late late late movie. I sing—anything that comes into my head—life is just a dream, da boodledy-boo, life is just a dream, sweetheart, and get hung up on the "Bear Went Over the Mountain," until a snarly police cruiser finds me out and drags along the curb beside me, the little monkey-Irish face on the man ready for a fight. Well, you can't help laughing at him and at his friend about the same size, full of his lofty purpose at the wheel of the police car.

"Come ovah heah."

"Certainly, officer." I breathe in his face with a grin. All right on that count, and God knows they'd never take me for a *femme fatale*. I like their wizened twin faces, chomping up and down on spearmint gum. It's fun of the city to send them out in pairs like this.

"Whaz all the noise faw three-tirdy in the mawnin?"

"There's a law against singing?"

"Three-tirdy in the mawnin."

"Say, those badges are nifty!"

"What's your name, Sistah?"

"I simply meant they have a lot of intricate work on them. . . ."

"What's your name, Sistah?"

"My name is Mary Agnes Keely." I resist an impulse to curtsy. After a good show of hat hitching with their thumbs, holsters fingered, flashlight beamed at my face, and the radio switched up, babbling calls to perfectly grand rapes and murders, they let me walk the rest of the block to my apartment. The charges proposed for "next time": disturbing the peace, creating a public nuisance, insulting an officer.

At home I finish off the bowl of figs. Lydia must be imagined without scope, no revelations for her, nothing large, wild, sweeping, no giddy indulgence but deadly grown-up enlightenment: all the slack passion of a reasoned religious conversion seen in the Savaards' life. Throw in the miracle if you must, Miss Keely, it's a crowd-pleaser, but let it be known that here no roses bloom in the snow, the wheel does not shatter at the virgin's touch. Dawn comes with a cold slanting sun to Ninth Street before I fall asleep in the back-breaking curves of our reclaimed love seat.

On Sunday—

There was a swan. Nature tuned in with a sunny day: my Prothalamion, how I had envisioned it since Major British Writers ten years back. There was a swan of chrome on Stanley's car. The car I'd never seen; he did not care to drive it to the city. Two-toned blue Ford, 1958 four-door sedan; clear vinyl preserves original silver-flecked seats.

I was late, having drifted in the wrong direction—swept by the wind-bag blustering of my own mind. I'd slept late on the love seat and woken to a long dozing reverie of precious thoughts—young flesh, great visions—cramps in my legs, the imprint of upholstery tacks buttoned up my arm. Stanley waited at the curb and bussed me. The wedding had been celebrated, bits of confetti, grains of rice on the floor mats. Something was amiss.

"Where did you get that hat?" Stanley asked.

"Do you hate it?"

"I've never seen you in a hat." We drove on a main street. *Brooklyn:* Stanley's world of homely low buildings, the neighborhood stores, the Moroccan Hippodrome, a public school.

"Is that your school, Stoshie?"

"We lived over near Coney then."

He took a sharp turn into a half-block that dead-ended in a lumber yard—a row of narrow wooden houses separated by the width of a driveway. Here there are no flowers. What matter, what matter, love of my life, that cement steps descend directly to the sidewalk—what matter as our ship comes in.

Stanley's jacket, made for leisure occasions, didn't put me at ease. The house, the family, the food, the glory of our nation (there *was* a portrait of Kosciuszko in the parlor). Against our marriage day which comes ere long . . .

Only the Polish patriot appeared to greet us, hung directly over the television screen so one could look up from the lively history of the present to the doped mezzotint eyes of the past, exulting in each suck of air. Here the flowers were strewn in my path, tile tapestry of roses.

"Those people," my mother had always maintained in one of her liberal cries, "use linoleum in the front room, which is nothing to criticize. It's cheap for them and they keep it clean." Well, Miss Snoot, you've linoleum on Ninth Street. But that is where we're camping out, isn't it? On our big adventure trip. It's not for real and true where we live, now is it?

Take heart: these are forward-looking people; Gilt-rod Modernissimo Suite. Stanley is home. Look where he hangs his jacket on the leafless tree they forgot to burn for dead. Look at his face for Christ's sake in this mounting hysteria about objects. Turn away from the three-D picture of that same Christ at his last supper.

"Stoshie?"

"Ag," he said, "take it easy."

"Hey, Ma," Stanley called. "She's out in the kitchen. Didn't hear us when we came in."

His mother appeared, wiping her hands in a dish towel: "What are you doing in here. I heard when you came in." She was thin, with dyed blond hair and a young face painted on, but her age showed through her magic glass slippers: veins, corns, with opaline polish on the toenails that made them look like those nasty shells that look like nasty toenails. All over her dressing gown clumps of orange roses larger than life.

"Take your things off," Mrs. Sarnicki said, "make yourself at home."

I wore gloves and the hat—Lydia's hat. It was intended to cover a multitude of sins—mostly myself naked against the quick tight skin of the lovely boy. But what I had envisioned as proper attire for the big day at the Sarnickis' now seemed heavy layers of hot woolen stuff. Helen, the sister, sashayed out of a back bedroom in a robe like her mother's, only her roses were scalding green. Oh, there *were* flowers. With jivy movements and a smart languid smile, Helen pretended to be still in her twenties. She and Mrs. Sarnicki shared the bleach bottle between them.

"Well, how do you do!" She landed hard on her consonants, batting the words out in an elegant manner. "At long la*s*t we meet the girl, huh Stanley."

I don't imagine the Sarnicki women believed in me before I appeared in their house, and now that they saw me they didn't much care. What had I expected? Black aprons from the old country? The strong warm welcome of simple people. The honor of my fat body in their house. What had I rehearsed? The dodging Protestant affectations of the cut-glass Irish.

In the kitchen Mrs. Sarnicki pulled out a swirl of violet fiberglas. "Sit down, honey." A molt-no-more bird perched on the limb of neva-wilt forsythia.

Helen looked up from scraping her nails with an emery board and regarded my hat. "You been to church?"

Gently Stanley took the hat off my head and put it on top of the toaster and Yes, I said, chuckling to show them the barrel of laughs I am, with luck I'd made it to the last Mass. They took in my dress and the black sack I carry to the office (bulged out with a wad of the boy's poems and the bottle of Beaujolais), coolly, uncritically, as though I were the native of some faraway land.

"I've got such a hang-over." Helen collapsed at the table, while my love opened a can of beer.

"Want a glass, Ag?"

"She just come from church," Mrs. Sarnicki said.

Stanley walked out of the kitchen with a wink in my direction. It was obvious he ignored them, did not even see them, a habit of long standing.

"Show her your bridesmaid dress," suggested Mrs. Sarnicki.

"Stanley tell you about the wedding?" With effort, hands pressed to her aching head, Helen took me into the bedroom. A Southern-belle construction, raspberry net, hung on the closet door: hoop, ruffles, ribbons, a shawl.

"We all had different colors." By some witchery Helen swept away the net skirt, revealing a slick satin gown, nothing on top but two breast cups overflowing with artificial buds. "It's very praktical. You could use it for evening later on." This seemed unlikely to me, and I think it did to Helen too; the flowered robe clung to her body, skin and bones, as she sank onto her bed with a groan. In her stripped-down bridesmaid's dress she would look about as sexy as a raspberry popsicle.

"My God," she said, "have you ever had a hang-over?"

I wanted to say Yes, I had a choice one yesterday and

just a wee little touch of emotional gung-hover this morning, and the way things were headed . . .

"I caught the bride's bouquet." She roused herself to find this decaying object under a raspberry horsehair hat which she modeled. The illusion was one of evil masquerading as innocence, a diseased cabaret girl in the jollity of prewar Berlin. Her teeth overlapped, but *exactly* like her mother's, and her skin had been bad fifteen years ago; now the pits were not quite hidden under a thick layer of flesh-colored make-up. She held out her hand, displaying a minuscule diamond, the size and value of a peppercorn.

"I guess you're next."

Out in the front room I found Stanley.

"Boy, that dress," he said with a low guffaw.

"She's sweet," I whispered.

"Come on, Ag, settle down." He pulled me to the couch.

"Not here." I drew away from him. His touch was dishonest. Here in this house he had preserved himself in a hostile silence, an insulting blindness to things. The heart clogs when it no longer answers the simple questions: "You like this purse? These shoes? How about these curtains? This Plexiglas chandelier-*cum*-spinning-wheel? And when she comes on in those lamé pants? Wasn't she a riot? Isn't he a scream?" The heart grinds like an old motor stiff with sludge—the deceptive kindness of another bitter word unsaid. Helen and her mother lived here, sponged the tables, plugged in the Last Supper, washed the chenille pussycats who frolicked on the toilet tank. They kept it all going. The girl with her pretentions to youth and beauty, the old woman with thick rheumatic knuckles. A little color, a little life—nuts to dowdy aprons and dim good taste. I don't blame Stanley. All my fruitless tight-mouthed years back home: we live any way we can; but the heart is apt to conk out and leave us stranded forever. And why would Stanley *want* to touch me in my fatuous Sunday clothes.

A man with blurred features pushed in the front door,

Bronislaw, Helen's beau. He poured himself a drink and said: "Hair of the dog that bit you."

Called to the table, we loaded up with stuffed cabbage, kielbasa, derma. Except Mrs. Sarnicki, who said she couldn't take Polish food—"I love it, but it don't love me." She went to the stove and pulled out a TV turkey dinner which she ate off the aluminum plate it had come in. Conversation centered on Irene and Joe—their names under silver bells on our napkins. Where had they gone on their wedding trip? It was a mystery. Niagara? The Adirondacks? Too cold, Helen said. Forced to another cabbage roll I asked why they had not waited until June, and Bronislaw laughed. The women turned on him with their opaline claws. Irene and Joe were exposed for hot-blooded animals, gone off just in time. Virginia Beach? Hot Springs? Daytona?

We nibbled their dry wedding cake. I smiled at Helen, "Did you sleep on it?"

"She got enough nuts in her head already," said Bronislaw. "I feel lousy." He shoved back from the table, his features grown more indistinct now, as if someone had put a hot iron to the face of a celluloid doll.

"You're hung over."

He left and we heard the television set from the front room. "It's a rotten practice game from Florida," Helen said.

"How much you want to bet," asked Mrs. Sarnicki, "they went to Miami after all?"

And Stanley walked out the back door without a word.

"That surely was a good dinner."

"I hope it wasn't too spicy for you. Polish food," said Stanley's mother, "I love it, but it don't love me. I'm glad you got a good appetite. My son described you as *tall*."

"Oh, I'm a big girl."

Her mind skipped a notch as she was rinsing off a plate. (Sweet tap run softly till I end my song.) "I had Helen when I was no longer what you'd call a young woman."

"Is that so?"

"Yes, that's so."

Helen, sensitive girl, rattled the pans. "Wasn't it horrible," she said, "about that woman in the Bronx gassing her children."

Mrs. Sarnicki went to lie down—she did look exhausted under the painted face, her mouth puckered with age, drawn tight with a string of crimson. Pulling back the kitchen curtain I angled for a glimpse of Stanley. Where had he gone? The Appalachians? Point Pleasant? Only the tail was visible, the impertinent ass of the Ford sprinkled with diamond droplets of water.

"Every nice day," Helen informed me, "Stanley washes his car. He likes everything kept clean."

What did she see with that flibberty quick look? My navy-blue dress—it had picked up the foul leavings on the boy's floor. Lydia had worked over it with a damp sponge, but the soiled cuffs, the rumpled pleats told my story.

"Don't mind me," I said. "Go ahead and watch your game."

"I hate baseball. My mother and I usually go visiting or to a movie on Sunday."

I had spoiled their afternoon. "So," she said, taking on the responsibility with an audible yawn, "you would probably enjoy seeing Stanley's room."

I followed her up the back stairs, her bony hips swishing in a curious effeminate strut. She paused for a moment in front of a door with a "Do Not Disturb" sign from a motel in Provincetown, then with a surprising sureness and a sweet malicious smile, so out of keeping with the crass liveliness she had assumed, Helen turned the knob and there was Stanley's room. A fantasy, room of the mind's desire, not the senses: teak-and-rosewood Scandinavian, steel and glass, the unbelievable strong hues of "accent" colors, shelves full-up with expensive art books. It was handsome, empty and bland. I thought of a housewife leafing through a gorgeous magazine, wanting so much, projecting into beautiful worlds, sweeping down the staircase in her gown by Stunello, swanking her guests with the Frenchy credenza and two Siamese cats. How much Stanley cared to make this secret place. What sterile little pleasures must be here enacted. The walls were hung with large paintings, boldly signed Sarnicki '63, copies of what was being done last year —each in a different style: a splash, an optical problem, stitched canvas, a return to magic realism. Not painted but done by some shabby designer's method, and God they were bad.

A hell of a lot you know, Mary Agnes. So I argued with myself; yet I knew that Stanley's dabbling was no better than that old oil in our dining room of a pin-headed moose backed into a purple sunset, gazing out at me with scum on his eyes, and the signature of my mother, '19.

"This one used to be squares." Helen pointed to a black canvas with two dung blobs, "and before that it was green with all fruit like set on a table. It was very—ah—vivacious."

I longed to take a knife and scrape away the wasted years for Stanley, to find a nicely drawn picture of his mother sitting at the kitchen table, or a plaintive young Helen realized in tender pastels. This was the reason he followed Flo's linoleum so carefully—it was an awful threat to his own furtive effort; these fashionable doilies decorated a private world that never took chances, never reached out to life at all. He must know, for his eye was sharp at the drawing board, that Flo had done wonderful things to my floor, and he had not yet seen the final glory of her colors. I would draw the mat over Flo's work. I would plant myself heavily in some obese piece of furniture and never let him see.

". . . always been artistic and had some very unusual friends."

That's my slot: unusual friend, only I've put an air pump up me lately and I'm blown up, mostly in the head, so if I'm not securely weighted, watch out, I'm off like an old Zeppelin over Brooklyn.

"Stanley says you write."

"I do."

"Anything I might of heard of?"

"Lord no!"

She swished out the door, offended, and I trailed after her hot green roses, but the scent was lost. Downstairs I picked Lydia's hat off the toaster and found my black sack on their empty violet chair. We rallied for the final round: madly giggly gay, I said I'd be going out to help Stanley wash his car, and how nice it's all been and thank your mother without disturbing . . .

"As a matter of fact," Helen said, "I think she was hung over."

In the front room I passed Bronislaw, who had melted into a snoring puddle—against his wedding day, which was a hell of a long way off.

"General Kosciuszko, I bid you farewell. Let me know how the Yanks come out in the double play."

Stanley was deep in the Simoniz stage. He polished the Ford's fender with a long sweeping gesture, insistent and obscene. I could have kicked its whitewalls.

"Say, it's getting cold again, Ag. Why don't you go inside?"

"They're all asleep. I'll go on home now, Stanley, if you'll take me to the subway."

"She isn't finished," he said rubbing her blue thigh, "and I wanted to show you something."

"Your room? Helen showed me."

He reddened, threw down the polishing cloth. "God damn her. I never let them up there."

"She only meant to be nice." Why did I defend her? My room at home, I suppose—how my mother loved to invade it—steal the light bulb, hide the books. Once I had recovered a term paper on Blake's aphorisms from the garbage—beet juice wept down every page: all the years of crap we hand one another.

"Get in the car," Stanley said. "You might as well go as put up with more of their . . ."

He backed out of the driveway fiercely—the hose left running. "I never let them up there, Ag. I wanted to show you the room myself. They're never supposed to touch things."

"We just looked." I moved over to sit close by him in the car. The confetti and the rice had been swept away. "I love you, Stosh—" (In spite of your room, because of your room, having looked in on the saddest sight, your room, I love you now in a much more poignant . . .) But he took the pleading in my voice to mean in spite of Helen, the kielbasa, the bird that never flies.

"Aw, they can't help it," Stanley said, caressing the wheel, "they can't help all their dumb . . . I should have got out long ago."

At the subway we sat in the car and kissed in a stone winter sunlight which had returned to end the day. Holding tight to the signal switch, Stanley looked at me and tried to speak, once, twice. The pressure in the car mounted: a still, unbearable weight of time.

"Ag?" he said at last.

(I thought: he will ask me to marry him.)

"Yes," I whispered, "yes—"

"What did you think of my paintings?" Stanley asked. And I did not lie.

"They were very interesting." I had caught Helen's *g* and I could not shake it all the way back to Ninth Street, dreaming of what might have been, crying over spilt milk, kicking myself on the subway which ran swiftly and so ends my song.

I returned the hat to Lydia, who was badly splotched from her old-fashioned fruit-juice treatment of the common cold.

"How did it go?"

"It went."

"Oh, dear!" And as though it had a connection, she said, "This afternoon a boy came to the door asking for you. He was quite *pleasant*."

"Yes, he is."

"He ate four bread-and-jelly sandwiches and drank a whole quart of milk."

"Ah, yes," I said fondly.

Lydia was titillated by what she figured was the wild absurdity of it all.

"He said his name was Hart Crane."

Yes, I could see him standing up to her seriousness, his eyes transfixed, the apostolic beard aglow, "My name is . . ."

"What *is* his name, Ag?"

"Hart Crane, I presume."

She went early to bed. Left to my guilt I broke open the Beaujolais, intending one toast to the Sarnickis' dinner which did not love me. By the time I had worked my way to the cooking wine (slightly turned), the tears were scorching my puffed chipmunk cheeks. My mother, my poor old mother, forming stones inside her like an oyster, she who always envied Lil's Bulova with the diamonds set round, or big as golf balls maybe, she who could never afford to play anything but the minnie, wee indoor sports of the poor. Boo-hoo-hoo, I sat in the hall and called my brother, Francis, to say I'd be coming up in the morning with my sterilized mask and my surgical gloves. I said that, and I remember using the word pimp and reciting the Corporal Works of Mercy—all six of which I can get through without a flaw.

Francis said: "We don't want you, Mary Agnes. You'd better not show your face to us ever again."

Another Friday—

All week I have stayed here, afraid I would forget if I walked out into the street with all the new people. I don't think I've missed anything: the absolute gagging inclusiveness, wasn't that the point? There's a piece of sky missing, and the hunter's elbow, duck beak, dog paw in the blanket folds . . . What a scene! Man with his sporting gear on the never-ending kill, that bright golden haze on the meadow . . . and me able to blast it with one whack on the bedtray.

I don't answer the phone now. It's just Sigal screaming for words to grip the nation. I've led him to believe that his temperamental Wunda Fairy will only muse to me this week in the intimacy of my boudoir. Or Stanley calling me to dance on the greensward in my hermaphrodite garment. I have led him to believe I am down with no more than a physical sickness; but we know, now don't we, that it is a fatal case of writer's cramp.

10

——◆◆●◆◆——

One Two, Buckle My Shoe—

This time it was Mary Agnes Keely on the train. She
dismayed her fellow passengers with her sneakers and a
voluminous Polynesian gown with swirling jungle flowers
that hardly detracted from the enormity of her. But no
one laughed; she was a sad sight, straining to put up her
suitcase, the scarlet flesh on her arms quivering—sweating
heavily as she arranged her book, a carton of chocolate milk,
and a big black handbag in the empty seat beside her.
Stragglers looking for seats passed her by, sensing an un-

bearable trip next to the strange fat lady all settled into a housekeeping arrangement: her book to crack open, her bag to search, milk to slurp. The book closed itself up. Another loud slurp up the disintegrating straw. The book—it was Mallarmé—was soon abandoned, and a yellow pad (pages and pages of smudgy blue scrawl) turned till she found a clean place, a smooth page which she felt with her hands as if it were a piece of stone she was about to cut into. Across the aisle a delicate man with rings and glove-leather shoes looked away in disgust: something about the fat woman as she clicked out the point of her pen, the excitement in her eyes, the visible working of her mind, made him feel he was witnessing a private physical act.

She wrote:

THE WISE VIRGIN

Once there was a virgin who loved an idiot. This was known to all in the village of Olde, and the townspeople stood at their doors to wonder at the virgin as she led her big boy to play down by the brook. There she would sit upon a rock, as virgins will, and take the wild flowers he gathered for her endlessly—endlessly as only an idiot can, repeating the simple acts of plucking and bringing and shuffling off again to pluck, to bring. In the autumn when the flowers were gone he brought her berries and pebbles equally pretty. Soon all of the girls, her virgin friends, came to agreements with young men in the village who offered them silver cups, cows, coffers, and college degrees; even the banker's daughter, affectionately called "bruknozie" (Little Bent Nose), was paired off with a kindly widower who kept a carriage and rolled his own cigarettes in the old fashion.

Yet each day, summer and winter as the years went by, the virgin led her idiot to play. It is said her parents died of spiritual fatigue during the great typhus epidemic, and

the day after they were put in the ground she took her beloved simpleton into their house. *His* family no one remem-
bers, the mother a faceless servant, the father a magistrate,
or itinerant thread salesman, which sounds more likely. In
any case they lived without plumbing in the virgin's home.
She embroidered the idiot's shirts and taught him to use
a hankie, which she pinned to his sleeve.

He loved her—oh, he loved her with such grunting devotion. Legends grew in the neighborhood: the poor unfortunate had walked twenty miles to the south of the
mountain to pick her the first blackberries; he had run
through a burning field to save her; and he had not slept
for weeks when she had bronchitis that unforgettable winter
of ——. Once—only in one instance was he unfaithful: he
lost his heart to a huge goiterous rabbit, a grown bunny
kept by one of the village children, son of an ex-virgin as
it happened, a woman known for her wicked tongue. The
story is that the virgin, kneeling by the rabbit's cage, im-
plored her idiot to come home, promising waffles and Kool-
Aid, prikosh and a dozen Dixie cups with bluish photos of
beautiful people on the tops. With begging cries she pulled
at his legs, but he shook her off, for idiots are always strong,
and with a lovesick nasal whimper he offered more weedy
nibbles to the trembling bunny mouth. Poisoned, that rabbit
was found dead in its cage. It may have been the bitter married woman, not the virgin, or her little boy (children are
cruel), or the idiot himself who all unwitting fed his dear
Flopsy a bad mushroom.

The women grew old, and their young lovers—once
young, once lovers—put on weight, slept over the news at
night and all remarked with envy how young the virgin was,
how slim and merry perched on her rock receiving love
tokens: daisies, goldenrod, wild phlox, the lilies that grew
by the brook. Of course the idiot did not age—they never
do—but gazed always upon the world with infant eyes,

happy to be praised for each posy, vaguely troubled by the cottontails that scampered through his wood. No one could reckon how old they were, that pair, though one senile grandmother claimed to have gone to school, actually to school, with the virgin when there was only one master to teach—some nonsense of that sort—in this run-down part of the city. The young were skeptical, snickered at the feature article in the Sunday Supplement which claimed the virgin had sacrificed everything a woman desires to care for the witless man. Surely hers was a better way, a life purer in its motives than the busy-work that makes a life for ordinary women. Later, these same young people said with reverence: "She was beyond us. We could not understand."

There came the inspiring beauty of their deaths—it was toward the end of the Revolution when the Fascist troops were withdrawing through the mountains to the north. They had gone as usual, the virgin and idiot, to the brook on a misty winter morn, where he brought her mica stones and snow-veined twigs—until he sighted on the far bank a colossal bunny with thick neck and wobbledy ears. He ran at the apparition bellowing whoops of joy, and was shot down at once in the icy stream. It was merely a young soldier on reconnaissance, wearing radio equipment on his back and a muffler against the cold morning air. The virgin fell on her fool, screaming out curses on all rabbits. So the city was alerted; all were saved.

In the public park there is a shrine by the brook where the new virgins come in spring with floral tributes and fresh prayers. She is immortalized with a classic saint's face, an unperturbed girl with stone curls, with irises nicked into the smooth-sanded eyeballs that look down without expression on his heavy granite head that rests in the unyielding folds of her skirt. An inscription on the pedestal reads, "Blessed are the . . ." (here a word or words are obscured

258

by a growth of common rambler roses) ". . . for they shall be this day in Paradise."

By the time the train arrived the fat woman's hands were covered with the leaky chemical in her ball-point pen. She rubbed them on her dress, which had devoured worse marks of sloven eccentricity.

"Heave-ho," she said, bringing the self-absorbed passengers to attention. They drew back and watched her juggle her suitcase off the rack, a trick she played broad, made into a good number. Then she started up the aisle, the book in her teeth, pages of yellow paper under a sweaty arm, her suitcase kicked before, and the big black handbag whacking her knees with each step.

"Heave-ho," Mary Agnes called once more, and descended to the platform. The conductor and every passenger in the car were with her; it seemed for a moment that they might all cheer now that she was safely to ground.

A slight young man with a lordly air came forward and took her suitcase. His face had a ghastly beauty, as though patched and sewn, reconstructed after a terrible accident. He mumbled something.

"Thanks," she said, searching beyond, over his pale blond head.

"Henry Savaard." His smile was tremulous, and his voice, too loud this time, was still uncertain.

"Gracious, but you're different!" Mary Agnes stood half a head taller than Henry Savaard.

"How do you mean different?"

"Different than I imagined."

This didn't answer the question; he had lost the usual ways of dealing with people, all the easy talk, and was bound in mute perplexity. With wavering eyes, with a twitch of his mouth, he asked to know what this woman had in mind.

"For one thing, you're too blond." Mary Agnes began an honest reply. He opened the door of a neat 1952 Chrysler with Indian blankets tucked over the worn seats. "And you're not big . . . because Lydia said you liked sports I had you with the physique of a football player. Actually, you're like the Apollo I saw at City Center."

Life is more accurate than art, she thought, more telling in its details. This is a lovely small man-boy, not a coarse high-school hero.

"I never got my weight up for football," Henry said.

Of course not. And the town was far richer in old trees and gardens than what she had invented—which went to prove to what lengths, to what dangerous lengths her imagination would have to take her to make the world in stories and plays carry on with a semblance of life. The entire weekend proved how flabby she had been to dwell upon scenes of violence: cinematic versions of madhouse capers which could not begin to match the solemn slow horror of Lydia Savaard and her husband working their way through the day.

Driving by a shingled mansion that held its own with an ageless copper beech of scorching perfection, Henry said that Lydia had wanted to come but was baking a pie. Often the trains were late and the oven unreliable.

A burnt-sugar smell filled the house. Accepting Lydia's flustered genteel kiss, Mary Agnes said it was only the juice boiled over. So long—it seemed years—since she had left Ninth Street—and couldn't it use one of Lydia's cleanings now. The roaches were back, just appeared one day under the saltines. But no memories were wanted; the oven was unreliable, the recipe vague. Each effort was a serious business—setting the table, washing the dishes—meant to prove a general competency. The wind blew a napkin, a cup chipped in the sink, and the Savaards asked themselves were things going right, had they perhaps been significantly careless or unaware.

". . . slippery hands."

"Invest in a plastic dishpan."

"Weight the tablecloth with rocks."

"Turn the glasses upside down."

"Build a trellis."

"Buy rubber gloves."

It gave Mary Agnes a headache to listen to them examine every move, trenching in against petty disasters, to hear so much about so little. It shocked her to think that Lydia was twenty-five, Henry a year older, for they were no longer young: their faces were guarded as if decades of misfortune had taught them never to show delight or even betray a pale shadow of annoyance. They walked stiffly up and down the stairs to their bedroom for a forgotten sweater or a pair of sunglasses, all trussed against emotional rupture —both thin, medium-brown bodies—alike in the shirts and trousers of their team. Mary Agnes lazed in a deck chair in her exotic gown—reading but not minding the afternoon fancies of Mallarmé's faun while the Savaards toiled in the garden beds. What they grew was exact. They talked about it: bookish discussions of grafting, pruning, spraying. Henry leapt across the yard to Lydia's rescue: it was a matter of the exact juncture at which to clip the rose, to encourage this bud, pinch off that. Shifting heavily in her chair, Mary Agnes considered the boring long time it took to play God, to decide what was safe and wise. If only all could be reasoned in their way they might perform miracles of growth and endurance.

It gave her the headache, listening to each hedging move; but by Sunday afternoon she had come to respect the Savaards. Mary Agnes, who was out for all the wild jigs that would bring her to that zany big dream world where the artist is suspended, Nijinsky-like, found that she admired the intricate formal sets which Henry and Lydia danced. Two disabled people, straining hard—surely they would make it. The garden, their child perhaps, was enclosed on three sides by a wood, and on the fourth they had put up a new raw fence. Over the fence the green lawn swept along the drive up to the Savaard house. They did not go there.

Old Mrs. Savaard came through the trees with a wheelbarrow full of books and china and unstrung tennis racquets. The big house was to be rented for the first time that summer; she was cleaning closets. Were these things wanted? They were not. She was a strong woman with wispy white hair that made her seem a bit cracked as she sorted through her wheelbarrow of junk.

Mary Agnes was struck by her failure to envision Mrs. Savaard—more disappointing than her failure with Henry. All she had from Lydia's stories was the broad black lines of malice and pride: an embittered queen quick to torture. This served "The Romance of Lydia Savaard" too well: a stock villainess had been called for—to play against the tender wife (shallow innocent) and Godnick (kindly cynic). But there was not enough in this set-up to justify the death and reclamation of Henry (hero *manqué*), the last vengeful act of a dying social system. Mrs. Savaard played a fuller role. With one skinny arm she lifted a cast-iron chair into the shade.

"What is it these people are called?" She turned to her son. ". . . name like a dog."

"Terrier."

"Yes, a dog. And they have peculiar ideas about the house—"

"They are having a canopy made for the back terrace," Lydia said, "in case it rains on their parties."

"With drapery at the side!" Mrs. Savaard showed no contempt for the dog people. She had found that an amused abstraction from the world was a possible mode. ". . . sketched out like a stage design. They are in the theater."

"Terrier is in television," Henry reminded her.

"Drapery out of doors, and what was sent from Altman's? An asparagus pan, and the season is almost over; and what was it . . . ?"

"Flowered sheets," Lydia supplied.

"Yes, I've made up the beds for them . . . with anemones, some with orchids. They don't look clean." Mrs. Savaard's voice was classic, sweet, like a piece of old music deep in the mind. Mary Agnes believed every word, and her toleration of the world as the funniest sort of place seemed clever, even original. She asked Miss Keely if she would like to come up in the afternoon—it was Saturday then—and see the house before the dogs took over.

In her fresh-flowered tent Mary Agnes trudged up the drive to the big house. She left Lydia and Henry in a crisis over three strawberry vines—

"Only ten bitter berries."

"Shriveled."

"Feed them? Dress the soil?"

"Hormones," Henry commanded in his imperial mutter. No, there was nothing up at the big house they wanted. From his tone Mary Agnes felt he would never go there again. In twenty or thirty years' time they would be putting up strawberry jam right here at the cottage.

When Mary Agnes finally made it, puffing up to the grand front door in the sun, she knew the house was worth any effort. So much dark dead ugliness, way beyond Lydia's range of description. The good rugs were in storage, and Mrs. Savaard had put down mats for the people with a name like a dog, but aside from the rope-and-anchor *motif* carved in the woodwork, there was no indication that this was a summer house. There were special cabinets everywhere: for guns, for fishing equipment, for bows, for trophies, for dog prizes, for horse prizes—like a club no one belonged to any more. They walked hurriedly through dim, polished rooms out to the restaurant-size kitchen, where they drank "Reel" lemonade. The one sight Mrs. Savaard pointed out was a special pot built into the stove to steam twenty lobsters. Whimsically the old lady stuck her head in it, wondering if the Airedales would find it useful. The lid was thick with dust and she wrote the word PIG with her finger. She had wanted to show Miss Keely some books she found in the attic: a complete, moldy edition of Zola. What, she asked in that melodious voice, hard, inventive as a fine tune, can I get for them?—and changed the subject, not wanting attention, withdrawing behind ancient eyelids: she was devoted to extrasensory perception.

She had seen her husband on the first landing of the stairs dressed in the loincloth of a Javanese sailor. "I asked if he wasn't afraid of a chill, and that's how I discovered it was Java, Miss Keely. He said it was always warm in Tanjung-priok. That tureen—the ladle is mended; still, I think I'll put it out of their way."

To Mary Agnes the tureen looked like chowder for fifty. She knew the Zola was worthless, but she told Mrs. Savaard she would not take any of the volumes now; it would be a shame—one never knows—to break the set. She would inquire around at secondhand bookshops.

"My husband's dealer is dead. I now belong to a rental library in a gift shop—which is closed all winter long."

They wandered back to the murky void of the large front hall, built to receive active men with golf clubs or hunting gear, and Mary Agnes was about to say good-bye when she felt the dark walls whirring and had to stumble to the nearest chair. The old woman's eyes were on her. An able brown hand came out in a gesture—not a touch or caress, more a blessing, an indulgence in the air.

Mrs. Savaard pronounced it like a gypsy: "You are going to have a child."

"Yes," said Mary Agnes, "I didn't think it showed."

"Ah, I see," said Mrs. Savaard, oracular, floating off into her unperturbed vision. What did she see? Not that Molly Mick has got herself in trouble. Not Henry's humorless struggle with the reasonable world. Not Lydia's disfigured body. Not the heavy dark house that needed vulgar sheets and canopies, draperies, the yapping, baying dogs in their spectacular television décor, if it was ever to come to life again.

"I see that you will have a child and it will be a girl."

Back at the cottage Mary Agnes drank two glasses of milk, then dashed out the back door to tell Lydia about her revelation. Henry was in town buying bean poles, so she let herself down on the grass with a thump. "Listen," she began. "Listen!" she begged. Lydia was scratching white powder into the ground. "You never gave me the idea that she floats around that mausoleum with her hair flying. She *communes* with her husband."

"You're impressed, Ag? She can't remember the Terriers and their canopy, but she argued them up to the last penny. She figures it all for us: this house we must live in again, and I'm to go into the city and bring my work back. She's getting Henry set up to carve decoys and refinish antiques by the fall."

"It's got a power," Mary Agnes said with awe. "It's going to hold together with everyone transmuted and grown up to the so-called realities."

"Don't be foolish. There are times I wish I were back on Ninth Street in that crazy apartment, fighting the roaches; and other times I look at Henry and think he'd rather be back in the nice safe nut house." She turned her head to the new raw fence which closed them off. "We have our keeper."

Mary Agnes agreed that Mrs. Savaard might be in charge, and breathing the sea air like an underprivileged city girl she said, "It's worth it."

"Hell, yes," Lydia said grimly. "We all know it's worth it."

"This is the prettiest place I've ever been."

"It was a great showplace."

"I mean here." Mary Agnes pushed herself up and lumbered around in an elephantine pirouette. "I've put on a lot of weight, no? I'm more than pleasingly plump?"

"I didn't want to mention it, Ag, but I think you could be more careful."

"Careful? I'm a big fat momma."

Lydia laughed.

"I'm *enceinte*."

"What?"

"Knocked up—you know that one don't you? There's something cooking in the old oven."

"Oh, Ag!" was all Lydia Savaard could find to say. "Oh, Ag, Ag," she repeated in a mournful chant.

"*She* knew it. And I thought I was so clever in my billowing gown."

"Oh, Ag, does Stanley know? Won't you marry him now?"

"First: he hasn't asked me."

"Oh, Ag, Ag."

"Second: it's not his child."

"Ag, Ag."

"Stop that!" Mary Agnes swung round again in her clumpish dance. "I'm a big fat momma, big fat . . ."

"No. No." Lydia caught her by the skirt, her young-old face set in tight morality. That was her solution: Protestant Lady on the March to Save American Girlhood.

"Who is the father?" she demanded.

"I don't really know."

"Oh, Ag!"

"That is, I don't know his name, but I know him. He knows me—better than any man alive."

"One of those artists," Lydia hissed as though it were a curse.

That evening Henry Savaard served up a diluted version of his disastrous charm: pet names for his wife, college-boy jokes, sophisticated patter that must have been deathly at cotillions—some of the old razz-ma-tazz for hefty Miss Keely. The ruined prince was called upon to display the power now gone. He kissed the ladies, poured the wine, told ghost stories on his mother after she had drifted off into the night. He sang a sweet French folk song—

Je fais pipi sur la grazon
Pour rompetez les papillons

just dirty enough to entertain a child. He told a story rich with lewd details, punctuated with diffident smiles, of his uncle who as early as 1938 was known to accept money for introductions to the right people.

Lydia wallowed in happiness. "*See*," she said with each adolescent sigh, "see what it's all about now." The ultimate fan, one-woman claque. Yes, Mary Agnes saw the great tenor who had lost his voice—playing musical comedy now, but no amount of technique could cover the faults. And when Henry went in for the brandy, Lydia, conscientious still, whispered, "What will you do? Whatever will you do?"

"Who knows. I suppose I shouldn't drink too much of this wine."

On Sunday morning the Savaards were back to watching each other, calculating the next breath they would draw together. It was then that Mary Agnes, stuffing herself with sweet buns to ward off morning sickness, finally sensed that their efforts were somehow noble. It had finished for the Savaards: they had gone out of life, but like a medical miracle in the newspapers they had been sucked back in after their hearts had stopped. With great care they could go on. Their invalid existence was precious to them. Henry was an ineffectual boy, barely worth saving, but Lydia was a woman with dimension now who could afford to let Mrs. Savaard manage the details. When Mary Agnes ran into the house to be sick, Lydia turned to her husband and announced the dreadful news.

Implying that they could face up to anything, they said, "Let us help." Dead serious they were, the Bobbsey Twins on another adventure. Mary Agnes ate a bun and laughed them down. She saw them as a bungling pair of midwives (boil water, swab the table) figuring directions from a dusty medical book out of the great attic (thread the needle, *see* under *Suture*, and pray to God) as a screaming new life passed them by.

While they waited for her train the Savaards asked what she would do. Two earnest faces pressed down on her, until she finally evaded them by hopping to the tune of "*Je fais pipi.*" They started at her again, opening and closing their unsmiling mouths at once.

Together they struck a fantastic chord: "You must come here and stay with us." And they would go through with it, Ag knew; they would take her in with her little bastard and set out a strawberry plant for them both.

Fanning herself with the book of poems, she cried a little. "I read that your body temperature goes up five degrees— in my condition." What could she tell them: that they were little soldiers and her battle wasn't going to be fought with hand weapons? They stayed on the platform and waved to the fat lady till the wind blew her peculiar dress up and out like a full sail. She was going—it was more decent to turn to each other and worry unto death about the shortest way home.

"Everything here is new," said a glimmering girl. She had picked up the phrase from a man with a nobbledy cane across the room who looked as though his judgments were important.

And how do I know? It doesn't at the moment have to do with Madam See-it-all Naratrix who can catch the words as they fall from the lips of one character (say the craggy old king of the art critics) and spirit them across the room into the mouth of some other dupe (let's have a self-styled starlet in matched mink paw with a good ear). No, the girl did say this when I came into the gallery. She spoke to me because I am so outlandish (red canvas trimmed with rope that night), people take me for a considerable personage. That's all they can do other than call Bellevue. And again, when I had elbowed over to the Marsala *con uova*, the critic, raising his gnarled scepter, repeating what was already the cliché of the evening, said to anyone who would listen: "Everything is new here."

You guessed it: Flo Schwartz's big opening at the Galerie Uptown. It is June, the last gasp of the season. School will be getting out and Flo is *in*. All her work—after twenty years in a firetrap—stuck with triumphant red stars: SOLD. She can work with spittle on blotting paper now (massive dissolution in spongy absorption) and they'll buy it.

Now button your lip, Mary Agnes, there's no room in this moving world for your harsh words. Just because you're out, out on the street with one suitcase and a shopping bag full of MSS, over four months gone. It's been done, dear girl, and it's old and out—that is to say, like the Savaards' carrying on with their inspiring drama of personal relations, your end, too, was written back in another century. The misused maiden fallen in a watery culvert waiting for the wrongs of society to wash her further into the mire: done and old and out.

I came home elated from my weekend at the Savaards'. Now that I had spoken about the child I could feel it move in me for the first time. I realized that it would have a body—the perfect shape of humankind developing once more, defying the boogie machine with his ten grillion wires that retain the facts of civilization while we forget our keys and what day the garbage man collects.

I put that down just to show the maudlin state of self-indulgence I was in when I arrived at Ninth Street in a taxi. And pride—oh I was all blown up: the idea had struck me on that mesmerizing choo-choo ride that I might do something altogether grand with the story of Lydia Savaard now that I had set eyes on the lost palace and the happy farmer's hut. All I had to do was go back and paint in the shadows, bring up the values. . . . Choo-choo, I would have to take care that I never allowed the disproportion of a scene not understood just thoroughly "researched"; Pierce-Arrows and Pear's Soap undercut by the CCNY sensibility of Morton Godnick (alias Wishengrad, pussycat of the psycho-scientific syndrome) . . . woo-woo through the cardboard tunnel, and only think what an extraordinary case you have after the heart massage has brought them back . . . puff-puff, off I go. Only suppose these people are playing some highly original game: three-dimensional chess which I don't know from parcheesi?

And climbing the stairs to my apartment I was sure I could attain the power to know what was required of me: how to levitate instead of giving out at the second landing. Steam engines gone, still we will say choo, choo-choo—laughable old fools to our children—for the next fifty years.

Mrs. Mertz was waiting for me on a camp stool.

"Don't bother your key," she said, "it's open for any tramp wants to muck it."

And so it was. The panels of the door broken in, jagged torn mouth to the fun house. Flo's masterpiece, *Œufs à la mode de l'Armstrong* as it is now titled, was cut out of the floor. It must have been a neat job getting it down to the street. They had knocked out one of the high windows, frame and all, and those faded velvet drapes, tied back to keep the scene always in mind: night, day, street, people, cars, dog, turd, tree—choked city tree breathing polluted air, sending its tap roots to the sewer—dopey, dumb tree. It would live, but something was over: the curtain was drawn.

"Leon is sick." Mrs. Mertz paced back and forth with her sore-footed walk in the place where the floor was now bared to pleasant old parquet. "Sick he couldn't even talk to you. We went to my sister in Long Beach. She says stay over, relax!"

I said I was sorry. That was not true: I was sorry only that Mrs. Mertz had not seen the memorable piece which Flo had made of her linoleum. "It was a bas-relief—like a sculpture," I explained. No answer, a plucking at her stiff curls recently turned red. "It was—it is a big, beautiful painting."

"Nice bums you got for friends, Miss Keely. I tell you I'm sick here, *here*," her heart, "and from you I've got no security."

I said I would pay somehow, and found that Mr. Mertz had already made out an estimate which she had in the pocket of her nautical culottes. Also if I was out by the end of the week they would not call the cops.

"Hold everything!" I made a frantic dash across the room. There behind the rubber plant my papers were untouched. "Thank God," I cried. Histrionic no doubt, swaying, clutching my yellow pads.

"You pregnunt?" Mrs. Mertz vibrated with curiosity. She hadn't been around sixty-plus wise-apple years for nothing. "Very nice girls. One divorced. The other pregnunt."

"Nunt." It was a scary negative I'd never heard: *no, none, null, nix, nunt*. "I've put on a little weight."

She shrugged and stepped out through the gaping door. "That weight you put on lying on your back." A matter-of-fact statement, kindly even.

"Really Mrs. Mertz, I've told you that I am sorry—"

"For you I'm sorry, believe me."

That was how I found out about Flo's opening, or, rather, I found out by picking the entertainment section of the Sunday *Times* out of a litter basket over near Wunda-Clutch on Monday morning. Schwartz at the Galerie Uptown. I was not invited. Who cares why? Not me, not Mary

Agnes—Ma Keely with the home cookin'—no, nunt. I'm as like to have my dough risin' as to be able t'go way up there in the Sixties with them artist fellas.

Scene to be done as a monologue by an actress with face many times lifted, wearing the hat, shawl, and lace-up shoes of Ethel Barrymore in *The Corn Is Green*:

They were all my children . . . all of them. Sweet boys always watching their waists, how they jibed me when I fixed up their favorite potatoes; dear fags, always watching their tight little pants, and the girls, pale things, never et more 'n a titmouse . . . Ah, but those lean heterosexuals shoveled it in: macaroni, rice, pie, puddin'. How them youthful bodies burnt up the starch. Burnt me up too, pullin' on my skirts for more, Mommy, more. Still, they all come along nice. There's Mordecai from my first litter, all shaved and dressed in clean suède for the uptown trade. Nunt, nunt, I'd say many a time, this little chick nunt goin' ta make it with his peep peep peep, ain't nobody payin' him no mind; and see him now, cock o' the walk with that sweet thing from Mount Mary-on-the-Hudson. How-dee-do, Mordecai, son!

"How-dee-do, Ma," he says, "I'm just telling Ryan O'Brien here whose Daddy is buying *Broken Yolk '62* for his private chapel how we used to care in the thirties when I was painting Post Officers for the WPA." He's always on like that, full of the gassy humbug I love to hear 'cause I unnerstand it; then one of the young'uns'll turn on him, poor Mordecai—oh, many's a time—screaming: "Care, care, care is Nunt, Daddy-O."

We-eell, all my little ones! Ginny scrubbed, holding Chutney's mocha hand, both of them with weddin' bands and dressed up like they's going to the interracial square dance down at Folklore U. Heidi-ho, Ginny, it's Ma. It's Ma gave you all that cereal and listened to you blab off at the mouth when you come in from a date; it's Ma, Ginny girl . . . Ginny. Autistic temperament: some of them's born like that. We had her tested and she came out nunt. "Nunt!" I says to that psychologist fella. "Well it's true she ain't read Pope, but she sure can fake her Proust." Some of them's like that—ashamed of their Ma. I don't unnerstand their new music, seems like there's no tune at all, only shoutin' and a lot of dirty thumpin' . . . Land sakes, when I was a girl—back straight, chin high—oh the lovely nunt, two three, nunt, two three. Smile! Smile!

All different these days. Here's my Flo, the best of the pack, had a paper route when she was five years old, drew real pretty pictures of the cat sleeping on the window seat, big Tom we had that time, and Flo didn't miss a trick—put in every whisker, white boots, place his ear was ripped. Now it's all new, all these eggs she done.

"It's the theme," she says, "Ma, it's the big theme." Well I don't see hows anyone couldnunt of painted all the yellow circles . . . now that's just between you and me, not to say yellow isn't one of my favorite colors, always has been none the less, the yolks in the whites—*Tempura 1, 2,* and *3*—have a little more to 'em, but the plain *Albumen* ain't so much to look at, or that *Sunny Side Up* all mottled like a wash dress I had once from down at the Boston Store, nice enough pattern, Flo, but I wouldn't wear it to church. Shake a mop, will ya, Ma—that's how they talk to me. Egg, egg, egg, egg crates all pasted up into some fistarus. Well whose goin' buy something like that'll fall apart . . . 'member once you kids built that club house out back all came to pieces the first rain we had. And nunts to you too, Miss Flo. Well, ain't she toast of the town? So, I'm not complaining, it's simple that I don't unnerstand. I said that girl'll make her way and make the fashion, not follow like the rest, mark my word: nunt. Nunt in this world gonna stop Flo as she never suffered from egomania or had to compensate to overcome basic insecurity or any of them other childhood diseases.

Famous Flo is listening to some old boor tell her she is new, and new is best, and everybody wants it while the paint's not dry. Everybody's afraid to have it next year or day after tomorrow 'cause it might be gas pumps back in, or Coke bottles, or Billy Rose's Aquacade or Florentine boys with pillbox hats. Makes a body nervous guessin'. *Poached* I like, you have that lovely piece of buttered toast to contemplate. "Oh, Ma," the children say, "bake off."

Spanish Omelet is bought by the museum. What museum, dear? *The* Museum, Ma. Ohhhh.

Yes, well I wouldn't want my lamb, Famous Flo, to hear for all the world, but I'll tell you it's a sin, a mortal sin, to let your omelets get all tough like that on the outside, like some nasty flapjack is what this is; well I don't care, they all turn on their Ma and say, "Oh, Ma, you don't understand." I always have to take it from my babies when they get to the snotty stage—"Oh, Mother, honestly, don't you *see* that's what makes it so moving and indicative of our society." . . . I *care*. An omelet ought . . . "Oh, Ma, slip a stitch; ain't nobody thought indicative in twenty years." Well I *care* an omelet ought'a be light 'n tender, there's enough ugliness in the world, I don't have to lace into my good corset and come all the way up here . . .

Coddled is goin' out to Dallas, but seems to me Guggenheim got the bargain: linoleum, a nice big piece'd do a small room, ever got tired of looking at it, nice pattern too, all gold, red dots, lumps and rounds, nunt show the dirt. It's a relief from the chicken eggs—set ya thinkin', all these people quit shovin' it might set ya thinkin' about bugs and fish, other birds *lay* their eggs too, and here Flo has made them all, all stuck in the marble and can't ever hatch . . . oh, it makes a beautiful panorama scrambled together, but it's a horrible awesome concept caught in the mind's eye, heart of hearts—I can't bear to dwell upon it too long . . . "Ma, will you go scrub a tub."

I'm just gonna set here in the Saar'nin chair watch you

young people have at each other 'n think a where you kids'd be if your ole Ma didn't cook 'n wash 'n work her fingers to the . . . Nunt! Jesus, Mary and Joseph, but I know that fella—Chat-e-laine. Owns what? Owns this Galerie Uptown. He's lookin' straight at me don't know who I am. My bifocals playing tricks? I coulda sworn he was the foreigner goosed me that time at the Danbury Fair. Oh, I'm not surprised you laugh at your old Ma, turned up again years later with another proposition—different context but the same line—N-u-n-t, as you might expect. It's the same all over the world. And what's wrong with the mystery man turning up to show the grand design, as it were? Is a few old ideas come in mighty handy when the Ice Capades is back in and flowers done in human hair and nobody'll take an egg you threw it at 'em. "Baste a turkey, Ma!" Listen, I know that flip-wrist is Chatelaine, who, *Primo:* gave me a set of empty rooms at considerable profit to himself in which to display my ignorance, who, *Secundo:* obviously put Flo and her pack on to me, so's they spotted me in that saloon and said let's serve this lady a treat for she'll be pleased to pay, who, *Tertio:* must *not* recognize me in my fully developed form in order I can avoid the scene in which once again I would debase myself before his bright, rapacious European eyes—"Oh, Ma, husk your corn!"

Well, they come a long way from Avenue B, my chicks, my lambs, my fluffy ducks, Famous Flo and supportin' cast . . . and still they don't know to put out a bite of somethin' tasty. All blaa, blaa about the big 'n extensive theme is new, blaa, eggs, blaa, blaa, well that don't stop my stomach rumblin', eggs over there, one chicken-eatin' little plate of 'em, deviled. Scuse me, pardon, *pardon see vu play*, I'll jus' have this lil' one with the parsley trim: no salt, taste like a chalky . . .

"Oh, my Holy Virgin, Ma, you ate *Deviled Eggs* was goin' in the Rockafellas' private collection."

———

Three, Four, Close the Door—

I have put Stanley off for over a month. Nothing I say on the phone convinces him that he is still my only love— as that sort of thing goes. (Don't kid yourself—that sort of thing goes fine.) After the dud trip to Brooklyn we had our usual lunches for a while and were able to blame Helen and Mrs. Sarnicki for our own midget spirits on that day. It gave temporary relief; next we drifted into being busy, evasive—Lydia moving out, the retail campaign launched at Wunda-Clutch, so many grand spring days for Stanley to wash his car, and me with all my stories to put down la-dee-da. Now he calls daily saying he has a surprise for me. Threatens to wait in the street. And what am I to say: bold, defiant with a telltale sob in the throat, "I have a surprise for you, too, Stanley boy."

Though he might not guess. Stoshie thinks I just wear funny clothes. It's what makes me a very unusual friend, along with the cooking and writing. But Flo knew at once. She put her hand on my belly—right in the midst of her rich important people—and said: "I can tell from your shape. Projectile. It will be a boy." I admired her for that —no questions, the fact met straight on; you have to hand it to Flo and her troupe, they'll be damned if anything as ordinary as an unwed mother will startle them. It is a human prospect. It is good. Strange that just as I am through with them they may take me seriously.

It moves toward the end of the day at Wunda. Sigal's already off to do a little business in new white golf shoes just out of the Abercrombie's box. Listen, I didn't want to say anything but they usually change at the links. Never mind, the little man will carry it off. He's rented a car to take him out to Cedarhurst in style.

As soon as they heard him clomp out to the elevator, *Mira! Mira!*, the radio was turned on full blast in the packing room. *Arriba!* We all cheat—I spend my time here on

276

my own work. Oh, I scribble off what's asked of me: Wunda Fairy mincing "Prest-O and off you go!" Or consumptive photographer's model in glamour gown claiming she made it herself—well almost by herself, at which point the eye is compelled to the omnipresent Fairy tickling the girl's ribs (where once the zipper dwelt in days of yore). Anything you say, Mr. Bert, is O.K. with me, as long as you don't waste my time. Of course it's what they wanted all along. They feel, here at the office, that I'm finally broken in. So I am: it means nothing more than a paycheck to me. Zip and Clutch, how I have depended on them for my liveli-hood: the bedraggled past and the tinseled future. Had I really wanted the past to win out, to be the real thing, and the future to be laughable, no more than an improbable adventure?

That was a false start.

Now look at my flowing robes. Here's a beginning: no closures, no sniggling small mechanism or woven device, a perfect garment falling free from the body, room for growth, nothing more than a cord necessary to draw the folds to me in infinite arrangements. Now it is the only dress for me.

In this city is *now:* New York—not Paris or New Haven or Decaysville-on-the-Housatonic, which are someday, once, then, all dreams and memory, places in the mind. Now is the city wearing the movie strip of Forty-second Street like a glad scar, and all the Medieval Virgins standing on one hip up at the Cloisters, and all the Modern Virgins standing on the other hip before dress racks in Lord & Taylor's; and the Sam Scime Hygienic Grocery, and boys in Lederhosen going up to the Top of the Six's; and those Puerto Rican families who stand on the curb waiting to cross with lots of beautiful children with scabby scalps; "Bird lives" and a high-toned beggarwoman on Fifty-sixth Street wearing em-broidered nylon sweater sets; and the mystery of Queens, the Bronx, Richmond, which turns out to be the humdrum soap opera of people living. Make up your own list: you might want to start with the Three Little Pigs in the Children's Zoo or Pius XII big as death in the vestibule of St. Patrick's Cathedral, "Goyim Go Home," or those minor African officials from the UN wandering through Macy's, riding the escalators in their French eyeglasses and new suits from Barney's—it's all good clean fun and will give you the essence of right now, but remember it is a parlor game; don't get choked up and send your efforts around to arty magazines.

I'll be leaving here soon to go across the city and meet Stanley with his surprise, and oh yes, I'll be leaving Wunda-Clutch soon—their insurance won't cover me after the fifth month. Time is important now, now that I feel the child at all times, a presence. I am no longer sick in the morning: I am filled with tides of energy as though my heart, my veins, my blood, my nerves know this is their greatest moment—we've hit it this time, Ag! I put on a cape and go out into the streets to Stanley.

If I had not started thinking again about the city my meeting with Stanley would have come and gone with mechanical grace, like the neon signs circuited to flash on and off. But I was wild, euphoric, by the time I arrived. We met on Third Avenue in a pretentious 1890's barroom dreamed up for college kids.

"What will you have to drink?"

"Nothing at all." I couldn't say I had lost my taste for alcohol. I dared not ask for a glass of milk. I was hungry— I am hungry many times a day—but the place looked like imaginary food, as if Flo's *objets d'art* would be served up on a thick white plate like those cute plates in old barrooms.

"See all the boys in seersucker. They're out of school. They take this for real." Such a happy trance had come upon me that I suppose I didn't speak one sensible word to Stoshie. I was possessed by the city again, as I had been

278

when I first came to New York to live. But I had neglected her for my own life. I had lived *in* her as much as any native; I had started to work. And in a sense it was the movement and variety of the city that had given me my whole past, like a gift from a shop I had been afraid to enter; or more likely I had been afraid to buy anything except the mimsey cocktail napkins, to put down my thirty-five cents' worth as a cover for the truth. Now that I was to be put out on the sidewalk by Mrs. Mertz and would soon be cut loose from Wunda-Clutch, I was thrown upon her once more.

"Now," the city said, "now is the horror, now is the nightmare, now is the sweet dream."

"Mary Agnes, I've wanted you." Stanley Sarnicki held my plump hand across a table with a red checkered cloth. He was the same, the very same. What had I hoped for? A disfiguring wart. A contemptible tie.

The color rose in his face. "Aren't you hot in that thing?" he asked.

"No. It's my rain cape. I thought this morning it might rain."

"Let's get out of here," Stanley said.

"See the make-believe sawdust they have on the floor!"

"Let's go." He breathed with the urgency of passion, as though . . . as though we could go back to my cot on Ninth Street and lie down again.

He took me two blocks uptown and we entered a white apartment house which was not completed. He pushed a button in the elevator. We rose through the smells of damp cement, unseasoned wood, odorless paint. He opened the door of an apartment. The white dust from the plasterboard was still in the corners, and Stanley's furniture, those beloved pieces from the shrine in Brooklyn, were already settled in the room. Stacked along the scrimpy baseboard were his paintings, one lapping over another, a harrowing retrospect of art in the sixties while the years are still upon us. The big window looked out on another white brick apartment house with the seniority of one or two years. I wondered if living in this room the ghost of an El would thunder by and disturb my sleep, for I knew at once the place was offered to me. Pulling my cloak to fall loose about me, I sat on Stanley's Swedish couch. In the kitchenette he made Martinis.

"Home Sweet Home," I said, putting the drink aside.

"My furniture looks good in here, don't you think, Ag? I was going to ask you . . . I shouldn't have gone ahead without asking . . ."

"It looks right, Stosh, absolutely right. Coming over here I had a vision of the city as a gigantic heroine of today, and even 'little old New York' with the tar scraped off the cobblestones and the shutters back in the windows is a mere frippery worn to deceive, but so obvious—like a woman with a hunk of costume jewelry. She has a history—what girl worth the trouble doesn't—but it's now she stands before you, mysterious, dazzling, immediate. There are regions you will never know. Dark blocks. Evil lots. Flowers bloom twenty floors in the sky for one thick-faced fool who doesn't know them by name."

I thought I had taken the right line; nothing could be more offensive than an image spinning out to generalities at the moment when Stanley Sarnicki wanted to say look here, we have our whole lives ahead of us (not true), let us not think of the past, my dear, let us think only of this bungalow, for out of much sadness and oppression comes a richly deserved . . .

"The city hangs there like some big saloon nude stretched over a bar—seductive and funny, too much, too much for anyone to handle." But I could not hurt him. He wanted me, this block of manhood, hulk of capability, cornerstone of reality, to yak on in my "nutty" way if I must, wanted, if there was no other possibility, to assign the empty bedroom to my child. Someone could make a hero of Stanley.

His proportions are right. He is fair. Someone could move him into this cheaply built place and let him act freely, love wisely, burst out the very walls of the standard-size rooms—paint brave pictures. But the child was not his.

I leapt up as lightly as I could, "Look, the molding has pulled away already."

"Every building has to settle," Stanley said.

"My apartment on Ninth Street, you can reach up, up, and it's a lovely ceiling with decorations they made in those days, in each of the corners and there in the middle for the light—ah, what pains people took once, what care . . ."

"You just finished telling me a big story about—"

"Did I? Yes. I meant that though Ninth Street has a past you'll never hear anything through the walls."

"I never liked it."

"You didn't?"

"I never liked that place. The hall is dark. It's a barn. The bedroom is depressing."

"Think of all the chances you had to tell me that."

"Well, I'm telling you now. I've rented this apartment. I sold my car. It's a new start—only two blocks from my office."

"It reminds me of an apartment I knew once, only that window faced out on the river. It was very much on the edge, you know; you felt like you were on the edge of the whole city; the whole operation was on the very edge. Do you have anything to eat?"

"The stove's not connected."

"I mean some cookies or crackers."

"Do you eat to live or live to eat, Ag?"

"Thank you very much."

A silence.

"Flo had her big opening last night."

"Why don't you take off that ridiculous cape?"

"Last night Flo had the opening of her show. It was called 'Mrs. Schwartz Puts All Her Eggs in One Basket.'"

"Uh, is that where you've been?"

"Yes, that's where I've been. I'll bet you could paint one of her plain yellow yolks and sign it Sarnicki '65."

Another silence.

"I'm sorry, Stanley, because I really think it's nice you have a hobby."

"Take off that goddamn cape. What are you going to wear, a fur coat on the Fourth of July? What do you want to be, some fat crazy character?"

"Yes."

"Finish your drink and we'll go out to eat."

"I'm not hungry."

(This is the last silence. I must find the courage to write a play with this silence. And let it go on—a real play with this long silence given to the actors. He drinks, stirs. She makes certain adjustments. As the silence grows the audience is stunned, restless but dumb, held by a cultural commitment. A man coughs, a woman—the actor, the actress. They volley with the cough. It has passed, this silence, through tragedy, through wonder, through technique into an old gag. Then, exasperated, tearing off her cloak, pulling her dress over her swollen belly, the woman shrieks: "My body has a purpose now." It comes as a flat statement: a moral supplied for morality's sake—a comfort all the same, a kindness.)

I said: "Don't you think, facing *in* like this, to the center of the city, that you could have quite a normal life. You could do all the things people do."

"I suppose so . . . Look, don't you want to go out and have some supper?"

"I have an awful lot of poems to read."

"Mary Agnes—"

"Stanley—"

I went home and stared at the shelf of packaged foods and canned goods I vowed I would finish before I left Ninth Street. There were some remarkable meals coming up: sardines and pickled pears, chow mein and blueberry muffins, and I would cry at each bizarre combination. I might have put a match to every word I had written and entered the credible years of hamburgs, French fries, apple pie, up in the white modern city. It was not possible, with my love-child coming. (I still amused myself.) Someone could make a hero of Stanley. I would not make him a victim. But I spent the rest of the week dreaming that I *might* have gone, knowing that I would not have gone in any case.

It had not happened in one shot—so to speak—I hardly ever believe that stuff about the girl from the nice family who makes one mistake: the boy and I had met on five separate and distinct occasions. In one place or another we worked out the perfect dialogue and repeated it, our ulti-mate confessions. Were we living? Like others? Did we breathe? Could we do anything? Anything at all? We did what we could for each other. And the boy—I heard at Flo's grand evening that my Lycidas had sailed to Europe with his mother, safe and dry, and was going back to college in the fall. What boy? I asked. With the beard, they said. That fink. That fool. That hope of all the ages.

All night long the baby moves *in utero*, exercising while I'm prone and the pull of gravity not such a drag. It's a restless scrambling, poor thing, like a dog trying to settle it-self. This quickening moves me, Miss Keely, once more to the highroad. I must find a place for us, that's for certain, a home. I must write that story I have in mind about a dog—all that about Jim Neary and my mother and the bitch Lassie. Parallel to the tale of me and Stanley, though with nothing of the picaresque about it. Intersecting the history of Sherry; but it must be a cool neat line: a story told. *I* must be out of it, no scene-stealing with a wink or a face pulled behind the speaker's back. No strategy. Put it down. There—expect nothing. Well, it won't matter where I am as long as I can lock myself in with paper and a refill for my pen, as long as we have food and a bed to lie on—feet up for my varicosities. But first let me say that I have found yet another door closed to me.

(What of Lydia, of Stanley, those who would take you in? You're mighty particular, aren't you, Miss, in your condition?)

I wanted to go where I can care for nothing but my work and the foetus stretching and curling inside me. So I went home. That's right, I got up at dawn and ate the last can of tuna in the apartment, figuring I would be able to step through the door early and avoid the parting scene with Mrs. Mertz. I almost made it down two flights when I heard my telephone—six o'clock it was in the morning. A base reflex made me drop my suitcase and the shopping bag stuffed with all my writing. I ran back up to answer.

Lydia said that he was dead: Henry Savaard gone down at sea. The Terriers had moved into the big house with their new equipment, and one of their toys on a trailer hitched to the back of a Mercedes-Benz was a sailboat they did not know how to sail. Every day Henry went up and looked at the boat, touched it. Finally he offered to rig it for them and get it in the water. He hitched the trailer to his mother's car and started down to the bay. Old Mrs. Savaard—she was living with them now—ran after him with a pair of Top-Siders and said she had never seen her son so like himself, not in many years. No storm came up. The sky was plumed high with clouds; bright sun, good wind. One saw clearly in all directions. They waited, two fabled women, for their man to return; and the old Chrysler waited down by the shore, until it was too late. The Coast Guard dragged for him during the night. There was a mark on his head where the boom came round and clouted him—as though he had forgotten, Lydia said, as though he had forgotten what he once knew best. Though I know nothing of sailing, I imagine it was a great change out on the water after his niggling small boats in bottles. What was it worth if all the mother's vision was in the past, if she could not sense that day an evil wind? What was it worth for Lydia to become a person, to go to all that trouble, now he is gone?

Desiccated plots: the senseless death of the hero; we still demand it.

And so there was Mrs. Mertz waiting for me in her bare feet: gnarled overlapping toes, pared bunions, fuchsia nails.

"I've been speaking to Leon," she said in that strained unlovely language, Jewish-grudging, the big comic heart of our city: ". . . what is your private concern is not our business. You got troubles I don't want you should be out in the street with."

"Thank you."

"Don't thank. Pay the rent."

"But I can't pay the rent," I said. "I'm going to my mother."

"A girl should be with her mother."

"There's a lot of rubbish up there if you can use it."

"What about your friend?" asked Mrs. Mertz.

I thought of our collection of Woolworth plates and pans, our "seconds" from Macy's white sale, two peeling wicker chairs, the cast-off dinette suite. I thought of Lydia's cottage, emerald silk against pale fruitwood, the flourishing garden.

"She won't be needing it."

"I wish you luck," said Mrs. Mertz. She meant in face of all the odds.

Going to my mother was not outrageous. I counted on a bed, and I would be free to lock myself in, not to listen to a stream of silly blather which had no meaning for me now. I would not be in exile: all states were mine. I had my child. I had my work. The only outcast would be that spinster huddled under a student lamp wearing her illusions into rags, long ago. *She* might have told you that Rimbaud was nursed by his sister, Baudelaire died in his mommy's arms. I wanted nothing but the bed, a glass of milk and a sandwich handed in at the door. But the door was closed to me. I knew my mother had been ailing, would not be in her full power, and I even figured how she would relish me, come back in disgrace. She could recoup her losses. But the door was closed.

The house was blue, bright as a sleazy nylon dress in a rack of gray-brown garments, but the job was finished. It was allover blue. Was *this* why I left? This slight offense among so many? I had not taken a key, or if I had I'd lost it. The door to the hall was locked. I rang the bell. An edge of paper stuck to the glass, and, standing in the heat with my suitcase and my bag of papers, I recognized the last of the wry-headed eagle. My father had gotten hold of an NRA sticker down at the firehouse, and wasn't she mad—sticking it on the front door to show there's a wealthy gentleman can throw his money away. I rang the bell again. It must have been summer heat, my body burning, for that was last year's Red Cross. Hadn't I made out the check?

A young woman with gray hair came down from upstairs where the tenants lived. Always different tenants—she couldn't get on with them. The woman looked—I don't want to make things up now—she looked frightened of me.

"Mrs. Keely is in the hospital," she said.

"Still?"

"She was out for a while over to her sister, but they've got her back in . . . again." She had said too much, telling me like that of my mother's doom, and shut her door slowly on the tip of her nose.

It was no short trip to the hospital, or, carrying a load it seemed longer than I remembered. Down our hill and up another—I didn't imagine the curtains drawn back, the eyes of the dead forgotten people on me. No life in the streets; well, there never was—it was always behind the curtains. I could hardly believe they were still here, Dunn and Ford, Krause and O'Toole—it seemed too long ago to still be going on. They are all drugged on brown velour couches in the front parlors and rise up once a year to peek out the window and condemn some bit of fun: if you draw a hopscotch on their sidewalk or run a stick along their fence. It seems they had children, but the children are gone.

Here I see the river, or the cracked mud where the river was and may be again, though I'd never swear to that. I wished I was turning in the other direction, down to the Reddi-Zip factory so I could pass those pink, green houses I had such a pathetic . . . fixation (there's a weakling word —fixation) on, those houses the Italians dolled up. I won't admit I loved them. That would be harking back to small hopes, or condescending—the great man come back to survey his humble origins: "Ah'll never forget sliding down that cellar door. We didn't know where the next unpretentious frame house was comin' from, but my father was a wise and gentle man, and he upended me and went at me with a rusty tweezers and Ah'll never forget his words and I hope the American people will never forget what I tell 'em in this intimate portrait—

" 'Son,' he said, 'God put those slivers in your ass.' And I cried. I cried that night."

Terrible indulgence. To come near the factory is a danger, for they might spot me, even like this, and call me names —not that I'd mind, though why expose myself to an emotional scene when I'm eating for two? God knows what their Miss Keely (she's not got all her buttons) might say. I managed an excellent curtain at Wunda-Clutch to get my severance pay. I said it's either me or that fairy goes. You can't have two women in the same kitchen, though I wouldn't vouch for her sex. Bert Sigal didn't think that was too bad so I went on to say I didn't think his fibrous tape was all that much of a miracle, indeed no miracle at all, when you consider the Assumption, or those women who live for years on nothing but a drink of water and the Eucharist. Bert said he didn't think I ought to bring religion into it and I said I was only talking about natural phenomena. At last he fired me, so I'm two weeks richer.

This climb to the hospital has always been famous in our town, almost as famous as the climb to church. The very ground will be damned if it makes anything easy in our physical or spiritual existence. Yes, it's a hill to the hospital, and I'm sure they thought I was ready for a bed. My breath had given out. I couldn't ask for my mother's room.

"K-eely . . . Keely," I gasped at the receptionist.

Two student nurses snickered at me from a doorway. What's the matter, girls? I thought you saw everything in a hospital.

"You can't go up there."

"I came all the way from New York."

"We don't care where you came from."

"I'm her daughter."

"Then you better sign here, Mrs. . . . ?"

"Mrs. Crane," I said and I wrote down the name: Mrs. Hart Crane.

"You better not climb the stairs. The elevator's . . ."

"Thanks. I know the way." I know the food-smelling ramps, thank you, and the Virgin Marys stationed at the end of the halls over withered gladiolas, and the solarium with badly printed Catholic magazines, the ambulatory shuffling about in bathrobes—all of that. From my father's hernia, I know, from Mae's mastectomy, from at least three hemorrhoid sufferers (whose names shall not be given), the alarming indignity of pain: I know the way. Before I reached my mother's room the great tidal wave of sickening memory had risen up from the ammonia pail in the gossip-ridden corridors. I was sucked under. Not all my skill in the free-wheeling world mattered here; I knew this way, with its coarse statements and digging nuances, better than any other.

By what fantastic effort will I drag myself up through this disaster, an act of God.

Miss Starch Ass said I might as well go in. You might as well let a brass band in, for all she'd know. My mother was breathing—that's all. The rasping finale to a querulous life. There was nothing to her: she looked . . . looked about the size I used to be. All the flesh was eaten away, only the hillock of her stomach with the growth, cruel comment on the old days' *en bon point*. Surely the skin, the nails were already dead. I picked up a hand: it was dry.

"I'm sorry. I'm sorry," I said to my mother. All night this woman sat with me when I had chicken pox. She cooked a thousand memorably bad meals which I ate. She let down my hems. She wanted me to be blonde and sweet.

"I'm so sorry." She only wanted me to be pretty and wear little white shoes.

Miss Starch Ass Connolly? Connell?—she was one of those people who had always been around—came in and smoothed the pillow as though there was something worth doing. She spoke in a thunderous hush: "Your brother will be here later. He's staying with one of the sisters. They always come in at night."

"How long?" I asked.

"They can keep them a long time," she said. "Her heart is strong."

The inside of my mother's arms were covered with needle marks, mere punctures in deflated black skin. The flesh had not risen in angry wounds; it did not look sore as we know it. Looking me over, the nurse said, "I start a feeding now when they send it up, and she's down for another transfusion."

I walked over to the sink behind a screen—big broad bollocks of a thing in the mirror, with red eyes.

"It's always hard," Miss Starch Ass told me. This is what she said when her cases came near the end. "She has some lovely flowers. Would you like to see them? I put them outside."

"No."

We went back to the side of the bed together, bravely.

"I put a little water in her mouth with a spoon. It gets so parched."

"Yes."

"You have to be careful though it don't choke them."

"Oh!" Yes, it was *Connell*. She had a sister who drank, deaf as a doorknob, taught Spanish at Central High.

She left on some contrived business, but stuck her head back in the door. "Agnes?" Miss Connell called in a loud whisper. "It's Mary Agnes, isn't it? Will you take her rings off? I've wound them with tape, but these colored fellas who come in to clean . . . you never know."

"Mom?" I said clearly. "Mother?" Knowing that she could not hear, I told her about the child that was coming, I told her about my work. Knowing she would never understand, I told her that it made me weep to see the permanent grown out of her hair, leaving her natural as a small-waisted country girl, and that I must contain all of it—all—coolly in my mind while the artifice burns in my heart. Now that she could not listen I told her she was not as bad as I remembered—the way you might tell the truth to someone you love. She rasped on and on; and then, in absolution, taking a full glass of water I poured it into her mouth. Most of it dribbled out down that white, white skin, but enough went back into her throat. And gag, gag . . . Ag, it sounded like, in a soft complaining. I was happy to give her the last word.

11

---◆◄◆►◆---

AUDIART, AUDIART

Upstairs in the Public Library the lights were going out.
On the ground floor the little man in charge of the newspaper room had put out the last sleeping bum and was
jangling his keys, afraid to lock up before the clock struck
ten. On the first stroke a woman started down the stairs,
the last one left in the library aside from the staff who
would go out the back way past the time clock.

"Good night," she said.

"Good night, Miss Keely," said the man. He was in
charge of locking the outer door as well, so he waited for

her to pass. She stood in the doorway, drawing back for a moment.

"Did you forget something?" he asked.

"No," she said with a quick smile.

"It's raining," he remarked and scurried around behind the heavy oak door to kick the hook out with his foot. On the last stroke of ten he turned the latch inside.

It was not true rain, but a soft mist in the air coming up from the river. Miss Keely waited against the building with her books pulled to her breast and then began slowly to descend the wide cement steps that led to the street. She was giving Jim Neary a start up the hill.

Not that it would matter if they met, for they were friendly still, but they no longer walked home together every night as they had last year. It had all started when they both turned up in front of the bulletin board where the reference librarian had posted the answers to the radio quiz. Their mothers, idle widow-women, were following the Lucky Call Quiz over WICC and wanted to be sure of the right answer in case the lucky phone call came their way. It was always some fact about the World Series or geography or the French and Indian War, which Mrs. Keely and Mrs. Neary confused with the answers from the day before. Jim laughed about the Pot of Gold.

He waited, after their first walk, for Mary Agnes Keely to come by at the end of her evening studies, and they would start up the hill together, a long, slow climb, for Jim Neary had a bad leg which turned down on the ankle with every step. They were neither of them young. She was past thirty and painfully thin, a tall, alert woman often smiling foolishly. For years she had worked as a secretary at the zipper factory. Nights she went to extension courses in the high school or down to the teachers' college in New Haven. He taught the fifth grade but had ambition, so he was always taking courses, too, and was set on a high-school job in history or social studies. Though he was near forty Jim maintained a boyish manner—he had red hair and light freckled skin and well-developed shoulders that he carried high, above the limp.

They got on nicely in their talks. He found that she was bitter at being left on the vine and left to work for her old mother. Her wit was cruel, but if he kept her on her studies—it was poems and stories she loved—then she was a pleasant mixture of cool intelligence and fire. He treated her to ice cream at Friedman's Dairy. That way it was longer home and his leg grew tired, but that way he could study her for a while in the fluorescent light. Her hair was brown, cut short so she wouldn't have to bother with it. Jim liked the look of her thin clever face, unadorned. Everyone said she'd be a teacher when she finished up her credits, but she told him no, it was for herself she studied.

Mary Agnes had not always gone to the library to work at night: she had rigged up a desk with a lamp in her bedroom that suited her, and there was some pleasure in closing the door against her mother; but after a few nights at the library—she had been using a literary history she could not afford to buy—Mary Agnes felt the easy routine of their meetings and thought she might offend Jim Neary if she wasn't in front of the bulletin board at closing.

On Thursday night he went to class, and on Saturday morning she went in to New York to a course in Shakespeare at Columbia. It was the first time she had attended a real university. The distance, the famous name, gave her a sense of the world. She would tell Jim when they walked up the hill on Monday night about the play she had seen in the afternoon, or the pictures if she had gone to a museum. She never told him that sometimes she visited her cousin, a beautiful, rich woman considered a Jezebel by all the family. Once she heard him explaining to nosy Miss Gleason behind the circulation desk that Miss Keely was a student at the School of General Studies; with respect in his deep voice it sounded almost grand.

Their walks became more open in the spring, and her mother was saying she could do worse than a man with a teaching position. As far as Mrs. Keely could find out, the Neary boy hadn't gone through one of the operations on his leg for several years. So the mother grew somewhat proud about it all and said it took an educated man to appreciate Ag. After church she took to having conversations with Mrs. Neary, a woman who'd had a hard life, she said. And she didn't hold it against them they came up from the south end: it was only a matter of a few dollars, she presumed; they were not all born "pug Irish" in tenements down by the river. Things became better at home for Mary Agnes now that she was going with Jim Neary. There was less wrangling with her mother about the scorched blouses, the tasteless food, the bills for worthless items at the stores, and this peace was such a blessing that she found herself softer with all the annoyance of her life.

In fact, she made a little game out of seeing Jim. She curled her hair and wore low heels to seem his height. It was a quaint old-fashioned courtship they both knew: no cars, no dancing at the roadhouse. Twice he kissed her when he took her home from the movies, and she ran up into the house sure that everyone on the block had seen. She did not think she loved him but felt a strange moving pressure when he drew close to her: his body was large. When they were little all the boys said Jim Neary exercised to make himself that big on top. She wondered if it was true.

At Easter, when her brother Francis came down from Buffalo with Joan and the children, Jim hobbled up the front steps with a pot of tulips and a bottle of Blue Grass cologne, a maidenly scent he'd chosen instead of the muskier perfumes in the drugstore with suggestive French names. He sat with Francis cracking nuts at the dining-room table and they talked about politics and about Francis' work with the FBI.

"Well, don't waste your time checking up on me," Jim said, "though I was no friend of Joe McCarthy's."

"God rest his soul," the mother said. Even Francis laughed at that.

Once toward the end of the school year he asked her if she could miss a Saturday at Columbia and come with him on a trip to the whaling museum at Mystic. They would go on a bus from New Haven with the Connecticut History Teachers' Association. She hunched over and drew in her cheeks, knowing that she couldn't tell him that Saturday morning was what she lived for, that he couldn't ask her to give up the lecture on *Antony and Cleopatra*. Instead she told him that she had made a date to meet her cousin in New York.

"Why do you want to do that?" he asked.

"It's Mary Elizabeth, you know, who lived with us when we were kids."

"Yes, I know," he answered curtly. "I wouldn't forget her." They walked on for a block before he said, indifferent, "I hear she's married now."

"Yes, she married," but Mary Agnes did not say that her cousin was divorced and trying one thing or another, one man or another, in a life of desperate luxury. "We usually go to a fancy restaurant or one of the clubs she likes. Last time the bill was nearly a hundred dollars for the three of us," she cocked her head proudly, "—with wine."

Jim felt that he had offered her a cheap provincial outing, and they went on with their simple evening walks at ten o'clock. That summer he found an American History course at New Britain State Teachers' College, and two nights a week she went over to Trinity in Hartford for Modern Poetry. When her mother asked why she had to keep studying when everything was going along so nicely with Jim Neary, Mary Agnes left the house in a rage. She knew that she didn't want him any more, that if there had been a moment when she envisioned herself not as a queer Miss Keely but as an acceptable Mrs. Neary, it had passed. Some nights she stayed home at the desk in her bedroom, feeling guilty at first, shut in on a summer night, but then her mood would change as she read poem after poem, going back to figure a line, to get the rhythm of it right. She read during her lunch hour and in the morning before her mother got out of bed: it held her days.

One night at Friedman's Dairy she tried some lines on Jim from *The Man with the Blue Guitar*, but he was only interested in her. It was hot and his carrot hair was soaked with sweat at the temples. She knew from the way he moved about under the table that his leg was giving him some trouble. He told her the teachers' supplementary pension plan was sure to go through the legislature this year. "I derive great satisfaction," he said, "from my fifth-grade class, from a lesson that's well taught—it's a shame to waste your knowledge and your talent."

"But it is only for myself," she cried, "why is that so hard to understand?"

A week went by and they were both busy writing papers, then on Saturday he came to her house with a cardboard box containing a trembling small dog, a collie. "It was off by itself," he said, "away from the litter."

She thought he gave her the puppy in a final effort, that there might be this live animal between them. Her mother, who hated dogs, said, "Oh, Ag, she reminds me of our Jip. Remember Jip we had when you were kids?" She did remember her father running in the back yard with a mutt he had brought home from the firehouse, but that was long ago. The dog had died of distemper within a few weeks.

"What'll you call her, Ag?" asked Mrs. Keely.

"It's up to you," said Jim, brightly.

Mary Agnes lifted the puppy from its box. It clawed at the air in a helpless paddle until she drew it close to her narrow chest. Its eyes were a deep amber full of certain pride.

"Audiart," Mary Agnes murmured to the dog, "Audiart, Audiart where thy bodice laces start, as ivy fingers clutching through its crevices . . ."

"What will her name be, Mary Agnes?" Jim Neary asked.

"Audiart," she said, "Audiart."

After he had gone home Mrs. Keely railed at her daughter. "He can see you're making a fool of him, Miss. What kind of name is that for a dog?"

The mother called the dog Lassie and said it was a nuisance. For the last weeks of summer Mary Agnes and Jim had the collie to talk about, but then they tired of the subject and stayed away from the public library at night. She began quarreling with her mother again, mostly over Audiart, who was growing into a gangly young dog, but the mother said Lassie was high-strung and stupid: she wouldn't go on the papers; she was fussy about her food. Mary Agnes loved the dog and took it for long walks up and down the hills, waiting patiently for it to sniff at every post and tree. She took it up on the bed with her and stroked it with a wire brush. The underside of the dog's body was purest white and soft, so new it seemed, not yet grown in with the coarser coat of hair. She knew that holding out for some magic she had turned her back on too many chances. "Audiart," she whispered to the dog, thinking of the brazen sensual image, the lush breasts laced in, the shadow of cleavage which the passionate troubador could touch only with his song. It was her favorite poem. "Audiart," she whispered; but the dog answered to Lassie.

The name of Jim Neary was never mentioned in the house. Mary Agnes petted and kissed the dog before she went to sleep. She liked the feel of its warm body curled at the bottom of her bed, though in the middle of the night it always whined at the door to be free to wander through the rooms of the flat.

One cold night in November she came home from work and went to the front hall closet for the red leash she had bought for Audiart. Her mother, folding the evening paper, said, "Francis stopped by today."

"*Francis* stopped by!"

"Yes, he was on business to Boston and he came through this way; but he couldn't wait, he lost time as it was."

"Oh," Mary Agnes said. There was a strangeness in the air, and she went to look under the kitchen stove.

"Audiart," she called softly to the nest of old blankets, "Audiart."

"Lassie's gone off with Francis," the mother said. "I thought she'd have more life with the children than she'll ever have with us."

"How could you do that?" Mary Agnes wailed.

"I don't mind a cat in the house," the mother said, "but I never liked a dog."

She knew that there was no way to get the dog back— it had been given to children. When they went up to Buffalo to visit Francis at Christmas she found that his wife, always a priss, had not wanted Audiart; she could not tolerate its hairs around the new baby. Mary Agnes locked herself in the bathroom and stayed there when they called her out. She would alarm the children, they said. She would ruin everyone's Christmas. At last she appeared with dry eyes, and Francis, who never had much heart about such matters, took her aside. He explained that he had given the dog to a nice family with a big yard.

"May I go and see her?"

"No," Francis said, "that won't be possible."

"Why not?" she asked.

He said he had given the dog to a man who worked at General Electric who gave him information and they did not meet each other in public.

"You gave Audiart to a spy!"

"An agent," he said, exasperated, "a special agent."

She said she couldn't see the harm in seeing a dog, that it was silly to think a dog would betray the country. She could not eat any dinner and went up to the attic bedroom to read.

Two days after Christmas Francis told her to get into the car, and the mother, tired of helping with the baby, said she would go for the ride. They drove to a cemetery outside of the city. A soft snow fell over the graves and decorated the headstones. Though there was no one in sight they walked through the plots, pretending they were visiting their dead. Mrs. Keely complained of the cold and asked what they were doing out here. Then a man drove up (they could not see his face) and opened the back door of his car. A dog jumped out. The collie had grown in a month. She looked tall and handsome as she ran free among the gravestones. She squatted at a large memorial. They waited.

"Audiart," Mary Agnes called, "Audiart!"

The dog veered off around a polished obelisk, and then the mother called, "Lassie!" in a shrill command. At once the collie stopped its doggy business and looked at them; then she dashed across the fresh light snow, jumping the graves. "Audiart," Mary Agnes called again as she came near, but the dog passed her by. Barking wildly she leapt at the mother in joyous recognition.

"Good Lassie. Nice Lassie," Mrs. Keely said sourly as the dog danced at her feet, and then Lassie leapt at her again with a violent wet kiss and the mother fell back over a sunken headstone nearly hidden by the snow.

That night Mary Agnes was the first to see her mother in the strange hospital after they had set her hip. She came to the side of the bed and gazed down at the dead plaster of the white, white cast.

"Well," the mother said, "you didn't want to look after a cripple and you got one after all."

12

————◄●►————

I have burdened you with so many events. What does that mean?—that I no longer respect what happens unless I make it, or that I feel things will happen in any case; that I cannot, as I have tried to do, set them straight? Silly palaver. There is still the child, the great event to come. That at any rate is what I am led to believe comes to pass in time. I once thought up ways to pass the time, elaborate rituals of washing, clothing, feeding myself, working in an office to this end. Now I *use* time—every last scrap of it—and I do not have to be so particular about the hour or the day. The child has grown large, risen high in my abdomen only to fall for the first time, maneuvering to be born. This was called "lightening" in a book I bought coming through Grand Central—a book they have taken away. Detailed drawings of the foetus in various stages of gestation offended the head nun, Mary Immaculata, which I might well have guessed after the way she instructed me to dress behind a bathtowel held in my teeth. Now in my solitary confinement I am free to do as I please.

I've lost track of when I came—when they brought me, though I recall at the time the doctor said I'd waited too long. He was not talking to one of the substandards sent here by the Juvenile Board, he said, but to a grown and educated woman.

"Thirty-seven," I said, for I'm not sensitive about my age and still have the knack to figure that. "Thirty-seven, and think of it, Doctor, because I imagine you were born not many years before we entered the war, and by that time I had developed a classic case of Christian guilt and knew algebra and the Latin declensions. Beyond a cheap emotional value, looking at ourselves in this way has little meaning."

He is a pudgy young man in a green cotton suit who might be described as nice or even pleasantly frank if he were not dipped in a thin coat of textbook sympathy. I asked, "Why is that suit green instead of white, Doctor?" thinking we might come at something significant here.

But he only answered, "White isn't used much any more. You should have tried to control your intake of starches, Miss Keely. Now it's an uphill fight. You should have taken proper care."

"Well, I read that book. Compelling! Couldn't put it down! The absorption in a purely *physical* . . ."

Baring his square white teeth, which exhibit years of the expensive dental care his mother believed in, he lost the lubricious charm of a would-be gynecologist and ranted on about the harm such books do in the hands of laymen.

"Why didn't you go to a doctor?" he asked. "Were you ashamed?"

"No. I have a lot to be ashamed of in my past—thirty-five degenerate years—but now I'm leading a useful . . . an inspired existence."

"You have a weight problem."

"I've always had a weight problem."

"Do you realize the strain that is put on your heart, maintaining that excess fat?"

"Listen, I've always been at least twenty pounds underweight"; and I detected thick exasperation in his medstudent eyes.

"Don't you see, Doctor, that during the past two years, on some day, if only one day or one hour in one day, I must have been precisely the weight indicated on the insurance company folder for a female, thirty-five to forty, height five-eleven. The perfect *norm*. And what a splendid idea to attempt to recover that day—worthless, like the claim to some dissolved empire, and yet there was a moment of physical perfection for me—on that day, neither constipated nor . . ."

I was not co-operating. What's more, he was distressed (only mildly) to hear that I had fatigued myself on three occasions by running down the front path and trying to hitch a ride to New York. My blood count is a disgrace. I do not urinate with proper frequency. And though they take me to this young man in green—I'd say once in every week—we do not warm to each other. He has cut down on my food, substituted vitamins and a diuretic.

I can't say I care much for their cooking anyway. Institutional food. This *is* an institution—a home for wayward girls, though there is some confusion in my mind about it, for I am in a room by myself now. They watch me and have taken all my things away except the bag of papers. I did create a fuss, I'll grant that much, hollered and rolled my eyes, called convincingly upon their prominent saints in a moaning, rocking, reverent liturgy. The dresses—all right, if the colors ran in their machines downstairs and made the usual mess, I couldn't be less concerned about what I have on—in the nature of an unbleached muslin hospital sack with ties. Shoes with the ties taken out, "so you won't 'trip,' Miss Keely."

"Yeah, Sister, and my name's Fatty Arbuckle."

"Please, Miss Keely!"

"That's all right. I can't reach my feet any more."

Chair. Table. Bed. Crucifix on the wall—not bad, white plastic glo-in-the-dark with hangnail edges from the mold—needs no more than a good exposure to the light to recapture a jazzy luminosity. Light on the whole poor, whereas in that first place, the ward, a row of unrelenting bulbs hung down the aisle—there where no one read and where I worked only by the most extravagant mental contortions.

They put me in with five hard young girls in varying stages of pregnancy. The oldest was seventeen and they had all been in homes before—for stealing, soliciting; but only two had ever been on dope, which they smoked without much craving in the back rooms of identical newsshops down the block from identical high schools. I asked them a number of questions, not out of any journalistic interest in their "predicament" or their "generation," but to try to get hold of their dreamlike existence, their inarticulate sojourn in a world they do not find fantastic. And I questioned the nun. It was only curiosity that made me ask why I was thrown in with this distracting lot; and it was because we all wanted to keep our babies if possible.

"If possible!" I cried. "I can feel his heart beating in me."

She suggested that I pray to God—how else would she have it?—and not upset the other girls, though in fact it was the girls who stole my papers, and the one who could read best was stumbling over the words in an uninflected drone while the rest crowded round, cracking gum, squabbling over the prize transistor radio. I'm well out of it. Al-

303

ways one interruption or another. They traded comics, hid their screen scandals, had the bets going as to who would go into labor first, second, and so on. Always something to break my thought: a nun with pieces of flannel we were to sew into garments to make time fly.

"You haven't started your baby's clothes," she said one day when the girls were on their third nightie.

"That's not my line."

"You must prepare for your child."

I said I *was* preparing (why pester her with my problem; at that time I was establishing a chronology), and she suppressed her anger under, "Mary, Mother of God, pray for us!"

The six of us from that room were herded to Mass. Now they don't bother me with it, though I'll admit I found it a change from what I remembered: the basket not passed and no sermon, to make it a short service for us. At Communion the youngest boys ever seen flipped doilies over the rail, as if the swollen penitent girls who straggled up the aisle were not quite clean. I suppose that is the point, only they make it too often. There were also nightly excursions to the Television Room where we sat in unhealthy darkness shifting on our hams, all the inmates of good behavior, watching. . . .

The pains have started. For the record, if you will bear with one more fact, they started when I began to write this last . . . and when they come every twenty minutes I am to inform the young doctor in the green cotton suit. But every minute is too full and flows into the next and the next. The pain is here at last in great satisfying heaves.

And the sisters in cream wool with black crosses of an order I don't recognize. They have extremely clean hands and wear gold wedding bands, which is nice for them, I'm sure.

"Will you tell me the name of this place?" I asked when I first looked out of my daze at one of them.

"This is the Good Shepherd Home."

"I prefer to be in New York," I said, knowing that at best I was in a town outside of Hartford. They have their ways of keeping me here—the private room, liver injections, food of some sort, the unsullied backside of their weekly duplication *The Virgin's Transcript* (on this I write). It's indicated, not too subtly, that Francis got me in here through influence. Say, that ought to be a devastating scene: Francis putting the pressure on Monsignor McGivme. How often he comes in handy! But I miss the hot summer nights in the city, the crisp fall nights: people in the streets; women in rolled stockings; the ape-man in the window in his undershirt; toughs lolling on the hoods of parked cars; the inescapable wet heat of summer in the apartments; the inescapable dry heat of winter rising from our stuffed furnace, withering the nasal membranes . . . everything to be seen and listened for, to be felt . . . Still, it won't be long now with the pains started, yes, I would say closer together and, oh yes, with increasing force; and I will go back with the baby. That is where I lived. You know that. The city: it is my home.

One day when I was still in the ward, Sister Mary of the Bloody Innocents came in with a basin and a gray doll—not dirty, but gray, intended to include the several non-Caucasians in our group without being overly specific—a tasteless counterfeit, though real water was used in the demonstration. We were to practice bathing the thing, and they passed it around carefully in a towel, tested the water on their wrists, poked it with cotton swabs, dusted it with talcum—all of that. I could see the girls were serious, even the worst of them, and at the end the sister handed it to me. A hollow dummy with synthetic skin, lifeless color, Dynel hair rooted in.

"Please, Miss Keely," the sister said, "you must support the baby's head."

I tried but could not. The whole kit—baby, basin, swabs,

305

and water—crashed to the floor. The girls and the nun shrieked at me. I don't know why; they were only playing dolls.

It was then they moved me away and began to question me about my mother. The connection was obvious to me. Some acts, I told the green obstetrician who is the only doctor they have on hand, are involuntary, while others, nourished in the mind, contain more truth than we know. And then the third, vastly inferior pot of acts, those performed with reason, can sustain us all indefinitely with cups of watery broth. I've lost my taste for it.

He said he would not fence with me.

That's it exactly. I've finished with all your games.

If I change my position, stand over the table, sit in the chair, lie on my side in the bed, it detracts from the intensity of the heaving pressure. If I ask they will give me something to help, but then what of the last possibility to be dealt with: my death?

So! the mark on the page grows faint and I must write over the scratches. Entrusted to Lydia Savaard, a note. Not sent to her, but *written by* her—prefixed *and* affixed let it be, and I will slide back and forth on the high-wire in between . . . and I'll not have her write in the manner of an editor's comment (I find *Merry Apples* to be exactly what is needed in the Five to Seven Reading-for-Fun series, whimsical fact that will satisfy the growing desire for reality) . . . rather more in the style of one nice lady writing about her friend—

I take it on good faith from the Little White Sisters of the Desperate that this work has not been tampered with in any instance, that it came to me exactly as the author arranged it before her untimely death.

Or timely death—some things must be left to others, some choices yet. And put down the statistics, which are easily available, of the number of women who die in childbirth— a figure no doubt extremely low, given the wonders of modern medicine; add a disclaimer from the doctor with technicalities: languid labor, narrow pelvic structure under deceptive layers of flesh . . . this isn't fitting for Lydia to put her name to. Though she is inviolate, I cannot impose and put her hand-in-hand with that flabby young man.

A more feminine elegy: *Mary Agnes Keely was not young. She did not take care of herself. She labored for many hours before she called another living soul—until it was nearly too late even for the child. As for the details given by the resident physician, I do not credit his stories. She chose a solitary way.*

They sent a priest to counsel me and I said I had no argument with my mother for over two years. I asked though if he might find out where they buried her— whether it was next to my father or in the Walsh family plot, for there had always been some dispute about who was to pay the bill for the Perpetual Care. Embellishments of that sort are magnificent, though I feel I have moved beyond into a place with brilliant exclusions—"Listen, Father, my folly will be grand."

The priest opened his book, fluttering the weightless pages edged with incurable red, and I could not guess from his drained handsomeness whether he had given me up or the world entirely. He switched the white ribbon marker for black as though the cards come out that way.

"Is there anything else, Miss Keely, you want to tell me?"

"I'm anxious to know, Father, do you drive a black Chevrolet?"

"Yes."

"A simple model, two doors—"

"Why yes!"

"Gear shift—"

"No, it's automatic. I'm not much of a sport. Please, Miss Keely—don't cry."

Even the room. Here I lie upon the bed and hold the sides of the mattress until the stitches rip, and with effort take the pencil from my teeth and scribble against the wall until it comes again. I've no complaints. This cell has been a palace for my work. I have been going over and over my pages with this orange pencil, a good No. 2, which I hide in the hem of the drapes. Here I am completely free. No more trips to be jolly with the girls, or little exercising walks on the grounds with my feet crushing the dead leaves, no more nights in the TV room where we watched comedies about families living in cute houses whose sorrows are based on a mischance like catching mumps when it is time for the junior jamboree . . . no more of that. Only once under protest I was led out to a special event—under protest; they said it would "take me out of myself"—a movie, *Rainbow on the River*, with Hattie McDaniel and Bobby Breen, and when the lovers kissed (their names are lost forever) Mother Immaculata put her hand over the projector and the girls hooted and hissed. Who cares—a dry meeting of closed mouths. No more of that.

Now the pain lives on within the moment of its ebbing. Yes, I must call for that dim young doctor. Always trying to reckon my time. What's it to him, *my* blessed event? He was an annoyance, asking again about my mother until I told him—Hot damn! I had finished that story off and it was the one thing I was satisfied with—a regret surely that I had not told her the blue on our house was a stroke of genius. That color—I would have passed it by for a pale leaf-green, a timid statement. Then he gave me more of the pills so that ten, fifteen times a day I have to stop in the middle of sweet half-formed ideas and dribble myself away in the toilet.

Best not to let him have a chance at Lydia Savaard. She would take his words to heart. Let her sign this note with the plump open hand of a school girl—

I do not know the truth about Mary Agnes Keely's life, more than any other reader . . . I do not think that she ever intended us to have the facts. "Henry Savaard," for example, is alive. He has not sailed a boat since his first breakdown, which is described here with great inaccuracy, as are the particulars of his illness and the furnishings of our house. All that is beside the point: what difference [Lydia must see in the end] *that we are reduced to department-store mahogany, which she has kindly corrected to the Biedermeier we favor, if she has in fact got at us in every meaningful respect.*

Here the bare essentials. The simplicity grand. I hope to show this room to my child while I lie in and nurse him, while he is still able to comprehend, before we go on our high-swung bus into the city—back into life. I cannot stop the pain with words, or forget the demands of the moment. Now I cry out for help . . . Now . . . Here, I will say to my child, your mother burst forth upon the whole dry world and knew . . .

The child is beautiful to us. The lawyer, mentioned here as Mr. Godnick, is arranging the legal adoption. We can never be, to speak in her words . . .

"Please, Miss Keely—"

. . . the Big Fat Momma, but we will take her child and do the best we can . . .

"Please, Miss Keely—"

. . . and knew she had triumphed, that it was no great sin to be, at last, alone.

A selection of books published by Penguin is listed on the following pages.

For a complete list of books available from Penguin in the United States, write to Dept. DG, Penguin Books, 299 Murray Hill Parkway, East Rutherford, New Jersey 07073.

For a complete list of books available from Penguin in Canada, write to Penguin Books Canada Limited, 2801 John Street, Markham, Ontario L3R 1B4.

SOLO FACES

James Salter

Solo Faces is a novel as extraordinary as its subject—men who climb mountains. The men are Vernon Rand and Jack Cabot, locked in a fierce rivalry forged in a deep friendship. Above all, it is the story of Rand and the purity with which he gives himself to the mountains, and the subtle but sure revelation of the loss of that purity as the story follows him from the rock faces of California to the icy majesty of the Alps. *Solo Faces* tells of bravery and death, trust and betrayal, and, finally, a peace fought for and won.

PANAMA

Thomas McGuane

At once outrageous, comic, and horrifying, this is the fourth novel by a young writer who has been compared to Ernest Hemingway, William Faulkner, and Thomas Pynchon. Chester Hunnicutt Pomeroy is an overnight celebrity who has become an overnight disaster, his mind fragmented by an overdose of sensations both natural and drug-induced. His only purpose is to win back Catherine, his estranged companion of better days. Chet's pursuit of her, his frantic, bizarre wooing, takes place in corrupt and eccentric Key West, Florida, where the demoralized lovers struggle through their appalling comedy. "A wonderfully written novel that balances suffering and understanding . . . a love story with the correct mix of hope and desperation"—*The Village Voice.*

BEFORE MY TIME

Maureen Howard

Laura Quinn, forty years old, a successful Boston journalist and the mother of two, is established from the outset of this witty, insightful novel as a woman settled in her situation. When a rebellious eighteen-year-old relative, Jim Cogan, comes to her Cambridge household from the diametrically opposed world of the Bronx, Laura's universe is profoundly shaken. Maureen Howard's precise, exactingly crafted prose carries this story of a woman's growing self-knowledge, of familial ties and conflicts, and of generational differences into the realm of revelation.

FACTS OF LIFE

Maureen Howard

In this extraordinary autobiography (winner of the National Book Critics Circle Award), Maureen Howard brings all of her novelistic powers to her own facts of life. Within the broad categories of "culture," "money," and "sex," Howard goes beyond the confines of the traditional autobiography in a book of startling originality. She evokes the wonder of common things and the strangeness lurking in the seemingly obvious with great charm, wit, and energy. "Maureen Howard is a talented novelist who has never written anything so concentrated and properly disturbing as this memoir"—Alfred Kazin.

THE DOGS OF MARCH

Ernest Hebert

In the New Hampshire hills tame dogs turn savage at the start of spring, pursuing winter-weakened deer through thinning snows. It is a senseless and cruel pursuit—the awakening of some primitive instinct in dogs supposed to be domesticated. Howard Elman also feels pursued—he is unemployed, his wife suffers from hysterical paralysis, his son rejects him, and his rich new neighbor is plotting to take over his land—and so in Howard, as in the dogs of March, there is a sudden surge of violence. . . . "What makes *The Dogs of March* a brilliant book is Mr. Hebert's ability to portray ordinary people. . . . He catches them so exactly that one feels a rush of love and recognition, of common humanity"—*The New York Times*.

NOCTURNES FOR THE KING OF NAPLES

Edmund White

This hauntingly beautiful novel is an evocation of a lost love—a love evoked through a ghostly sequence of nocturnal visions . . . of New York, Spain, Greece, and other places whose exact locations are not revealed. Following a strange, elegant, and musical order of dream-images, these "nocturnes" recreate the longings of childhood, the regrets of the pleasure-seeker, the bitterness of desertion, the ambiguities of homosexual love.